From the archives of the Comptrollerate-General for Scrutiny and Survey

TRAITOR'S FIELD

Robert Wilton has held a variety of posts in the British Ministry of Defence, Foreign Office and Cabinet Office. He was advisor to the Prime Minister of Kosovo in the lead-up to the country's independence, and has now returned there as a senior international official. He divides his time between Kosovo and Cornwall. His first book, *Treason's Tide*, won the inaugural HWA/Goldsboro Crown for debut historical fiction in 2012.

From the archives of the Comptrollerate-General for Scrutiny and Survey

TRAITOR'S FIELD

arranged by

ROBERT WILTON

CORVUS

First published in Great Britain in 2013
by Corvus, an imprint of Atlantic Books Ltd.

9 8 7 6 5 4 3 2 1

A CIP catalogue record for this book is available from
the British Library.

Hardback ISBN: 978 1 84887 819 8
Trade paperback ISBN: 978 1 84887 839 6
E-book ISBN: 978 1 78239 017 6

Printed in Great Britain by the MPG Printgroup

Corvus
An imprint of Atlantic Books Ltd
Ormond House
26-27 Boswell Street
London WC1N 3JZ
www.corvus-books.co.uk

for my parents
for a past
for a future

TRAITOR'S FIELD

Introduction

As you may be realizing, I can't resist stories of hidden hoards of documents and dirty work by anonymous agents of the state. An acquaintance who knew that I was researching the seventeenth century recently sent me a photocopy of the following letter. It was written more than three hundred years ago, by the Reverend Henry Minafer to a friend of his named Rowse. (There's an enticing possibility that this could be Sir Francis Rowse, who would become one of the most notorious scoundrels in an age where there was some pretty stiff competition; he was reputed to have once quite literally sold his own grandmother.) We don't know what happened to the letter between September 1701 and July 2010, when it was part of a bundle of correspondence bulking out a collection of autograph letters sold at auction in Exeter. Given Minafer's insignificance, and the uncertain identification of Rowse, the letter has no intrinsic value.

Lincoln's Inn, Chamber XIII, the 9th of September 1701

My dear Rowse,

you may, I dare venture, have heard of the remarkable Discovery in my Lodgings. But I write to you of this, and of one yet more peculiar Aspect, because as well as finding the Story of interest you may, given your Acquaintance with the Lord Chancellor's Circle and with such privy Matters, be able to offer me some wise Analysis or Counsel.

I have lately taken these Lodgings in the Inn, from Mr Thomlinson — you may remember him from the

University, altho' I fancy that like myself he was a Year or two before your Time. He has suffered me to have some Improvements done, the Rooms having been untended for some little While. It was during these Works that one of the Joiners — with not the first of his Demonstrations of Clumsiness — accidentally thrust a Beam up through the Ceiling of a short Passageway at the top of the House. It was determined that a larger Portion of the Ceiling should be removed to assist tidy Restoration, and it was this that caused one of the Men to perceive, in the Roof Space thus attained, two small but sturdy Storage Chests.

Of these Chests I should first say Something. They were of thick Wood, but stoutly cornered and banded with Iron, and, remarkably, lined with both Copper and then Leather — and thus Proof I fancy against every possible Assault of Nature.

It is naturally the Contents that have drawn greater Attention. They were nothing other than many hundreds of Papers of an official Tone, all seemingly dating from the Middle of the last Century — most indeed from the Period of the second King Charles's Exile. How they came to be gathered to the Chests, and thence secreted behind this false Ceiling, One may only speculate.

I of course looked through the Documents with great Curiosity. I could remark no particular Theme nor Secret, but nor were they trivial: these were the workaday Correspondence, One might say, of the Government itself — the Orders, Responses, Judgements and Communications of the State, with every other Name a Minister, a General or a Prince. In my casual Perusal, I should say at this Juncture, I noticed a number of Documents marked with a rather curious official Seal, depicting a Device or heraldic Mark not familiar to me.

My Mind at Last turned to the proper Ownership and Holding of these Papers. I fancied that Someone in Authority ought at least to be aware of their Rediscovery, and I thought it likely they might be considered confidential — or at the least official Property — even now. Thomlinson knew nothing of the Business but, with his Approval, I contacted my Friend Herrick, who as you know conducts a certain Amount of legal Business for the Treasury Ministers and for the Court. Through him I was subsequently contacted by one of the Secretaries to Sir John Somers, informing me that the Lord Chancellor's Office would wish to secure the Papers.

Yesterday, shortly before I was due to depart for Evening Service, I was visited by a Man named Isaac Jilkes — another Clergyman, as I immediately remarked — who said he was from the Lord Chancellor's Office, and who repeated their Interest and asked if he might glance at the Papers. I naturally acquiesced, and hoped that my Servant could offer such Assistance and Hospitality as he should require, in my regrettable but unavoidable Absence. I believe that he departed a little While later, professing himself grateful and satisfied. This Morning, as heralded, two Clerks and a Secretary from the Lord Chancellor's Office visited me and collected the Papers.

The strangest Circumstance of all is this: in showing the Secretary through the Documents, and remarking as to their Variety and Interest, I looked instinctively for the official Device that had previously caught my Attention. I could not see it, which at first I reckoned little because there were in Truth not a great number of Documents that had carried it. But as I went through the Documents more intently, I could find this Morning not a single One with that unique and distinctive Marking.

I immediately interrogated my Servant, who denied any Knowledge of such Papers or their Movement, and is in Truth so unlettered and so incurious a Fellow as to have paid them little Heed in any Case. I determined that, for some Reason, the Reverend Jilkes must have removed all of those Documents bearing that strange Seal.

But the Lord Chancellor's Officers disavow any knowledge of the Reverend Isaac Jilkes, and I can find no Record of such a Man. I must then ask, what was He? What was his Interest in the Papers, and whither has he gone? And if he is truly not known to the Office of the Lord Chancellor, then how came he by Knowledge of these Papers?

You, Rowse, who were always the Man for a Mystery, may with your wider Experience of State Habits have some Light to offer me on these Events. In any Case, I find my Mind much eased by having shared them. I beg you to accept my good Wishes, and remain,
Your Friend and humble Servant,

Henry Minafer

The papers discovered by the Reverend Minafer above Mr Thomlinson's ceiling are now acknowledged as one of the great documentary troves of British history. Given by John, Baron Somers, the Lord Chancellor, to Sir Joseph Jekyll, the Master of the Rolls, after whose death they were bought by the bookseller Fletcher Gyles and then, after his death, edited by Thomas Birch, they were finally published in 1742. We know them as the *Thurloe State Papers* (British Library 195.h.2) and they remain a unique and essential source for historians of mid-seventeenth-century Britain, and in particular for that remarkable rootless period between the British Civil Wars and the Restoration of Charles II, during which a collection of soldiers, lawyers, radicals and visionaries tried to create a new kind of government and a new kind of world.

What happened, though, to the strangely marked papers stolen from the collection in 1701, by the man calling himself Reverend Isaac Jilkes? We can't know. But internal evidence raises an intriguing possibility: could they, perhaps, have found their way into the archives of the Comptrollerate-General for Scrutiny and Survey, rediscovered recently under the library of the UK Ministry of Defence? Was Jilkes a representative of that extraordinary organization, tasked with retrieving certain papers of particular sensitivity before they could become public? Again we can't be sure. Perhaps only the Reverend Minafer could tell us whether his missing documents form part of the source material for the following narrative, recounting another phase of the strange history of the Comptrollerate-General.

As before, the strategic framework of events for this account, between 1648 and 1651, is common knowledge. The detail is drawn directly from the archive of the Comptrollerate-General for Scrutiny and Survey, along with other relevant sources currently available (specific documents are referenced with the SS prefix, or equivalent; references are not given here for the many other documents that have contributed colour and background). The exact play of dialogue and emotion is of course my conjecture, consistent with the data and tending I hope to illuminate rather than distort what happened. If my fictionalization of these incidental elements inspires the reader to their own investigation of the facts, so much the better.

R. J. W.
February 2012

5

Prologue

The Passing

Dawn on the moor, the cold and wary light silvering the stagnant water, and glistening on the grass and the frosted heaps of dead.

The river slips drowsily through the early morning, wide and flat between the flood plains and unexcited by the promise of the sea just a few miles ahead. It has hurried seventy miles in the darkness, south from the hidden dales of the Pennines, then turning to the west to elude the first forays of the sunlight. By the bridge, tiring, the water slides furtive around the obstacles in its flight, the boulders and the tangled, clutching lattice of reeds, looking for the shadows under the stonework. It creeps past the white face of a man slumped in the shallows, trying not to wake him with its sting against his skin, rummages in the sagging sodden jacket and through the breeches, washes over one bare foot and chuckles away into the gloom under the bridge.

A hand plunges down and grabs the jacket, pulls the body over onto its back, and a dead arm splashes among the reeds. *A musketeer, from the uniform; Scottish presumably.* The face is already puffy after a night in the water, the eyes stare shocked into the morning light, and a black-toothed mouth gapes. *Not a good face: born roughly, lived worse.* A few bruises and rips, but there is no sign of a wound on the body, no bloody sword swipe, no punched hole from a musket ball. *Drowned.*

Mustered in some god-forsaken slum with the promise of excitement and a penny a day, a month or two raping and foraging your way through northern England, and your warrior heritage splutters and chokes to death in a stream as your comrades clamber over you to get to safety.

Still the glazed eyes gape.

You're not who I'm after, anyway.

Above, dark against the morning light, a weary shake of the head. Then two great splashes as the man pulls away and tramps out of the water. Around him, the corpses sprawl. Tracks through the mud and reeds show where men have dragged themselves to safety or to collapse, and the bank is scattered with hunched brown forms. Some have the wild distortion of violence, thrown by a ball or ripped open by a flailing sword. Others, from wounds or exhaustion, have collapsed peacefully into the grass and never woken. They could be a herd of cows at rest, faces buried in this pasture; so battered and muddied in the dim morning, the brown shapes seem to be slumping back into the earth. Around them the debris of battle: swords and muskets; pikes held by dead men, and broken pikes abandoned by live ones; bandoliers, belts, hats and boots, purses and bags; dropped, flung, forgotten or wrenched off by the early scavengers. Death has come down the river like a tempest, and he has ripped this army out of the ground and whirled and torn and scattered it across the plain.

A too-practised glance around the bank. At least forty men in this immediate stretch – fifty, say. And all King's men. By this point it had been a rout.

A sigh. The man stiffens. The sigh again, harsh and hoarse, rasping through the grass at his feet. Another musketeer, huddled up like a baby in the mud. The man crouches, an instinctive hand on the body's woollen cap, then another on the shoulder – he can feel how thin the man is through his sleeve – and he carefully rolls the body onto its back. A stomach wound, and it's savage. A pike in his gut many hours ago, and nothing will save him now. The face is ghostly, the eyes closed, but still the hissing comes from the throat.

The man stands, checks around him, pulls the jackets off two nearby corpses and lays them both over the faintly shivering body beneath him. *Go quickly, boy. Nothing left for you in this world.*

A clean face, untouched by sickness or years. A thin, terribly young face. A face drawn in charcoal on paper: the boy is white, and his stomach, two hands frozen feebly at it, is ghastly red.

Stralsund. Breitenfeld. Lützen. Memories of three decades of conflict; a continent of death. *I have been here too often.* The man pulls up his gaze.

More of them had died on the north side of the river, hesitating to splash into it or trying to get to the bridge, cut down by a final cavalry charge when all their powder had gone. The water's clean now: the blood has long ceased to flow, and the current has carried it away to the Irish Sea. But the boulders and the grasses around are rusty in the dawn. Above them, the carcases have formed a breakwater on the bank, piled two and three deep, a mess of uniforms stuck with swords and musket barrels and pikes and arms and legs.

Movement beyond them, against the distant shadow of Preston town. The man drops to a crouch, eyes narrow, face gnarled around them, watching for the movement again. *I've come on too fast. This battle is not yet over.* Horsemen: a patrol out from the town, perhaps. *This is still contested ground.* The horsemen coming on towards the bridge. Drop among the corpses? But his richer, cleaner clothes will stand out. *The bridge.*

Hawk's eyes on the distant movement, the man scurries low over the bank again, against the side of the bridge and down into the shallows. This time his boots slide silent through the water; no splashing, no clumsy movement. Under the bridge, crouching against the curve of the arch. Eyes adjust to the gloom: a body in the shallow water, and he heaves the torso up onto his knees.

The horses are nearer now; he can hear voices, echoing weirdly off the water and through the arch. Even if anyone glances under the bridge and sees a shape, they will see the legs and slumped body of a corpse before they see anything else.

I had no choice. I cannot wait. I have to know where he is.

The thump and rattle of horses on the bridge, then over his head. The patrol is heading south – for Wigan, perhaps.

The man spends twenty minutes crouched in the gloom and the chill water, a dead pikeman on his lap.

He was refighting the battle in reverse. From its scattered fringes of debris, men who'd crawled to die under hedges or lay shivering of wounds and fear in peasant kitchens, he was tracking the chaos inward through the channels of panic to the heart of the slaughter, back to the first shock of contact, the first ugly rattle of sword against pike, the first gasp of understanding that death is really loose and hunting you in this place. He knew that gasp.

He'd come through Wigan in the middle of the night, and fugitives had still been staggering into it gibbering of Cromwell's horsemen behind them. Every bedroom held a wounded Royalist officer, every corner of alley and ditch a soldier. The Roundheads would be on them by now – he'd glimpsed the rearguard as he'd skirted the line of flight, knew it wouldn't stay to guard anything for more than an hour – and the town would be under military law. That meant door-kick searches, and looting. It meant arrest at best for those wounded officers, and herding and robbing and nasty acts of vindictiveness for the rest. By now the Royalist fugitives would be fleeing south again, with the local villagers starting to pick off the stragglers.

But not the man he was looking for. His man should have been with the command party, but was not. He'd caught up with the command party in a churchyard outside Wigan, wide-eyed and leery of Roundhead ghosts in the darkness, and they had shaken their heads and shrugged and waved thumbs over shoulders and hurried away to the south.

So he had continued north, working his way up parallel to the road, through a witches' night of moans and cries and half-glimpsed shiftings in the blackness. Shouts of orders and of self-reassurance emerging from the void, then explosions of thunder and vicious metal rasping and the crackle of muskets as the Roundhead pursuit threw itself once again on the dwindling rearguard. He'd moved among riderless bewildered horses, suddenly pale in the gloom, among gasping fugitives, half-man and half-beast and scurrying away into the hedges as he passed, and among the dead.

Nearer the river, the sun's first tentative advance coming across the plain, he'd come on another devastation: a graveyard of wagons, empty or overturned, smashed boxes thrown around them in the dirt. Hamilton had lost his baggage train as well. Happy pickings for the Roundhead infantry: a Duke's household on the move, gold plate and silver and rich cloths, and. . . and papers. The first breeze teased a few scattered pages among the boxes, and they fluttered at him. A hissed, vicious expletive into the dawn.

Then there had come a shout from among the wagons – a sentry, two sentries. He'd waved and kept his distance. And so to the bridge, through the dead men.

His legs, his back, feel dangerously cold now. His boots are good – most important part of the uniform: *Stiefel vor Stahl*, like the Brandenburgers used to say – but they can't keep out this damp cold for ever. No sound from above, so the stiff old back stretches up and the numbed legs slip through the water to the bank.

The bridge itself is a shambles. Shattered soldiers – Scottish musketeers again – are sprawled all over the narrow way, thick in the dust and slumped over the parapets. The northern end of the bridge is choked with bodies, and they've been dragged aside to allow the cavalry to pursue the fleeing Royalists, or lie broken by the horses charging over them. Here, as the ground opens out towards Preston, the uniforms change. These are Roundhead dead – pikemen, mostly; the bridge was won hard, by men rushing again and again into barrages of musket shot, until at last their pikes could reach the desperate bodies trying frantically to reload and reprime their weapons.

I'm too exposed here.

The eyes can see the battle in the dead men. He's come through the flight in the hours before dawn. The struggle for the bridge, the close-quarter wounds and the vengeance of men who've paid too heavily for their objective, is easily told. But here? The few bodies leading to the town tell a fast assault against the detachments who'd found themselves cut off by the fall of the bridge, and are now either prisoners or scurrying back to Scotland. The main thrust of battle has come from the right, along the river. A lane nearer the water, no bodies but badly churned: Cromwell's legendary cavalry, no doubt, his ironsides, and there had been no one to stop them: the troops trying to defend the bridge had been caught in the flank and caught hard. Another shake of the head.

The trail of death leads away from the river's edge along a muddy road, and he walks it slowly, eyes and ears wide for signs of pursuit. *This is still contested ground.* He reads the battle in the uniforms and in the deaths. A clump of men entangled together – the same clothing, the same symbols tucked in their caps – means a standing fight; musket wounds mean the same. English soldiers among the Royalist dead, now. *Langdale's men. Have you died with them, Langdale, you old goat, or have you survived again?* Cavalrymen, too, and their horses. This fight took many hours, and every fifty yards of it was a mad screaming assault by pikemen and riders on musketeers and on other pikemen, a hacking swirling orgy of noise and metal, the cold fire of a wound in your side and the screams in your ears, and the mud treacherous beneath your feet. They're sodden with it, all the dead men: their blues and reds are a uniform stupid brown, so that it's harder to tell Royalist from Roundhead in their slippery death, and their hands and hair and faces are smeared and clogged and turning brittle grey.

He walks those yards, and he refights those hours, in the faces. *Mannheim. Magdeburg. Vlotho. Too many dead faces.* Pain: screaming cheek-slashed chest-cut pain; groaning gut-shot pain. Exultation: glory; malice; madness. Shock: so surprised; so frightened; so cold; so this is hell. *I have become an accounter of deaths.*

A horse slumped in the mud, two pikes buried in its great chest, face stretched out wild. The rider half beneath him, a sword protruding from under the edge of the chest armour. *You saw that coming and you couldn't do anything about it, could you?* The helmet grille grins up at him. More horses, shot and stabbed and bled, and he knows the screaming that these beasts added to the carnage as they died.

Why did Cromwell stay north of the river?

It's the smell that's lifted his head, nose instinctively seeking higher ground. The wounds are more savage here, the putrefaction more advanced, and the sharp syrupy rancid stench of death and shit hangs low over the carnage. His wider gaze brings him the other bank of the river, the fuller scope of the battle. A chase is fun but futile; nothing more than a clumsy violent race, and the man more determined to escape with his life will always outpace the man more determined to loot what he's left behind. Properly, logically, Cromwell should have come south of the river, to block the Royalist advance.

Cromwell got lucky: with the terrain, with his opponent. *Or perhaps the Godly warrior has the devil in him like they say.*

Faces at peace, and faces now in an eternity of disquiet. Faces molten and faces viciously distorted and faces absent, with the indiscriminating violence of war. A slumped man with his throat cut in the aftermath; a body naked from the waist down, white and silly in the morning, fancy boots and breeches long gone and worth nothing to him now. The dead in heaps, grey and glistening in the frost.

Further away to the south there's movement again. Another patrol, perhaps, or off-duty men on the scavenge. *The battle is not done.*

The lane drops below the surrounding fields, and the bodies cluster like flies around the mud.

This is where it started.

The wounds tell him. The sheer volume of death tells him. He's walking on the bodies now, bodies torn and shattered by the violence, bodies that drowned in the mud. He remembers the endless rain of yesterday as he galloped across England, and he sees today what he was too late for then: the bleary blinking through the downpour as the endless attacks come across the fields, the slippery hacking in the sunken lane as finally a wave of men breaks through the musket fire to the pikes, the gasping for breath and for a mouthful of water through the torrent, the vast onslaught of noise.

Why did Cromwell stay north of the river?

This is where it started, but still he has not found his man. The battle was thickest here, and longest. There will be more officers among the dead. There should. . . but no, their finery will not betray them now, because it will have betrayed them already to the scavengers.

A naked torso. He wrenches at the slippery shoulder; sure enough, the face tells breeding. But not his man. The blackened chest tells close-range musket fire.

A glimpse of brighter cloth at the bottom of a brown pile of death, and he's on his knees rummaging in the squelch of limbs and wounds, the eyes wide with horror and the mouths packed with mud, until he pulls another pale unknown face towards the light for the last time.

Have you somehow slipped away?

The forward edge of the sunken lane, knee-deep in bodies and the wind stinging his ears, trying to see the very first instant of battle, the first fact: a shout of alarm, a musket shot, a thunder of mounted death coming across the Lancashire fields.

He turns away, towards the distant huddle of the town. Much nearer, there's a single oak, and as the wind gusts again something waves to him from behind the trunk.

His boots and legs belong more to the earth now than to him, brown and misshapen and pulling him down with them as he tramps up out of the lane and over to the tree.

You poor fool. Was this what you wanted?

The old man is sitting against the tree as if asleep. He reads the wounds in the torn clothes. The old man has taken a deep cut across the shoulder and a worse one in his side.

Did it feel like heroism? Did it feel like manhood?

The man wasn't really so old, but dying has hurried things along. The face is the distant empty grey of the morning sky beyond. The eyelids hang frail and wrinkled above the hollow cheeks. He had staggered away from the carnage to die, seeking some final moment of privacy, some last trace of the privilege for which he fought. The oak kept its secret well from the scavengers.

He makes a swift search of the body: pockets, but also boots and sleeves, pulling the dead weight away from the tree to be sure he has missed nothing. A few coins, which he leaves. Three or four rose petals, likewise. Then, inside, stubborn among the distorted clothes, a folded piece of paper. He pulls it free, glances at it, and black frown lines rip across his face. This he takes.

The dead face coughs.

Surely not. And something like frustration flickers in him. He crouches closer to the face. Hand against the temple; finger and thumb pulling up the eyelids. There is something stubborn still at work in the old head. Ear and cheek tilted close towards the lips, trying to isolate a ghost of a breeze in the cold morning.

Surely not. He checks the wounds again – especially the side, pulling the clothes uneasily away from the gore, teeth set. These wounds will not be endured for much longer.

Then voices in the wind. A glance behind him. There are men on the bridge again. The eyes come back more intently to the face, to the wounds.

There is no such thing as capture for this man.

For a moment, the two old faces are close. Two grey men alone in the wilderness of the death-blasted moor, ghosts of a fertile age long past.

As gently as he can, he pulls a ring from one of the wounded man's cold fingers; it catches on the old rolls of knuckle-skin. Then he pulls a dagger from his mud-clutched boot. He places the blade tip against the old man's breast, and a simple kiss on the forehead, and then he pushes until the dagger's hilt comes hard against the body.

Thus passes the Comptrollerate-General for Scrutiny and Survey.

1648

The Kingdom in Twilight

'There's men, Miss Rachel, in the trees.'

Brown eyes came up fast from the book. 'In the trees?' Her body seemed sharp, strained; she felt the muscles pulling at her to stand up.

'Yes, miss. Just across the lawn. They might – they might be coming here, miss.'

She was up and across to the window in four long lithe steps, the sweep of her dress hurrying behind her.

I cannot remember when I was not afraid.

Stubborn raindrops still held to the glass, and the pale spread of the front garden flickered at her crazily, distorted and strange through a hundred panes. The garden was a fresh breath of green stretching away, but the oaks fringed dark around its edges.

Among them, the black shapes of men were moving.

~

VERITAS BRITANNICA
Liberty under God in a Kingdom under God

he Lord GOD has shown thoſe who would need it new PROOF of His great MERCY to this our troubled land. At the town of PRESTON in Lancaſhire he has ſmitten with righteous VIOLENCE the upſtart band of Traitours and Scots and Criminals and Cut-throats, which had invaded England with clear and foul intent to uproot the cauſe of RIGHT and GODLY government. The Lord GOD saw fit to grant His armies complete VICTORY, and the invaders are ſundered UTTERLY. General CROMWELL was His inſtrument, and he has harried the fugitive raſcals without compromise or heſitation, as befits the proper execution of GOD'S JUSTICE.

With the ſpurious claim that they were ſupporters of Kingly governance, the invaders croſſed the north of England with much devaſtation and blood; now that army is broken at the hands of the RIGHTEOUS, and thoſe few who eſcaped deſtruction, their cauſe being quite loſt, are returning with violent haſte whence they came, or being captured, wretched and pitiful, by General CROMWELL. General CROMWELL came up on the invaders, under the traitour Duke of HAMILTON, on Auguſt 17 and, finding them ill-diſpoſed athwart the river RIBBLE, fell immediately upon, his conviction being rewarded with complete SUCCESS. The treaſonous HAMILTON and his crew of generals fled at the firſt trump, leaving behind their moſt wretched followers, who died by thouſands. Among their DEAD on the field were SIR JOHN HOUGHTON, THOMAS FERRAND and SIR GEORGE ASTBURY, known for a cloſe adherent and confidant of King Charles.

This is the final CATASTROPHE for the coterie of CORRUPTED and MALEFICIENT adviſors that ſurrounds the King; their avowed intent to uſurp the cauſe of TRUE and LOYAL government having been ſo confounded, which can only be accounted the WILL OF GOD, they muſt now be ſtripped away from the King's perſon as the traitours they are, leaving His Majeſty in direct and proper relation with his loyal ſubjects and their PARLIAMENT.

The door slammed open against the wall, the noise gross and wrong and sending her instinctively backwards, and a soldier was standing on the threshold. He had a smashed grin in a stained and unshaven face, a caricature of impurity and mischief.

'What's here, then?' Big eyes patrolled the room, smiling at the effect of the door slamming and his own words, and then widening with an uneasy excitement as they absorbed the long brown waves of hair and the full sweep of the female body.

He said it again – 'What's here, then?' – but the words were a hesitant substitute for anything better to say; a little tongue wandered over the lower lip. Rachel Astbury tasted revulsion in her throat. Her breath came in an uneasy hiss.

The man began to sway towards her. Was he drunk? Or was this shamble his broken norm? Some stiller part of her brain was telling her that she couldn't even be sure this was a Roundhead, a soldier of Parliament, and not a fugitive King's man.

But then, what did that matter?

'Who's this, then?' He seemed to be conducting a dialogue with his own sly mind. Three yards away he stopped, and his spread hand came up and then travelled down over the undulating image of her body, as if gauging it, or practising the movement.

'Eh? Who, eh?' Somewhere in the house there was a shout, and hurrying steps.

He was swaying forwards again. 'Does the lovely lady have a name, does she?'

She'd rehearsed this scene so often, full of tactics that now seemed somehow obscure, and fears that had by contrast solidified and sharpened.

'Rachel!' But it was not her own voice, and she stood for a moment with her mouth open and her name stumbling on her tongue. 'Rachel!' – Mary's voice, nearer, with footsteps distinct on the flagstones.

Now there was another figure in the doorway, but it wasn't her sister. Another soldier, and there was no way out and no way in for anyone else.

The man was a yard away, eyes wide and hand trembling. The backs of her legs pressed hard against the edge of the bench and her upper body shrank away clumsily above them; her hands clutched at their opposite wrists and against her bodice, in obvious show of defensiveness.

The hand came up again and this time it was right in front her face, dirty fat unsteady fingers reaching for her throat. She felt the palm flesh under her chin, the fingers pressing her skin against her jawbone. 'Rachel!'

Mary was a pale blur behind the soldier in the doorway. Her own focus was wholly the face looming in front of her, every bloodshoot distinct in the eyes, the black hair-stubs sharp on the nose.

The teeth appeared as individual characters in the smile. 'Rachel, is it now?' The little tongue wandered over the lip again, and the mouth pulled open in preparation for some horror. Her fingers scrabbled clumsily at her cuffs.

'Come on, matey.' These, from far away, were not words she could distinguish. 'Hurry along, won't you? The Captain—'

A whistle squealed somewhere, and the vast face flickered in irritation. 'That's us,' the other voice said, 'hurry along.'

The mouth moved closer to hers, and the eyes widened, and her fingers fumbled like frail trembling heartbeats, and then the big egg-white eyes shifted and the focus broke and the hand dropped from her throat and reached behind her.

The man stepped away, staring intently at the silver goblet that the hand now held. 'Lovely,' he whispered, 'lovely.' He looked up at her again, and there was no intent or malice in the eyes any more. He was human again, and simple, and there was a strange innocence to his greed.

The soldier swayed briskly to the door and followed his comrade out, still watching the goblet held proud like a torch, past Mary shrunk close to the wall.

Rachel Astbury collapsed to the bench, the little dagger came free of her cuff and fell from her useless fingers, and she began to shake and gasp uncontrollably, huge painful sobs that lurched in her chest.

—◦~◦—

Astbury House was everything the Captain hated: complacent, rich, Royalist – and not even bold about the fact. Standing in the hall, stolidly fighting his own weariness, he was trying and failing to maintain his politeness in the face of the wheedling of the lord of the manor: always happy to receive the Army, bravest of men, my house is your house, especially if you can eat with a fork, surely no need for the rank and file to be loose in the premises, perhaps we might come to some arrangement?

Sir Anthony Astbury was everything the Captain hated too, and for the same reasons.

He knew the type. Bit of genteel service when the going had been good, retired hurt once it was clear that the King's was a lost cause. Paid his fine to hang on to the estate, God bless Parliament and now please leave me in peace. He could afford to lose some linen and trinkets.

Then two younger women – daughters? – edging in in the wake of the last of his scavengers. The daughters were rather fine, weren't they now? One was sort of stern-looking, and the other was sort of wild – bit upset, perhaps. He hoped there hadn't been anything too nasty. The good Lord knew it was hardly surprising: keep a man in camp for months on end with nothing but small beer and the sad old whores who followed the army, brittle cackling boisterousness and eight kinds of pox, and why wouldn't he go a little moon-crazy when he saw something like this – something so lovely and so fresh, and frankly just so damned *clean*? Had to be careful, though. A village tart found face-down in a ditch didn't seem to register with anyone now, but the gentry tended to complain when their women got knocked around, and complaints would find their way sure as the sun back to him.

That stern one, now. Probably a bit stuck-up, she was, and that was fine; might like to look after a man. Bet she'd run a tight home. And hidden fires inside, perhaps.

The old man was still whining on. Been most devoted in his just obligations to the state, Sir Somebody Somebody could surely vouch for me, paid up prompt and regular. *Bet you did, too: all above board and please go away with your dirty little war.* Sir Anthony Astbury wouldn't be fighting six men for a licey mattress in a tavern tonight.

And now these two London men had appeared. Sombre, black-coated men; something to do with checking or collecting the fines of delinquent Royalists like Astbury.

Proper puritan clerks, the pair of them; quiet and superior. The old man had stopped talking at last, and was watching him anxiously. Just a faint calculating arrogance in the eyes.

The Captain wrestled wearily with his bitterness. *Lord, what wouldn't I give for a warm companionable bed?* 'Sir, these few supplies we have commandeered are deemed essential for the functioning of the Army;

you'll be given tickets of receipt as usual.' *And much good will they do you.* He heard the words falling from him as if from a distance. The old man was about to interrupt again. 'This land is at war! Rebels are up in half the counties of England. Your little luxuries are less important than the survival of the state.'

That had stung. 'Luxuries?' The sneer was emerging onto the face again. 'How—'

'And I'll gladly get your friend in London to come and explain that to you. Or Oliver Cromwell himself, how would you like that?'

Lord, I am so weary.

Unnoticed, one of the London men was standing beside him. The voice was a low firm murmur, inaudible to the others. 'Captain, if we need General Cromwell, I'm sure I could pass a message onward when I'm in London.' The Captain started to scowl. *You smug, miserab—* But there was no attempt at superiority in the face of the man in black. The large eyes looked rather sad. 'Otherwise, perhaps we'll leave the politics for today. I don't envy you, having to settle these men somewhere tonight. And they should have had enough time with the silverware now.'

The Captain managed a heavy smile, nodded slowly. He glanced briefly at the old man, a curt nod to him, and turned and left.

The man in black waited, still, listened to the door close. A solemn nod to the two women, and then he stepped towards Sir Anthony Astbury. But for a moment his glance snapped back to the younger woman, stunned and wild and glaring at him.

Night brought a brief illusion of security to Astbury House. Nothing could be seen from the windows, not even the ominous trees. For a moment, instinctively, Rachel Astbury felt that this smaller existence, behind its locks and bars, was warmer and safer. But the night brought the wind, roaming the estate in the darkness, and stirred up faint animal noises somewhere close by, and the endless creaking of the doors and timbers of the house. In the darkness the family was smaller, and more alone, and the threat outside vaster and less knowable.

After the departure of the soldiers, and the two men from London, her father had at first contrived a little triumphalism. But his pretence at having seen off the intrusions of the world was as transparent to himself as to his daughters and servants, and he quickly relapsed into peevishness. A silent supper, and a brusque prayer, and her father had gone to his study. By some unspoken agreement, and knowing that he would not want company, his two daughters followed him regardless. They sat out of his eye-line, very close together, Mary reading and Rachel sewing.

Astbury House was the tiniest fragments of light and sound in the darkness. Scattered candles in gloomy rooms; the rhythmic sweep of pages under Mary's fingers, and the restless rustling of papers under her father's; occasionally the closing of a door by a servant somewhere else in the building. Outside the wind, and the patrolling birds. If the house could hold its breath, maybe it might not be noticed.

Three mighty hammerings barked into the gloom. The front door; and the knocking was still echoing around the house as Anthony Astbury's head reared up wild-eyed.

Perhaps it had been a trick of each of their imaginations. A clumsy servant. A thunderstorm. A heart.

For a moment Astbury House perched in silence.

Two more great slams at the door, and they all three flinched.

Anthony Astbury had to go. A servant would open the door, but he had to be there. Dragging his brittle courage from its hiding places, Astbury stood and walked on uncomfortable feet to the study door and so into the hall. He threw one glance at his daughters as he passed, accusing them of forcing him to confront the limits of himself.

Rachel found that her fists were locked tight, the material clenched to a rag in them. *I do not know how long I can live like this.* She looked up, and found Mary watching her.

'I have to see.'

Mary nodded. They both stood. By the time they reached the door between study and hall, their father and one of the servants were at the front door, each with a lantern. The two old faces shone and shadowed as they moved.

Then the servant was grappling with the bolts. They heard the hard metal reports as the house loosened its armour, and there was a sudden rush of noise as the storm charged in through the door, throwing the servant back against the wall still clinging to the latch. The wind buffeted back and forth on the doorstep, and they saw their father peering into the night.

After a wary moment, he ventured a step forward, and lifted the lantern higher.

'Great God!' he said, and the words rang shrill into the storm. 'Is it you?'

Any reply from whoever was hidden outside was lost in the noise, but then a shadow had stepped forward over the doorstep and was helping the servant shoulder the door closed. A hat, a broad back, high boots flickered in the lantern light. Suddenly the roar of the storm was silenced with the door's slam and the falling latch. The bolts slid heavily back into place.

The shadowed stranger had said something else, and the Astbury sisters saw their father's face turn to them and say with unnecessary volume, 'We'd better talk in my study.'

They understood, and stepped quickly forwards into the hall and aside.

At last they saw the stranger, as Anthony Astbury led him past them and into the study. A tall man – taller than their father, anyway, and broad with it. An older man, surely; but his physical strength and straight back made him younger. Thick grey hair, as far as they could guess in the distorting glow of the lantern, and the face was ancient and hard.

The stranger was like an old rock, and as he passed them pressed flat against the hall panelling he looked at each of the sisters with unconcealed interest. There was something alive in the dark eyes and the mouth, though they gave no hint of a smile.

On a framework of pikes and the lower branches of a slumped oak, the servants had contrived a rough shelter of blankets and cloaks and scavenged sheets.

Under it, huddled in their own cloaks, three men wriggled fitfully for more comfortable positions among the oak roots, and watched in the lantern light as the material above them grew sodden, bulged down, and began to drip.

'Where is Traquair?'

'I did not see him, your Grace.'

James, First Duke of Hamilton pushed himself up against the trunk, shifted his backside irritably, and watched the lantern.

'You said you know this place?'

'No, your Grace. I heard a name mentioned – a village. I didn't know it.'

The rain flicked heavy and incessant on the blankets, and somewhere out in the night there were the shuffles and mutters of unhappy horses and soldiers.

'Your Grace, they say that Traquair may have. . . may have taken his own road.'

'Deserted, you mean?' The word stung oddly in the Scottish mouth.

'Surely not, your. . .' What was the point? 'Perhaps an hour or two back along the road, your Grace.'

A grunt. 'Clever Traquair. But maybe we'll prove him wrong, eh?'

'Well spoke, your Grace.'

'Herefordshire is in arms; Lingen fights for us there, didn't you say? We will join him.'

'Indeed, sir. We've not had word of him since Chester, but. . .'

The Duke's shoulder had begun to chill. He shifted it a fraction, and felt it clammy. He forced himself not to look at it, not to think of the trunk running with rain. He would hold this position until the end of the conversation.

'Not Pontefract?'

'No, sir. Pontefract holds out, but it's too risky. We'll not make it.'

Hooves heavy in the muffled muddy world outside, and furtive calls.

A murmur through the damp shelter. 'General Middleton? A rider, General.'

Middleton had been silent. Now he glanced at the Duke, and scowled. An undignified scrambling, and he pushed his way out of the shelter on hands and knees, swearing at the water on his neck.

The Duke, head a little forward, stared at the damp wall where Middleton had gone, watching through it, straining for his return. *The things I have suffered for Charles Stuart.*

The General was back within a minute, a sudden shuffling beast in the gloom of the shelter, shaking head and shoulders like a dog. He brushed the water from his face and rewrapped himself in his cloak before he spoke.

'Sir Henry. . .' – he saw the anxiety in the Duke's face, and his shoulders and voice dropped – 'Sir Henry Lingen is beaten, your Grace. On the same day as yourself.'

The Duke's eyes narrowed, and he pushed his head back against the trunk. 'Then Herefordshire is lost to us also.'

'It is lost to us, your Grace.'

Outside, the shapes of indeterminate beasts drifted unhappily in the darkness. Across the unmixed black of the land, the faint foggy lantern glow coming through the drenched blankets floated in the void.

—◦~—

Mary and Rachel Astbury ambushed their father when he was ten feet short of his bedroom, two translucent ghosts in their nightshirts, and his surprise was immediately irritation: 'I told you—'

Mary had retreated a little, but Rachel was still square in front of him. 'Father, who is that man? What's happening?'

He focused properly on her face, the beautiful eyes angry, the skin glowing in the candlelight, and then on her older sister beside her, dark and watchful.

'I have news.' He tried again. 'I have sad news, girls. My brother – my brother George is dead.' He looked into their eyes again, wondering if he was supposed to say more. He found that each of his hands was being held. He tried to form more words, swallowed them down again with difficulty. 'He was killed in a great battle, for the King.'

He pulled his hands away, touched a white slender shoulder with each, and stepped back.

'I'm sorry, Father.' Mary.

'I'd rather not—'

'Who is that man, Father?'

Rachel again, of course.

Sir Anthony Astbury gulped for words. 'I regret to have to say that he is your kin,' he managed eventually. The eyes fell for an instant. 'Kin to your poor late mother, at least.'

He could see the surprise in their eyes, the interest. 'Pay heed to me, girls! That man will not stay here long; I shall see to it. You are not to speak to him, nor give him opportunity to speak to you, nor on any account to allow him to be alone with you.'

With his sudden vehemence, their interest had become bewilderment. 'To your beds now. In the morning all will seem easier.' He was talking as much to himself. He looked up, and was visibly irked to find his daughters still gazing at him. They turned quickly to go.

'He—' They stopped, and the two faces turned back to their father; two re-conjurings of his beautiful young wife, come back in the storm to haunt him, along with her strange and troubled family history.

'He is Sir Mortimer Shay.' The voice dropped to a mutter. 'Mortimer Shay in England again, and in our lives.'

—•—

The Groom of the Stool. Early in his reign, His Majesty, being a less convivial man than his father, had decreed that he would be accompanied at his most intimate proceeding by only one of his attendants.

William Seymour, Marquess of Hertford, was accordingly alone with the King as he knelt to complete the refastening of the King's breeches.

His Majesty, Seymour had learned – and this was the subtlety that had made Seymour the most trusted of the King's attendants – did not like to receive ill news when with many men, not caring to have his vulnerabilities or frustrations observed, this having a tendency to exacerbate his blush and his hesitancy of speech. His Majesty did not like to be in any distress of mind before or during his intimate proceedings, believing this disruptive to the good rhythms of the body and thus detrimental to the health.

So it has to be now, then. Seymour, still on one knee, held his head bowed for an extra moment. Still on his knees, he shuffled backwards a pace and made an exaggerated show of checking the rearrangement of the King's garments. Inconceivable that His Majesty could be allowed to seem in the slightest way foolish. Then he stood and stepped back.

He held out a bowl of warmed water, and the King carefully washed his hands, the small pale fingers exploring each other slowly and reflectively in a rare moment away from the world. *Imprisoned by the father; opposed the son; rejoined him in time for his defeat and incarceration.*

He held out a towel, and the King carefully dried his hands. *The wrong side on every occasion, and fate has decreed that I, that have scorned this family over two generations, shall at the last be closer to Charles Stuart than any man living, and tell the hours of his misfortunes.*

He held out a smaller bowl, of rose water, and the King carefully dabbled his fingers in it, each hand in turn and each tip in turn flickering in and out of the liquid. The King's head is bowed still, watching his own fingers.

He held out a new towel, and the King carefully touched his fingers on it. The King likes to believe that he is alone, even when he is not.

'Your Majesty.' The King looked up. The King should speak first. The King knows that Seymour would only intrude in this way if he needed to impart news privately.

The wide sad eyes gazed at Seymour. 'Your Majesty, I regret that we have ill tidings from the north.'

❧

From an inn in Leeds, the Sign of the Boar, riders went south and north and east to the sea with messages. The messages were addressed to four different men in four different cities: to John Fenniman, of London; to Jacob Hoy, of Edinburgh; to Pierre Mazzini, of Paris; and to Pieter de Gucht of Amsterdam.

Shay had hesitated over London. It seemed unlikely that he would get a reply from London. But one never knew.

The message was the same in each case. The writer, Francis Padget, was interested in acquiring a copy of the *Codex Walther*. A friend of his, Mortimer Shay, had once recommended the recipient as a man who might be able to assist him in such matters. If the recipient was able to oblige him, he should reply to Francis Padget at the same address in Leeds.

Francis Padget did not exist. John Fenniman, Jacob Hoy, Pierre Mazzini and Pieter de Gucht did not exist either. But there were other men in those four cities who, if they still lived, and if the circumstances allowed, would be alert for messages addressed to those names, and would be able to provide proofs of identity sufficient to receive the messages. Men who would know the real and dramatic meaning of a reference to the *Codex*.

Mortimer Shay did exist, and he would be waiting for a reply.

In the first pale whisper of dawn, a short, stout man kneels in a copse of trees near the town of Colchester. Again he looks all around him. Again he empties his mind and concentrates all attention in his ears.

The cold is a hollow ache through his body, scalding his cheeks and his hands. The promise of warmth is magnified by the parallel promise of safety. The longbow in his left hand he can explain – a rustic eccentricity – don't a man deserve a rabbit if he can get it, in these bad times? The arrow in his right hand will get him hanged.

Ahead, vague in the grass, he can see Parliamentarian sentries wrapped in dew-covered cloaks and drowsy. Beyond them, two hundred yards off, loom the walls of Colchester. His breaths come fast and short – fierce puffs of steam in the morning.

An arrow from a longbow in even moderately competent hands will cover those two hundred yards and could cover as many again. The two hundred will do, and precise accuracy is not necessary. Again the slow, staring perusal all around to his left and then to right. Again the ferocious intensity of listening.

The only movement in the ghostly grey scene, he rolls his shoulders, sets his knees solid, and with one fluid motion fits arrow against string and pulls the string back in a mighty heave until the feathers tickle his ear, holds – for pride, for one long breath – and then the arrow is away with a hiss into the dawn.

A faint rattle as the arrow hits the town wall, but he does not hear it: frozen in the posture, then again the look around, again the listening, and he is away at a crouch through the undergrowth, breathing free and dreaming of breakfast.

Soon after – the treetops are silvering, but the army of Parliament still sleeps in grey – a small door opens in a shadow in a cleft in the walls of Colchester. A figure stands still, and watchful – first for any sign of life from the besieging army, then scanning the ground nearby. The arrow was aimed at this point, and he sees it almost immediately. Another check for movement nearby, four purposeful strides and he has the arrow, and is back at the door and safe inside. The door has been open for considerably less than a minute.

He waits until he is back in his lodging room, the arrow tucked into his coat, before unwrapping the message from the arrow shaft.

Five words only are on the paper, and something dies in his hungry gut.

Again he is hurrying through the town, and now its chaos offers him only tragedy rather than defiant hope. Crumbled walls, burned houses, a hollow-cheeked woman staring wild at him, the blanket-covered mounds of dead, the stench, two soldiers cornering a cat, a dead-end – yesterday there was a road here, and now it's blocked by a mess of rubble and timber – a smear of blood on stone where some other animal has been caught and killed, a listless soldier trudging nowhere, a forlorn flag.

He has not heard conversation on the street for many days. There is nothing to say, and other people's faces offer only despair, and shame.

The sentries know him, and don't care any more, and soon he is knocking at a door, entering, handing the paper to a dapper dark man interrupted while pulling on his boots. The man takes the paper but still watches him.

He shakes his head.

It's a decent face in front of him: not handsome, but good. The siege has turned it inside out, the flesh becoming hollow. He has marked the change day by day, complacency becoming piety, for that is what hunger will do to a man, and it's somehow more noble now. Something flickers, uncontrolled, around the mouth. The decent man breaks his gaze and looks down at the paper.

Hamilton's army destroyed. Invasion scattered.

In the third week of August 1648, a stranger was travelling the land around Preston. North to Kendal, east to Skipton and Halifax, and south to Wigan, he moved from tavern to tavern and to the occasional sympathetic private house. He asked after friends who had been involved in the fighting, selecting the army according to the likely inclination of his host.

Where he found a soldier – a fugitive Royalist seeking some kind of absolution, a Roundhead ready to take a drink and give his opinions – he gathered details of the Preston campaign: the men and the movements, the manoeuvres and the tactics.

It was a waiting time, a time of frustration, worse because Shay didn't know what he was looking for in the conversations. They were merely a way to pass the hours, and to do so as productively as possible. He was storing up facts and ideas, as if for winter. Information, like Oliver Cromwell, had a way of coming back at you when you didn't expect it.

<hr />

Thus Colonel Thomas Rainsborough: a pale, domed head with golden-brown hair falling in thick waves behind it; the crown hairless and so emphasizing the strange pallor. Hooded hawk's eyes under high brows, a small vivid red mouth. A golden wisp of moustache brushing the lips. An elegant angel of a face.

Colonel Thomas Rainsborough at prayer: the eyes lightly closed, the face even more uniformly pale, the lips flickering with devotion, nibbling at the words and whispering them intimately to the infinite.

Colonel Thomas Rainsborough at the siege of Colchester. On 21st August the defenders sent out five hundred of their womenfolk to beg for food. For there might – even after the frenzied skirmishes, after the starvation and the barrage, the endless mad explosions of stone as the balls shattered the fabric of the old town, shattered history itself, after the bitter heckling and the nasty violences, after the poisoned bullets and the thumbscrews and the matches lit under fingernails, the violation of the tombs, the desecration of the bodies – even after all this there might still be pity and charity and a gentleman in the besieging force.

Uneasy, frightened, ashamed at their weakness as beggars and their implied weakness as women, the crowd drifted towards the besiegers' lines. There was an uncomfortable shifting among the encircling forces as they realized what was happening, shouts and gallops and hasty consultations. Colonel Rainsborough, roused from prayer by an orderly who knew that of all things one never roused the Colonel from prayer, ordered a volley of musket fire over the heads of the women.

Still the herd shuffled forwards, leaderless and random and faces down, towards the Parliamentarian lines. Four of the women were grabbed – a shifting, a murmuring of alarm, a nascent moaning among the others – and Colonel Rainsborough had them stripped naked. Laughter across the field, the unbeautiful animal laughter of men as men, and fear: nakedness is what comes before violence; nakedness is what comes before violation; nakedness is what comes before death. After nakedness, anything is possible.

Then he sent the women back. Lost between worlds, dumb and hungry and stripped of humanity and hope, the herd drifted back into the besieged town.

The things I have suffered for Charles Stuart.

James, Duke of Hamilton sat heavy on his horse. The compact body was slumped, the clothes battered. A hard freakish wind threw gusts of rain at man and horse, blustering and dropping, roaring in the ears then vanishing, and as suddenly launching the deluge from some new quarter. The road east from Uttoxeter rises gently, and the Duke found himself at the top of a shallow hill, surrounded by the incessant, exhausting storm and the surly remnant of his army.

There was some further obstacle, some new delay. His mind was numb to it all now.

Another flurry of wind and rain at his back, and his neck hunched instinctively. The large eyes flicked around. It had been a long time since he'd really looked at his army. Too much mutual resentment. Too much shame. Now that he glimpsed it, he realized how small and straggled it had become. The regiments empty-ranked and intermingled. The few horses hang-necked. The riders slumped like their commander. The weapons carried careless and awry. A musket dropped at the roadside, a ribbon trodden in the mud, a blanket wrapped around a shivering head, the wordless squelching trudge, and the faces that would not look back at him: drowned faces, sullen, beaten. The unearthly force that was Cromwell, the long meandering flight across the country, the sudden alarms and the sleepless nights, and the eternal furnace of wind and rain, had eaten and shrivelled the army like some vicious plague.

'The men'll go no further, your Grace.' A voice at his side.

Head up suddenly with the anger and the pride, and damn the rain. 'The hell they won't! I'll talk—'

'Your Grace!' The hand white on the Duke's arm – uncontrolled, improper. An uneasy release. 'That would be. . . perhaps a risk. And beneath your dignity.'

'Then they can rot here. We'll away!' The wind blustering up around his face, catching the words and swallowing them. 'Come on, then!'

But again the wrong hand on the Duke's arm. 'They won't. . .' The words caught. 'They won't allow us, your Grace. Too many of the officers have already fled.'

'Aye, I wondered where Langdale had got to.' The Duke's heavy features dark and scornful.

'The men. . . insist that they will keep us here at any hazard.'

James, Duke of Hamilton: a low black cloud, hanging solitary on the little hill.

＊ ～ ～

In the final week of August, the stranger shifted base eastwards, from the districts around Preston to the districts around Leeds. It was unlikely that a reply would come yet – there was certainly no chance of anything from Amsterdam or Paris – but something was just possible from London or Edinburgh. He read news-sheets and pamphlets wherever he could find them, for they were all the information he could get for now. As he travelled, he sounded casually the opinions and loyalties and characters of innkeepers and farmers, shopkeepers and clergymen. Where they were promising, he probed – tested, challenged, encouraged, reached out. One never knew when one might need a good hand or a good heart.

⁓ ⁓

'George Astbury is dead. On the field at Preston.'

'What cause had he for that? It was neither his inclination nor his duty! The man who holds that office is supposed to stand above the fray, to work outside the world. What did he think he was playing at?'

'You must ask him when you see him. Until that time, we who are left must shift to survive as we can.'

'We always thought him an uneasy choice. Who is to follow?'

A pause.

'Shay.'

'Shay? Do you offer me an opinion or a decision?'

'I offer you a fact. Shay is in possession of the field. He has the experience. He is reassuming control of the organization. He fulfils the office.'

'Mortimer Shay is a living chaos. Shay is misrule; Shay is mayhem; Shay is blood.'

'These are not settled or normal times. Cometh the hour, cometh the man.'

⁓ ⁓

Uttoxeter's main street was slick with mud, dragged on a thousand boots and softened and smeared over the ground by the rain that still fell steady.

In the middle of the street, face to another of the sky's grim clouds and cloak gusting and whipping around him, James, Duke of Hamilton stood silent and defeated.

In front of him, watching uneasily and trying to maintain his composure, was a Roundhead trumpeter: the most junior of soldiers, the most humiliating of conquerors.

This, then, was the final illumination of the character of the men who had beaten and hunted him. This shaming was more ruthless than anything inflicted in the fields around Preston. The old world and the old ways were to be dismantled and trodden into the dust.

The storm battered and soaked the two men, the Duke and the soldier, facing each other in the mud and unable to speak, watched by a thousand empty eyes in windows and gutters.

The things I have suffered for Charles Stuart.

———

Sir, these are the news from Colchester, this day the 27th August. The town is very like to fall tomorrow, so this may be my last despatch to you. If you have not already, please now consider this knot of the net broke. The besiegers cut our water three weeks past, fresh food as I told you is long become fable, and I doubt that there remains one solitary dog horse etc living and if it does so it must be the miserablest scrawny beast and still sold for a King's ransom. We are become, all of us, from Lord Norwich down to the lowliest, miserable scrawny beasts, and I fear we would fetch no price, nor may we avail that King no ransom of hope or support. Lord Norwich and the aristocrats and Sir Charles Lucas and the soldiers are agreed that the routing of the Scotch army at Preston, which I learned privily four days past and which Sir Thomas Fairfax in the besieging lines around was blithe to let us know one day later with much cannonado of celebration and sending of kites into our walls, renders our endurance futile. There is none to come to our aid, and none to whom we might provide aid. For weeks past we have convinced the people of this town and the soldiers among them to endure the worst privations that ever civilised Christians saw, such that all that inhabit this place be nothing but maggot-fed ghosts and skeletons, and the extremity of their suffering and this with much sickness and outrage from our foes leaving them in their spirits closer to beasts than human souls. Now even the smallest child if it yet draw breath knows of the rout of his Grace at Preston, and no longer will they accept any entreaty to logick or to honour to undergo one further minute of privation, nor in truth dare we offer such entreaty. For sake of duty to Christian mercy we are obliged to end the great sufferings of these honest people, not the least of which have been our ever more desperate and brutalised soldiers who have not scrupled to use violence and fire to secure for themselves what little sustenance there may be, and offer ourselves to the hands of our besiegers and the will of God.

Discussions began between Sir T. Fairfax and our own Council shortly after the news of the disaster at Preston had spread, and the terms of surrender are near agreed. There was a movement by some of the hotter bloods in the leadership to cut their way out of town and force the parliamentarian lines, but it was thought that the people of the town would thwart this purpose and in truth I doubt the strength and spirit of those who would have attempted it, so frail and so forlorn are we become. From Fairfax the men are promised fair quarter, the town must pay a fine, and the Lords and Gentlemen must become prisoners of mercy and trust that there yet be Gentlemen in the armies of our enemies in this God-forsaken time. General Fairfax is known for a good man but much worn down by this decade of war, as might be any man with half of his sensitivity, and among his officers Colonel Rainsborowe is held as an epitome of pitilessness and implacable cruelty, a self-reputed breaker of inequalities and instrument of God. If I have sure means of saving for you my papers and the Directory I will do so, otherwise according to our practice I will ensure their destruction at any cost. For myself, I may have no certain expectation. I hope that I have done my duty, and I hope that I may meet my fate with honour. I give this message into our usual trusted means, and myself into the hands of the Lord. My respects and humble services to you, Sir. Most faithfully, A. P.

[SS C/S/48/9]

᷍

Leeds on the point of evening, turning cold as the sun drops behind the buildings: a rider out of the far north appeared in Eastgate Street with the first candles. He held his horse at a walk, inconspicuous and able to keep alert to the town around him, to read the faces and mood. He only once had to ask his way, quietly, of a shopkeeper on his way home.

Having seen the Sign of the Boar, he kept the horse walking, passing the inn without breaking step. He only stopped when he reached the next inn: took a room; saw his horse lodged.

Then, in the first gentle gloom of evening, he walked back along Eastgate Street and stepped cautiously into the Sign of the Boar. He bought a drink, watched the room for half an hour. Only then, and with the inn room quieter now, did he step to the bar and ask for Francis Padget.

∽ ∽

ROYALIST THREAT IN THE CITY: RESULTS OF INTERROGATIONS CONDUCTED AUGUST 16. 1648–AUGUST 20. 1648

There is wide expectation in the city of some tumult, in the favour of the King and the Prince of Wales and the Royalist cause. There has been yet no effect of the battle fought at Preston, and the City remains uncertain in its loyalties and restless for some improvement in its conditions. Significant preparations have been made for a rising, presumably rallying the trained bands to their formal allegiances. Browne is spoken of as commander, or perhaps Hollinge, and there are wild rumours of secret preparations of yet unidentified infantry and cavalry detachments. Such forces would of course enable the King's adherents to dominate the wealth and importance of the City of London, and would present a grave danger to General Fairfax at Colchester while General Cromwell remained so far from the capital.

[PAPERS OF THE LONG PARLIAMENT, M/48.102,
PHILADELPHIA UNIVERSITY LIBRARY TAKASHI COLLECTION]

∽ ∽

Dearest Cromwell,

this by way of caution or encouragement, for as usual our Parliament does not act with the same vigour, clarity, and integrity as our Army. Notwithstanding your victory of the week past, for which every man here

has given his thanks to God humbly and right heartily, both the House
of Commons and the House of Lords have this day repealed the Vote
of No Addresses, thereby enabling their negotiations with King Charles
to resume immediately, and I think that this be their aim. I perceive no
sign that the approach or the ideals of Parliament's commissioners in
treating with the King would display any of the strength appropriate to
our cause, to your recent success, or to the slippery history of the King in
such proceedings, and I rather think that as usual they hope to hurry to a
compromise by the straightest route.

My love and my duty to you,

O. St John

August 24. 1648

Fleet report, August 26.: inshore scouting vessels report that the ships of
the Prince of Wales, which were thought to be making eastward for the
continent, have turned and are bound for the mouth of the Thames. We
can report no healthy spirit among the crews of our own craft anchored
in the river, and beg leave to present our most urgent concern at the
uncertain and ominous prospect.

The preacher's voice soared and rasped, his shoulders rising and falling
and his hands conjuring the words out of his chest. From the doorway,
many of the actual words were lost, but the tone of the voice was clear,
its exhortations and accusations, its bitter denunciations and soft
prayers.

There were two men in the doorway, one in the uniform of a Roundhead
cavalry officer, the other in heavy practical civilian clothes.

'You want him?' murmured the first.

A shake of the head. 'No need to interrupt. No point in making it worse.'

The man in question could also be seen easily from the doorway. Seated in one of a semicircle of chairs, the most powerful man in England stared with rigid attention at the preacher, jowls slumped and swarthy and large eyes unblinking.

The cavalry officer murmured, 'Not good?'

Another shake of the head. 'The south's alive with Royalists, and while the Army's fighting up here the Parliament's getting ready to give it all away again. He's going to be furious.'

When he visited the Sign of the Boar again the next day, the rider found a message for him from a man passing as Francis Padget. An hour later, he was out of the city and trotting steadily towards a certain crossroads.

He slowed the horse as he came within a hundred yards of the crossroads. It was a well-chosen spot. The land was flat and open all around; nowhere for either party to have set a trap. He kept the horse at a walk, peering ahead to the crossroads, around him, occasionally unobtrusively over his shoulder.

At fifty yards he saw the shape of a man on a horse, under an oak by the junction. His own horse's ears pricked up, and the rhythm of the walk altered for a moment. He checked that the bag slung by his right leg was open, and let the horse walk on.

Mortimer Shay watched him come: watched the rhythm of the horse, watched the posture of the man, checked all around himself, focused on the road beyond the rider leading back to Leeds. Eventually he eased his horse out away from the tree and into the roadway. As it emerged from under the shadow of the branches, the animal shied at the sunlight, and the hooves stuttered on the ground. Shay found himself blinking in the sudden glare too, forced himself to keep his gaze on the approaching rider despite the orange pain in his eyes.

The two horses edged closer to each other, hoof-beat by hoof-beat on the uneven ground, the men watching each other with the same rhythm: the face, the body, and quickly around; the face again.

Shay said, 'Have you travelled far, pilgrim?'

'I have, and I've farther still to go.'

'God and the King's justice go with you.'

'God save the King.'

They had stopped still, close enough for the horses to be sniffing at each other's manes.

Shay scanned the face again, and the poised body. He saw the bag slung loose at the other man's knee, and stiffened as he saw the pistol butt protruding from the opening.

He forced his eyes up to the man's face. The envoys of the Committee were implacable. If Shay had been marked for death, no words would save him now.

The other had seen the stiffening of his body, saw the intensity in his eyes. Shay held his body firm; a sudden movement could provoke his death regardless.

The other man moved his hand slowly down towards his knee. Still he held Shay's eyes. Slowly, he wiped his palm on his thigh, and the trace of a smile came to his lips.

'You must be the friend of Francis Padget.'

'I am Shay.'

A nod from the other. 'I have heard something of you.' He held Shay's eyes for a moment, and then his gaze dropped. Shay held up his left hand clenched, and the man examined the ring that glowed dull on the little finger.

'You've come from Edinburgh?'

'I have. Whither else did you write?' The accent sounded strained, as if the man was uncomfortable with the conversation.

'London, Paris and Amsterdam.'

A nod. 'We have sent to each. You will receive no reply from any but us.'

Shay waited.

The rider said, 'My message to you is simple enough, sir, and I hope it suffices.'

The message was simple indeed: the message was a single word; a place.

Shay repeated it once, and the other nodded, and pulled at the reins of his horse. 'I'll leave you to your road, sir. Leeds will not see me again.' He stopped, and gazed respectfully at Shay. 'I pray that God go with you on your journey.'

MERCURIUS FIDELIS

or

The honeſt truth written for every Engliſhman
that cares to read it

From MONDAY, AUGUST 24. *to* MONDAY, AUGUST 31. 1648.

FRIDAY, AUGUST 28.

On this day at about 6 of the clock was ſeen over Oxford with great alarm by many perſons there a great black cloud, & ſhortly it did appear to run with blood, which was taken as an omen of great woe for ſome though it was not known whom. On this ſame day were found divers other ſigns of ill-portent, among them a cow of Reading that did give blood and not milk & a plague of dead fiſh at Marlow.

On this ſame day alſo occurred after long and deſperate trial the fall of the town of Colcheſter. As it ſhall ſurely be ſeen, the black omens of heaven were both for this defeat of proud men & alſo for the ſhameful and barbarous handling of the vanquiſhed. The ſtruggle of Colcheſter had laſted fully two months and one half, & the oppreſſed within the walls were teſted with many and growing torments, ſuch as no water and great ſickneſſe and the foul uſages of the enemy. The townſpeople had reſort to eat their horſes, & the horſes the dogs, & the dogs the cats, etc, & them all riven with maggots and plagues. The EARL of NORWICH, and Sir CHARLES LUCAS, and Sir GEORGE LISLE, and the other Lords and Gentlemen having command of the defences, were reſolved to proſecute their ſtruggle to the uttermoſt, but the women and the children did cry unto them GOOD SIRS WE HAVE NO FOOD AND ARE SORE HUNGRY AND AFRAID and when at laſt there was no food more they ſought terms.

Sir THOMAS FAIRFAX, commanding the attacking army, had according to all the normal uſages of war and the habits of

Englifhmen promifed quarter and good treatment for all, but he fhamefully broke this promife and Sir GEORGE LISLE and Sir CHARLES LUCAS were murdered by the foldiers. Sir CHARLES LUCAS was fhot firft, and he died in the arms of his comrade. The foldiers faid to Sir GEORGE LISLE that they were fure to hit him and he replied that I HAVE BEEN NEARER YOU WHEN YOU HAVE MISSED ME.

This was the fouleft deed that I think ever was done in the hiftory of the war in thefe iflands.

[SS C/T/48/4 (EXTRACT)]

—⁓—

Another day, another crossroads outside Leeds, and another rider clumping towards a rendezvous.

Shay waiting by the junction again. The hooves of the approaching horse stamped slow enough to be counted.

Something seemed... the rider was a woman. Shay wondered what story she had for her journey south. Perhaps there was a servant in town, or back along the road.

She rode well: steady, flexible. Instinctively, Shay looked optimistically at the face. Not a fair woman, but a strong one – dark and sure.

The same exchange of greetings, the invocations of a captive King and a disputed God, and again Shay showed the gleam of the ring on his finger. The woman nodded, and Shay knew she was reviewing the protocols in her head. Now she looked up – still there was no relaxation in her face – and spoke.

Again, a messenger had come full two hundred miles to pass a single word: a name.

—⁓—

Some days later, a letter arrived at the Sign of the Boar in Leeds, addressed to Mr Francis Padget. It was put by, as letters were, for travellers and local residents. It was a full week before a large, older man appeared in the inn and, having taken a drink, asked whether there might be any correspondence for Padget. The letter was produced, the drink finished, and the man disappeared back into the town.

Once well out of town, and alone on the road, Shay pulled the letter from inside his coat. No obvious sign of tampering, though it was rarely possible to tell – unless you were dealing with complete fools, and the decade had taught the royal cause hard that it was not.

The letter was from Jacob Hoy, bookseller of Edinburgh. He regretted that he himself could not satisfy Mr Padget's desire for a copy of the *Codex Walther*, but he had heard it said that Master Peter Staurby had – no more than a year ago, anyway – been in possession of one.

Staurby. Shay read the name again, then replaced the letter in his coat; he would destroy it in the first fireplace he reached.

He rode on, only half conscious of the pale morning around him, the wet fields.

Staurby. Something about the name. Something – *Good grief. Astbury, you old fool. You fool of a schoolboy, you amateur.* The old man had not died too soon; the system had to be gripped, and quickly. *The age of such games is past; this is a new world.*

He could not assume that the place was not being watched, which meant both that his approach must be unremarkable but also that he could not make any sign of watching himself. Behaviour intended to escape scrutiny is dangerous enough, but nothing so much as behaviour intended to detect scrutiny exposes a man to it. So, no circuits, no dawdlings in the street, no adjacent vantage points, no more significant scanning of his surroundings than a man might reasonably do to find his way.

The house of Mr Farthing, he had learned from one courier. The town of Stoke, he had learned from the other. In the town, discreetly, he learned that the house of Henry Farthing was better known as the Jug – an inn.

Shay liked inns. No one could remark on a man entering or leaving an inn at most times of day or night. A man could stay in an inn for a few minutes or a few hours and not be remarked either way. He was also pleased because it suggested that Astbury had shown some sense in managing his messages: knowing Astbury, he had feared hollow oak-trunks and loose flagstones.

Shay rode up to the Jug at unremarkable pace, and left his horse in the yard. There was a rich, fat smell there, and his instinct was assuming horse shit while something in his brain told him he was wrong. He stepped into the inn. It was a warm morning and the fire wasn't lit, but the chairs were more comfortable by the chimney and he sat there for an hour, drinking steadily. There were three other customers for different periods of his stay, and he responded to their casual bites of conversation.

Then he left: watching the little details of the rooms, the faces, the movements of people in the street outside, he left – got on his horse, trotted steadily out of town.

The following day, at around the same time, Henry Farthing heard faintly the sounds of an arrival in his yard – the calling for the ostler, the whinnying of a horse – and glimpsed movement through a small back window. A moment later the new arrival was in the main room of the Jug Inn.

A man getting on in years, but big and healthy by the look of him. A man of power, Farthing felt. Did he remember the man from before? Yesterday, even? So many faces.

The man ordered a drink, and sat – the chair wasn't a strong one, and it creaked badly as he dropped into it – ruminating near the door.

There was another drinker in the room – a trader from the square, in out of the day just for a moment's ease, been here a quarter-hour already and wouldn't be much longer – and then sure enough he was gone.

The big man still sat in silence; half asleep, sort of. Eventually he seemed to find himself. He looked around the room – at the window, at the door – then stood and walked towards the bar. Farthing watched the looming figure, tried to read the expression.

'I'm looking for Henry Farthing.'

'Me, sir.'

It was a strong face in front of him – big-featured, and worn, the lines deep between the brows and crackling around the eyes. 'You keep messages, papers: have you anything for Peter Staurby?'

Farthing felt his eyes widening in his face. That name. So rarely heard – sometimes letters were collected in person by one of two faces he'd come to recognize, and sometimes the letters just disappeared during a busy day – and hearing it revived an old unease.

'I – I'll check, sir. One moment.' He turned away into the back room.

The name was an ulcer, flashes of discomfort and never quite forgotten. He was doing nothing wrong – surely, he was doing nothing wrong. But the Staurby correspondence was trouble and, in an age without law, trouble preyed unpredictable and vicious like a snake.

When he returned to the main room, the stranger was halfway between bar and door, watching him intently, somehow on edge. A man alert to surprises; a man who would be trouble and attract trouble.

He swallowed. 'Just two, sir.' The man was back at the bar, nodding once. 'I don't – I don't recognize. . .'

Grey, cold eyes stared into him. Then the old man lifted his fist, and Farthing saw the ring: a flash of the first remembered pain of this business, years ago now. He looked up into the eyes, nodded with a little frenzy, eager to placate. 'Thank you, sir. I'll be sure to remember.'

The man took the papers. 'Don't remember too hard, Master Farthing.'

'No. No, sir.'

'I don't know that Staurby will be getting many more letters. I might need to collect for other friends, time by time.'

'Of course. Anything, sir.' He opened his mouth to speak – couldn't manage it – tried again. 'Some papers have been destroyed, sir. It was the instruction. Burned. After every week, if not collected.' He waited for the reaction.

A pause, and then the curtest nod. 'I'm pleased to hear it. For now you will continue the same system of precautions exactly.'

'Of course, sir.'

Something rapped on the bar, and Farthing's eyes snapped down.

A gold coin. 'Thank you – thank you very much, sir.'

'A tidy inn this, Master Farthing. Good luck to you.' And the big man was gone.

As Shay stepped back into the inn yard, the smell was nagging at him again – not horses, surely; sweeter, more exotic – and finally he saw it: an apothecary's shop backed onto the yard too: a dark doorway, green things in its shadows, strange small sacks and boxes around it.

The name – Staurby – would need to be changed.

For a moment, Shay had wondered at what he might have missed in the letters that Farthing had dutifully burned. The thought faded quickly. *If I am to fret, it must be about the book.*

But now he felt something building in him, some excitement or strength. The men of shadows had decided to legitimize that unknown knife-thrust on Preston field. Now he had ears in every significant chamber in the kingdom, eyes on every desk. Now all England spoke to him. Once again, he was master of the network of the Comptrollerate-General.

The first of the two reports retrieved from the Jug Inn was the last report out of Colchester, written on 27th August and rightly predicting the town's fall the following day. Shay read the summary of the last futile flickers of pride and nobility with irritation suppressing sympathy. The second report was much shorter, and more recent.

> *Sir, this by my hand but to pass you the words of another. I learn that Sir Thomas Fairfax has completed his new dispositions in and around the fallen town of Colchester. The people of that place, with one day of warm thin soup in their bellies, have quite forgot that they ever knew or had a King, and the blood yet undried where poor Lucas and Lisle were slain. Colonel Thomas Rainesborowe is detached by General Fairfax to join the siege of Pontefract.*
> *Faithfully, T. S.*

[SS C/S/48/10]

Sir Mortimer Shay: away from Stoke now and a shadow against a beech-trunk under the low roof of its branches. *And why in God's name do I care for Colchester's hungry and for this Colonel?* A shake of the head at his predecessor's diversion of resources into inefficient irrelevance.

Once again, he reached into an inner pocket and removed the page recovered from George Astbury's body on Preston field. A simple report – almost routine – from inside besieged Pontefract, and he wondered at it.

———— ~~~~

At least once in a week, usually on a Saturday when the King slept in the afternoon, or when he had adequate other company, William Seymour would beg permission from the castle Governor to walk down to the river. The begging was a humiliating business, and the answer inconsistent, but the Governor was not a bad fellow – and where, after all, could he really get to on the island?

His regular path took him down through the town – the temporary sensation of freedom, of air that was really his, enabled him to endure the wide eyes of the peasants, the pointing – to where the Medina river became the estuary, and so on towards the sea.

Always a sentry came with him. It was a routine of habit, of discipline, for he had nowhere to escape to and they probably wouldn't care if he did. But it confirmed that he was different from other men now – a member of a new and more select aristocracy, of the isolated, the unfree. The world he had roamed had shrunk now, to the world of that little majesty in his closely watched rooms in the castle, to the castle grounds, to the views around the Isle of Wight from the battlements, to this one merciful breath of air, the fetid closeness of the town and the empty freshness of the river.

It was colder today. Autumn was slowing, shrinking towards death. The riverbanks were darkening as the leaves turned and fell, and the colours were becoming simpler and starker: the grey flicker of the water, the sterile wall of sky. There were few boats on the estuary, and no travellers on the path today. Ahead, a rowing boat had been pulled half out of the water onto the bank, two men pottering slow around it.

He strode on, feeling his stride lengthen, enjoying the feel of the path under his feet, solid ground and his to walk on. Once they were clear of the town the sentry would drop back a bit – they hardly felt comfortable with each other – and he could pretend that he was alone.

'Seymour.' The sound jolted him.

The unexpected sound and, he realized, the knowledge of his name.

One of the men at the boat – he had reached it without noticing – standing against it now, looking along the path towards the sentry then murmuring a word over his shoulder to the other boatman. The other glanced up, then just stood and ambled away past him in the direction of the town. The first man had turned towards him again: an old face, worn but hard –

'Shay!'

'A word or two, if you will.' A glance back along the path, and he pulled off a rough and shapeless cap. 'Please preserve your calm and your stance. I am a humble river man, you are bored enough to talk to me. Your sentinel will give us a few minutes, I imagine.'

Mortimer Shay, leaning against a little fisher-boat in anonymous working clothes, a ghost from history come out of the waters in the middle of the Isle of Wight, not a mile from the King. Seymour said, 'We thought you dead, or abroad.'

'I am returned to office.'

'The devil you are.'

'Nevertheless.'

'I rather think the King decides such matters.'

'I rather think the King should begin to listen to better advice.'

Seymour's shoulders dropped. Eventually he nodded.

'By all means check with the Committee. You will have channels of communication, no doubt.'

'Be sure that I'll check, Shay. Where is your Committee now, whoever they are? Fled with the rest?'

Shay shifted in the sand. 'The Committee is everywhere and nowhere. I presume that most are abroad now. One or two in Scotland, perhaps.' He looked up towards the town and the castle sitting over it. 'None, I'd imagine, is here. Confinement does not sit naturally with the Committee.'

'But you're not sure where they are?'

'I'm not sure *who* they are. I can hardly be sure where they are, can I? How does His Majesty?'

Seymour hesitated. Out on the water, two ducks were drifting with the flow, and his eye followed the movement. 'He lives outside this world, Shay.

I think he bears this waiting – this eternal, damned waiting – better than any normal man might. But the little indignities of confinement irritate him. The disrespects. The dependences. He is often peevish.'

Shay nodded. 'Our misfortune in finding ourselves a Scottish papist for a King.'

'His Majesty is no papist, Shay, and it's treason to say it!'

'Papists are lively fellows, in my experience, but fragile. Scotsmen are miserable but enduring. Either is perfectly tolerable, but they're an ill combination.'

'Shay—'

'The waiting must continue.'

The voice had been immediately firm and unchallengeable. 'We wonder whither it leads us.'

Shay shook his head in sudden intensity. 'That's for the priests, Seymour; the future – destiny. The King must just survive today – and he must do it every day. You must help him to it.' Seymour shifted uneasily. 'There is no alternative to the King! While he endures they must inevitably turn to him. If he endures, he wins.'

'Easily said.'

'The Army and the Parliament are different, Seymour, and they want different things. But for now, they each need the King. Easy enough for you, do you see? Merely by existing, the King tries and worsens the differences among his enemies.' He snapped a glance towards the sentry, still a way off and indifferent. A rough smile. 'Keep at it, Seymour. You've endured decades; you'll manage a few weeks.'

Seymour nodded uncertainly. He too glanced towards the sentry, and instinctively lowered his voice. 'Is there no chance of escape from here, Shay?'

'I'm sure I could contrive three or four chances, if you gave me half an hour's thinking on it. But I cannot advise it, Seymour.'

'You cannot—'

'As the situation stands today, there is not a strong military force in these islands for him to rally to. Even if there was, it would only unite his enemies, and we would have to depend on a grand military victory that shattered Cromwell once and for ever. These many years we have not found the General or the army to do it.'

'France, then. Or Holland.'

'If he escapes to the Continent he is never returning, Seymour. Know that. We would lose the kingdom for ever.' A dark shake of the head. 'Believe me, it is better as it is. Patience, old horse.'

Seymour's face wrinkled uncomfortably. 'And in the meanwhile? What do you do?'

'I must take the measure of our friends in the provinces, and especially in Scotland.'

'You hope for a new army in our cause?'

Shay shrugged. 'Oh, armies are easy enough to come by, and Scottish ones are cheaper than most. Victories are a little harder. And the politics is harder still.'

'What, then?'

'Oh, we may do a little mischief yet. Between the soldiers and the politicals, the men of money and the men of God, the upsetters of the altars and the upsetters of all society. Between such a muddle of strong-believing men, we may cause a constant squabbling as will restore the King to his rightful place above them all.'

Seymour watched him doubtfully, and then let his focus drift out into the river and the fields beyond it.

Eventually the eyes drifted back. 'Shay, do you really not know the names of the men behind you?'

Some flicker in Shay's dark eyes, something old, something wise or something evil: 'I have some ideas.'

'I had been sure that Sir—' but now Seymour found Shay's hand reaching towards him, open. 'What in heaven are you doing?'

'Asking you for money, your honour. Your sentinel is approaching.'

'What?'

'Give me a coin.'

'A coin?' But he was reaching for his purse now, hearing slow footsteps crunching along the path behind him, and he thrust the first coin into Shay's hand.

'He's still coming on. Turn, notice him, and then reassure him.'

'When do I get my coin back?'

'You don't. Times are hard, Seymour. Fare you well.'

A new voice startled him, the sentry's from over his shoulder, and closer than he'd imagined. 'All well, your Lordship?'

Seymour turned, found the sentry ten paces away: 'Oh – yes.' Stepped towards him. 'Yes, quite well.'

'That fellow not bothering you?'

'No. Just a fisherman. Pleasant to talk to someone new for once. Pitiful fellow, really. Only wants money.'

The sentry nodded, and drifted away again. Seymour turned back to Shay, but the bank was deserted. Out in the river, the little rowing boat was making steadily for mid-stream, the man at the oars pulling smooth and looking away over his shoulder towards the sea.

MERCURIUS FIDELIS

or

The honeſt truth written for every Engliſhman
that cares to read it

From MONDAY, SEPTEMBER 28. *to* MONDAY, OCTOBER 5. 1648.

MONDAY, SEPTEMBER 28.

THE diſſemblers, hecklers and lawyers from the ſelf-juſtified PARLIAMENT are now gone to viſit HIS MAJESTY, preſenting their tricks and ſhams like ſo many Eaſtcheap gypſyes. They do prate of liberties and Preſbyteries and other games that we know to be but lies, and none need doubt that HIS MAJESTY is proof againſt all. He is reported moſt well in his health, and exceeding noble and eloquent and moſt effective in his dignified engagement with the raſcals, who preſume to call theſe negotiations, when they are but impertinence. Even theſe trifles are too much for the radical men of the ARMY, and certain ſaucy fellows from the provinces ſuch as LEICESTERSHIRE, who, being intemperate and uncompromiſing and UNGODLY men, do cry againſt any diſcourſe with HIS MAJESTY THE KING, ſo it may be ſeen that the rebels are both upstarts against the LAWFUL AUTHORITY and in dischord among themselves. These are the plagues and pestilences by which the LORD do test HIS CHOSEN PEOPLE in the desarts of their existence, before HE do lead them to the greater GLORY that shall be theirs.

TUESDAY, SEPTEMBER 29.
Meantime, all loyal eyes in the Kingdom are turned unto the proud castle of PONTEFRACT, the last bastion yet standing against the usurpers. General Cromwell, like a wolf, has surrounded the castle quite and prowls about it with much noise and maleficient intent. Conditions among the garrison are, we may assume, of the direst, and yet we learn that these GENTLEMEN do continue to bear themselves like TRUE and STEADFAST CHRISTIAN SOULS, determined to follow the example set by HIS MAJESTY and resist the offences of the unworthy. They are now in the fourth month of their confinement.

[SS C/T/48/7 (EXTRACT)]

In proud Pontefract, the gentlemen scurried hunched between the towers. Even on days when they weren't attacking, Cromwell's soldiers found it good sport to aim speculative musket balls over the walls, and periodically a patch of stonework would explode in fragments as a cannon found its range, blasting yellow shrapnel and dust over the defenders.

They were thinner gentlemen too, now, and sickly.

'Halloo! Miles Teach!' Miles Teach turned, ducked, and scrambled along the parapet. 'You've been in the fray as usual.'

They crouched, heads close. 'Their usual morning exercise. No trouble.' Teach nonetheless brushed instinctively at his coat front, and again tried to wipe his grimed face, hearing his breaths coming hard. It wasn't that he felt ill; just permanently tired. Poor sleep; poor rations. He knew the signs.

'How do they at the east wall?'

'Well enough. Buckerfield may be a fool, but he's brave enough.' He tapped the other's chest – easy enough in their clumsy proximity – where something bulged. 'What news from the world, Paulden?'

'I'll show you.' A dry grin through the dust. 'He's written again.'

Teach looked up. 'Has he indeed? We have a friend in the enemy camp, it seems.'

⟞ ⟝

In those days the old town hall in Newport was still relatively new – Newport itself was already old. The grand grey stones of the town hall squatted complacent by the square, while the smaller lesser buildings around it did their best against the autumn winds, and the rain that had not seemed to stop for a year.

While Charles Stuart, King of England, Scotland and Ireland – though at present holding sway over no more than a relative handful of followers and servants in one suite of rooms in one building in this small town on an island in the far south of one of his kingdoms – negotiated with the representatives of his upstart Parliament, he did so alone. While he fenced with their demands for a restriction of his rights and powers, while he exercised in law and theology and philosophy and rhetoric, while he danced in languages, in Latin that tapped precisely at the panelling and French that drifted among the hanging fabrics, he was allowed no advisers with him.

In that innocent time – while autumn lasted, at least; while there were still stubborn gnarled leaves on some of the trees and green on the hills above the town – one still did not accuse a King. Even criticism was veiled. So the manifold ills and sufferings of the nation were nothing to do with the man at the heart of them – in the eye of the storm, so to speak – but instead ascribed to the evil intentions of his advisers. Wicked designs, wilful lusting for blood, Popery, even treason: any charge could be levelled at the King's advisers with increasing freedom. The King's advisers were the offence; they surely could not be part of its restitution.

Besides, Parliament knew Charles Stuart for the slipperiest man in his whole realm, and a slippery man was more likely to slip if not steadied by his counsellors.

The King's advisers were suffered to remain in an ante-room, behind a curtain. Through the heavy material they could hear the voices of debate: the high, wheeling flights of His Majesty's arguments, his little erudite witticisms fluttering the curtain tassels, his occasional angry retorts buffeting at the folds; and the rumbling murmur of the negotiators of Parliament, implacable or entreating, frustrated or sure, and apparently endless.

The ante-room got its light from a single, tiny recessed window, and from two candelabra. Six men slumped in its gloom, rich-coated shadows, watching the candlelight flickering in each other's eyes, the strange alien glow from the window catching a bottle of wine. Intermittently one would lean forward to catch some particular point in the muffled debate; shortly he would slouch back. The room stank of cooked meat and of men.

Furtive murmurs from their confinement:

'His Majesty is in good fettle.'

'His Majesty is not immune to blunders, but these London lawyers would do well to recall that they trifle with a most educated man.'

'The most widely learned, surely.'

'How long has it been now, today?'

'His stutter is often much diminished now.'

'Lord, how I loathe these cheap invocations of the people's interest.'

'What will it avail, this learning and debate of the King?'

'Little village demagogues. Inns of Court mountebanks.'

'We are advised to delay. To procrastinate. To work on the divisions of our enemies. The longer His Majesty may talk, the more time they will have to fall among themselves.'

'Advised? Advised by whom?'

'You have better counsel to offer us? His Majesty has other men working for his interest, and other channels of communication to London. We must play our part.'

Charles Stuart, a small man exquisitely dressed, poised but comfortable in a large and ornate oaken chair, feet perched elegantly on a stool to disguise the fact that they would not reach the ground. A magician conjuring theories from a sphere of legitimacy beyond his audience, and spinning word tricks out of his lace cuffs.

Thus Charles Stuart:

An old Jew in Madrid showed me a clockwork bird in a cage: a golden bird, tiny and exquisite, that danced in a ring and whistled and flapped its wings, all with the turning of a key.

A shrivelled, obsequious man. But fastidious, I think, and proper in spite of his faith. In a world that despised him he had created another more perfect world, a world over which he had absolute control, a world of order and beauty, a world protected in a cage.

I find that the Lord has set me to spin in this cage.

How ugly you are. Your drab, heavy weeds and your pedantic hectoring, your uncomfortable courtesies, your common choleric English pudding-faces, your tiresome wrestling with words, your insistence on sharing my company.

I do not have to listen to these men, do I? I am not like other men. I am not made for this bullying, this forced communion with other humans, this dirtiness.

There will come a time, I think, when I must leave my perch and fly this cage.

You will prove to me? Your entire error, Master Glynn, with your books and your precepts and proposals, your vile temporizing aristocratic friends beside you, your clumsy studied indignities of confinement, your fundamental error is to believe that we dabble in a matter that is susceptible of proof. You may prove to me the earth round or flat; you may prove to me triangles and spheres. Prove to me black white, if you will. But these things of faith and Kings, these are of a different cloth altogether. These are not given to us for debate or for consideration. They do not become true because we juggle numbers and compare theories and decide them true.

They may not be changed like an ill-fitting doublet; they may not be reformed like a wilful lad; they may not be reordered like pans on a shelf. They simply are, like the stars or the sun, like the weather, like the very earth itself, and we may merely decide how to conform ourselves to them.

And still you drone. Theorists native and foreign. Empty threats. Pathetic entreaties. A Christian instinct to conciliate; a holy compromise.

Do not you understand? I cannot trifle with these perfect glories! The throne, the religion, these were not given me for my amusement and contingent use, to be gambled with, or traded like so many tinker's trinkets. This was my inheritance, given to me in trust for the good of all my people. The right ordering of the state is our heritage and our defence. The true religion is God's, and God's alone, and we must account ourselves thrice blessed to be allowed to share it. To toy with the state is treason. To toy with the religion is damnation, and for us all. While Europe has burned in a hell of intestine chaos these three decades past, we had lived at peace one with the other, tolerant of our varieties within the embrace of God. Your innovations, your experimentations, your Parliamentary meddling, would set us all adrift for eternity.

I wish my fallible voice could be trusted to impart these truths aright, that you would understand and believe.

The Bishops are the interpreters of the Lord God Himself, and I am His regent. Do not you understand that if I give up the Bishops I give up the soul of all my kingdom? The Bishops are divine. This ordering of society is divine. This ordering of society is mine!

I must not seem to weep. A Prince must have no private side for the world. Brother Henry twisting my ears until I wept. A Prince must have no emotion. The King so scornful of his pale and feeble second son, court pranks and blustering words, until the second son became his heir. Then such a pathetic race to make me fitted, the ghastly forced hours of paternal counsel, an old man desperate to mould his youth anew before death overtakes him.

What have I done wrong that I am thus tormented? The Son of God suffered for the sins of other men. Surely, this land has known every manner of sin for ten years or more. I have striven to protect my people and protect my faith, to do my duty as I saw it. In what has lain my sin, that my God should punish me thus?

Why do these men not understand me? Is there no one in this realm who could have been my fellow?

——— ~

The old manor house huddled in the foothills of the Peak District, local stone and lack of show, as if to convince the violent world of politics that it was more of the natural world than of the human, and could be left in peace. The guests, as Shay watched them from the edge of the room, were such as might be found after some great battle or calamity: battered and world-worn and dull-headed, clothes and eyes that had seen too much of life in the last ten years.

'Shay, surely? I did not know you were living still.'

'As you see.' His face offered no warmth, and the forgotten acquaintance drifted away. *Perhaps none of us here is living still.*

Not a forgotten acquaintance. Roger Savary: widower; East Anglia, but that would hardly be comfortable now; son killed at. . . Edgehill? Early, anyway. Now huddling here on the high ground as the flood destroyed his old world.

And then a flash of a girl across the room. There were young people here, after all. This one would be. . . not yet twenty, surely, but woman enough. The clothes were worn, but that only heightened the bright glow of her bust, thin sharp collar bone and the creamy sweep down to her breasts, dramatically pure flesh against the old linen. Behind her a man of her own age in a coat too big for him, watching her face, her open smile.

Shay felt his own chest move, the blood in him. *Yes, Roger Savary, I am living still.*

'Mortimer Shay,' and there was genuine warmth in the voice. It was the warmth that made him turn.

'Sarah! My lady Saville, how are you? Does me good to see you.' And it did, rather to his surprise. Not a particular friend or a particular memory, but a link with the past who had somehow kept her vitality.

She was examining his face with interest.

'You're about to say that you're surprised I'm still alive, I think. Everyone seems to find it strange.'

She smiled, then shook her head impulsively; a girl's gesture. 'I would never doubt that you would live.' She smiled again, and glanced back over her shoulder. 'Some of the young men were asking about the grim stranger standing on the edge of the room. I fired their interest with wild stories of your past.'

He grunted. Had he had her ever? Not that he could remember. There had always been prettier, wilder, more passionate women to be had, under the floating layers of dresses, behind half-closed doors, after hours.

'I'm grateful for the invitation today.'

She shrugged. These gatherings would be happening frequently, as this ravaged society herded together for reassurance, for warmth. 'You've come over from Astbury? How is the place these days?'

'Survived well enough. First time I've been there for ten years or more.'

'We were sorry to hear about George. You were kin, weren't you?'

'Through his brother's wife. You saw much of him here?'

She considered it for a moment. 'Occasionally, once the worst years of the fighting were over. It's hardly an easy journey here, but we've little enough society in these parts. He was here a few times in a few years, I suppose. Recently less. He was. . .' – she hesitated as she strayed into the world of politics and men – 'increasingly busy, I think – in the King's service.'

Shay murmured neutrally. He hadn't thought to hear of George Astbury here, but would take the insights where he found them.

'And you?' she said. She went to touch his arm lightly, but hesitated as if suddenly aware of his sheer size, and when her fingers finally brushed his sleeve they came with more charge. 'Your interests—'

'My own. As always.'

She nodded, as if this had satisfied her curiosity. 'George was last here very recently. Probably only a week or so before – before the battle.' She tried to push the war back beyond the hills. 'He seemed. . . rather changed.'

Shay looked round into her face. 'Changed?'

'He was always rather serious, wasn't he?' She smiled. 'When we were younger I found it almost – almost attractive. But that last time he was more. . . worried.' Shay was still watching her. 'Perhaps he was just concerned for the fate of the army. He'd been with them for part of the journey down from Scotland, and. . .' – she looked up at him hesitantly – 'I suppose you men can tell when the crisis of a conflict is near.'

'Yes, perhaps that was it. Was he talking about the army?'

'No – no, of course not.' It would have been as much indecorous as indiscreet. 'He seemed fretful. Talking of this and that. Pontefract.'

'Pontefract?'

'It's not that far.'

'I know where it is. Why on earth should he fret about Pontefract?'

Lady Sarah Saville shrugged, and smiled with a shyness out of place on her fifty years. The affairs of men.

'I once asked him why he was interested, and he said that Pontefract would tell him much.'

What had Astbury been fussing about? He was more curious than concerned.

Her face was closer to his suddenly, and Shay felt the breath of her whisper. 'If only you'd been able to ask Marmaduke Langdale.'

'Langdale?'

The voice was an excited murmur; she was a girl again. 'He was here!'

Shay glanced quickly around; her behaviour more than her words was going to attract attention. There were two young men – three – several yards away, and they looked down as he saw them. For a distracted moment he wondered whether they would see him as competition for the girl across the room.

'Langdale was here? You mean – after Preston?'

Hissed excitement still: 'We sheltered him for a night.'

He smiled. 'You're a good woman, Sarah.' It was genuine affection, and she could tell. 'Did he talk about Astbury?'

'Only about his probably being dead. But he mentioned Pontefract, too, and so I mentioned Astbury.'

'Langdale was fretting about Pontefract as well?'

'He was trying to get there, I think. Something about "his men".'

Shay nodded. 'Those who fought with him during the main years of the war. Many are now besieged at Pontefract. He went in that direction when he left here?'

'I don't know. They – they captured him. . . I suppose not long after.' She said it tentatively, not sure whether he knew.

'Mm. I'd heard rumour.'

'He's in Nottingham Castle.'

'Is he, indeed?'

'It's—'

'I know where Nottingham is.' He smiled to take the edge off his asperity. 'You're well-informed, Sarah.'

She was suddenly serious. 'These are my people. This is my world.' There was almost hurt there, too. 'You will allow me not to forget it, at least.'

He nodded, sincere. *Is it war or is it just age, this insistent accounting of the mementoes of the past?*

'It's wrong. It's wrong for a man – a good man, and he's not young – to be locked up like that. Weeks now, I think.'

'Knowing Langdale, he'll have made their lives more miserable than they have his.'

But suddenly her fingers were on his arm again. 'You could do something! You could get him out!' Her eyes and mouth were wide in the dream. 'Oh, do it!' It was desperation, an empty clutching at a vision of a more heroic past, more romantic. 'Save him, Mortimer.'

There was movement near them: the three young men were watching them more openly, and Shay wondered how much their voices had carried. Sarah Saville had followed his glance, and now looked back up at him with more composure, a little more height.

'I was never a fair woman, Mortimer, but I was always true.' She said it with dignity, and only a little embarrassed smile at the end marred the effect. 'I charge you with this; say it's a quest. If you have no greater, make this man your interest. Prove that something good and daring may still be done here.'

His eyes had been elsewhere, calculating. It was ridiculous, of course. Now he turned to look her full and blatant in the face, and the eyes were big and hard, and then they narrowed in intent, something animal. Her eyes widened in reaction, a faint flush of excitement and alarm.

Sir Mortimer Shay, roaming once more the houses and hearts of England.

'Astbury died at Preston. Shay has his place.'

'How came Shay by the office? By no pleasant means, I am sure. Was he fighting for Cromwell that day? He is uncontrollable.'

'He is unstoppable. He held the office briefly before.'

'He was removed from the office, and with high good reason.'

'We may add persistence to his list of qualities.'

'I am right glad to be out of England.'

Sir,

    *Cromwell, Fairfax and St John must work continuously to keep the
scales in balance. For whereas on the one hand they threaten the Scots
with the Army should they fail to surrender Berwick and Carlisle, so
on the other hand that same Army is in a ferment and may not fully be
relied upon. September is now spoken of as a month of mutiny. The
so-called Levellers have petitioned Parliament again for their radical
claims, and the regiments in the north — those same who would be most
necessary should the Scots seek battle again — have been loud in their
support. The Army that Cromwell unleashed in this land threatens to
escape his control quite, and those renewed rumours seem most credible,
which do say that he himself contrived to remove the King from Army
control last winter for fear of some outrage by the Agitators and Levellers
in the ranks.*

    Faithfully, S. V.

[SS C/S/48/17]

Shay spent a night in an inn outside Derby. He would have preparations to
manage in the town during the next days, and further preparations once
he reached Nottingham.

He was the only man staying in the inn – indeed, the only man to step
through the door for the hours he was there – and he spent what remained
of the evening sitting in silence with a jug of wine, trying to keep his head
turned to judgement and not memory.

Warm and desperate for life, Lady Sarah Saville had offered Langdale
to him as a quest, and as amusement for his interest. *And what if it serves
the King's interest as well?* He needed to understand what Astbury had
done with the Comptrollerate-General – principally the book. He needed
to understand what had preyed on Astbury's mind in those last days:
Pontefract, and the field at Preston. Sir Marmaduke Langdale was a rare
link to that.

Besides, even an empty exploit against the new regime would serve a purpose. *The complacency of these Parliament men might stand a little shaking.*

Three men followed Shay on his meandering journey, always a mile or two behind, and he did not see them.

Until its final deliberate destruction, the old Nottingham Castle rose like a vast and solitary yellow tooth from the uneven gum of the surrounding landscape.

The first Richard, back from crusade wild and strange, with grim leather-skinned companions and new engines of war, had laid siege to the castle as part of his campaign to recapture his kingdom from the partisans of his brother. The third Edward had come of age here, seizing his usurper stepfather in a night-time ambush with just a handful of friends and a subconscious inheritance of right. The centuries and the sieges had left it broken and rotten, a relic of an older society with crumbling walls and fallen roofs and Roundhead soldiers trying to keep it defensible and warm.

On a morning in October in 1648, a man appeared in the heart of the castle, a shadow suddenly on the yellow-grey stone in a forgotten corridor. He sensed his way through the castle, feeling his way by memory, adjusting to the rhythms of fallen masonry and half-heard sentries' footsteps.

He was prepared for violence: a sentry or two might need to be subdued or killed, and such men could easily disappear unnoticed for an hour or for ever in the shambling ruined maze. But it was not necessary. An hour of observation showed that, through indifference or calculated routine, the room now being used as a cell was not closely guarded. The man slipped through the cold tunnels unobtrusive but assured, the scuff of his boots echoing weird in unknown staircases and holes in the roof. He pressed close to the cell door.

Sir Marmaduke Langdale: the hair was grey now, the heavy eyes sagging, but still the great beak of a nose thrust itself proud and ludicrous into the world's business. Age had given it a certain nobility. On the young Langdale, obsessed with discipline and supply as they marched to the Rhine, it had been merely comic. *But that was nigh thirty years ago.* He watched the gaunt grim face a second more, framed in the iron-crossed window of the cell door. Now a hero two or three times over, in a losing cause.

A furtive delicate click from the lock; the cell door squawked briefly as it opened, and again as it closed. The narrow face lifted instinctively, soured at the interruption, and then caught in surprise as it recognized the intruder.

Langdale took a great breath, and then swallowed it. 'Shay!' he whispered, hoarse. Sitting high in a wooden chair by the window, he slumped back into it.

'Afternoon, Langdale.'

He spoke at normal volume, and the General set his tone accordingly. 'I tolerate a certain indignity in my current circumstances, Shay, but I absolutely refuse to share my confinement with you.'

'They haven't caught me, yet. I wandered in on my own account.'

This didn't seem to surprise Langdale. 'Last we heard you were in Holland. I'd thought you long hanged.'

'You're out of luck.'

Langdale stood, and they shook hands like old oak branches creaking in the wind. 'You want to borrow money, presumably.'

'Merely ask a question of an old comrade.'

'Don't come the old comrade with me, you misbegotten bandit.' Langdale returned to his chair. 'The lack of furniture deprives me of the pleasure of not offering you a seat.'

'I need to have an ear anyway. What was George Astbury doing on the field at Preston?'

'I feel you've spent your life keeping furtive watch, Shay: fathers, husbands, bailiffs, sergeants-at-arms. You have passed your every minute of existence in some pursuit or other that must be hid from other men.' He folded his hands primly in front of him. 'Why do you want to know?'

'You know old Astbury. A worthy fellow, I'm sure, but I doubt he did a reckless act in his whole life. He'd been given no place in the line of battle, surely?' Langdale shook his head. 'And he had no business there. Yet I found his body not thirty paces from that midden where you fought the day out.'

Langdale's heavy eyebrows had risen. 'He did die, then? I had heard it said.' The beaked face twisted sadly. 'Not a warm man, but a decent one. He was terribly in earnest that day.' The eyes were gone back into the battlefield. 'Bustling everywhere. He would insist on checking everything with the scouts.'

'The scouts?'

'Jumped on anything they reported. Rode out to see for himself. Back again, quiz the fellows, check the map, off into the field again. Well, you know how scouts are.' Silent agreement from Shay. 'Solitary, nervy fellows. Didn't like this much. Ruce – Scoutmaster that day – he got very unhappy about it.'

'What did Astbury think he was doing?'

'I couldn't imagine. He was pretty dismissive about Ruce – thought he was just a low fellow, a mechanical, didn't credit him for any initiative. When he started bustling around me I told him straight not to interfere. He'd got into a kind of fever over when and how Cromwell might catch us out. Cromwell' – the words became sharper and more pronounced – 'has a way of bewitching men.'

'Mm. He mention Pontefract at all?'

'Astbury? Might have done – siege still going on, people were thinking about it – but I don't. . .' He turned to Shay. 'Yes. I do remember one comment. We were talking about it – there were fresh rumours – usual fatuous chatter; you know how it is. Came to old George, and he looked very thoughtful, and he just said, "There is sickness there." That was the word: sickness. Sounded rather final.'

What was Astbury's obsession? The repeated references to the place; the last letter in his pocket. 'Meaning disease, you think?'

'That is what sickness means, Shay, yes. But I can't speak for George Astbury. Ask him yourself, in the unlikely event you end up in the same billet. He seemed damned bleak about it, that I can say.'

Shay was silent. 'I had rather gathered,' Langdale went on, examining his folded hands and then peering hard at Shay, 'that Astbury was starting to interest himself in intelligencing matters.' Still silence. 'That might explain his interest in the scouting, I mean to say. Same sort of business you always seemed to be dabbling in. Stuff you never talked about.'

Slowly, Shay produced a malevolent smile. 'Quite,' he said. Langdale's face was sharp and hard and full of distaste.

～ ～

The journey from Coventry to Nottingham was fifty miles, and the two Parliament men plodded most of them through a wet afternoon along muddy Derbyshire roads, cloaks hunched around shoulders and the few words lost to the wind.

The region was still uncertain: angry hunted Scots were loose and lost and roaming wild, and little bitter deeds of Royalist violence could catch a man anywhere. So they had an escort: one fat levy, hardly the pick of the new Army, which told them what they needed to know of their own significance. The soldier trotted behind them, walked behind them, stood behind them, and had done all this for many days, and John Thurloe could not recall a single word from him in all that time.

They had found a good room in Kegworth, dried their clothes and eaten and slept well, and the fresh morning had shared their rejuvenation. They rode to Nottingham with the sun brightening their faces and the green of England around them, and the old castle gleamed across the landscape as they approached the city. Webster was kin to the castle's Governor and wanted to pay his respects, and then they might find a good lunch somewhere, and for a few warm hours England seemed a place where a man could find life pleasant and even pleasurable.

Strangely, into Thurloe's reverie of pleasantness kept striding the image of Sir Anthony Astbury's daughter, as she had done intermittently over the previous weeks, proud and shaken and angry, hair awry and staring at him venomously.

As they approached the main gate of the castle they were overtaken by a messenger on horseback, brisk and businesslike and high in the saddle as his horse rattled over the drawbridge.

～ ～

'How did they take you, old ghost?'

Langdale's face twisted into a scowl. 'In an alehouse.' He offered the words precisely, as a gift to Shay's scorn.

Shay just nodded, and winced slightly at what Langdale's mighty pride had been through.

Langdale shrugged. 'It was clear they would take me that day or night. Better to go with a hot meal and dry boots.'

Another nod. The shared precepts of three decades. Shay said more softly, 'I saw the field. Your men stood fast like gods.'

The old General just shook his head. 'Even I would not have believed it of them. They were annihilated, and they would not run.' Another shake of the head, back in the sunken miry lane, then he looked up. 'Shay, I am right sick of it all.'

'You've life yet.'

'Perhaps so – for which I should thank you, I suppose.'

'Me?'

'I thought you came to rescue me.'

'Not particularly. I just had that question.'

'I see. I'm pleased to be of service, Shay; you know me.'

'Indeed. Why? Would you like to be rescued?'

'I ask favours of no man, Shay, least of all a pirate such as you.'

'So I assumed. I also assumed that if you wanted to escape you'd have done so. Crumbling old ruin like this.' His head was bent to the door again.

'Quite. I have made preliminary work with two of my gaolers. One is a man of true and passionate belief, God save us all, and that's always fertile ground. The other is healthily corruptible; young wife, too, he tells me, and that sounded promising. A couple more days' conversation and I'll come and go as I choose. But not much point until I'm rather surer of the ground outside. I don't mind escaping, but I'm too old to run hither and yon to no purpose.' Langdale pulled his cloak around him and settled comfortably. 'You were wont to dress a little more showy, Shay. Why those drab black weeds today?'

To the Governor of Nottingham Castle
Colonel John Hutchinson, Lord Radcliffe
From the Committee of Security of the Parliament of
England, met in London, in harmonious association with
the Army Council

Colonel,
be forewarned that envoys of this Committee shall visit you this day,
with the express and specific purpose of scrutinising the good-holding
and condition of the prisoner Marmaduke Langdale, General in the
illegitimate and rebellious Army of the upstart King Charles Stuart.
Our envoys may interrogate the prisoner as they deem fit, and will judge
of their own accord whether he may be better removed to some other
strong-hold for his further interrogation and prosecution.
   We send formal greeting to you, Colonel, fully cognizant of our
respective offices, under the love and protection of God.

[SS C/T/48/01]

'Well, Langdale, this has been pleasant enough; but I've business elsewhere. I'll bid you good day.'

'Good day to you, Shay. My regards to Lady Margaret.'

'Unless you want to come with me. . .?'

Langdale looked up. 'Is that an invitation? A request?'

Shay shrugged. 'If you like.'

'Well, if you're asking me. For fellowship's sake, then.' Langdale was up out of the chair with surprising speed, and heaving hurriedly at his palliasse. A loose stone pulled away, and he was pushing a book into his jacket, a knife into his belt and a ring onto one gnarled finger. Shay gestured him to stillness briefly in the doorway, and then they were out into the passage.

They moved cautiously, from safe point to safe point, corner to stairwell to shadow, and it took fifteen minutes to reach a section of passageway dominated by a large wardrobe. The wood was dark and crude, and starting to rot.

'Here; give hand, Langdale.' With two men at it, the wardrobe pulled away from the wall easily. In the shadow behind it Langdale saw dimly a darker shadow: a narrow opening in the stone, a gateway to some other world.

A soft sigh of understanding. 'The Prince's passage; I thought this was mere legend. This is how young Edward broke into the castle. And how you got in.' The old General glanced at the man beside him. 'The cupboard must have been a bit of a heave for your rotting body. How do you know these places, Shay?'

A dry smile in the gloom. 'The little practical curiosities of history, Langdale. I collect them.'

—∼——∼—

Colonel John Hutchinson had no interest in being Governor of a crumbling wreck of a castle far from London, and no hesitation in demonstrating it. The long dark curls and the neck-cloth showed elegance, but the pale skin and the hard, indifferent eyes showed the more austere man within.

He accepted the greetings of his two visitors with no more than basic courtesy, and politely asked after the family of his kinsman Webster. He was clearly confident of his superiority as a Member of Parliament to these two mere clerks.

'Tiresome up here, you understand me?' Irritation and disdain in the voice. 'I gave up my regiment because I had a greater duty in Parliament. But if I can't be there, I'd rather be in the field with my men than acting the sentry here.'

His visitors murmured their sympathy.

'All very well for you men, trotting the countryside with no responsibility and no greater calling. All most pleasant for you, I'm sure.' He picked up a folded paper from his table. 'And you make your arrangements pretty tight, don't you? We've barely received your letter.'

'Our letter?'

The paper was brandished with more energy. 'Announcing your visit. Only just got here.'

'What letter?'

Now openly angry, and waspish: 'You've come to talk to the prisoner Langdale. We're getting him ready now.'

'We came to bid you greeting, nothing more. We sent no letter.'

From the open door to the corridor: running boots on the stone, and shouts.

~ ⁓ ~

'Langdale: another question.' The voice was a murmur, the attention focused elsewhere.

'You become tiresome, Shay. I thought you knew everything.'

'Why did Cromwell stay north of the river?'

The old beaked face was immediately grave, and somehow sadder. 'It made no sense. By all the calculations of convention, it made no sense. And yet there he was, suddenly and unstoppably. I had many hours to ponder the matter, every minute of them evil.' He focused on Shay again. 'You think somehow he knew our dispositions? Scouted us out?'

'I wondered.'

Langdale shook his head slowly. 'They say he can smell the secrets of a field: the terrain, the placement of the men. It's unearthly.' The lines of the face sharpened and crackled; Sir Marmaduke Langdale was back in the sunken lane again, his men drowning in mud and Cromwell's horsemen coming at him in waves that would never end. 'He is a force of nature herself, Shay. He has the devil in him.'

Shay listened in silence. A military opinion from Langdale was truth. 'I never thought to hear you superstitious.'

'In thirty years, and as many slaughters, I've not seen the like.' Another shake of the head. 'I think it's much simpler, Shay; no secret, nor complicated calculation. That man hungers for battle, for glory and for slaughter, and when he sees them near he comes at them by the straightest road.'

~ ⁓ ~

The cell empty, the prisoner Langdale disappeared: Governor Hutchinson had acted fast, his deeper frustrations channelled into anger at this new outrage to his dignity, anger at those who had allowed this embarrassment, anger at his two visitors for somehow being linked to it. Instant orders to one of his Captains had spread throughout the castle, and soldiers had clattered through the warrens towards the abandoned cell.

The Governor had himself visited the scene, had returned still angrier from his private maze, now unfamiliar and treacherous to him. More orders. A message to the town. The main gate to be closed. He had been leaving to resume his personal oversight of operations when another sentry had hurried up to him, a bustle of breaths and equipment: a cupboard had been found awry, a hidden passage behind it – the Prince's passage of legend. More orders: urgent pursuit into the tunnel; soldiers to leave through the main gate and make for the lower meadow with all haste; another message to the town. Then the Governor was striding off again into the maze.

A Captain was left in Governor Hutchinson's chamber in case further information should arrive and need to be carried to the Governor. Everyone else was caught up in the search, with one exception.

John Thurloe sat silently, upright in a simple chair, frowning at the folded letter that still lay on the table.

Shay and Langdale had passed forty minutes in companionable silence on a crumbling spiral stair that twisted up into the open sky. Two minutes after the pursuit had passed by the entrance to the stair, they were back down it and away towards the opposite side of the castle.

'A waste of a secret tunnel if you ask me, Shay.'

'I don't. Most likely it remained one of the thousand secret conveniences of our history, but over three centuries I can't guarantee it's not become known. And I may have been seen.'

'Now what, then?'

'Now you're my prisoner, Langdale.' An irritated shake of the grizzled head. 'I'll take that knife, and I'll bind your hands.'

'I preferred my plan. I liked the sound of the gaoler's wife.'

'So why did they send the letter?'

'Sir?'

Thurloe's head snapped round. 'The letter, Captain. The forged letter from the Committee. What was its purpose?'

The Captain shifted uncomfortably, shook his head. 'I'm afraid I don't – To distract us, I suppose. Put us off our balance.'

Thurloe launched up out of the chair. 'But it put us on our balance!' He aimed a slow and deliberate kick at the leg of the Governor's table. 'You people clearly weren't paying much attention to General Langdale, and the first thing that letter made you do – very natural – was go to check on him.'

'A bit lucky, then?'

Thurloe smiled and shook his head. 'This wasn't about luck.' His head was columns of figures, tumbling Greek declensions, the mental disciplines of his youth; he felt the warmth and thrill of rigorous thought. 'What was the effect of that letter? To send us to the cell to check the prisoner. What was the effect of sending us to the cell?' The Captain kept opening his mouth as if to try to answer, but Thurloe was looking through him. 'To have us find the secret passage. What was the effect of us finding the passage?' The questions and answers came steadily, as if by rote. 'To have us chasing into it.'

'And we'll try to block the end, sir.' The Captain's efficiency found voice at last. 'Supposed to come out somewhere in the lower meadow.'

'Which is where?'

The Captain thought for a second and pointed to his left. 'Roughly that direction.'

Thurloe nodded. The castle around him, a shambling warren of holes and tunnels and mistakes and possibilities. He pointed a long finger in the opposite direction. 'And does the castle have any gate or door on the other side?'

'Help him up then, man!' The sentry, sullen but quick to take an order, bent to the task, but Langdale had gripped the saddle with his tied hands and swung himself over. Shay on his unfamiliar horse skittered beside him, stared down at the sentries as if in thought. 'Can you two find mounts?'

'You'll need men with you, sir?'

'I've a troop outside, but. . . No matter. Shouldn't have a problem with this old relic.'

'Pox-raddled, dirty traitor!' – and Langdale lunged at him; Shay batted him back into his saddle. Ahead, the gate swung open.

Thurloe striding through the castle corridors, deducing his way through the maze with the Captain trotting behind him calling suggestions; and then Governor Hutchinson loomed in front of him as he spun round a narrow turn. 'We've got him!'

A confusion of limbs and words and thoughts, then: 'Got him?'

The Governor, breathing hard and somehow heated: 'Got Langdale. They're taking him away now – that third man of yours and a couple of my men.' He glared at Thurloe: 'Your man's a bit damned rud—'

'A third man?' A second of confusion, then instinct faster than deduction, and Thurloe barged the Governor aside and was charging through the warren, the Captain still clattering after him.

Shay was at the gate, ducking his head under the arch as his nag clopped ponderously over the uneven stones.

Ahead, through the gate, a short wooden bridge and then open ground. Something snagged in his hearing, some imperfection in the stolid rhythms of the castle. The hooves trod hollow and heavy over the stone.

He had Langdale's horse on a long rein, following behind him, the old General slumped and scowling.

'Stop those men!'

The horses' ears pricked up, and the heads of Langdale and the two sentries whirled up to seek the sound, but Shay had yanked on the long rein and kicked viciously at his horse. Beyond the open ground the trees. If they could make the trees. . .

Thurloe, a frozen moment as he saw conspiracy happening in front of him, and then he was stumbling down rough steps, hands snagging and scratching against stone, the Captain above him repeating the shout: 'Stop those men!'

A uniform meant an order, and the nearest of the sentries lunged for Langdale's horse. Shay was through the gate, but the unknown horse wasn't having it. It hesitated, skittered round, and backed into Langdale now accelerating through. The old General swore, pulled at his horse's neck, kicked into the flanks, but now there was some new pull on him, the beast swerving odd and heavy beneath him. Then Shay moving past him back through the gate, the horses squeezing and shuffling, a flick of a knife to release his hands, and Shay lashed out with his boot at the man clutching the saddle. Suddenly free, the knife grabbed and in his belt, Langdale kicked at his horse again and was away through the gate, Shay spinning and hurrying after, with the man in black no more than a strange stain across his blurring vision.

Hooves rattling and echoing on the planks of the bridge, and now there were more men closing in on it from the other end. Langdale's horse reared at the sight of blades, and there were three, four soldiers blocking their way. Shay kicked his animal into the charge and for once it obeyed, but there wasn't the distance to gather speed. One man went sprawling, but other hands were scrabbling at his legs, reins, saddle. A blade appeared and flashed in his hand, and another man went down with a scream, but he was slow now and stopping.

Away towards the trees, beyond the soldiers, there were shouts, hooves drumming hard and free on open ground.

Thurloe had reached the gate, barging through the sentries and roaring them to action. As his boots thumped onto the bridge he saw the two fugitives bucking and grappling with soldiers: saw one soldier grabbing at one of the fugitives and half pulling him down, saw the fugitive, an older man surely, reacting with weird calm and pushing a pistol back under his armpit and firing and the soldier tumbling away. The fugitive swung upright, the horse wheeled, and for a moment his eyes met Thurloe's. And beyond them all came three riders, haring across the open ground with heads bent low over their horses and swords levelled as they accelerated towards the bridge and the mêlée. Thurloe was halfway over the bridge when the riders struck. The soldiers staggered, fell away in one furious tempest of blades, scattered, and now all five horsemen were free and away and making, unstoppable, for the trees.

Shay, General Langdale and their three rescuers rode their horses hard and silent for five miles, sometimes by road and sometimes across country. Shay had rapidly assumed the lead, and the others followed automatically. As they'd approached a junction, one of the unknown three had pulled level with him and beckoned to the north, open fields and the distant shadow of the hills across the land. But Shay had shaken his head briefly and bent again to the horse, sitting heavy and intent and urging the animal onward. With a shrug and glance of frustration at his companions, the younger man had fallen back and followed.

As they came over a rise, Derby appeared on the horizon in front of them, and then disappeared again behind trees as they rode on. Shay slowed to a trot, turned in the saddle and beckoned the young man nearest. A pale face, long fair hair, and he trotted nearer and started to speak.

Shay cut him off. 'The wood, ahead there. You three will skirt it southwards until you reach a track running north by west. You will take that line until a junction with a dead elm. There right, and so shortly into the trees. We will regather there.'

'But—'

'We must take the road now, and the road becomes more open and more travelled. They will be seeking news of five riders, not two or three.' Shay saw the puzzled, irritated expression. 'You are a hunted man, now, and you must learn fast. The first lesson is that you don't have time for explanations.'

'But can't we—'

'You can do as you're bid, or die on the road where you are. No more than a trot, now.'

John Thurloe had spent a full hour in silence. He stood at the door to the now empty cell, reached for the handle, then stopped himself. He stood looking at the slit of darkness into the secret passage, took a breath and stepped towards it, then stopped himself. Then he walked back out of the castle as he had come in – the conventional route – and found his way by indifferent sentries to the external entrance to the passage.

He entered the castle again, as the intruder had entered, scuffling and stumbling through the caves until a boot-tip kicked a rough step, and so up in darkness until the faintest whisper of light promised life again and the old wardrobe. Then he walked softly to the cell, and this time, after a moment, he opened the door and entered. He stood. He perched on the edge of the palliasse. He noted the hiding place in the wall. *Men of concealment. Men of initiative.* He sat on the chair. He listened. He left the cell, trying to elude the door's creak.

He was trying and failing to forget the trick with the pistol, fired back under the arm: an expert's trick, instinctive and immediate and sure.

He was clutching at spirits he could neither quite recall nor be sure of, these men who were not like him, spirits from a different time or a different world. At one point, the hot red face of Governor Hutchinson had thrust into his vision again. The Governor was embarrassed, and confused, and trying to find a way in which Thurloe and the Committee for Security were responsible for what had happened today. The words came singly and incoherent, and Thurloe had just looked at him, silently, and eventually the Governor stamped away back to his violated lair.

The secret passage. The cell. The passages between them and the passage leading to the other side of the castle and the escape.

There had to be somewhere else. There had to be somewhere to wait while the foolish Parliament men bumbled around in the cold warren of tunnels, while they gaped stupidly at the empty cell and summoned the courage to step into the darkness of the Prince's secret passage.

There were any number of places: side tunnels, abandoned chambers, piles of rubble. *Compensatory lengthening affects first aorist forms whose verbal root ends in a sonorant.* Did the spirits know this place or were they guessing? The secret passage; the escape through the opposite side of the castle. Were they desperate or calculating? The distraction; the bravado. Discount places with inadequate chance of concealment. Discount places that might be simply or accidentally checked. Discount the indefensible, discount the dead-ends.

In Attic and Ionic Greek, the sigma in the first aorist suffix causes compensatory lengthening of the preceding vowel. It must be a place between the Prince's passage and the areas where the Governor and the guards were most likely to be. The spirits needed the pursuit to go past them into the cell and the passage and that side of the castle – clattering and shouting, confused and angry, red faces and conflicting orders – leaving the way clear to the other side.

Thurloe at a junction of passageways, looking at the grit around his boots, looking at the patterns in the flagstones, looking down the passage in front of him, past a stairwell entrance to where the dust swirled idle and golden in a column of light from a hole in the roof above. *In Aeolic Greek, the sigma causes compensatory lengthening of the sonorant.* They must have waited for some time: *The letter will bring these foolish Parliament men to the wrong part of the castle, but I can't cut the time too finely. I don't know how long I'll have to wait for the foolish Parliament men to snap at my bait. I can't risk them coming before I've reached my hiding-place. Where might I sit in relative comfort for an hour or so?*

Twenty steps up the spiral staircase Thurloe found a spot where the grit had been brushed away by a pair of recent backsides, and scuffings beneath where four boots might have rested for a time. *This'll do. We can hear the foolish Parliament men scampering past below, we can slip out smart enough, but we'll have time to get ready if someone does by some chance come up here.*

He sat down beside them – on the step below, anyway, as a younger man might.

These men – the one who broke in, at least – they knew this place. They know places like this. This is their country, and it always has been, and I am an interloper. The remarkable business of the letter. *Was this all fantastic chance?* The effectiveness of the timings, the smoothness with which the foolish Parliament men fitted into the plan. *He knew when the letter would arrive.*

He knows our systems.

The eyes widened a little, and the staircase was momentarily colder. Thurloe pulled his cloak closer around him, and forced himself to settle back against the ancient smoothness of the centre pillar.

But they cannot have known that I would come today. They did not know of me. He passed the rest of his hour in more companionable silence, wondering at the men so close to him.

Hot and uneasy and exchanging empty expressions of uncertainty and bravado, the three riders followed the tree line to the track, and the track as it led into open country and to the elm, and then turned as instructed and dropped into the welcome gloom of woodland again. In the shadows they hesitated, their horses breathing heavy and rummaging in the long grass that fringed the roadway.

A rustling from the undergrowth, and the two older men emerged from the trees, shadows from the darkness. Again the first of the three made to speak, and again he was ignored.

Shay led them a further mile, until the wood ended in sight of a watermill, and beyond it Donington. He held them there for several minutes, dappled under the leaves and still silent, while he watched the mill intently.

Eventually he led them down. The mill-owner met them at the gate of his yard. Shay murmured a word to the man, a word that the others could not catch. Without a reply or a glance the gate was pulled open, and Shay was gesturing his companions into the yard while he took a final full scan around them and then followed.

He was the first to dismount, legs falling heavy and tired into the mud. 'We change horses here.' Langdale slid down too, stretching his legs uncomfortably.

'But this is my horse, and a good one!' Another of the young men.

'It may be recognized, and that makes it a bad one.' He nodded towards the mill-man. 'It's his now. The horses will be dispersed. Do any have a well-known mark? A brand?'

Confusion, shakes of the head, weary and unhappy climbings down and then the three young men were standing forlorn in the mud as their horses were led away, the mill-man examining them with satisfaction.

'A mill in the middle of nowhere, and you arrive unannounced and with a single word the man will do your bidding and swap your horses – risk his life?'

Shay turned. The dark-haired one: medium height and compact, quiet-spoken but swallowing irritation. Shay said, 'There are times when one needs a bed, or a horse, or a friend. One is wise to cultivate such arrangements.'

He looked at all three of them, and then with old courtesy shook each by the hand before stepping back.

'I'm grateful to you, gentlemen; that was a closer thing than I had conceived it.' The three had straightened a little; young men, faces proud and clean and open. *Did I look like that a lifetime ago?* 'Might you honour me with your names?'

The compact figure took a step forward. The moustache was not yet a success, but there was nothing frail in the dark brown eyes or the voice. 'Thomas Balfour, sir, and at your service.'

'I am glad of it, sir.'

The pale young man spoke, clear strong words from the well-boned face. *Lord, the beauty of the young.* 'Henry Vyse.'

The third stepped forward, but there was a grunt from behind Shay, and then Langdale's growl: 'Vyse? Son of Bernard Vyse – of Kent, and Sussex?'

'Our lands are all forfeit, General. But I am still the son of Sir Bernard Vyse.'

Langdale nodded. 'A man could make no prouder boast. And your mother was Hester Carraway.' A nod, and Langdale grunted again. 'Give thanks to the Lord nightly, young man, that you got from your father your heart but not your looks.'

The third man, heavy-set and slow-spoken, was Michael Manders, and again Langdale was interested. 'Your father was beside me at Marston, young man. Losing him was as bad a blow as the battle itself.'

'This was no longer a world in which he cared to live, sir; and he wanted no other death.'

Shay was still staring into the blue eyes of Henry Vyse; the jaw was solid Vyse, whatever Langdale said, but not those eyes. *Hester Carraway, by God.* He saw a smile, heard a laugh through the decades, sighed a growl at the opening of a bodice. *If I had sired, Lord, might it have been sons like these?*

Vyse spoke. 'What happens now, sir?'

'It will not be the season for Generals for some while. I must get Langdale abroad.'

'How?'

Manders. Shay's eyes narrowed and hardened at him. 'Secretly.' He looked at the others. 'Take a mug of beer in the mill here, but do not stay for a second one. Return to your normal pastures, but not for three days at least and not without well spying the land.' He gave them a heavy nod. 'Again, my thanks to... Why did you come after me, by the by?'

Vyse again: 'You... looked a sporting gentleman, sir. A man for a deed not a word.'

Manders, louder: 'Not enough of that in these days.'

Three of the King's bloods, standing in the mill-yard dirt. They'd have been too young for most of the fighting. The clothes were of good quality and fine style, but not new. Balfour's in particular were worn, and perhaps even repaired in one or two spots. A last so-ho! for the old world.

Vyse added, 'Lady Sarah Saville said that your cause would always be a good one.' *Ah, Sarah, if only that were true.*

Shay smiled heavy. 'You're bold young men, and sharp.' He looked at each of the three faces in turn. 'I will have need of you. A message will come. You'll not know how or from whom. But there'll be no doubting it, and when it comes you'll oblige me by not hesitating.'

Vyse's eyes widened a fraction. Manders started to speak, stopped, and then merely nodded.

'Good lad.'

Then the two older men were up on their replacement horses and through the gate and away, and even the memory of them seemed doubtful to the three left standing stupid in an unknown mill, looking at each other and their muddy boots and trying to recall how they came there.

⎯ ⌣ ⎯

Doncaster early on a Sunday: the first of the sun rising out of the distant German Sea, turning the tower of St George's pale, so that its stones seem more a part of the opaque sky in which it stands, alone and aloof on the edge of the town, than of the shadowed, furtive streets that scurry from its base.

In them, the town is starting to stir, with its first shiftings and scratchings of morning. Stray dogs begin to snuffle and forage in the gutters. In

Frenchgate, in the shadow of the town wall, two sleepy whores stare up sullen and bleary at a window across the street, in which a trim maid is getting dressed. From somewhere, a thoughtless hammering and clattering of wood as a stall is assembled. At gates and junctions and doorways across the town, from the river to the ruins of the old leper house of St James, sentries shift feet, and swap hands on the pikes that prop them up, and try a different shoulder against a pillar, and nod and droop and scowl and roll furred tongues around sour mouths in the weird drifting half-world between sleep and life.

From the St Sepulchre gate, shouting and then the rumble and rattle of hooves at the trot.

A military town now, Doncaster, but comfortable with it: the base of operations for the siege of Pontefract a day's march away, it bustles confident, with the self-righteous imperative of duty and no danger. The soldiers thieve and scuffle and harass the girls, but there's money enough flowing, for the innkeepers and the tailors and the smiths, for the pimps and the dips and the dice-sharps, and the town feels prosperous and satisfied as it wakes.

The hooves echoing from different corners of the town now, tricksy and unsettling and unseen in the winding streets. The heavy breaths of horses standing in the High Street. Uninterested glances from sentry posts and windows. Words to a soldier, insistence, a shrug. Boots on a wooden stair. Voices again, then shouts and the vicious hiss of swords drawn, a grabbing at half-dressed men, wild eyes and anger and fear, and boots on the stair again and the sentry with a blade at his throat and the doorway to the High Street explodes in figures, wrestling and dragging and cursing. A scuffle around the horses, the animals edgy and shifting and hard to mount. Shouts, orders, boots slipping clumsily out of stirrups that won't stay still. Always the shouting, exhortation and intimidation and the Lord God invoked for all sides and purposes on his violated sabbath. 'Move, damn you! Up! Mount up!' Sword-points at breasts, a pistol jammed into a shirt front. 'Up, damn you, or die here! Help him, then.' Glances, curses, a chance, a lunge and a sudden frenzied scuffling, clumsy grappling for arms and weapons. 'No! We don't—' and blades are rattling at each other and the Doncaster morning finally snaps in a pistol shot, and a scream, and now the swords cannot be stopped because blood can smell blood, and the swords are bickering and chattering and nothing is certain in the scrum of frightened animals, and from the muddle of shouts come more cries of pain, affronted and furious, and final. A moment of stupid bewilderment, because the works of men are inexplicable to themselves above all, then insistence and orders and the hurried sheathing of weapons and the grappling with saddles and reins, and the horses whirl and stutter, and then the hooves batter away down the cobbles like musket volleys.

Two men die on the cobbles, pale and half-dressed and shocked, and cold.

⌒ ⌒

With a mighty thump, both of the pair of elegant doors burst open and before they had slammed against the walls the explosion himself was in the room, the big features angry, the hands still held high and flexing and unflexing as if looking for something to throttle, striding forward unstoppable by any earthly force. 'Rainsborough is dead!'

Oliver St John was standing on a low platform, head held high, one hand cocked against his hip and the other poised in elegant gesticulation, the long lace cuff rendering the wrist apparently lighter than air; his breeches were deep and heavy black, which only emphasized the richness of the doublet, brown turning to gold: a Chief Justice of England, and he looked and felt it. He raised an eyebrow.

Cromwell needed a Royalist cavalry troop on which to vent his anger. 'Hacked down in a Doncaster street while the Army snored!'

St John contrived not to lower his chin, but the eyes dropped into a frown. 'God be with him and grant him rest.' He glanced at the man working in front of him, hands still full of palette and brushes and now staring uncomfortably between his patron and the newcomer. The man had never met Master Cromwell, but Master Cromwell was the most dangerous man in the country. Master Cromwell was also, very obviously, in a black blazing fury.

'I pray that he may. He is unlikely to do as much for us.'

St John frowned again, sighed, and then waved the artist away. The artist retreated hurriedly and happily, head down and still clutching his tools.

'Not to imply anything less than complete Christian charity in you, Cromwell, but Rainsborough was hardly a convenient person for us.' He stepped down from the platform and strolled to the easel.

'He was a brave man, and a man of princ—'

'Spare me.' St John peeked round the easel at his new eternal self. 'For us, he was a damned dangerous nuisance.'

Cromwell would not stand still. 'He remains so. Thomas Scot and his group are crying murder and conspiracy. They will not accept that this was a Royalist assassination. Rainsborough is like to be their first Leveller martyr, and they will use him to make all the mischief they can.'

'Of course.'

'They demand an investigation.'

St John nodded. 'Then we should give them one.'

'Scot himself is our chief intelligencer. You countenance unleashing him – in his current mood? He will upend society – he will upend the Army, if he can.'

St John was scowling at his other face. 'Mm. Not him, of course. But I have a better man.'

'I have better men digging privies.'

A pained smile. 'More apt, and more able. I got him some clerkship – Cursitor's fines – and use him on discreet errands. A man of great shrewdness and great good sense.'

'Godly?'

'Not ungodly. I don't think we need bring our Lord into this overmuch. Baines!' The last a roar, and a head appeared between the doors immediately. 'Baines, find Thurloe. Find him wherever he lurks, and have him to Master Cromwell before day's end.'

<hr/>

MERCURIUS FIDELIS

or

The honeſt truth written for every Engliſhman
that cares to read it

From MONDAY, OCTOBER 26. *to* MONDAY, NOVEMBER 2. 1648.

WEDSNEDAY, OCTOBER 28.

RECENT events do ſurely ſhow that the Lord GOD doth puniſh wickedneſs, and that as he ſo briefly allows the unrighteous their vain hopes, ſo doth he reward the righteous for their faith. Every phenomenon in nature, ſome men believe, hath its oppoſite, ſo the nettle hath the dock etc. Perhaps likewiſe in the affairs of men doth the LORD guarantee a right balance and equanimity, ſeemly unto his creation. On October 28. there died at Wincheſter Lady Blanche ARUNDELL, widow of Thomas, Baron Arundell of Wardour, and ſhe was buried next her heroic huſband in their vault at TISBURY. Rightly doth ſhe lie beſide her huſband, for ſhe proved equally a warrior and a true heart. The ſtory of her defence of her houſe at Wardour, aſſiſted by the mereſt of her maids and ſervants and children, againſt fully one hundred times their number of mercenaries and rebels, is become a legend of the rightful ſtruggle in this Kingdom and a worthy ſign of the defiance of Kingly government againſt the cankers that ſo beſet it. The loſs of ſo great a heart to the loyal cauſe might be taken as a victory for the rebels, but that we may all rejoice that the Lord GOD hath taken unto himſelf so precious a ſoul.

THURSDAY, OCTOBER 29.

Not more than one day after, the LORD showed his juſt command of nature. Having taken off a righteous ſoul and thereby given the unGodly cauſe perhaps to rejoice, he cauſed the deſtruction of an unrighteous ſoul, and showed the faithful a full meaſure of his mercy and truſt. Colonel Thomas Rainſborowe was the most brutal of men, if such he may deserve to be called, that ever took up arms in the misbegotten cause. He was a self-proclaimed leveller of society, a breaker of the right order of the world, who had shown his inhumanness in every action of this war in which he partook. While taking his ease in Doncaster, musing on the starvation and further deprivation of the poor inhabitants of Pontefract who yet resist the onslaught of the unGodly, he was slain in the public street, like a cur or vagrant, in an heroic sally by a few of those men he thought to have bottled up in Pontefract. This act of valour was the bravest yet by the defiant defenders of that town, and yet may not we see in it the hand of the Lord GOD himself meting his rightful punishment upon those who would upset the proper order that he has commanded?

[SS C/T/48/9 (EXTRACT)]

Oliver Cromwell: Member of Parliament but the greatest threat to that Parliament; the most devout of men, and the most brutally effective in war; the pre-eminent General of the age, victor of innumerable battles and two wars; the man with the word of the Lord in his mouth and the scourge of the Lord in his hand. Oliver Cromwell, staring up at him from behind the table, two great dark eyes glaring out of the heavy features.

John Thurloe stood silent, slowly unclenched and then clenched one hand, tried to hold the mighty stare.

'Master St John reports you a man of tact, a man of intellect, a man of determination.' The voice seemed to come from the heavy timbers of the table.

'I owe Master St John much.'

'You neither challenge nor endorse his description.'

What game is this? Cromwell the man of prayer. Cromwell the man of war. Thurloe thought for a second, and then shook his head very slightly.

'St John reports you a man to be trusted to the uttermost.'

'I own a duty to my masters, and a duty to my God, and I hope that I know when and how to choose between them.'

A nod. A pause. 'You are not a voluble man, Master Thurloe.'

Thurloe smiled slightly.

Cromwell nodded again. 'I like that.'

Sir,

    the assassination of Rainsboro by a sally from the Pontefract garrison has put Cromwell into a fury at the slow progress of the siege. His fire is the greater, because the radical men of his clique, principally the republican Thomas Scot, a sympathiser to the so-called Levellers and still spymaster to the Parliament, saw Rainsboro as their own particular hero. They have been quick to cry treason and half-heartedness in all directions, and they now present this incident as a test of the commitment of Army and Parliament to reform. Irregardless of policy and strategy, Cromwell must satisfy these radical men or risk a break with them.

    A man called Thurloe has been set to investigate the affair at Doncaster.

    Faithfully, S. V.

[SS C/S/48/23]

Colonel Thomas Rainsborough died many times, and had lived many lives, in the letters and pamphlets that recorded his death. Each page, each leaf in the whirling autumn storm, told its own particular truth.

Colonel Thomas Rainsborough had been a coward and a warrior, a traitor and a crusader, a monster and a saint. He had lived a life of humility, of kindness, of purity, of peace, of passion, of hatred, of debauchery, and of blood.

He was killed by knives, by swords, by pistols, by a fall from his horse, and by a strange and terrible pox that crept over his flesh in the course of one night and left his whole body cankered and grotesque. His last words were for God, and against God, for a King and for a Republic, of defiance and of fear, and when he opened his mouth only a vile grey phlegm oozed out.

He was left a blooded, broken mess in the Doncaster street, and carried into the sky with face perfectly unmarked.

Angry men in mobs tell their own truth, and thousands of them – it may have been two thousand or it may have been ten thousand – marched through London in Rainsborough's funeral. It had rained for two days, and continued to rain, drooping the rosemary sprigs in their hats and the soggy ribbons of remembrance. The roads were mud, an oily treacherous swamp under their boots that only encouraged them to huddle closer together, arms around shoulders or hands clutching the coat in front. Snaking through the ancient streets, the crowd steamed and splashed – a stumbling, cursing, seething organism looking for a way.

From an upstairs window, Thomas Scot watched the procession with bright, exultant, calculating eyes.

'Those trepidatious men in the Parliament shall not ignore us now,' he said. 'This land has seen its last King.'

The man beside him nodded fervently.

The crowd slithered on past them through the street. 'Equal justice under God!' rose thin and strong from somewhere ahead, and then thousands of voices gave the echo: 'Justice!'

＊＊＊

John Thurloe arrived in Doncaster more than a week after the death of Colonel Thomas Rainsborough, but the death still hung humid in the air. He could feel its weight in the attentive performance of the guards at the gate; he could see it in the sullen faces; he caught it in the first glances of alarm whenever he entered a shop or a room.

Thurloe did not know soldiers. They were increasingly present in his life, standing inappropriate on the edge of discussions or disfiguring doorways, surprising rough colours and heavy boots and the embarrassed clatter of metal. But they remained alien and out of place, like wild creatures or coarse language in the chapels and chambers he inhabited, their brutal honesty and anonymity unsettling.

He did not know them, but he could sense the strains in the behaviour of these men: the melodramatic performances of routine with musket and gate; the over-loud interrogation of his name, his purpose, his hostel, his purpose again; and the sour black discontent in the faces. Uniforms and walls were becoming less reliable indicators of allegiance, and it discomfited these violent worshippers of order.

He found a room in an inn – he'd be sharing, but the landlord wanted to encourage quiet-seeming, thoughtful men who weren't soldiers, and so he'd only have a preacher and a horse-dealer for company – and reported to the garrison commander.

The General looked tired and harassed: a large bright uniform at a small drab desk; a body and a face for joviality, now sagging. He stared into the order from the Council for half a minute, and Thurloe watched his thoughts: irritation at interference, suspicion at a civilian, unease at the break in routine, worry at the further impact on his disgruntled men of a stranger prodding around their lives, relief at being able to pass on to someone else the taint of this unhappy case.

Eventually he looked up, and just nodded. 'Well, there it is then,' he said. 'Look, Master. . .' He peered at the paper again.

'Thurloe.'

'Thurloe. There's a war on, you know that?' Thurloe just looked at him. 'Damned difficult affair this. No need for more trouble, you understand? Men are unhappy.' He waved a fist in a slow thoughtful circle, as if stirring a pot of his troubles. 'Radical ideas. Hot tempers. Difficult business, a siege.' He nodded to himself at this wise precept. 'Sickness. Expectations.' He looked up at Thurloe again. 'London!'

Thurloe thanked him, hoped politely that God would add his sinews to a speedy victory, and left.

———— ◆ ————

The reports began to creep towards Shay from the extremities of the country, hidden or crudely encyphered or anonymous. From Cornwall and the Highlands and all points between, men wrote of their loyalties and their fears, their strengths and their vulnerabilities. In his head, Shay began to draft a map of his own private kingdom, a kingdom with its resources and its strongpoints and its lines of communication. Then, at first cautiously, he began to feel his way around this kingdom, and to reckon its possibilities.

Thurloe walked one irregular loop of the town to absorb the layout and the atmosphere. He was here to enquire into a business among soldiers, which made him uncomfortable, and he invented suspicion and hostility in each crowd of uniforms that he passed in the street, every impassive sentry whose eyes followed him.

From fences and door-knockers across the town hung sodden sea-green ribbons: memorial tokens for Rainsborough; the badge of the Levellers. In a square, in front of an inn, a mane of the ribbons hung from a pole, and sprigs of rosemary had been stuck into the cracks and hinges of the inn gate. This, then, was where it had happened. The gate was closed, the inn nursing its shame. Thurloe walked on, out of Doncaster.

He had been given a rough outline of the raid, and followed its course: from the open fields, through the St Sepulchre gate in the west and so back into the town again. He watched the scattered clusters of soldiers in the fields, trying to understand why they were placed as they were, and they watched him in return. He observed the routines at the gate, trying to ignore the fidgeting sentries. He walked into the town, saw the street leading to the violated inn, saw the other streets, down which other Royalist horsemen had ridden in diversion. Some of the raiders who had sallied out of nearby Pontefract and raced back in triumph would have been local men; they would have known Doncaster's streets.

There had been a plan here; this was more than an ale-fired frolic.

Sir Greville Marsh had fifteen trusted men, muskets to go round, and regular meetings of these loyal souls. In Lincolnshire, a network of local gentlemen could muster one hundred and fifty men, fifty of them mounted. Sir David Davis could raise all the Welshmen he wanted, but they would need paying and probably training and they wouldn't come before spring. A group of London merchants would advance money for men and supplies, if they were promised certain commercial advantages by a victorious King.

Shay absorbed it all. The local groupings, the secret places, and the money; the outraged gentlemen and the stolid yeomen, the sportsmen and the chancers and the mercenaries; the man who would betray his castle for a price, the horse racing meetings where Royalists would gather, the friends in strange and useful places. Sometimes a little inspiration, and he'd store it for possible future use. Sometimes a frown, at the fragility of these scattered forces, with their mixed motives and their hesitations and their foolishnesses.

Shay discounted none of it. This was the terrain on which he would fight his battle.

⁓

Back at the garrison headquarters, Thurloe found the General's Adjutant, a man of his own age, tall and pale. The man's ready assistance had been promised by the General, but when Thurloe caught up with him on the stairs of the town house that the Army had commandeered, arms full of papers, he saw hesitation and discomfort worsening the man's apparently habitual frown.

He found a room for Thurloe on the ground floor – undecorated, spare, just a table and chair; found more chairs elsewhere. Thurloe wondered what the room was used for, either by the Army or the normal inhabitants of the place. Having passed on the summons for those Thurloe had asked to see, the Adjutant returned to find Thurloe slouched on a chair at the table, and hesitated in the doorway.

'I shall sit with you,' he said after a moment. It wasn't a question. He took a chair a short distance behind Thurloe's shoulder; it would be an appropriate position once the interviews started, but for now the two men stared off in the same direction, the Adjutant gazing at Thurloe's shoulder and Thurloe gazing at the room and confirming where in the house he must be.

After thirty seconds like this, Thurloe scraped his chair round to face the Adjutant.

'Difficult time, I presume,' he said.

The Adjutant waited.

'Must be difficult to control and sustain men in a drawn-out siege. Then to have this business.'

A pause, and then the Adjutant nodded. His eyes were watchful.

Eventually Thurloe smiled, shook his head. 'Cheap tricks. I'm sorry. No more parlour conversation.'

Slowly, the Adjutant smiled. The eyes were still narrow and thoughtful.

Thurloe's words stayed low, but quickened. 'Colonel Rainsborough was known for a leader of the radical interest in the Army. The so-called Levellers.'

Another pause. Another nod.

'Ribbons and rosemary all over town. A powerful force in these regiments, I think.'

Nod.

'Isn't it strange that a movement of equality and new freedoms should flourish in an organization more hierarchical and more rigid than any?'

The Adjutant's face opened; the eyes moved instinctively in thought. 'Or perhaps it's very natural.' Then he shook his head. 'No; that's facile.' He thought again. 'The levelling men are happy enough to be led. But they desire to be led on their terms, by men of their own timber. And as for the freedoms. . . men must sometimes ask themselves for what they fight, and freedom is a goodly cause.'

'Thousands of men – armed and trained men – determined to change society.'

'This land has known a decade of blood, Master Thurloe. If nothing changed, would that not be futility indeed? May we not hope for something good at the end of it?'

The first of Thurloe's soldiers knocked and entered. Over three hours he saw them, singly or in twos and threes, hostile or obliging, taciturn or garrulous, disrespectful or oddly afraid. All of them, through some element of mood or phrase or posture or expression, demonstrated their concern that a civilian should be talking to soldiers about soldiers' business. Thurloe wrote it all down – the impressions, the phrases, the facts. And always, over his shoulder, the Adjutant sat silent, and Thurloe could read his expressions from the reacting expressions on the faces of the soldiers when their eyes flicked over to him.

The advance pickets – the squads posted out in the fields, utterly surprised by the horsemen who had exploded out of the dawn – told of the speed, the sheer unstoppable number of horsemen, their desperate resistance against the horde, the eventual weight of numbers. One older man explained to the civilian in earnest detail the role of the skirmisher, required to give only limited resistance before withdrawing. Thurloe listened politely to it all. Trying to avoid too obvious a challenge to their battered pride – *No doubt a man on a charging horse must by weight alone be able to scatter a number of dismounted men, so I assume it natural that a relatively small number of riders must always in military affairs be able to displace a larger number of foot-soldiers* – uneasy shiftings in seats, hasty glances at the Adjutant – Thurloe tried to get a more accurate estimate of the number of raiders. Wondering at the dawn – *Since, as you say, you'd been awake and alert for some time, you presumably had some idea where the sun was* – eye-freezing confusion – he tried to establish the direction from which the assault had come, and some idea of the time.

The extremely rough idea suggested that there had been a gap between the charge through the pickets and the forcing of the gate. The soldiers had dispersed into the undergrowth, only to emerge once all was obviously clear. They had been simply ridden over rather than defeated, as the absence of wounds suggested: surprised, removed as a factor, and forgotten as the raiders continued towards the town.

The story from the St Sepulchre gate was similar, told with the same hesitations and inconsistencies and exaggerations. But here there had been a fight at least: there were wounds, and men he could not interview. This west entrance to the town was really gateway rather than gate, the contest determined by surprise against sleep, and by the presumably considerable advantage of charging horses. Thurloe tried to scrabble for clear details among the broken recollections: again an idea of time; again an idea of numbers; any suggestion of structure among the raiders – commands, leadership. No, there was not, and little frowns and glances told him that this was something only a civilian might ask.

'For the riders in the town, are there witnesses?' They were alone again for a moment.

The Adjutant shook his head. 'We asked around, of course. A few people glimpsed them as they passed. I can give you one or two liars who will tell of their encounters. And I can show you the routes the riders took. I also have two townswomen who saw definite portents for the raid in the days before: one during that night. We should not discount such things.'

'Nor do I. There was no suggestion of contact with anyone in the town during the raid?'

'None. They were noticed by few. It was early, of course. I believe that those riders who did not carry out the assassination itself were intended to distract and delay only if necessary. They do not appear to have sought attention.'

And so to the killing itself. The Adjutant had a score of reports of screams and curses, second-hand retellings of heroic last stands against impossible odds, and one substantial and detailed description of the movements of the ghost of Colonel Thomas Rainsborough in the hours after and before the death, but only two witnesses.

The first was the inn-owner, a dapper, prudent man, and Thurloe felt something in himself uncoil at the first non-soldier he'd seen in hours. But the man, words kept as carefully as clothes, had nothing useful to say: awoken by the sound of an argument, as so many mornings would be in this military town, and then shortly afterwards from the street the noises of anger and then violence and then death. He left, feet soft on the boards and Thurloe disappointed that the civilian had offered nothing more than the military.

The Adjutant's other witness had seen more than the rest of Doncaster taken together. He had been sentry on duty outside the inn that morning. Some riders – *How many riders?* – three or four – *Think! Think of the faces* – four then, four riders had stopped at the inn. *How did they come? Charging? Trotting?* – a gentle walk, nothing to remark. They claimed to bring letters from General Cromwell for the Colonel – *Was such a thing normal?* – normal enough. The sentry had fetched the Colonel's Lieutenant to the door, and the riders had repeated their mission. The Lieutenant had authorized the opening of the gate. Three of the riders had gone into the inn yard with the Lieutenant, and one of those had stayed in the yard with the horses – *And the fourth?* – had walked off with his horse. The sentry had to keep an eye outwards, but as he'd said one of the men had stayed in the yard – they'd exchanged a few words while they waited – and the other two had gone up to the Colonel's room with the Lieutenant. Then, a few – *How long?* – a few minutes only, and they'd all come down again with the Colonel – *How come down? In what order? How disposed?* – it was difficult to be clear, it all got very confused very quick, but probably the Lieutenant and the Colonel and then the two men behind, and he wasn't sure but there'd been something about the Colonel that looked angry – Colonel was often angry but he'd looked sort of uncomfortable angry – and then it was chaos because someone had grabbed him by the shoulders and yanked him back into the yard and then the Colonel and the Lieutenant were hurried out and the riders with them with their horses and then he went to get up but someone had lamped him properly in the face and he was sort of stunned, and they'd pulled the gate to behind them and he was still coming round properly when through the gate he heard shouting and then fighting – *Fighting?* – fighting: swords and pistols and shouting, and by the time he was up and out the riders were gone and the Colonel was lying dead in the gutter.

The man's face had reddened in his own breathless retelling, and he ran out of words unexpectedly and sat blinking and gulping for them for a moment, and then subsided. The Colonel had meant something to him. Thurloe wondered whether Leveller soldiers distinguished themselves in any way by badge or sign. He said, 'And the Lieutenant?'

The Adjutant's voice came low over his shoulder: 'Died in the street with his Colonel.'

'That was him. Of course.' Thurloe sat still for a moment, wrote a few lines, sat silent again. It didn't seem much. Was there something else he should ask the sentry? He tried for descriptions, but the sentry could only give generalities. Had any of the riders been obviously in command? The sentry wasn't sure, but maybe one had told the man to stay with the horses, before going upstairs himself. Thurloe nodded, and murmured distracted thanks. The sentry checked with the Adjutant, and stood and walked away. Catching himself, Thurloe called a fuller thank you after him.

Finally the escape from the town. A soldier in indeterminate uniform had sauntered up to the men guarding the northern bridge out of town, and started a conversation. There had been no sign or sound of alarm from inside the town. Suddenly a large party – Fifty? A hundred? It was impossible to say – *That seems a lot of horsemen to have made no sound in the town, surely* – had charged them from the unexpected direction, scattering the guard and escaping to open country and to Pontefract. Only later did they realize that the mysterious soldier had gone with the raiders. With the exception of some immediately discounted scars and disfigurements, Thurloe got no useful information about him.

Again, there was a plan here: great nerve, and a plan.

'Not a very impressive picture, I fear.' With the door closed behind the last relieved witness, the Adjutant was watching for the reaction.

Thurloe shrugged slightly. 'I wouldn't know. That's for their General and their God.'

He was feeling uncomfortable. He had nothing to report but the obvious, nothing to add to facts already known, no comment to make more legitimate than the speculations of the dozen pamphlets that had already covered the story exhaustively. Nothing to take back to London, and nothing to justify the faith in him of St John and Cromwell.

'What did you think of Colonel Rainsborough yourself?'

The Adjutant watched him carefully for a moment.

'His men adored him. He was their own particular hero.' He caught Thurloe's eye, and smiled. 'Soldiers are boys, in truth. Simple values; simple pleasures. Licensed irresponsibility.'

'You haven't answered my question.'

'No, Thurloe. I haven't.'

'You didn't like him, yourself, I think.' Something furtive and shocked crossed the Adjutant's face. 'Pardon me: that's not a fair question.'

'The Colonel was a brave man, and bold. An attractive character.'

'A soldier to be loved by soldiers.' There had been something of sympathy, surely, when the Adjutant had described the Levellers' politics.

'Quite.' The Adjutant moved a paper across the desk; hesitated; moved it back again. He didn't look up. 'Some criticized a. . . a recklessness; a brutality.'

'I understand.' The Adjutant was a little sympathetic to the Levellers; or perhaps just a little scared. Either way, it told something of their influence.

'Soldiers can be civilized men, do you know?' The question came as a genuine appeal. 'And those who mistrusted his politics mistrusted. . . what they saw as – as populism.' He licked his lips slowly. 'For our cause he was a. . . problematic figure.'

Thurloe nodded. 'He still is.'

CHAMPIONS OF THE KING'S HIGH-WAY
OR
THE NEW ROBYN HOODS

The ſtories of the capture of Captain Edward HOLT are like to prove fantaſtical, for even if the Parliament men laid hold on him he would eſcape by-and-by and leave them graſping at the empty air, as when the MAGISTRATE at LEEDS ſaid to him, Sir I do not give you leave to challenge this authority, and great HOLT said, Ha ha then Sir I ſhall take my leave, and with one vault he eſcaped by the window, stopping only to kiſs the hands of divers ladys. HOLT is known for a ſupremely large man, and his cunning is the equale of his ſize, as when in April he robbed the baggage of General FAIRFAX when it was guarded by ſixteen men. In June he went into LANCASHIRE and on the 11. he was ſeen in BURNLEYE and on the 12. he was in LANCASTER and in between he took three purſes from a coach near Omſkerk.

And his BENEFACTORS are only the ſympathiſers of the Parliament, for he has ſworn that he ſhall take not a ſixpence from an honeſt man, and he has ſaid, Shall they call me villain if I puniſh only villains, and all of his earnings he returns to thoſe honeſt men who have ſuffered the extortions of the Government, and in YORKSHIRE three barns and a CHURCH have been repaired at his expenſe.

Such an one is alſo Sir Miles TEACH, known for a very daſhing gallant ſoldier and a jolly REPUBLICAN of the roads, for he knows no ſuperior or maſtery by law as he rides, and ſince the men in LONDON have determined that they may do without the Laws of GOD and the King in that corrupted City, they muſt perforce ſuffer that they exerciſe no law themſelves upon the highway. For as HOLT truly ſaid, The CHAOS and INJUSTICE they have ſpread I ſhall ſend back to them ten-fold. Sir TEACH was always renowned for his daring as well as his pleaſant ways, and indeed the Ladys know him for a ſwordſman as much as the Gentlemen, and when from a Parliamentary hireling he takes a purſe, from the LADY he will like take but a kiſs, and who ſhall ſay which was the loſer?

TEACH was ever a cloſe companion of His Majeſty The KING, and attended him in many places, but it was remarked the one occaſion he would forſake the KING'S preſence was if there was chance of battle, for he is the braveſt man and at NASEBYE of ill-renown he killed ſeven Roundhead men and a Colonel. Now he contines his war upon the KING'S high-way, and ſtill the Parliament men do loſe their impure blood and their ſtolen gold. He is ſometime a companion to Captain HOLT, and it is known that in Auguſt near SKIPTON they had a CONTEST which would take moſt gold in one night (this was ſaid by ſome to be on the 4. Auguſt, by others on the 5.), and in the morning they counted and they had won equally, and the Roundheads and the Committee-Men and the turn-coates had suffered equally, and it is ſure that the good people of that place were the gainers.

To the Lord President of the Council of State,
being a report on the late events in the town of
Doncaster, and the death of Colonel Thomas
Rainsborough.

Sir,

at around dawn on the 29 October a party of Royalist raiders surprised the western entrance of Doncaster town. It is probable that they came from besieged Pontefract, but this is supposition merely. Their number has been much exaggerated and may not safely be assessed, but their movements and achievements would indicate a party of a dozen at the very least and perhaps some twenty, altho' many more would seem unlikely. They scattered the outer pickets by speed and weight of charge, and subsequently surprised the St Sepulchre gate. Inside the town they separated into smaller units, some for contingent readiness and one group of four men riding to the inn where lodged Colonel Rainsborough. Three of these gained entrance by a ruse, and brought out the Colonel and his Lieutenant into the street, where both were killed. The raiders regathered to make a forced escape from the town by the north, whence they fled towards Pontefract Castle.

Although timing is of course vague, there was an interval between the scattering of the pickets and the assault on the western gate — during which time, incidentally, none of the pickets found himself able to reach the town to give warning — which suggests a degree of calculation and control to the exploit. This is confirmed by the restraint and certainty with which the party behaved once inside Doncaster, some spreading to be ready to make distractions in divers quarters should that prove necessary, some making direct for the inn. The deed was foul, but it was executed with strategy and decision and skill. The measured and unsuspected approach to the town, and the knowledge of the dispositions of our soldiers thereabout, likewise suggest a system of scouts and spies.

Others more fitted to judge may consider whether there was negligence in the fulfilment of their duties by the defenders of the west and north gates, by which the raiders gained entrance and exit. But it is not possible

to find evidence of any collusion by those men. There may have been
such, but surprise and confusion seem adequately to explain the exploit.

[SS C/T/48/10]

———— ∙ ————

The King's advisers, now always in shadows and murmur.

'The negotiators have gone. This phase is done.'

'Parliament must needs think on the King's answers.'

'We cannot wait!'

A huddle of hunched shoulders, tense and belligerent in the gloom of the ante-room.

'The negotiators are desperate for an agreement with us. They told me so.'

'They have not got that agreement. They are gone because their cause is hopeless.'

'Delay will worsen the divisions between Parliament and Army. The King has done most skilfully.'

'Delay will push the Army to intervene. The King is lost!'

Wild eyes flickering candlelight at each other – frustrated, angry, captive, lost, uncertain.

'The calculation has changed. The King must be got away.'

'The King refuses!'

'He must be counselled. I am advised—'

'Seymour, I grow tired of your secret voices. Who are these men and why should we heed them?'

'We speak of the safety of the King, and of the realm!'

'We do not know wherein lies that safety. I tell you we do not know now!'

Charles Stuart, huddled in the large oak chair, alone:

Oh, how I have yearned for this silence. No one stares at me, no one asks questions of me, no one can see my hands, my height, my uncertain lips. No one waits for me to fail or to weep. No one to trap me now.

I beat them. Their armies and their books and their theories, they thought they had me at disadvantage; they thought I – they thought that I, the King – could be manoeuvred and wheedled. I beat them. I was cleverer than they were. Perhaps now a little respect. Perhaps the whispers in the London streets, the clever lawyers at their dinners, perhaps these will say at last that Charles Stuart is a King indeed, and a King truly for England, and a wronged man.

I hope that they were satisfied. They seemed so disappointed. I had thought their entreaties, their genuflections, mere masque-show; but they left apparently so disheartened. I hope they will give good report of me to their Parliament. They are my people, I am their King, and I am doing as I see best. If only these people would understand me.

But perhaps they will be angry. I have delayed them; I have temporized and cavilled. I have double-dealt with the Army in the same hour. Will they be angry with me? By what right could they be, with me, their King? But they will be angry nonetheless. They were always angry, because I am clever and I am different. Would that they could once understand me. Would that they could love me for who I am.

There was a new face among my advisers; the hunted sheep. A dark, grim face. A face I thought I recognized, and somehow an ill memory. A spy? Or was the face even there? Was this not some angel of darkness that I alone could see?

Escape, they say. I would I were free of all of this. There have been periods of my life – there have been facets of myself – when I have felt truly comfortable: a fit body, a fluent tongue, a right man, a right King. A trusted horse, moving sure beneath me, and us alone in the trees. Henrietta, and a moment of utter trust together, all discomfort and sin forgot. Did the old King somehow see me in these moments? There have been gardens, there have been hours, there have been alignments of my body and mind, when I have felt truly free.

But if I attempt to fly, it will only make them angry. If I show that I have kept my word, if I tarry regardless and do my duty, then perhaps they will see that I am a King to be trusted. A King to be loved.

Withal, I have nowhere to turn, and nowhere to fly. I am in the Lord's snare; I am in the Lord's cage.

One foot shakes on the velvet stool.

Through the window, in the market square, the sudden rattle of many hooves on the cobbles, and shouts. A rescue? Of course not. New soldiers sent by the King's enemies. But why? And then a rude hammering at the doors below.

Late in the evening in Grimsby town, the rain driving hard out of the darkness of the sea and bustling through the streets, and the wind buffeting unpredictably out of the blackness, a cloaked and hooded man slipped into the Anchor tavern. A respectable place, the Anchor: too close to the waterfront for most of the townspeople, but kept too strict for the common fishermen. A place for cautious tradesmen and sober captains. A place grown tired and silent through the years of war.

The cloaked man, back pressed to keep the door closed against the wind but ready to be out in an instant, checked that the tavern room was empty before letting the latch close fully and taking the last step down.

The landlord watched him carefully, and continued to watch with a mug and a rag held still in his hands as the man crossed the tavern towards him.

The man reached the bar, wet his lips uneasily, and murmured a single word. The landlord's eyes widened a fraction, and then he nodded.

The cloaked and hooded man said no further word that night, and he said nothing when, in the hour before dawn, he stepped down from Grimsby jetty into a fishing ketch that bobbed and chattered in the black water. The mooring ropes were pulled in while he was still steadying himself on the unfamiliar deck, and the ketch slipped away towards the dawn.

Thus Sir Marmaduke Langdale escaped England. The veteran of all the great battles of the nation's terrible decade, hero of a dozen desperate charges into history, slipped away in the mists. He would go on to Venice, to war against the Turks at the other end of the Continent, but his journey began with a whispered word in an empty Grimsby tavern.

Sir,

Cromwell's opinion is much altered these last weeks, and I think this do foreshadow great change in the direction of proceedings in London. But three weeks past he was most modest in manner and belief, ever–mistrustful of the King but in his considerations of how to deal with the King very ready to find terms with all colours of men within Parliament and without, looking for this Assembly or a newly elected Assembly to dictate the policy, and saying I do desire that understanding between all Godly people which the Lord hath promised us be they Scottish or English, Jew or Gentile or Presbyterian or Independent etc etc, and most conciliatory also to the Leveller interest.

Now he can no longer find in his heart such latitude. He is grown much heated at the temporising of the moderate men in Parliament, as much for the giddy reversals of their positions as for the positions themselves, such as their readiness to show leniency to those who lately led the armies into England, even unto Hamilton himself, and what Cromwell perceives to be an over-enthusiasm to treat with the King at all hazards. He cannot find mercy for those who sought as he sees the matter to bring foreign dominion over England, and he cannot find patience for the deliberations of Parliament, and his talk is turned most wild, as it concerns the tolerance by the Army of this Parliament and of the King himself.

Faithfully, S. V.

[SS C/S/48/40]

Sir Mortimer Shay sat on his haunches in a derelict fisherman's hut on the south coast, the earth floor littered with pebbles and weed and bones and shells, and the air as sharp and cold as if the salt crystals were gusting solid through the window holes, and he watched the white sea and wondered at the character of Oliver Cromwell.

Through the doorway and beyond the sluggish water of the bay, the spit of land stretched across his vision and on the end of the spit he could see Hurst Castle. In this castle, sited in perfect definition of defensibility and framed by a dead sky that defined bleakness, was his King.

Oliver Cromwell had changed his mind. Or, rather, Oliver Cromwell had observed the factors in his world – the divided Parliament, the restive Army, the fickle King – and, as the currents in them had shifted, that mind had recalculated how to sustain the progress and the stability it desired.

Shay didn't like the sea. He'd crossed it more than once, and every time been the first man hurrying off the boat when solid land was reached. He didn't like this vulnerability in his temperament. He didn't like the undependable shifting under his feet. Through the rotting bleached door frame the sea stared back at him, one vast dead eye with the grey castle its pupil.

The Army had seized the King, and brought him to the mainland, to that castle. With him, the balance of power in the land had shifted dramatically, and now Parliament waited like a cornered hen.

One of the window holes darkened and blurred suddenly, and then there was a figure in the doorway. Shay was up from his haunches immediately, wincing and irritated at the clumsiness in his knees.

The figure looked uncertainly at Shay, then back the way he'd come, and then to Shay again for reassurance. Shay beckoned him with a flick of his head.

The figure stepped in cautiously, one step only and blinking hard to catch the face in the gloom. Then the eyes widened in surprise. 'Upon my oath – I had not expected to see you.'

Shay shook his hand, and held it for a moment. 'I'd be delighted if you forgot you'd seen me. How do you?'

Something between a gasp and a laugh from the other man. 'I. . . for myself. . . well enough, I suppose, in these strange days.'

'Good.' Shay stepped past him, and glanced briefly left and right through the doorway; then he returned to the back wall.

The newcomer stayed on the threshold. He leaned against the doorpost, in an attempt at nonchalance. 'London – is – in – ferment.' He weighted the words emphatically, trying at jocularity. Then London crept up behind him, and he remembered it, and shook his head. 'Ferment.'

Shay waited.

His visitor stood upright again, nonchalance abandoned. 'The Army has purged Parliament.'

'Purged? How?'

'Soldiers at the door. Three days ago now. Arresting some; refusing entry to others. Those in favour of seeking agreement with the King.' The words were hurried. He didn't want to stay. 'A hundred men or more. As many again now stay away from fear. What's left is. . .'

Shay let the pause hang, before picking it up. 'A Parliament ready to try a King, would you say?'

'A Parliament ready to do the Army's bidding, whatsoever that may be.' The dead voice came suddenly alive. 'What has happened in this land? Even two weeks ago – one week – there was no question but that the King would be at the heart of any settlement. For all the blood, for all the complaints and cries against him, his acquiescence to some settlement was still desired by all. Now there's every chance we are to be the first Christian land to make a public criminal of our own sovereign.'

Shay realized that he was trying to look past the man, through the doorway to the dead white water. To the castle? An instinctive fear that the King might be bundled off somewhere else unless he kept watch? Or was he just looking for the sea itself? Mortimer Shay needed to see his enemies.

Head tilted to one side, focus over the man's shoulder, he said flatly: 'Oliver Cromwell has happened in this land.' His focus shortened, to the shadowed face in front of him. 'I mistook him, I confess. I thought him merely the blunt instrument of the independent men in Parliament, the luckiest of the Army's commanders.' He took in a great acrid sniff, fish and salt and the cold bleached air, and shook his head once and ominous. 'I begin to see it now. He has a greater perspective than any of them. A clarity of vision; a clarity of purpose.'

His gaze was out to sea again. The shadow said crossly, 'He's ruthless; he's unprincipled.'

Shay considered the face and then the figure absently, as if looking for Cromwell through them. 'Ruthless, yes. Of course. But in pursuit of his principles, I think; and that's the danger. He sees further, he knows where he's going, and he shows no scruple or sentiment in getting there.' Hard eyes, and a dark smile. 'I should like to meet this man.'

~ ~

The colours and life of Astbury had shrunk away into hibernation. The stones of the house were dulled without the sun, and Rachel Astbury walked through deadened gardens, as if the first cold of winter had scorched every plant and left them as skeletons of ash. Even the greens that endured had somehow hardened and blackened: they crouched low, hung back against dark trunks, reflected no light.

In the frozen landscape there was only one movement: Jacob's shoulders, rising and falling over a spade. Rachel moved towards him, as if to the last of life. Her exterior was all cold; she was trying to pull away from it.

She watched him a while: the flexing of the old sinews under the jacket; the steadiness.

'It doesn't seem possible that it can survive,' she said. 'That anything can ever be green again.'

He looked up, nodded respectfully. 'Oh aye, miss.' It was agreement and reassurance, and it was all she would get from Jacob. The ancient face nodded at her again, and returned to the spade.

'Nature. . . kills herself.'

He looked up, and considered this. Then down again. 'Knows what she's doing.'

She waited, but there was no more. Just the frosty rasp of Jacob's breathing, in the wilderness. She turned and walked towards the house, dreaming of a fire and trying not to feel her own body.

～

On 29th December in that year, the Army Council was visited by Elizabeth Poole of Abingdon, a woman known to speak prophecy rightly, a woman with God's truth in her mouth.

The Army Council, hungry variously for enlightenment or for exculpation, welcomed her with sober respect. A woman, of course, had no place in politics, and certainly no voice. One had to beware false prophets, and the Council in its experience of the gravity and grimness of the world knew the manifold deceptions and flippancies of women. But God's providence must be sought and welcomed wherever it may be found.

The Council had her sit on a simple chair, and stood around her, pressed close in their heavy uniforms and reverential glares. The room smelled of wet cloth, and men.

Among them, Elizabeth Poole seemed insubstantial, almost transparent: thinner, paler, odourless. She wore grey linen, and its elusive folds and shadows inhabited a different spectrum to the tans and blues that circled her.

She confirmed that God was at work in and through the Army. She described a vision: a strong man, capable and careful, healing a frail body. The strong men looked at the frail woman in their middle, and knew that the Army could heal England.

Through the fogged window there was a burst of coarse argument from the riverbank, rough, unrestrained shouts and laughter. The soldiers ignored the distractions, stared harder at the fragile creature in front of them, that their concentration might harden into faith and open them more utterly to the divine.

Elizabeth Poole murmured the rightness of their proceeding against the delegitimate King, urged them politely to fight for the liberty that God had vouchsafed them, whispered of the great test in front of them, and blessed them with the trust of God and the nation.

Slowly, some nods, and murmurs of 'Amen'.

~ ~

Thomas Scot had the invidious habit, or so it seemed to Cromwell, of placing himself always at the very edge of a man's vision. Never in front, never face to face. It made him perpetually a distraction, an irritation.

He was there now, a glimpse of complication, a promise of complaint. Cromwell turned his head to face him square, scowled, and then his eyes dropped again to the report.

> *Sir, I must beg leave to report that this day, January 4, the*
> *Parliament of Scotland has in its first act of business produced the*
> *strongest possible declaration against the current proceedings towards*
> *Charles Stuart, honouring him as the rightful and inviolable King*
> *of Scotland and expressing dark concern at what is perceived as an*
> *excess of religious toleration among those forces most influential*
> *in English politics. I shall send to you the full manuscript of this*

declaration at the first moment I have it. The Duke of Argyll,
notwithstanding his amity and hospitality to you but two months
past, has placed himself in the front line of this new campaign, and
will listen to no moderating counsel from myself or any other. It
is clear from the thing itself and from other correspondence I have
had that he considers it no more than politic to take so advanced a
position. A man of his ultimate changeability may fairly be taken as
bell-wether for the movements of Scottish sentiment.

[NALSON COLLECTION 24, BODLEIAN LIBRARY]

The mighty Cromwell nose twisted up in a big sniff of distaste, as at an acrid smell that would nonetheless not deter him from taking a full breath. He gripped the report in a slow paw, and thrust it over his shoulder towards St John, standing behind him.

'How many Scottish armies am I to be obliged to fight?' Scot's face opened theatrically at the question, a show of wise wonder at the mysteries of life, as if Scottish armies were an unknowable emanation of divine caprice. Which, it was beginning to appear to Cromwell, might well be the case. 'Must we inform the Parliament that this is to be a yearly phenomenon, an annual sacrifice, a celebration of harvest time?'

Oliver St John was smoothing out the crumpled corner of the report, stroking at it like a dove in his palm. 'The politics of it are hardly surprising, and the strength of the words a reflection of the weakness of the real threat. There is no army.'

'We cannot be sure. The border with Scotland is the broken door of our house, through which cold wind and pestilence will come unless the door be bolted or the pestilence purged.'

'I would counsel haste.' Thomas Scot's thin cracked voice, and both heads turned to him.

Scot smiled weakly, as if embarrassed that his words had carried. 'There is not yet an army, as Master St John wisely remarks, and there will not be one if we act quickly to remove that which would be its cause and its rallying-post – that is, Charles Stuart. But if we linger, we will permit the divisions and frailties of our weaker supporters to eat at our cause, and we will make such an army a certainty. Some preachers are speaking for the

King already – for his character, and for the impossibility of trying him. The Court is dithering. I have reports' – he laid his palm softly against his chest, as though the reports were kept there; perhaps they were – 'of their qualms and quibbles. Downes, for example, and Love. There is a cancer of divers men, all inclined to find reasons to oppose us, and if they should have time and place to cohere. . .' He let the threat hang, but then decided it too subtle. 'If they should attract leadership. . . the leadership of General Fairfax, perhaps, who is of course much loved among our people, then we should scarce have an army of our own to oppose against what Scotland might throw at us.'

There were just three of them in the room, and in the moment it seemed a small and lonely place.

'I would counsel haste.'

─── ──

Sir,

the trial is to proceed, regardless of disputes and doubts over the basis in law for such a proceeding. There is a grouping of men who will push it to the uttermost, even as to a threatening of the King's life, but there is agreement that such would only be to press him to recognise the legitimacy of the proceeding and thus accept the new Parliamentary order of things, and come thereby into a more peaceful and enduring relationship with his people.

S. V.

[SS C/S/49/7]

─── ──

On 5th January the Army Council called back the prophesier Elizabeth Poole, to hear more of God's intent. There was snow outside, and the heavy boots dropped slush on the floorboards, and the lattice windows fogged in the heat of the intent room.

Frail and bold, a divine sparrow among the profane herd of cattle, she confirmed their role as stewards of the nation.

She was more confident this time, looking around herself, making occasional darting contact with the glances of the big men. She reminded them that a steward must improve that which is in his care, but must not overreach his station. The King had betrayed his trust, and Parliament had betrayed their trust; the Army must not follow. From somewhere she produced a paper – a few less concentrated minds wondered at the workings of that whispering dress – and with it a clear instruction, which she would not weaken despite increasingly insistent and sceptical questions. The King might be tried, and convicted of breach of trust, but his person must not be harmed.

The soldiers shifted, uncomfortable in their heavy boots and coats, swapped glances, looked darkly at the glowing woman, looked away.

Tyrant, traitor, murderer, and a public and implacable enemy of the Commonwealth of England. Thus the King of that country, brought to trial by his people.

Every day now the Court must make some further innovation, of administration, of religion, or of law. The Court must move fast, to stay one day ahead of the implications of yesterday's innovation. If you stop moving you lose your balance and fall. Today the Committee is trying the King – for treason, until someone unhelpfully points out that since treason is an act against the King you can hardly charge a King with it, can you? It is an age of elaborate theatrical, and an appropriate setting has been designed for this unprecedented spectacle.

Westminster Hall: the stones and timbers of oldest England, a grand and solemn and austere stage. A raised platform at one end for the judges – magisterial, superior, all-seeing. A wooden bar across the Hall, to distinguish between judge and judged, right and wrong. Soldiers, because pikes and uniforms give an unchallengeable legitimacy to a proceeding, and because – well, because you never know. At the far end of the Hall two tiered wooden galleries, thirty-six hours of unbroken work for the carpenters, just pay them whatever they ask, because a spectacle must have spectators. Justice must be *seen* to be done.

Unfortunately, the actors keep forgetting their lines: members of the Court disagree with each other, say the wrong thing, absent themselves; sessions are cancelled; the soldiers have to be prompted to give their cries of support to the proceeding; their Colonel threatens to fire into the crowd; members of the audience will insist on heckling.

And in the middle of them all, tiny in his loneliness, the King. Another overweening oak chair – *Have they not the wit to make a throne of becoming smallness, rather than these oppressive giants?* – placed on a platform of rich ochre carpeting. From above, the highest points in the galleries, the King resembles a peculiar insect trapped in amber.

Held as if by some aura, none of the King's subjects may come nearer than ten feet. The carpet, the distance, the distinction: now that the King's majesty has finally come under open challenge, those who no longer recognize it seem to be according it proper recognition at last.

But who would wish to stand too close to this strange man, accused of all possible crimes against the state? For lifetimes the touch of a King has cured infection; now it seems that the King's touch has become infectious, bringing defeat and chaos and guilt.

There was a King in this realm sat in his throne and tried to hold back the sea. Perhaps I have that gift, that you hold yourselves so far from me. But your endless staring faces overwhelm me, your curiosity, your scrutiny, your scorn, and I know I cannot hold you back. Rather I would disappear, slip these heavy clothes and vanish as a spirit, become one with the yellow light that burns through the windows.

Has any King – has any man in his station and time – had to suffer such affront to his dignity? Such insults, such unbecoming aggression, such masquerade? I am become a mummery show to the whole people, a fighting cock. I am become the jester to my own Court.

This is unbelievable. This is unthinkable. This is not real. You speak a language of law that I do not recognize. You refuse to recognize my status or my arguments. I am merely a distant spectator of these bastard proceedings, which appear to me but dimly: an argument observed through a window; a conversation heard from another room. How far away these people are, how far England as I perceived it. This is no longer a world that I understand. I fly above it. I am a sparrow fluttering among the hammer-beams, looking down on this strangeness. I am gone, through the keyhole.

Behind the scenes, the arguments, the persuasion, the intimidation continue.

The Crown Inn, in Uxbridge, and Shay was sitting in a corner away from the fire when his visitor arrived. The man stepped in uneasily, looking around, saw him, looked a little sick, looked around again and approached uncomfortably, as if his clothes were wet or pinched him.

Shay said pleasantly, 'Sit down! Sit down!' and when his visitor was sitting down leaned forward and murmured through a smile, 'A discussion between companions over a drink in a good inn attracts no attention; trying to disguise your approach to a man with whom you're about to have an intimate conversation does attract attention. Relax yourself. Smile.'

His visitor did neither. He sat back in his chair, and then plunged forward. 'It is signed.'

Shay breathed in heavily, holding his expression even.

'It is signed. Death. The King is to lose his head. At the last, they insisted that the charge of treason be on the warrant.'

Shay merely nodded. Then: 'How many? Who?'

Another flash of nausea in the face. 'Fifty-nine. Bradshaw first, of course. Then Grey, and Cromwell.' A shrug. 'Those you would expect. Ireton, Marten and Lilburne. Hutchinson. Pride. Scot.'

'Hutchinson?'

'On the first day. He still smarts, that he let General Langdale escape from inside his very hands at Nottingham, and so brazen. Since that day he has burned for a revenge on Royalism.'

Shay's eyes had narrowed. His visitor waited – and then leaned in again. 'This is the headquarters of the Army itself! Why do we meet here?'

'That is why. The most trusted, the most sure men in the realm meet in this town.'

'You're – I was here negotiating with the King in '45, did you know that?'

Shay said nothing. He'd known. A man had few enough opportunities to exercise his humour.

Again his visitor's face was thrust forward. 'I want indemnity.'

'You want what?'

'Indemnity. Who can know how this will go now? No one has killed a King before. The preachers say the whole world could end. The millennium itself. We may yet see civil war worse than ever we have imagined it.' Shay seemed to be considering the notion. 'Who can know? But you must indemnify me – protect me if the country turns again. You must sign – or the Prince. The Prince must sign for me.'

Shay's mouth twisted, chewing the idea. 'One would tend to try for such a bargain before offering one's information.'

A flicker of panic across his visitor's eyes. 'But. . . I have. . . You must!'

Shay's old head was stone. 'I will speak for you when I can. For the meanwhile, I will have need of your service – from time to time. Forget us not, and perhaps you will be not forgotten.'

A sick nod. Then, eventually, with emptiness: 'What happens now? What will you do –afterwards?'

Shay's expression was open, the tone mild – the answer obvious. 'I will create such a chaos in these lands as will make these Godly men think their world upturned, and all the torments of hell upon them.'

His visitor stared at him, pleading for the reassurance or the joke, and then the strained face collapsed and the shoulders slumped. A breath, and then he flung himself up from the table and turned to go.

A moment later he was there again, hands gripping the chair back and head bent low.

'Thank you for not asking.' Shay looked up. His visitor was not looking at him, head offered low for blessing or execution. Shay saw tiny droplets of water on the swaying strands of hair; it must have come on to drizzle after his own arrival. 'Whether I signed. Thank you for not asking.'

Shay took his hand. 'You forgot to shake hands.' He smiled heavily. 'It's getting harder to stay alive. A man must shift as best he can.'

The Palace of St James, in London. Early in his reign, His Majesty, being a less convivial man than his father, had decreed that he would be accompanied at his most intimate proceeding by only one of his attendants. Now he crouches crimson over the pot, watched by two soldiers who are dutied to monitor him night and day, and who shuffle and flinch in their discomfort. The bringing down of majesty was not supposed to be like this.

Below, in a kitchen storeroom, murmuring through a gloom gusting with nutmeg and cinnamon and grain of paradise, two men:

'Shay, is there no chance of —'

'None. Do you have what I asked?'

A scrambling in a pocket. 'Yes, but—' A paper is taken firmly – scrutinized intently in the musty light and thrust into an inner pocket – and a ring.

'My duty and my respect to His Majesty. The new King will wear this, and will remember his father when he does so.' Two pairs of eyes stare at each other through the impossible. 'You will be safe, Seymour. I have seen to that. Are there other papers?'

'Some, of course.'

'Burn them, Seymour. Burn it all.'

Whitehall is the great theatre of the British Empire, the stage for a thousand years of history. Every significant actor in British history has entered or exited through its arches. In the warren of rooms and passages behind its grand façades, anonymous and gloomy grinds and spins the machinery of state. Behind the windows – blank, reflecting other façades, and the faces of the passing spectators – as much treason is talked as government.

What shall I say to them?

I believe that I have a good mind, a loyal heart, and a true soul – oh God, make my soul pure, grant me but this mercy that my soul be pure – but I have no good tongue. My tongue is the traitor in this house, the Judas in this garden. My mind and heart and soul would sustain me, but I know that at the last I must turn to my tongue and that it will betray me.

Grant that the betrayal be quick, oh Lord, grant me some last dignity. Let the kiss have something not unsweet in it.

Today England is killing her King.

He waits for his entrance, in the newest and finest among this complex of buildings. In this banqueting house, the King's subjects would come to see him dine, watch him eating beasts that it was death for them to touch, birds that they had never heard of, all from platters worth more than their whole lives. This lavish chamber, now the King's waiting room, his purgatory, had been his own creation: a light soaring escape from the mediæval that clustered around it, a defiant statement of modernity, of privilege, of divine possibility. Fate is this: that a man is instrumental in his own death; may he not at least create the scene himself? Above him the ceiling panels show his father's ascent to heaven. Allegory is everything.

The window burns in the sun. Such light; so bright. . . I shall vomit. Let me not vomit, grant me some dignity, my stomach revolts at this life. Grant that the pain be little, oh God, grant that the pain be little. How much pain can there be in this world? What is the worst pain that I have felt? What is the worst pain that I could imagine? What will I feel? Will it be a burning? Will there be a great light or a great darkness? They say that even once the head is cut that still – oh God, I am about to – I must not – please grant me at this last some little piece of dignity. Even the vilest of my people have more dignity than I. My whole existence has been a humiliation. My life has been an embarrassment of excrements, of insufficiency, of indignity. Oh God, my body is vile, you know, oh God, that I loathe it and would escape it, but grant me that at this last instant I might not suffer worse. Oh God, am I to die surrounded by laughter? Must my eternity be a soaken sheet, and shall my devils be cackling children?

Today, where they watched him dine they will watch him die. His death will end their suffering, heal their wounds, and purge their sins. It is his last touch of divinity, and what is a King for if not to live the life of his whole people in public and splendour? In a moment or two, he will step out through one of the impressive windows onto a makeshift platform, to a block of wood, to a man, to an axe. There is some uncertainty about the identity of the man; the axe is real enough.

A voice. I must move. If I move forwards perhaps I will content them more; I must try to content them more. Honestly, gentlemen, I am a man who desires you no inconvenience.

I am to step through this window and die. Will there be no more demands beyond that? What a sweetness, that I may at last satisfy this insatiable demand of me, this constant strife of fifty years, that I must always conform. How much must I do to keep you happy? Always there is someone, some voice, some requirement to conform, some inconvenience, some intrusion of other men into my world. Was it so much to ask that I could be alone and at peace? Lord, will I be alone and at peace?

The window is one blaze of light. Is this death, oh God, am I coming nigh to you at last? Accept my soul, oh God, for it is a soul that desires nothing but your love and I have fought for nothing but this, and into this golden glow I offer myself, oh God, receive me I beseech you, take me from this world for I am blithe to come to you.

But still I see my foot upon the boards. A little foot, I was known for a dancer, in Madrid they clapped me once, still a buckle and a shoe and this corrupted world. I live yet!

I have not escaped. I am still in the nightmare. How vast is this place, how infinite this multitude? They are about to laugh, they must surely laugh at such a tiny man on this vast platform.

I am going into the light and I leave behind me this darkness, and with my last breath I curse you foul multitude that you may all for your many torments of me know nothing but darkness and blood for the eternity that is left to you for you have been nothing but cruel to me and I tried so hard.

It is very simple. I need not worry about going astray in front of these people. When I move my hands forward, the axe will fall.

My hands are small. Henry: you have a girl's hands. These delicate hands will kill me. God has forbidden self-slaughter, and I am forced to break his sacred law. Oh Christ, is this the final torment, that I must cause my own death? That cannot be fair, that surely is not fair, that a man may damn himself against his will. Am I never to be given a chance of purity, am I never to be granted peace? I was forced to betray my friends to the mob to win support, I was forced to raise armies to fight for peace; and now I must damn myself to escape this hell.

It is very simple, the sign to the headsman. I have lived a life of ritual and command. When I move my hands forward, the axe will fall.

All the people of England are here to watch me. I have asked them to believe in me, and now they have come to see for themselves that I am real. And now likewise they will see that I am dead. If these are still the people of England, then I am still the King of England. Is this my last privilege, the uniqueness of my humiliation, the public destruction of me? My father the King: let your countenance smell of courage, Charles. But my countenance has never but betrayed me, father. It is no countenance for a King, nor yet for any littler courage. Your Majesty, I have dreamed for all my life that once you would look at me with love and pride. Father, what would I not do for your love? Ask me anything. Ask me anything but to be brave in front of this multitude.

What? Why do you stare? What more must I do to satisfy you? Why this sudden silence from the mob? Oh God, I must speak, they will not be satisfied with me unless I speak. God, why will you not bring me into your light already? God, grant me your peace, for I am full done with this world and I neither yearn nor care for one crumb of it, my God, I am your faithful servant and I know that in your mercy you alone will grant me grace for my loyalty.

On the scaffold, at last, Charles Stuart did not stutter.

When I move my hands forward, the axe will fall. I must not get it wrong. My cloak— Who is— How dare— But of course they must take my cloak. And today I must wear this foolish cap, because I am a fool and I must look a fool, and I must satisfy them and so my hair must not impede the blade. Henrietta loved me for my hair. She was wont to stroke it. But that was not in this life, I fancy.

I have never appeared so bare in front of other men. But shoes and hose and breeches and a shirt. My journey down from majesty must be seen also in my dress. Two shirts – why? This morning, of course. Being dressed for the last time. The last. The last, the last. And which shirt will your Majesty wear? I shall wear – but what will happen to the other? It is mine! Christ's garments were torn by the soldiers. My shirt will immediately be stolen, even while I live. None shall have it. I shall wear both.

I must keep moving, or they will be angry. The hands, forward. Oh God, I am your faithful servant. The block. Oh God, I am your faithful servant. The block. Oh God, grant me dignity at this last. Oh God, grant me the littlest pain that my faults have deserved. The block. I kneel before you, my father, I am blithe to come to you. Receive me oh God for I am thrust out into the void and I trust nothing but your arms outstretched to receive me. Father, why will not you love me? Father, will you love me once merely? The block. My hands, my little hands, Henry, when I stretch forth my hands the axe – reaching for the block – that is not the movement! I am not stretching forth my hands to die – will I never be understood in my life? Oh God receive your frail and humble servant, for I am yours alone. The block. I reach for – I will not touch the block for it is too solid and I am melting away into the light at last, oh God grant me the light for all I have done was in the hope of your love. The block. I bow my head before you oh God, oh God my father will you bless me? The block looms in my eyes, this clumsy lump of the world, the cuts, the blood, oh God my neck will not touch the block because it is too solid and I am light alone, oh God unto your arms I offer my sinful heart, oh God my father will you receive me, oh God my father grant that once I may satisfy you, oh God my father love me I beg of you, I open my heart, I open my shoulders, my arms are reaching for you God, oh God my father will you receive me, shoulders, arms, elbows, hands are moving, I am reaching for you oh God my father the light.

1649

The World New-Made

The news of the execution of the King reached Astbury House on galloping hooves, drumming up the driveway and stuttering to a halt at the front door. It passed by hand from courier to servant and servant to master, who received it red-eyed and heavily wrapped against the February morning, while the courier trudged round to the back of the house to beg some breakfast, breath hoarse and boots creaking on the frosted earth.

Anthony Astbury received regular letters of news from London, and as usual his daughters heard the world from his lips, his eyes blinking tears at this final affront to the dignity of the society he knew.

Mary and Rachel stopped listening after the first sentences, and stared at each other. A King was the pinnacle of the structure of the world, the keystone of its proper order. If a King could be killed, then the world was now without margins. It knew no bound or restraint, and anything was become possible. Without margins, the world above them was chaos; without margins, their world was bottomless.

Rachel Astbury stared hard at the table, trying to believe in a spoon, a beaker and half a loaf of bread. Through the morning windows, the world was blank white.

⁓

A life: the Reverend Roger Kempe was born in Witham, in Essex, and baptized there in February 1604. Little is known of his time as an undergraduate at Emmanuel College in Cambridge in the mid-1620s, although concern is expressed in one record that he had 'fallen to the company of critical boisterous men, and to loose practices' – with the implication that this referred to religious more than social habits. By

1630 Kempe was a vicar in a comfortable living near Bedford, known among the local gentry as a good companion, of essentially conservative outlook. He gained a certain notoriety as the probable author of a series of sermons published in 1637, *The Lord's Realm is a Garden; or, The Right Husbandry of the Kingdom of Earth*, which seem to criticize on behalf of local interests the impositions of Charles I's autocratic government.

In 1640 he was advanced to the living of St Matthew's Church in Northampton – almost certainly thanks to the influence of the Bishop of Oxford, since the Bishop of Peterborough, in whose diocese Northampton sits, was suspicious of Kempe but at that time politically weak. Despite his previous apparent criticisms of the King's rule, what survives of Kempe's preaching and writing from the first half of the Civil War reflects moderate Royalism – whatever the King's faults, he did not think it lawful to fight him. But in 1647, and certainly by 1648, Kempe's attitude swung significantly against the King: in his infrequent sermons he focused increasingly on the proper obligations a ruler owed to God; after the defeat of Hamilton's invading Royalist force at Preston in August 1648 he preached on the plagues of Egypt and the divine destruction of the forces of Sennacherib before Jerusalem. He may have been influenced by Charles I's desperate manoeuvrings to save his throne, but it seems significant that at the same time Kempe was given the entirely nominal post of Chaplain to the County Committee of Northamptonshire – very much part of the new administration.

Finally, during the winter of 1648–9 and the King's trial, three sermons were published in pamphlet form anonymously, but with Kempe widely suspected of having been the author. *The Lord's Justice, Being a Description of the True Duties of the People of God* was an explicit denunciation of Charles Stuart's deceits and sins, and a theological justification of the judicial process against him.

On the evening of February 5th, 1649, Richard Kempe attended a small and convivial supper with several of the influential men of Northampton, returning home after his household had gone to bed. On the morning of February 6th, Kempe's servant found his master seated at his study table, his throat cut and a blooded knife on the floor beside him.

It looked, of course, like a suicide. But there was surely no cause. And there had been strangers in the town. Such are the times.

———

Sir Mortimer Shay disappeared into the Welsh hills with the old feeling of release. His road dropped discreetly into forgotten valleys, wound past a ruined castle, twisted and split, opened out into fields, was lost on grey rock slopes, and found again by a wood. At last, the morning sky fragile over the squat peaks, he came home to the rusty brick manor under the hillside.

It was morning, so she was in the garden. He saw her first through the bean frames, and then bent over a line of colewort shoots. Darkest blue working dress, and a shawl of the same. As she stood, her back to him, he remembered the turns and slopes of shoulders and hips, like the hills. Under the cap, silver in the darkness of her hair.

His boots crunched on the path's stones and she stopped still. The night-blue shoulders tensed. Then she turned, her eyes closed for a moment, and they opened again and she breathed out a sigh that seemed to have been held for a year. He moved closer, and stood over her.

She raised one hand, and pressed the palm against his old leathery chest, fingers splayed as if to measure or draw something out.

Then with both hands she held the sides of his chest, gripped the arms, the shoulders, the wrists. She reached up, and cupped her palms under his scaly jaw.

Shay stood placid throughout. Now he bent to her, and placed a kiss on her lips.

'Hallo Margaret,' he said. She nodded slightly, and took in another breath, feeling it fill every corner of her. Rightness. She put her hand in his great paw, and led him into the house.

At the parlour table, he watched the tricks and flickers of her face, the stubborn handsome bones of brow and chin, with the old wonder.

'How goes the world?' she asked.

'They killed the King.'

'We heard so, even here. Poor Stuart: truly a brave and decent man, but he twisted himself quite inside out trying to be his own monstrous father. Were you in the killing?'

'I had rather tried to avoid it.'

'Poor Mortimer. So tiresome for you when the world goes awry.' She settled her hand on his forearm. 'And now you are putting it to right again.'

'We'll muddle through. There is another King, and he will have his birthright soon enough. No one expected the killing, and few wanted it.' He checked her face: he felt safe in its incisive understanding of the world. 'These people in Parliament, and the Army, they have kicked a wasp's nest: in the counties, in Ireland, probably in Scotland too. And now they will argue among themselves.' He took another mouthful of bread. 'How goes it here?'

'Well enough. Your wars have left us poor equally, and there are still some extra mouths fled from Denbigh, and that's long ago now.' She watched him chewing. 'There was a distemper in the pigs in many of the farms last autumn. The younger mare died.' He grunted. 'I sold two strips over towards the gut.'

'By the hawthorns?'

'There. A good young man. Gareth knows the family.'

'Good.' He settled his hand over hers. 'I can't stay long, Meg.'

She squeezed his arm fiercely.

The
WESTMINSTER GAZETTE

being an accurate record of all eſſential tranſactions of the State

PRINTED BY AUTHORITY

THE new-made Council of State has completed the deſignation of the various ſubordinate Committees by which the proper buſineſs of the State ſhall be duly conſidered and decided.

The High Court of Justice continues its consideration of the case of the Royalist rebels James, Duke of *Hamilton*, who commanded at Preston, the Earl of *Holland*, the Earl of *Norwich*, Lord *Capel*, and Sir John *Owen*, all charged with treason.

Passed the 22. February, an Act in Parliament authorising the impressment of suitable able-bodied and idle men into the Navy, and ensuring the more equitable sharing of prizes, which has been in the past a source of much dissent.

General *Cromwell* is reported still before Pontefract, having that place in tight grip, and by reports sent from Doncaster he has communicated to Parliament his satisfaction with the progress of that business, which report Parliament has received and found welcome.

Lately made Captain in the Army – *Akers*, William; *More*, Nathaniel; *Thorogood*, Ralph.

Appointed Clerks to the Council of State – *Burroughs*, Thomas; *Iles*, Roger; *Noon*, Matthew; *Thurloe*, John.

~ ~

Four eyes were staring at Thurloe, as if considering their supper – and then finding it rancid.

'Oliver St John himself commends this man to us, Master Tarrant.' Thomas Scot, Parliament's chief of intelligence, a pair of rheumy eyes protruding from a pale wilderness of wrinkles. 'Commends, I say. We may interpret: commands.' A black cap, white hair thick from under it, and Thurloe saw that the head shook very slightly at the end of each sentence.

The second pair of eyes was close beside the first – unnaturally close, in the face of a younger man trying to derive authority from his chief.

Scot still: 'And these days, I think we may infer another voice behind Master St John, doing the commending – and the commanding. Isn't that so, Master Thurloe?'

Tarrant was dark and thin, perhaps nearing forty, in a new black coat. 'Oliver – Cromwell,' he said. He was trying to sneer, but wariness kept the voice too low for it to work.

'A man who serves Cromwell, serves England and serves God – isn't that so, Thurloe?'

Thurloe was still waiting for a question or statement he could reasonably answer. 'Is there somewhere I should sit?' he said politely. 'Anything I can start to work on?'

Scot stepped away, leaving Tarrant becalmed by the desk, gazed at a wall of bristling pigeon-holes, and turned back to face Thurloe. 'I continue to press the Council to formalize this work, but still we are mere hobbyists. The new Government of England is infested with enemies. The dispossessed Court in exile. Plotters and financiers and intelligencers in the Netherlands. Royalist allies and temporizers in Ireland and Scotland. Restive groups in every county, waiting for a sunny day and a rallying cry to storm the nearest town. Agitators, seditious printers, counterfeiters, rogue preachers, false prophets, indifferent magistrates, sentimental peasants. And faint-hearts in Parliament, and even' – his head pulled back and his eyes narrowed, watching Thurloe's reaction – 'some men at the top of the Army, who would stop the calendar or turn it back a page or two, men who fear the honest instincts to liberty of those who have done the fighting.'

'Yes,' Thurloe said. 'Perhaps I should get to work.'

'Not everyone knows how hard it is,' Tarrant said. He leaned forward and added, 'It's hard.'

'Thank you,' Thurloe said. 'I understand.'

'No concerns about Master Thurloe, Tarrant. Thurloe was at the University. A lawyer. Master St John commends Thurloe's shrewdness and intellect.'

Tarrant didn't seem impressed by Thurloe's shrewdness and intellect.

'A particular friend of Cromwell and St John may work as he pleases, and we shall not presume to command him.' The tension in the cheeks relaxed, and Scot seemed suddenly wearier. 'We shall be grateful for your co-operation, Master Thurloe. Time by time you may profit by working beside Tarrant here.'

Tarrant did not seem impressed by this either. He led the way out, and Thurloe followed. In the doorway he hesitated, and glanced back, just as Scot glanced up from his table. A large ledger was open in the exact centre of the table. The old man looked at Thurloe uncertainly, as though surprised to find him there, and then with a faint discomfort.

'I have my views, Master Thurloe, and I apprehend that General Cromwell finds them extreme and over-exacting for his politics. But I believe that we are achieving a cause in this land – a great cause, a millennium on earth – and I will esteem any man who contributes honestly to that cause.' The chin was held high, the lips pressed, as if defying anticipated criticism.

The sudden sincerity was striking, and Thurloe nodded slowly.

***

The 26th of February: Lieutenant-Colonel Lilburne stands among the members of the House of Commons, who look down on him variously indifferent and uneasy. A troublemaker, Lilburne. Argue with himself when he can't find another. Imprisoned, pilloried, flogged in the time of the King. Popular causes at the time, of course, and perhaps we got a little caught up in the romance of the man; but with hindsight maybe it was disputatiousness rather than principle.

A trim man, Lilburne; dapper even. Tidy curls and a sprightly moustache. Still young, surely; but suffering has greyed and cracked his face, and the shoulders are thin under the black coat. He makes a point of standing very upright, but it seems to pain him. Damp prison cellars and the lash have bent him before his time.

As he starts to speak, the indifferent become interested and the uneasy become angry. He talks softly, Lilburne, through his fever-weakened throat, and that always makes them lean forwards. He has his hat in one hand and a paper in the other, and the hat seems to flutter, as if some unexpected breeze in the chamber will blow him over. The words are hoarse but painstakingly articulated.

Lilburne talks of liberties, of freedoms, and of truth. Lilburne talks of the new slavery in which England finds herself. Alarm and a broiling murmur around the chamber. He refers to the paper in his hand, and as he does so, and again, every man in the chamber focuses ever more closely on the paper, as if it is growing in front of them, or about to take wing, or burst into flames.

The sun shone unseasonably warm as Shay rode into Doncaster, and it heartened the day. In its light, the skeletal trees seemed to huddle more ashamed of their nakedness.

At the gate to the city, two crossed pikes barring his way, Shay yawned and shifted his weight in the saddle, aware of the clearest paths of escape to left and right and continuing to watch the face of the sentry who scrutinized him. The man's skin was terrible, a battleground of pockmarks and spots.

The sentry glanced up at Shay's face again, and winced fractionally – not a man who enjoyed being looked at – then he waved his hand indifferently at the pikes. It was enough to move them, and Shay trotted forward into the city.

But then getting in might be easier than getting out, of course. It was a risk coming here: a fortified place, and a military headquarters. It all seemed relaxed enough, but there were people dying in the fight for besieged Pontefract not that many miles up the road, and that sharpened the atmosphere.

Pontefract was the last outpost of Royalist defiance in the country, and here in Doncaster was supposed to be the man who was his one channel of contact through to the garrison. *I have to see the ground.*

Sleepy streets. An innkeeper trying with a wavering pole to re-hang the carved effigy of a bear over his door. The site of the old St Nicholas hospital. A church. Shay kept his horse at a trudge as he came alongside the vicarage. A modest house, though it seemed well-kept. It also seemed to be closed up: the shutters were closed, at least, and there was no hint of light or life.

'You wanting the vicar?' A voice, from behind him. 'Reverend Beaumont?' He turned without apparent concern.

Not a sentry. A shopkeeper? Not smart enough. A jobbing craftsman?

Careful. 'I want a vicar. Don't know his name, and don't care.'

'Reverend Beaumont,' the man said, as if confirming that Beaumont was the Reverend that all right-thinking people should want. 'You'll not find him.'

'Oh? Where—' Shay had the uneasy sense of a joke that he wasn't getting.

'He's up at Pontefract Castle. Swinging in the wind, he is!' And the man opened his mouth in a delighted grin, as if his handful of rotten teeth were the real surprise. 'They hanged him for he was slipping secrets to the Royalists inside.'

I need to be far from this conversation and this place, and fast. 'Oh, indeed?' Shay seemed to consider the fact, as if pondering a decision by the late Reverend Beaumont to be hanged. Then he shrugged. 'Should have minded his own business, I guess.' And he nudged the horse into a walk, feeling the lively eyes following him as he went.

From half a mile off, lost among the trunks of a clump of trees, Shay watched the jagged yellow peaks of besieged Pontefract. The fortifications rose spindly and uneven from the countryside, the lower walls running around and down the slope and away, in odd extensions born of fashions and contingencies in the history of defensive war.

Nearer, Shay could see scattered flags and tents, detachments of s oldiers on chilly sentry duty, the occasional cluster of riders moving across the scene. The Parliamentary Army had wrapped Pontefract tight enough. There would be ways in and out – there were always ways, to be found in knowledge more local or more ancient than one's own – but without being more certain he would not try to re-establish contact.

The letter – the last letter out of Pontefract to George Astbury, the letter that had been in his pocket at his death – was still in Shay's own pocket. With the besieged town in front of him, he pulled it out again, unfolded it, reread the simple message.

> *Sir, as you will well know, Cromwell was last week before the town*
> *and did much plundr. He did not trouble us here in the castle. But*
> *the damage done neareby will further upset the local people. And the*
> *effect on supplies for winter may only be guesst. Cromwell departed*
> *the 11th. Our younger bloods do still enjoy their raiding sorties into the*

countryside for cattle and men to ransom. The garrison is better
settld now since the agreeing of the Governing Council's articles of war.
T. M.

[SS C/S/48/1]

An unremarkable message, and so it would seem if intercepted; nothing in here of use to the Parliamentarian besiegers. There might be a hidden message in it, but not one that Shay could see using the usual codes and cyphers.

What was in here for Astbury? A short note, a smudged and worn paper. *What is in here for me?*

The largest Royalist garrison yet defying Cromwell's Army was cut off and alone. If they still sent out secret messages, those messages were not getting through. It was too dangerous to risk trying to pick up the thread: there was no knowing what the Reverend Beaumont had revealed before he died, no way of knowing what Parliament's intelligencing men might now be able to read. Pontefract was deaf to him, and dumb.

Sir,

I regret to report that on the 9th March James, Duke of Hamilton was martyred under the executioner's axe at Westminster, beside Lord Holland, and Lord Capel who defied for so long in Colchester.

The Duke faced his enemies with the same courage and dignity he had always shown — in defeat at Preston, in the flight thereafter, and in his confinement since — and his Creator with right grace and eagerness. Thus, he has followed his Royal master to the uttermost, and the similarities of their passing and their composure are the fittest compliment to his Grace that I can pay. I am relieved to report that his body rests in holy ground, and his soul no doubt in that better Kingdom.

At the last, I was able by privy means to secure the enclosed. Though his Grace could not escape this murderous clique, his name and his line will I trust endure and outlast them far. I beg you to give the enclosed to the new Duke, and with it a worthy report of the nobility with which his

brother fought for our cause, and carried his honour untarnished to the death and beyond.
God save the King.
P. V.

[SS C/H/49/107]

＊ ＊

The Hague: a plain reception room, cold walls and hard tiles and William Hamilton crouched over an excited terrier, stroking it roughly behind the ears. He looked up expectantly as the door opened, and then in surprise.

He stood, and waited for explanation.

'Your Grace, I bring you the gravest news. I—'

'What? I am no Gr—' Then the face opened in sore outrage. 'Oh, they havno'. No, they havno'.'

'Your Grace—'

'No. Ah, the foul, the foul cheating filthy – They havno'.' The head writhed and rolled on the shoulders, as if the pain of the death itself had passed with the title. 'My James – James, oh, you poor – No.' The face back to the silent visitor, breaths coming uneven and harsh. A cry, a choke of distaste and revulsion, and the shoulders swung ready to push out of the cold cell of a room, and then stopped.

The visitor's arm was stretched out steady, offering something in a precisely poised thumb and finger. Instinctively, Hamilton reached towards it. Then, strangely, his visitor had taken his hand and gripped one of the fingers, and now pushed a ring onto it.

William, Second Duke of Hamilton. 'God save your Grace.'

＊ ＊

Spring was tickling the extremities of the apple trees at Astbury House, and Rachel Astbury was walking among them trying to conjure dreams of romance or at least hope, when one of the maids came hurrying through the long grass with skirts held to knee.

Rachel saw her approach, and looked deliberately away again, trying to recapture the tree-scented suggestion of freshness in the air for one last moment. Then she turned to face the maid.

'Please miss, there's a man called here.'

'A stranger?'

'I don't know him miss, certain. He says—'

'You told him my father was away?'

'Course, miss. He asked for the mistress. Is that you miss, Miss Mary being away?'

A moment of hesitation. *Can I disappear from this world?* A moment of fear. *I cannot face any more shadows from the trees.*

Then pride. 'Yes. Yes, of course it's me. I'll come at once.' *Is any man on earth safe to me now?* 'Joanna!' Joanna turned back. 'Make sure John is there with me.'

After the fresh glow of the garden the house was immediately gloomy and obscure. Between kitchen and hallway she found the outline of John waiting for her. The steward's fading coat was reassuringly familiar. *But thin. We are frail vulnerable people here.*

He led the way into the hall.

The shoulders that she found when John stepped aside were not frail. In the pale grey light of the hall, the back of the visitor seemed larger and darker than everything around it. As he turned to the footsteps, the effect was not diminished: a strong chest, dark hard-wearing clothes – *there is no spring in this man* – and a heavy-featured face.

The face saw her, seemed to smile on an instinct, and gave a little bow. The eyes didn't drop with the head, but kept watching her.

'Miss. . . Rachel, I think.'

A hard hulk of darkness in the hallway, and she knew him with a little gasp.

'You're the – the man in the storm.'

He frowned, and seemed to consider this. Then he chuckled deeply; it was like water coughing in a pipe. 'Yes,' he said. 'I think I am that. But some people call me Mortimer Shay.'

'Yes. Yes, of course. Sir Mortimer.' She bobbed the suggestion of a curtsey. She didn't take her eyes off him, either. 'You're. . . welcome here, sir.'

He ran a heavy hand through thick grey hair. 'I suspect that I am not, Rachel. Your father does not, I think, cherish my presence here. A prudent man, your father.'

Some instinct of irritation at the condescensions of the older, of men. 'He is not at home. I shall decide whom I welcome.' She affected a moment's consideration. 'You are welcome here, until my father should decide otherwise.'

A smile spread broad over his face, and there was new interest in his eyes.

He wasn't just looking at her, but examining her too. Periodically his eyes would sweep slowly down her, over the exposed bust with her breasts pushing above the bodice, over her stomach, down to where her thighs moved against her dress and then her hem brushing the floor, and back up again. She took in a quick, uneasy breath, held her head higher.

Withal, he is a stranger, and I have let him into the house with me.

The consciousness of her vulnerability, and of his scrutiny of her body, made her more sharply aware of being a woman.

I do not know this man. I do not know what he does or what he is capable of. I do not know why they fear him.

— ~ —

The Parliamentary Army deployed around Pontefract were edgy, excited. Something was happening. Word was trotting among the ranks and tents and sentry-points: the Royalist garrison inside were close to surrender; had finally agreed to surrender; had surrendered already?

Thurloe was wary in crowds: crowds were unpredictable, irrational, inhuman. He stood among the scattered expectant soldiers, watching the castle walls two hundred yards off, and wondering what he was supposed to be seeing.

Not for the first time since they'd been standing there, Tarrant, a yard or two to his side, stabbed a sidelong glance at him. Thurloe's presence was unplanned. Word had come to Thomas Scot three days before that surrender was likely, and Tarrant had hurried north. Thurloe had ridden with him as far as Nottingham because he had a defaulting Royalist to investigate, but that case was delayed and so he'd invited himself to continue to Pontefract.

'You seen much fighting, Thurloe?'

Thurloe ignored him. He'd found it an increasingly satisfactory tactic with Tarrant. It unsettled him, too, which was amusing to watch.

There was a shout from nearer the walls, indistinct. Immediately the men around them shuffled, and murmured, and Thurloe and Tarrant strained to see what was happening. Gradually, the excitement subsided again.

'What are you fighting for, Thurloe?'

This got his attention, and he turned and held Tarrant's glance.

'I'm not fighting for anything. This land needs stable and good government if it is to thrive. There are some decent, able men capable of providing it. This fighting is a necessary phase we have to pass to get to that.'

'Would you have killed the King?' Tarrant presented it as a test.

'No.' There was a little sneer of triumph on Tarrant's face. 'But I don't care that he's dead. Why, what are you fighting for?'

'I'm fighting so men like me, without money and without university time, can make a life in this country. I'm fighting to be done with all the special groups of men who set themselves above – Kings, and priests and such. I'm fighting for the honest ordinary man against all the clever-clever men who just want to limit liberty and run the world for themselves.'

Thurloe considered this. 'There are more stupid men than clever ones,' he said after a moment. 'I think you're in with a chance. But yours sounds rather like the Leveller manifesto.'

Tarrant's eyes narrowed, and a smile started to creep onto his face. And then a hand landed on his shoulder, and he turned. A shorter, darkly handsome man. Greetings, and Thurloe was introduced to Lyle. Lyle was an associate who'd been based in Doncaster during the siege – Thurloe assumed this meant that he was Thomas Scot's channel of information in and out – and Lyle had facts.

Tarrant and Lyle exchanged a few sentences of murmurs, glancing at Thurloe, who affected to ignore them.

'Gate's open,' Tarrant said, holding his excitement back. 'Surrender ceremony in one hour. The Army's starting to take control inside, and the

Royalist middle ranks will be trying to get away. We're going to slip into the castle and see what we can find.'

He turned to go, and Thurloe stepped forward.

'You coming?'

'I'm coming.'

'You could get unlucky, University. You could get hurt.'

'Or I could get lucky, and you could get hurt.'

Tarrant scowled, and turned again and started to walk.

I could get unlucky. I could get hurt.

Thurloe followed, stride for stride.

Tarrant does not want me to follow him. I mistrust Tarrant. Ergo, I must follow him.

Outside the main gate of the castle, soldiers were beginning to drift together for the formal parade to mark the surrender. The open ground – a plain of mud after the winter and the constant traffic of the besiegers – was a scrum of drifting men, some in uniform and some not, and there were women among them. Small groups of soldiers were stopping and questioning individuals, apparently at random, though it seemed that a lie or a pretty face would get past them. As they neared the castle gate itself, the three of them had constantly to push past shoulders and skirt uniforms disinclined to move aside.

'Chaos,' Lyle said under his breath.

'There's supposed to be an outer cordon,' Tarrant said.

'Half the garrison could have escaped before they've even properly surrendered.'

At the castle gate, a platoon of pikemen was tramping over a wooden drawbridge that shuddered under their rhythm. Lyle, Tarrant and Thurloe kept pace with them and so passed through the wall, the yellow stone gouged and discoloured after the months of siege.

The platoon tramped on through the mud and turned a corner, leaving the three men in relative isolation just inside the new-conquered land. Sentries behind them at the gate; around them, among the houses and makeshift shelters that filled the castle precincts, half-seen in shadows and alley entrances, a handful of hollow-cheeked defenders, unarmed and suspicious. And suddenly Thurloe felt the strangeness of it all: *these gaunt dirty faces are my enemies, and my countrymen; we have fought to defeat them, and now we must find a way to reconcile them; the battle is over, but this still feels like hostile, foreign ground.*

'Get separated,' Lyle said, 'and there's still men who'll cut your throat. If you're coming' – this to Thurloe – 'you'd better have this.' And he pushed a knife into Thurloe's hand.

Thurloe took it instinctively, looked around more anxiously at the street, and then down at the knife.

I don't know what to do with this. I don't even know where I'm supposed to put it.

The hollow faces watched him, impassive. The three men began to squelch down the main track. From someone, Lyle had learned where the commandery was, and Tarrant and Thurloe followed a pace behind him.

Am I a conqueror? Thurloe wondered. *I didn't even know I was at war.*

Still the faces, still the hungry protruding eyes. This place had been Royalist, and then Parliamentarian, and nine months Royalist again, and now it was for Parliament once more. In every alleyway there was furtive movement. Commanders would have to risk the judgement of those who had defeated them. Soldiers could be imprisoned or transported. But the civilians who had survived in battered Pontefract would be wondering how to accommodate themselves again. Men might have to contribute to a fine; men might just drift away in the bustle and new ease of the besiegers. It was an unfastened place for now, this swamp of mud and wreckage, of lives and loyalties in transition. Thurloe glanced warily into the alleys and doorways.

The commandery was a ramshackle improvised hive, an old tower of the castle, built in the same distinctive stone, with newer generations of building added on in different stone and wood and plaster and even sheeting. The months of destruction had further disordered it, and the exterior was a madness of irregularity, like a building put together wrongly or inside-out.

Lyle led the way in, and up a short flight of stairs. Perhaps he knew the place of old; perhaps he was very confident; perhaps his information was good.

At the top of the stairs, an open chamber, and the three of them kicked around it for a minute. Scattered debris of a besieged life – mugs and helmets and chairs half-smashed for wood. A greasy pewter plate in one corner, with the skeleton of a small animal picked clean on it. A fire had burned recently in the grate, but the residue was ash only.

Lyle led them up another flight of half a dozen steps, a side passage leading off halfway up. As he passed it, Thurloe on a stubborn whim decided he'd had enough of seeing what the other two had already seen, and turned off into the passage.

The two other pairs of feet stamped up the steps away from him, and then onto a wooden floor somewhere.

Thurloe was in a short corridor, flagstone floor, a stone wall on one side, plaster wall on the other; three doors, two open. He peered through them, one after the other. Gloom, disorder, filth, stench. Humans as animals; there was no residue of humans as thinking, superior beings here, traitorous or otherwise.

He pushed open the third door. A man – perhaps his own age – bright red hair and a corresponding pale face – was squatting on the floorboards in front of a fire. He had a small barrel between his legs for some reason, and a lighted taper in one hand, and a tied sheaf of papers in the other.

The man's eyes and mouth widened in instinctive surprise, but then out of the madness of this dislocated world he contrived a wide, warm grin.

'Such a cold day,' he said pleasantly, and set fire to the sheaf of pages and laid it squarely in the glowing grate.

Out of the strangeness, Thurloe heard himself say, 'What was it?'

Still the man only smiled.

The foot of the sheaf was fully aflame now, and the whole was starting to curl. 'Why would you. . .?'

Still the steady smile, and Thurloe overcame the strangeness and stepped forward with determination. 'I want that paper!' Perhaps half of the thin sheaf was pricked with flames.

'Indeed?' Still the strange, sprightly calm on the pale face. 'How much do you want it?' And the red-headed man lowered the taper to the barrel between his legs, and lit a fuse.

For one insane moment he continued to squat there, grinning at Thurloe while death sparked beneath him. Then as the sputtering flame reached the top of the barrel Thurloe flung himself backwards into the doorway and as he lurched away he saw the other leaping in the opposite direction towards a window and then the world broke open in thunder.

A staggered second later, Thurloe was pulling himself up off the staircase, head ringing and back aching, and the world was a dumb-show. He stumbled to the doorway, and held himself drunkenly between its posts.

The room had ceased to exist. Half the floor was void, the rest scorched timber. The walls were black and pockmarked. The air was smoke and dust and fireflies of burning paper and splinter.

Thurloe lurched around the edge of the room, pressing against the warm walls and feeling the floorboards sagging under him, until he reached the window and stuck his head out. First he felt the precious gust of clear air, then he saw half a dozen people staring up at him, no more than mildly concerned by this new eruption in a whole world in flames. The red-headed man was gone.

—— ~ ~ ——

Shay stopped Rachel as she was crossing the hall. He was a few paces up the wooden staircase, and she looked up expectantly. A shaft of the morning sun pierced the windows over the porch and, in the gloom of the hall and its dark wood, picked out white a shock of his hair, an eye, a cheek and his teeth, and they seemed wild.

'Rachel, I was wondering if there was a private place I could use when I am here. To read. Letters and accounts from my own estate. You understand. Did poor old George perhaps have somewhere of his own here?'

Rachel was distracted for a moment by the tension between her recollection of poor old George as her gentle prudent uncle and his violent death in battle.

Above her, Shay waited, and she was aware again of his bulk. She never seemed to see his whole body clearly – it was always suggested, by shadows, much more of it unseen and looming near her.

'It wouldn't, I think, be wise for me to intrude on your father's domain.'

Flickers of smiles on two mouths, a shared understanding, immediately erased by propriety and – for Rachel – a faint guilt.

'Of course. There's a room very near to George's – your – bedroom. John will show you.'

The room found, and a key with it, Shay stood alone inside its closed door and tried to recreate George Astbury and his habits.

Even George wouldn't have been foolish enough to keep papers in his bedroom, with servants in and out twice in a day at least. And Shay fancied he'd not instinctively have mixed the over-human realities of his bedroom – smelly sheets and a full piss-pot – with his business affairs. He had checked the bedroom regardless.

But this room might do better. There was less of comfort in it than he associated with the old man. Perhaps that had helped him focus – a kind of austerity. George Astbury in his monk's cell, at his devotional intelligencing work. A small room, white plaster and dark wood. A corner room: two windows on the two outer walls, one of them over a window seat. A plain oak table; a chair with brown upholstered seat, and a solid footstool likewise leather-topped. A fireplace, swept; a plain mantelpiece above it at chest height, with one anomalous brass candlestick at one end.

George doing his duty. George sitting himself upright in that stern chair, papers on the desk. George would have been embarrassed to be caught with anything – flashes of their occasional interactions as boys, *fifty years is it now?* – so if he worked here he'd have wanted his papers here.

Nothing with desk or chair.

The floorboards well nailed-down. The chair leather unscuffed by boots – until Shay stood on it – and the ceiling unyielding. The fireplace stone-backed, *and instinctively George would fear someone somehow coming in and deciding to light a fire*. He checked the chimney anyway – and found it bricked up, solid. The window seat hollow, but its front firm and its top held in place by the panelling under the window.

Shay's mind tried to be George Astbury, while his knuckles rattled obsessively at panels and boards.

One of the slats of the side panelling a little loose, just over one end of the window seat. He picked at the crack, drummed his knuckles on the slat, worked at it with his hand.

The slat slid smoothly towards him and out. There was a small void behind it, rough brick and dust.

Enough for a few papers, but no more, and there would be no way to hold them in place. Shay went to slide the slat back.

And wondered again about the window seat. With the panelling slat removed, the broad plank would move along a fraction, and up. In a second, Shay had lifted it away to reveal a very satisfactory space beneath, at least a foot deep and about as wide and perhaps two feet long. He peered at the dust of the boards inside the space, wondered at the faintest square outlines in it. Boxes? Papers?

Withal, it was empty now. *Where is the book?* The few copies of the Directory were either still held by trusted men, or would have been burned if endangered. But the book was different: known to the fewest. *Where is it?*

Shay replaced the seat and the panelling slat, and left, locking the room behind him. The hollow under the window would need to stay empty, too; he would find his own hiding place.

'Did you find any skeletons?'

She was a light invisible voice in the window's blaze, as Shay came down into the hall with eyes slow to adjust.

He waited until he reached the floor, refusing to be thrown by the first thrust and waiting to pick his ground.

Now she was a shadow against the window and, as he stepped forward into the hall, a figure of dimensions and colours, and finally a face.

'My thanks for the use of the room, Rachel. All I need.'

It was a lovely face, sure enough, and it was watching him with self-amusement and precocious challenge. But a flicker of uncertainty crossed the eyes, as the conversation failed to go her way. 'Did you. . . find what you were looking for?' The fine chin was still up, provoking.

He waited until he'd shifted his ground, making it obvious that he was considering her face. 'All that I need, thank you.' He leaned forward. 'One shouldn't look for too much.'

He thought he'd made her complicit in his staying. She seemed to think she had gained a little ascendancy over him.

Rachel Astbury was altogether too pert.

MERCURIUS FIDELIS

or

The honeſt truth written for every Engliſhman
that cares to read it

From MONDAY, MARCH 19. *to* MONDAY, MARCH 26. 1649.

MONDA,Y, MARCH 19.

THE ſilly PARLIAMENT, which the day before had with great ceremony and pomp paſſed an ACT aboliſhing the MONARCHY, as tho' a herd of cows might paſs a decree againſt thunder-ſtorms, or the TURKS decide the price of fiſh in BILLINGSGATE, this day proceeded to paſs an act aboliſhing the HOUSE OF LORDS. Having thus aboliſhed a part of itſelf, like a man who do ſaw his own leg off for cauſing him to trip, we may hope that the PARLIAMENT now ſuſtain this work and ſwallow itſelf whole.

WEDNESDAY, MARCH 21.

Even as the PARLIAMENT did HIS MAJESTY's work by removing more traitors, ſo too did the ARMY continue its war with its own ſelf. On March 21. it expelled from its ranks OVERTON, thought the author of the recent tract againſt CROMWELL THE FOX, and ſome of his friends, for their radical diſſenſion. Like this the ARMY will peacefully aboliſh itself quite, and we ſhould be thankful for it. Doubtleſs theſe LEVELLERS are mere malcontents and ſimpletons, for the chaotic deſtructiveneſs of their NOTIONS may be ſeen by a CHILD, but they have ſeen the lies and vanities of the preſent leaders of PARLIAMENT and ARMY right enough. CROMWELL's anger at their frowardneſs is underſtandable, for they do ſhow him plain as the TYRANT he is.

THURSDAY, MARCH 22.

At DORKING on Thursday was put to the stocks one TAPPE, for preaching out-of-doors very mischievously, crying that all PRIESTS and PARLIAMENT-MEN and KINGS and GENERALS are but ants in the dung-hill, and that the DEVIL was at work in all rulers, and that he had seen JESUS standing by the town well promising vengeance on all sinners, and naming many other PORTENTS and SYMBOLS besides that betold the coming judgement.

SATURDAY, MARCH 24.

Until Saturday the brave men of PONTEFRACT castle maintained their struggle, but on this day their strength left them at last. So ends the defiance of a great fortress of LOYALTY and HONOUR against injustice and tyranny. Eventually the pitiful cries of the women and the most extreme privations that ever men endured forced the stout hearts to open the gates and seek for HONOURABLE TERMS. Like lions and true GENTLEMEN they resisted the tricks and tortures and salvoes and sallies of the HORDE, and many survive to continue the fight. Indeed, more survive than even their foes did know, for the ARMY refused MERCY for six of the defenders of the castle, but could not lay hands on them. Very like General LAMBERT and the Army thought to further weaken the spirits of HIS MAJESTY's loyal followers, their victims, by more executions and ATROCITIES, but not for the first time their policy miscarried. Even as the siege was ending, those BRAVE MEN that the Army hunted hid themselves in a SECRET place within the walls, waiting until the soldiers were distracted with drink and licentiousness, and achieving their FREEDOM. So then did the bravest of HIS MAJESTY's followers escape the snare, and so will TRUE SOULS prevail.

[SS C/T/49/2 (EXTRACT)]

Downstairs again, in Anthony Astbury's study and running his fingers along the spines of the books – more to stir thoughts than out of any insane expectation that the book he sought would be among them – Shay caught a glance of a face and turned, unsettled.

His sister. Now a portrait in an alcove. Politely reverenced; stored.

Ah, my Isabelle. Perhaps I'm glad you did not live to see what has become of your world.

He turned, and Rachel was standing watching him. Her presence was a jolt, and so was the bold echo of those brown eyes.

'You have the look of my mother,' she said. 'The cheeks; around the mouth.'

He tried to ignore it, began to move. 'She was only half my sister.'

'Even so.'

Shay turned fully to face her. 'Yes,' he said. 'It was often said. A far happier lot for me than for her.' He forced a smile, and turned away.

'Blood is the strongest bond.' Rachel said it too loud, and he stopped. He turned to find her surprisingly close, forcing her presence at him. 'Don't you find it so?'

He looked at her seriously. 'Sincerely, no. Not enough to be depended on. These last years have taught us that.'

'Sir George found it so.'

She was speaking with a child's petulant insistence, and a child's fragile boldness of stance, and he felt anger coming fast. 'Then he was a fool.'

'That's disrespectful!' There was genuine affront in her tone. 'He trusted me.'

Shay let a long slow hiss out through his teeth, not looking at her, and turned again and walked away.

'He burned his papers.'

The heavy shoulders stopped still, two black boulders in the gloom. Rose with a breath; dropped.

'His last visit here. Just before he went off to die in the battle at Preston. He carried the papers out and burned them. Jacob helped him. I saw, and he didn't mind. I may be a wo—'

Sir Mortimer Shay turned to face her again, and she recoiled at something in his eyes: a ferocity, a wildness, a capacity for – for anything.

He took a step closer. She started to speak, and stopped. Another step closer. Then his hand reached up in front of her breasts, and the finger and thumb clamped firmly under the fragile line of her jaw. His eyes flicked left and right, and she knew he was listening. She also knew that none of the servants would be nearby at this time. The first alarm overcome, her mouth nonetheless opened instinctively, but the heavy forefinger of his left hand rose slowly to his lips, and still his eyes bored into her.

He began to move forward, and his finger and thumb pushed against her throat, and she retreated, one clumsy step, another, and immediately she knocked against a timber with head and shoulders and rump, and gave a little gasp.

Still his hand was under her jaw, where the fine bone gave way to flesh: not hard, not choking, but with a soft certainty that held her trapped, her feet not quite flat on the ground.

'The girl is bursting out to be a woman, isn't she?' he said, a hard murmur. 'And the woman is bursting out to be free.' He shook his head. 'Believe me, if once you taste the world you dream of, you will wish yourself back in the cradle.'

The brown eyes – *beautiful; a doe, a falcon* – were wide: alarm; anger.

'Somewhere between the nursery and a dream of marriage you found that adulthood was a secretive place, and you found George Astbury more secretive than most. Now here is Shay, whom the world mistrusts, and he is more secretive than any. And you want to be let in, don't you?' He turned her chin a fraction. 'Lord, you probably want to decorate.'

He released her. But before his hand dropped away he lifted a finger and, apparently absorbed, ran it down one side of her satin jaw.

'One day, very possibly, I will need to trust you. One day, perhaps, I will come to you desperate for some help or protection that you alone may give me. And you should fear that moment as it were a snake.' He leaned closer. 'Trust kills.'

He left.

Rachel Astbury stared after him, venomous.

Shay had been on the track of his man for thirty-six hours. Fugitives from Pontefract could be traced easily enough, if one knew the right people to ask and the right kind of persuasion. This one was harder than some: a room paid for but not used; a false trail laid through a wood; the doubling back towards the fallen town. On foot now: disappearing, not fleeing. A man who cared that he might be followed, and knew how to avoid it. Nevertheless, Shay had the scent fully now, and had followed it to a stable on the edge of Wakefield.

He'd watched the stable for half an hour, and watched for movements near it. Only one heavy-timbered door, and he'd been ten minutes in checking through the gaps in the planks and feeling at the latch, and easing through. Eyes closed for the last seconds before entering so that his vision came quickly in the gloom, and he'd been fast into the shadow of a beam. Then more minutes working along the stalls, feet slow and ungainly up and gingerly down into the straw, past four silent, shifting horses. A sudden whinny from the first, now behind him, and he stopped; head still, eyes shifted back the way he'd come.

The beast caught his glance, and shook its head dismissively. He waited until he could hear the others' breaths again – waited until he inhabited the silence, knew its rhythms and corners. And so to the last stall, and the distinctive huddle of a body under a blanket against the wall.

A glance all around him, and forward. The blanket covered the body from boot to head. Nearby, the proper inhabitant of the stall stood watching him; a shiver of the sleek head, a subdued whiffle, and hooves shifted in the straw. Shay could see the crushed area of straw where the horse had slept, alongside the body.

That's wrong.

He spun, knife up in his left hand, but his wrist was caught in a fierce grip and he was back against a beam with a blade at his throat.

Dark flat eyes in a worn face. Killing eyes. 'You'd not planned on a knife through your neck, I think.'

Shay's eyes narrowed. 'Nor you a bullet through your belly.' And there was a click, heavy and loud between them.

The man pushed the knife forward a fraction so that it broke the mottled skin of Shay's neck, and allowed his eyes to drop for an instant before they flicked up again. It had been enough to see the pistol.

A flicker of life came into the eyes. 'Predicament.'

Shay smiled. 'Comfortable balance.'

'You're well-dressed for a horse-thief.'

'And you for a groom.' The man's clothes, as much as Shay could glimpse through eyes kept still by the knife at his throat, were of quality but not ostentatious. A soldier as well as a gentleman.

The man said, 'And now?'

'You're a fugitive from Pontefract, and no ordinary soldier. I have tracked you, but alone. I fancy we might spare each other the time for a word.' He breathed in carefully, and then there was another distinct click from the pistol.

The knife held at his throat a moment more, and then flicked away. The body seemed to relax, and the knife disappeared. A nod into the stall. 'Something told you the trick. At the last.'

'Mm. Horse wouldn't sleep so close to a stranger.' A small scowl of real irritation on the face. Shay continued to examine it. 'Man makes a mistake sometimes.'

'Some men can't afford to make more than one.'

Shay nodded. 'False trails. Traps. A man who lives a permanent ambush.'

'If you don't keep pace with life, you lose it.' He was examining Shay as intently. 'You seem to know the habit, sir.' The eyes widened. 'Wait: a man who tracks fugitives of the King, but not for ill; a man who knows every trick of the skirmish. Great gods. . . are you Shay?'

Shay's eyes went cold. 'Not a name it's safe to know, sir.'

A faint shake of the head. 'Nor, I imagine, to bear.' A quick decision. 'I am Teach.'

A slow nod from Shay. 'Yes. I thought you might be.'

———

Shay and Teach found an inn on the road between Wakefield and Leeds, tended by a squint-eyed girl and her shambling, purple-nosed father, who roamed from room to room exchanging silent accusations. Shay and Teach had a room, and a fire, to themselves.

Shay pulled three packaged papers from a pocket, and undid the first. 'How was Pontefract?'

'You know a siege, I think?' A grunt from Shay. 'So you know the conditions. The only question, ever, is whether the spirit and the water last long enough for relief to come.'

'And this time there was no relief.'

'We noticed.' He said it without humour. 'In the siege, in the end, men forget what they're fighting for.' He shook his head in distaste. 'Mere survival. Futility; and the women and children crying.'

'The command?'

'Well enough. Morrice; John. Colonel. I'd heard reports of weakness and vice, but I saw none of that, and he was tested enough. Some put him out as a deceiver, for he was Parliament's man before. He was bitter at them, right enough, and that made him determined. He captured the castle himself last year, and it was by patient planning and daring. As a commander: disciplined; respected.'

Shay's face was in the paper. 'What communications had you with friends outside?'

Teach turned to face him, careful. 'Some.'

Shay looked up, and then down again. 'Reverend Beaumont is dead; hanged.'

'And none shall follow him by my loose tongue.' He watched Shay a moment longer, and then smiled at his own caution. 'Very well. There was a way: a courier who knew a way out through the ditches and the slums, and would deliver messages to a church.'

'Who knew of this?'

'Two or three of us.'

Shay left the names, for now. He pushed the first paper into his pocket again, opened the second, and after a moment threw it into the fire, watching it flare and vanish. 'Did you ever know George Astbury?'

'What do you know of him?'

'He's another dead man, Teach – another man who can no longer be betrayed.' The head came forward. 'But a man whose work others must continue.'

Teach absorbed this, and nodded. 'He sent me into Pontefract. Probably flattering, but by the time we were living on dogs and cats I was cursing him.' A smile. 'Horses, dogs, cats, rats, and worms we kill. . .'

'. . . but the worms will revenge and have their fill.' A child's joke that defined men, and their smiles were forced. Shay went on: 'And Astbury encouraged you to write to him, perhaps.'

'He did. I had done so for him before, when I was in attendance on the King.'

Shay nodded, glanced at him, and looked into the fire again.

Teach had seen the glance clear enough. 'And you will have suggestions for me now, perhaps.'

'I could make a speech about duty and loyalty and honour, if it would help.' He was opening the third packet.

'Save it. I believe in none of them, not any more. But while I live I'll live as well as I can.'

Shay nodded again. 'Ireland. I fancy—' He stopped, gazing down at the open paper on his hand; 'I fancy the war will shift there.'

Teach's face soured, grim. 'By God, it doesn't get any easier, does it?'

'No.'

'I need to eat, Shay. I have no family, no estate. But I hope to. Eventually. When this madness is done.'

'I understand. You'll not be forgotten.'

'In Ireland? Whole armies have been forgotten there. When?'

'A month or two yet. But you could do me at least one service in the meantime.' He opened his hand: the third paper, with a very few words on it in an elegant script; and, wrapped in it, the coiled shimmer of a seashell. 'I'm summoned, and I may need a man at my back.'

<hr />

Lyle, Thomas Scot's man in Doncaster, operated out of a rented room above a dairy. Thurloe had the vague instinct that his having been blown up in the pursuit of duty entitled him to come and go there more freely, to a little more respect. For himself, his feelings wavered: a little heroic; somehow a little foolish.

Lyle, to be fair, had changed his tone somewhat: still patronizing, but with an acknowledgement that Thurloe had been blooded. When Thurloe walked in he was sitting at a table, surrounded by papers: handwritten reports; one paper with an odd pattern of holes spaced in it; printed news-sheets. He was reading one page and writing laboriously on another. He finished a word, and then his eyes flicked up. 'Hallo, Hotspur,' he said, and smiled without warmth. 'What you blown up today?'

Tarrant was standing against the window frame, arms folded tight together as if holding his energy in with difficulty. As soon as he saw Thurloe he was fully upright, frowning; then he subsided again stiffly. Tarrant's tone had changed little. He'd claimed irritation that Thurloe hadn't somehow done more. There was also, Thurloe thought, a faint sense of envy.

There was a large chest against the near wall and, for want of an alternative, he sat on it. 'Lyle,' he began; Lyle's eyes flicked up again. 'What was he burning? Messages? Codes?'

Lyle sat back. 'You tell me. You saw it.'

'Exactly!' Tarrant was up again. 'If you'd—'

But Lyle had carried on. 'That late on, I'd be surprised if there was any correspondence that hadn't already been burned.'

Thurloe absorbed it. 'Must have been hellish important. To wait that long. Then to risk your life for it.' Lyle nodded. 'Lyle, who are these people? I was at Nottingham, and—'

'The Royalists have their intelligencing men too,' Lyle said. 'They're desperate – have to be now – and they'll get worse.'

'They're a rash,' Tarrant said, pushing forward into the conversation. 'You're the expert, Thurloe.' To Lyle, with a sneer, 'Thurloe fixed up the report on Rainsborough's death, for Oliver St John. They're like a poison, Thurloe. They will infect this whole world.'

'But you must have some idea of them.' Thurloe was leaning forwards; now he settled back, trying to seem measured. 'You get. . . information about them. Reports. We have our spies, surely.'

'Look—' Tarrant, hot and then wondering where to take the initiative he'd just seized. He glanced down at Lyle, back at Thurloe, and then down again.

What battle is this, and what side am I on? What am I not allowed to know?

Lyle was still watching Thurloe.

Why did I write the report on Colonel Rainsborough's death, and not Tarrant, or Lyle himself?

'We're winning,' Lyle said.

'Logically there are two hypotheses.' Thurloe had slowed his voice deliberately. 'Either you're incompetent, an intelligencing man without any intelligence to pass. Or you're not telling all you know.'

Tarrant scowled. Then he returned to his window.

'You're clever, Hotspur,' Lyle said, and again the unconvincing smile. 'But where's it got you?'

⸺ ⸺

'Ready?' The shadow of a nod from Teach, single and firm. 'Don't fall asleep.'

Shay took a breath, and released it slowly. It disappeared into the rustle of leaves. Then he stepped forward from the tree line into thigh-length undergrowth.

On the opposite side of the clearing, another figure had done the same.

Shay peered through the gloom. A black cloak against the dark trunks, a black hat – and a mask of some kind.

He took another pace forward, the bracken pulling at his boots.

'Shay.' It was Teach behind him, low and urgent. 'He has a second – in the trees behind him. Two – three yards to the right.'

Shay nodded slightly, let his eyes wander slowly to the right. He couldn't see anything, of course.

Buried to the knees in the grey foliage, he and his reflection watched each other. Another step forward, and they were both on clear ground.

Three – four steps brought them to proximity in the centre, Shay forcing himself not to look at the trees, trusting Teach, watching instead the movement of the man in front of him. Controlled careful movement: a man of calculation, but not a man of action.

Three yards apart, and still Shay could make nothing of the features under the hat.

He stared into the mask nonetheless. 'Have you travelled far, pilgrim?'

'I have, and I've farther still to go.' The voice was low, firm.

'God and the King's justice go with you.'

'God save the King.'

Among the mess of rocks, the masked figure selected one and sat warily, watching Shay. He waited for Shay to do the same.

Shay gauged as best he could where the masked man's confederate was – there was every chance the confederate had moved, but he had to seek advantage where he could – and sat down so that the masked man was between them.

'You've come from. . .' – he knew he'd get no precise answer – 'overseas?'

'I have.'

'Into England. Now. An exceptional circumstance for the Committee, I imagine.'

'The English have assassinated their King, Shay; we may fairly describe the times as exceptional.'

Good boots – expensive; not hard worn. Cloak and hat meant nothing. Shay looked at the hands for a glimmer of rings in the last of the light, but saw nothing. Means of identification and distinction would be minimal.

'How lies the land?'

Shay tried to gauge the voice, through the mask. Not a young voice. But the man was not as old as he. Forty, perhaps. 'The people are stunned, for now. Cowed. Preston and the risings at the same time – Colchester, Pontefract, Wales – they exhausted enthusiasm and material.' The man was still and silent, waiting for him to finish. An intelligent man. 'But the killing of the King shocked many. There's discontent at the arrogance and impositions of the new regime. And the regime has its divisions: between some of the MPs and the soldiers; even in the Army, between moderates and the Levelling men.'

'Risings? A new royal army?'

'Not without something to rally to.'

'So it will have to be another invasion.'

'Yes. And not yet. Not this year.'

The mask considered this, then nodded acceptance. 'From Ireland?'

Shay growled distaste. 'Nothing good ever came out of Ireland.'

'Scotland again, then?'

'Yes.'

The cloak, the mask and the hat were all but lost in the evening now. 'The Scottish demands on religion are still too much for us – for His Majesty, that is.'

'The politics of Scotland are in constant shift. A month or a year may bring a new party to the fore, offering a different bargain. And you and His Majesty may have to bend a little, if you want the kingdom back.'

The shadow was silent. It was close to impertinence, and they both knew it.

'His Majesty looks for a new champion in Scotland. Montrose is in Norway, but would return if called.'

'Montrose.' Shay's voice was low, but there was question enough in the tone.

'You do not esteem him?'

'As a man, very highly. As a soldier, he is brave but reckless. And he is no kind of politician at all, and I think your man will need to be soldier and politician.'

'We have Hamilton, too. He grieves for his beheaded brother.'

'He may serve.' Shay shifted on the uneven surface of the boulder. 'There are no loyal men in Scotland: every man has served every master in his time, and the Hamiltons have been more slippery than most. When we can make a congruence between our interest and enough of the Scots, we'll find the man easily enough. For now, we must make a little time. Keep Parliament and the Army distracted. Weaken them if we may. And for that, Ireland will serve well enough.'

'You said nothing good ever came out of Ireland.'

'Nor did it. Indeed, a great many good men went into Ireland and did not come out again. In the chaos of that stinking primitive swamp of an island, we may find enough to draw in Master Cromwell.'

'Ormonde is still there. He made his peace with the Catholic Confederacy, and he fancies he can make that a military alliance in the royal interest.'

Shay nodded. 'Good. Then have him do it.'

'An alliance with the Catholics?' The masked man held up an instinctive hand, trying to block the onslaught. 'The late King suffered for a decade to avoid so open a stand.'

'The late King's policy was not a success. We must find our friendships where we can.'

'The Catholic Confederacy is volatile; divided. Could we depend on them?'

'The Catholic Confederacy is a squabbling snakepit of cut-throat barbarian peasants. I would depend on them for nothing but a knife in the back and an empty purse. But they must fear Cromwell and the puritans more than anything else. And that may bring them together and hold them together long enough to serve our turn.'

Only a moment's thought. 'We will send as much to Ormonde. And you?'

'I will do what I can to support the cause in Ireland and Scotland. I will ready our friends here for the King's eventual return. And in the meantime I may work a little mischief to keep the Parliament and the Army off their balance.'

It was fully night now. The mask was lost in the darkness, vision only hints of grey among black. There was a pause, and Shay thought he saw the man nod.

'You're the man for it. You have our trust and our blessing.'

'My respects and my duty to the Committee and to the King.'

'We are sure of it.'

They stood.

Shay said, 'And you now. . .?'

'Will be out of this island before dawn. Have you fully the threads of Astbury's operation now?'

A hollow grunt from Shay in the night. 'I have the communications. I don't yet know what game he was playing at the end. And. . . I do not yet have the book.'

'You do not. . .?' An aborted gasp through the mask. Words were unnecessary. The man took a breath, and said: 'You will find it.' It was not explicitly a command, and certainly not a reassurance. It was truth, because the alternative was inconceivable.

Shay's voice was low, solid, grim. 'I will find it.'

They each took a step backwards, cautious and uneasy in the gloom and the rough ground. Two half-bows, half-glimpsed, and the two men turned and disappeared from each other.

Sir,

Cromwell and the rest of the new-fangled Council of State are in a fury at the public sympathy for the so-called Levellers. They had thought, by their swift action in imprisoning Lilburne and the others who spoke before Parliament in that cause, to have crushed the protest and hushed contrarian voices. But the complaints of Lilburne and his Levellers, at the tyrannic arrogations of the Council of State itself, and at the offences against the processes and habits of English justice which they claim the Council has committed with its early dealings, and at the offences against the soldiers who put them in their current high position, touch Cromwell and the Council where they are proudest and where they are sorest.

The people of the kingdom know but that they suffer, and now a man has come who tells them why they suffer, and they are like to believe him, even though he blame the government itself. And this surely is most ironical, that it is the men who killed the King and who now dominate the Council who first taught England that its government may be doubted and challenged. By criticising the current regime in terms that magnified the virtues and responsibilities of Parliament against such impositions, Lilburne and his Levellers have most shrewdly stirred up a new spirit of righteousness among impressionable Members of the Parliament.

I think Cromwell and the Council do more fear the continued and growing feeling for these notions in the belly of the Army itself, which has always been their rock and their salvation. The shadow of the Agitators still stands over the regiments, and memories of democratic practices within the operation of the Army linger, but the threat of the power of the sword over the politicians, lately heard again from within the ranks, is no longer part of the policy of the leaders. While Cromwell and Fairfax and their kind have the Army, they have the Kingdom and none may challenge them. Should the Army weaken or fracture, set at odds by the radical and equalising dreams of the Levellers, they would be left as men naked in the public street.

S. V.

[SS C/S/49/21]

153

Shay read the report, and wondered at the attitudes, and reread it.

'Teach.'

Teach, sitting against the wall dozing, opened his eyes immediately, though his head and body stayed still.

'What do you know of the Levellers? What do men say of them?'

Teach took in a great sniff, and wriggled his shoulders.

'They are no kind of organization; an affinity of interest merely. A hodge-podge of ideas. A kind of disease in Parliament's Army.'

'I had them as fanatics and moon-gazers; ideas dangerous but fantastical.' Shay gestured with the paper. 'All these petitions and protests. What do these men truly want?'

Teach shrugged. 'They want more. They want better. They've had a decade of war and they want it worth something.' Another great sniff. 'Usually they want their back pay.'

'Freedom of belief, and the liberties of the people, and no trifling by Kings and Bishops with their folkloric nostrums. These are notions that Cromwell himself unleashed. Should he fear the Levellers?'

'I doubt that man fears anyone, save God. But you know it yourself: an Army can have but one loyalty. Once the men begin to pick and choose their cause, and ration their duty according to whim and weather, order collapses.' He stood suddenly, rubbed his rump, and reached for the wine bottle. 'Cromwell's great success was to build an Army around an idea and a discipline. Now he finds they have too many ideas, and it's costing him his discipline.' He took a swig, and washed it around his teeth. 'A different world from your German armies. You have a fancy for these Levellers, I take it.'

'Mm.' Shay was looking towards the report again. 'An enemy distracted and divided; that I fancy.'

❦

John Morrice and Michael Blackburn had been fully two weeks on the run. They were surviving on forest nuts and stream water, and vegetables scrabbled from the ground with their hands, and a piglet stolen near Huddersfield, clumsily slaughtered and part-cooked. They were surviving from ditch to barn, in shadows and half-light, never properly dry and never sleeping properly.

Morrice had some kind of fever. Since their escape from Pontefract they had made seventy miles, a waking dream of meandering, of stumbling.

The fourteenth night they spent in a barn, on sacks and old straw. In the small hours, Blackburn finally found sleep. Morrice continued to shiver and drowse.

He woke with the dawn, conscious immediately of the cold. He had never been warm. Reddened eyes flickered, and focused, and then widened, and immediately he flung a hand out to grab at Blackburn next to him. It took two rough shakes before the younger man woke, bewildered and protesting with questions, and then silent and staring like his Colonel.

Ten feet away, sitting with apparent comfort on a box and against a beam, a man was watching them.

An older man. Heavy built but carrying himself alert. He smiled.

'Good morning, gentlemen,' he said evenly. 'I let you sleep on, for I guess you need it. But we shouldn't wait for much more of the day.'

'Who—'

'A friend.'

'Why should—'

'Because if I wasn't, I'd have cut your throats or had you in the hands of the militia by now.'

Morrice and Blackburn had shuffled to sitting positions among the sweepings of the barn floor. They knew the truth of the statement; knew the vulnerability they had let themselves fall to.

'Since you're men of prudence and resource who have survived thrice over where most men would not once, it may be your humour not to believe me.' Again the smile. 'I approve. You may choose to reveal nothing of your systems and your supporters. From the looks of you, I should say you'd had few of either.'

Morrice said quietly, 'How did you come upon us?'

'I have. . . acquaintances, from whom I learn of things of interest hereabouts. Your movements have not gone completely unnoticed.' Another shared glance of discomfort between the two on the floor. 'Now, I guess you for fugitives from Pontefract.'

Again the mutual unease. 'I'll take that for a yes, if you don't mind. Names?' The two hollow, greasy faces pulled back and frowned. 'I've said that I could have killed you or arrested you if I'd wanted. You've no fear of arrest from me, and you may stick your head outside and check that I'm alone if you wish. But if you don't want my help, I'll bid you farewell and leave you to whichever of starvation and fever and the militia gets you first.'

The older man watched him sourly. 'Morrice. Colonel. This is Blackburn. Cornet.'

'Good. Perhaps it reassures you to know that I fear a deception as much as. . . Morrice?' A cautious nod. 'You're a prize and more for a wandering constable, aren't you, Colonel?' Morrice's sourness did not ease.

The voice suddenly sharpened. 'In May last year you met two men at an inn outside Leeds to discuss seizing Pontefract. If you're Morrice, you'll know the name of the inn.'

'How do you—' Morrice stopped, dumb. 'The – the Black Horse.' A moment of silence, and he added, 'Satisfied?' But the truculence was marred by a sudden fit of coughing.

'Well enough.' The stranger reached to one side for a small sack, and threw over two loaves of bread and a bottle of wine.

Blackburn ground the food into his face, utterly absorbed. Morrice chewed slowly, still watching the man opposite. 'Do I know you?' he said after a moment, and there was new respect in the voice.

Mortimer Shay frowned, checking for a recollection of his own. 'I'd rather you didn't.'

Morrice nodded. 'I understand. I have forgotten you again.' Shay smiled.

Blackburn looked between them uneasily. 'Who—'

'Quiet, boy.' Morrice glanced only briefly at his subordinate. 'There is an older, deeper world; and you go softly when you feel its shadows on you.' He gestured with his bread. 'We're grateful for the vittles, stranger.' His tongue cleared a piece of loaf from his cheek. 'What do you seek of us, or what do you offer?'

'Escape.' Hope and wariness flickering on the faces. 'Escape to the Continent, by quicker, surer means than you've managed in recent days.' He leaned forwards. 'Unless you'll stay in England to continue the fight. We're not done yet.'

He'd not expected otherwise of these shipwrecked men, but the uncomfortable flinchings in the faces were still a disappointment.

'We would, but—'

'We're excepted.' Blackburn, with a strange mix of bitterness and defiance. 'We're dead men.'

'Excepted?'

'In the negotiations for the fall of Pontefract, the Parliamentary commanders offered mercy for all but six men. We're two of them. They catch us, they hang us regardless.'

'Why?'

Again the hesitation, but again Blackburn picked up the conversation. Food and drink – and conversation too, no doubt; they'd unlikely exchanged a sentence in days; Shay recognized the signs – had restored a youth's self-assurance and pride. 'The Colonel for he led the defence against them so long. I for my part in – in a certain exploit.' He took a swig of wine. 'That's why we had to escape.'

'Exploit?' Exception was rare for those who had not commanded; some egregious little savagery on the edge of the battle, inflated by a victor's affronted morality? 'What – you mean the killing of that Colonel? Rainsborough, was that him?'

A flicker of discomfort again.

'Lad, if they knew enough to except you for it, you'll lose nothing by telling me, whoever I am.'

Blackburn chewed this for a second, trying to hold the pride in his eyes. Then he nodded cockily. 'That was him.' Another swig. 'That was him, dying like a dog in the gutter, and well-deserved.'

Shay listened with a kind of fondness. *Ah, the brittle bravado of the boys.* 'We had no fouler enemy, or so I hear.' *We old men have built our world upon it.* 'Lord knows why you chanced it, but it was the boldest thing.'

Blackburn was obviously used to the criticism. 'Maybe you'd say it was reckless, but—'

'Young man, I've been doing stupid things on battlefields these thirty years. You may trust me to know boldness, and to understand it.' It wasn't just flattery. 'Nonetheless, I admire your notion of a morning's sport.'

'They said he truly was a beast.' Blackburn was softer; the older man's respect had promoted him to a status with which he was not yet comfortable. 'It did our people good to see that we could bite back.'

'Indeed.' Shay stood, and walked to the barn door, and checked that morning had not yet come to the farm. He was talking as he returned to his little perch on the box. 'I have a curious wish to know more of that incident. A good tale, I fancy.'

'Wait, lad.' Blackburn found his Colonel's hand on his arm. 'We'll not put ropes around other men's necks.' This to Shay. 'You've had your fill from two desperate men, and we've told you no more than you'd get from any Roundhead sentry in Doncaster.' Morrice sat more upright, and then coughed harshly. The words came hoarse. 'But I'll not risk the name of one of my men. I don't send a man out to parley unprotected – not without the man opposite me has an equal stake at forfeit.'

Shay scowled. For some reason he wanted to hear more about the death of Rainsborough. *You don't know what you don't know.*

Morrice was managing to hold his eyes; Shay had begun to like this Colonel greatly.

Silence, and then a great breath. 'Very well. I am Sir Mortimer Shay.' He stared at them bleakly. 'With what else you know of what I can do, you know enough to hang me too.'

'Shay. . .' Morrice breathed the word in a wonder of memory. 'I thought I knew your face, sir, but it's twenty years since. Your name was become a secret whisper, or a curse.' He gestured as if to move Blackburn forward. 'Tell him the names, boy.'

'Sir?'

Morrice was still watching Shay. 'If he's true, he is the last best hope of England. If he's false, we are doomed regardless. Tell him.'

In April of that year, a stranger was moving among the regiments of the Army of Parliament. Perhaps more than one stranger. In the Army encampments on Blackheath, and at Salisbury, and perhaps elsewhere, a man might be felt at a shoulder, or seen behind a tent, or heard through a shifting screen of leaves. The voice – the voices – spoke of John Lilburne's honest cause, of the birthrights of ordinary Englishmen, of old liberties and new glories, of fair pay to the men who were dying on behalf of other men. The words breathed and gusted and echoed, as racy jokes and angry debates and promises pregnant with miracle. The Leveller cause was furtive talk around the fire and silly drunken boasting and earnest political persuasion. The voice – the voices – murmured among groups, and pushed hard and insistent at known agitators, and sometimes an officer would think he'd overheard something before settling back less easy to his routine. A shoulder was patted; a shilling was passed.

<hr>

Shay's first hearing of the death of Colonel Thomas Rainsborough was in a Lancashire barn, the occasional distant cock-crow a little stab of their increasing vulnerability.

'Guess you'd say there were four of us,' Blackburn said with artificial deliberation. 'Four who led it, one way or another. Five maybe.' He was cross-legged on the floor, leaning back against the ramshackle planks of the wall. 'It was the grandest thing you ever saw.'

'Four or five?' Shay tried to make the interjection relaxed, interested. He didn't want to delay in this stuck-out unknown trap of a place, but he didn't want to hustle the boy into inaccuracy.

'Captain Paulden – Captain William Paulden – he had the idea mainly. He spoke to Lieutenant Austwick about some men for it. Then they came to me' – a little glance at his Colonel in fear of contradiction – 'as my troop were known for lively fellows – rather jump a big ditch than a small.' He paused, wondering where to take the story next, and saw the question on his listener's face. 'And there was a civilian. Always close to Captain Paulden, he was. Name of Teach; Miles Teach.'

Teach indeed. The wildest dare, the quietest report of it.

'That was the four of us, anyway, with my men behind. Captain William's brother was with us, and he usually knew what was going on.' He'd leaned forward into the question, and now returned to his studied relaxation against the wall. 'It was the grandest thing you ever saw,' he said again, and this time Shay let him run. 'We'd all been locked up tight in Pontefract all those weeks, and then to be charging free across the country like that, wild and free. . .' Morrice started to cough again, and Blackburn waited for him to subside. 'We came out of the dawn at them, scattered their pickets while your eye was blinking, and charged into the town. Then we had to be more careful, see? Thing like this, it takes subtlety.' Shay nodded. It did take subtlety, and he wondered who had provided it. 'We'd got through the gate right enough, and the guards were all dead and fleeing, but we knew they'd spread the alarm soon enough. So we had to be quick. But we couldn't make a fuss. Way we were dressed, we could be soldiers from either side. Didn't want to stir anything in the street unless we had to. So now we're going at the trot, all calm and unthreatening, and all the time waiting for the trumpets to blast behind us!'

He was leaning forward now, the pose of magisterial narration forgotten. 'Discipline's the thing, you see?' Shay nodded. Actually, he did see: it couldn't have been easy to saunter through Doncaster knowing that an alarm would be raised imminently, that a small force could be surrounded and cut off with ease. 'But my lot, they're trained and practised. I sent them off around the town, this way and that, so they could deal with anyone who got excited. Planning, you see? That's the thing.'

Shay found an old warrior's smile from somewhere. 'Why, that's grand, Blackburn. You'd have to have a special troop for that sort of affair.' Blackburn nodded. 'And Captain Paulden and the Lieutenant, they came to you, did they?'

'Yes, sir, they did.' He nodded busily.

'And the planning? Who'd worked out all this careful manoeuvre?'

'Well, we each—'

'Paulden.' Morrice, quiet and firm.

Blackburn had the faint sense he was losing control of his story, and nodded again to confirm what his commander said, and repeated 'Paulden' authoritatively. 'Captain Paulden.'

'And they told you the plan?'

Blackburn hesitated. 'Yes – but no, not the details. No need for details. I had to provide the men. "Find a dozen or two good men" – that was it. Anyway, it was just a raid, a grand raid.'

The cockerel crow seemed to squawk more loudly into their dusty isolation, and from nearer by a cow moaned. They glanced at each other uneasily.

'Paulden,' Shay said deliberately. 'Do I know the name?' It was addressed to Morrice.

'The family have been true for the Crown all through. No great name or fortune, but they've given what they— Wait, I should be clearer. There were three brothers.' Shay's irritation darkened on his face, and Morrice hurried, words coming rough from the raw throat. 'One died fighting at Wigan during the Duke of Hamilton's campaign last year. Two were with us in Pontefract. William's was the idea to go for Rainsborough; William's was the plan. He died shortly after the raid – fever. The third brother, Thomas, rode with them. As the lad says, he was usually pretty thick with his brother.'

'And Teach?'

'Oh, he was involved right enough. Any conversation needed a bit of sense to it, a bit of experience, you'd find him there; and any deed needed a bit of spirit, he'd be there as well.'

The dull calls of the cattle sounded nearer again.

'Well then, youngster.' Shay to Blackburn. 'What of the death of Rainsborough?'

'Oh, I don't know who actually killed him. I doubt anyone does. It was confusion, you see?'

'Tell me.'

Blackburn was forward again, eager. 'We'd sent smaller parties of men elsewhere around the town. Captain William stayed out patrolling in the streets.'

'He didn't go for Rainsborough himself?'

'Not at first. He said he needed to be flexible. To command the situation where needed. I remember him saying to his brother, and to Mr Teach, to listen out careful for the signal.'

'So who actually went for Rainsborough?'

'Captain Thomas Paulden, Lieutenant Austwick and Mr Teach. And me, too. We rode to the inn, where Rainsborough was, all quiet and innocent-like through the centre of town, and nobody knew what we were after. Then Captain Thomas rode on to the north bridge to prepare our escape there.'

'So there were only three of you for the deed itself?'

'Had to be.' Blackburn temporarily rediscovered some of his superiority. 'Had to be inconspicuous. And now we've to get into the inn, see? The Lieutenant, he knocks and says, all confident, "We have urgent letters for the Colonel, from General Cromwell." We'd talked about this earlier, and it worked just to plan. The sentry, he was half-asleep, and he doesn't give much attention to us. Lets us into the yard, and then waits in the gateway. He's not looking at us any more. He doesn't know he's already admitted the biggest threat he'll ever face!'

'What then?'

Blackburn's eyes were alive, intent. 'Rainsborough's Lieutenant meets us, and he gets the same story, and swallows it, and he leads Lieutenant Austwick and Mr Teach up to Rainsborough's room. I stay in the yard – with the horses – someone needs to keep watch, see? Minute or two later—'

'Who was giving the orders?'

'Orders? No one, in truth. Mr Teach, perhaps; we'd got used to him as a man for a tight game. Few minutes later they're down again, Rainsborough and his Lieutenant being pushed ahead. Mr Teach says to me, "Get him in!", him meaning the sentry, and I immediately grab the sentry in and put him down and the others go into the street, and I put the horses out after them, and everyone's sort of milling around a moment, and then I see that the sentry is up and looking to interfere and I only had time just to put him down again, nothing fancy, knock him on the nose, always slows them down and makes them think a bit.' There was part of the young Blackburn that Shay was warming to considerably. 'But somehow it's started off in the street now, behind me, and I'm watching the sentry and trying to get out and still wanting to make sure he's staying down and then it's shouting and swords and we're all in God's hands. In the muddle Rainsborough and his Lieutenant go down.'

'Who actually killed them?'

'Couldn't say, sir. The others between them. Captain William Paulden, he'd turned up now. Mr Teach, Lieutenant Austwick – but I couldn't say which. Everyone was armed and angry, and maybe you know what it's like.'

Shay nodded slightly. He knew what it was like. He was lost in the scene for a moment. It had indeed been a bold and tight game. He watched Blackburn subsiding uneasily, tongue licking at lips still, the energy of the exploit echoed in the describing, and saw decades of young faces like him, uncowed by experience and the sentimental over-attachment of the old to life.

And he couldn't overcome a sense of unreality about the scene he'd heard described.

———

April 16. 1649 – Mary, d. of Sir Anthony and the late Isabelle Astbury, m. Sir Henry Lowell, Baronet, of Leicester.

Astbury House: the study: Sir Anthony Astbury seated at his table, straight-backed, eyes switching constantly from the words appearing tiny under his hand in the flyleaf of the family Bible, and the couple in front of him.

Sir Henry Lowell, Baronet, of Leicester returned his father-in-law's glances with indulgent respect. A decent man, Astbury: a generous dowry, with the prospect of the house eventually, and a handsome daughter, who would be a loved and loving wife and a fine mother.

Sir Henry Lowell had come through the 1640s well enough. Enough bravery at the start; enough prudence at the end. He had the wounds, heroically won, to impress a daughter; and the contacts, carefully cultivated, to impress a father. In recent years Lowell had kept his focus firmly in Leicestershire, and done solid and generous work with the militia, and the new men in the county knew him for a dependable man.

Lady Mary Lowell was silent, a little sentimental at this last formality of her father's, a little anxious at what Henry might be thinking, and newly alive and purposeful and happy.

Rachel sat in the corner, forgotten and futile and a little jealous.

———

Mortimer Shay, Colonel Morrice and Cornet Blackburn, now shadows in the dusk at the edge of a spinney, a grey-green world. The animals of evening were beginning to emerge, with odd calls and rustles among the leaves.

'This is the Preston road. Travel wisely and in the shadows, but as fast as you may, until you reach the inn. There a wash and a shave, and be gone before dawn. After that you may go more carefree; try to act so. You should have mounts by noon tomorrow. You may try for a boat in Liverpool or Lancaster, depending which road the wind blows you.' Shay looked into the two gloomed faces. 'You have the words I gave you safe in memory? The locations?'

A residual awe kept Blackburn silent. Morrice nodded. 'We do.' He reached out his hand. 'We owe you all thanks, sir.'

Shay grunted, and shook hands with both. 'These days His Majesty can give you little enough of glory or gold for your loyalty. God speed.'

He turned and vanished into the greyness.

———— ~ ————

The regiment in camp at Banbury, day retreating pale from the sky. As evening became colder and slower, the men huddled closer together, kicking at the ground with practised glances as they thought of sleep, warming themselves with convivial chatter. Life, in this evening, a dry coat and good men around you, seemed gently rather grand. Men sat in clumps, shoulders pressed together, the aloof habits of individuality long forgotten. Cards and knucklebones were produced and peered at with quiet concentration and laughter. Pipes emerged long and frail from inside pockets. Tales were told, chronologies repeated; history can keep you warm.

Hewson's regiment refused to go to fight in Ireland – and didn't that show the Generals at last? – one man told me a Major got punched in the face – musket it was, right up his nose – no more fighting until our Leveller demands get met – pay first – of course, pay first – except they can't pay first, pay ever, because they're bankrupt in the wars. (And didn't it feel strangely, wildly good that the real confrontation had begun?) Kicked them all out, though, no pay – so what? – no pay anyway. Whalley's regiment wouldn't turn out for their officers – seized their colours, they did – dug in – like a siege, they said – and tell us about Scrope's regiment. I heard the Colonel was in tears when they wouldn't obey. Not so smug now, are they?

And here we are. All the regiments of true believing men starting to gather, and then we'll see what the Generals say. The Army is now about men like us: we've reclaimed it from the hands and ideas of the politicians. Fellowship has become our cause, and the Army is fellowship.

The evening heavier. Eventually sleep.

Then the nightmare: the earth shuddering and the heads screaming and the drowsy clusters of men dragging themselves awake and somehow up, and staggering and clutching for shoulders and weapons and clarity and the nightmare is on them. The nightmare is Cromwell, vast leather-and-metal men on rampaging horses, exploding dark out of the night, monstrous grey-brown shadows with banshee swords and a madness of noise. The stupid stumbling self-protecting surrendering men are knocked spinning aside like clods of mud under the hooves. It's not even a fight: a rampage, a rout, a rounding-up of cattle.

Shay and Teach came to a fork in the road, a choice of muddy lanes.

'We part here, I think.' Teach's voice made nothing of it, and the face was blank as usual. 'Ireland's this way. I think I smell it.'

Shay smiled, and nodded. He took a long look at Teach, sure on the horse and implacable.

Then a whim. 'Teach: a last fancy, if you'll indulge me.' Teach waited. Shay pulled from his inner pocket the letter found on George Astbury's body, and stretched over the two horses' heads to pass it. 'You recognize this? One of yours?'

Teach took it, frowned, glanced at it, and then looked up warily. 'Yes. From Pontefract. How did—'

'It was among Astbury's papers. I wondered if there was some significance, above the ordinary. I couldn't see a hidden message in it. Some special cypher?'

Teach glanced at the page again. 'You couldn't see it because there isn't one. If the Pauldens or I had anything secret to pass, the letter would begin "Sir, I write. . .", and the hidden message would be encyphered in one of the normal ways.' He handed the paper back to Shay. 'This is – no more than it seems. Why?'

'I really don't know.' Carefully, Shay folded it again and replaced it in what had become its customary place in the pocket. A thump of gauntlets. 'Come safe back, Teach. Ireland isn't worth a man of your quality.'

Teach grunted, grim. 'I come pretty cheap, Shay.' Then he turned, and was gone into the mud.

<hr />

Colonel John Morrice, dangling at the end of a rope, seeking a composure to counter the burning of his shoulder muscles, and not finding it in the unbidden memories of how he had come to be where he was.

The journey to the coast so much smoother – their confidence growing with each warm day in dry clothes, each magical provision of horse or bed with the words provided by Sir Mortimer Shay. The decision – a quieter road – Lancaster rather than Liverpool or Preston – and so smoothly onward to the town. Then the misunderstanding – dusk in the Three Mariners – a watchful man – unease – the word – the confusion – suspicion – escape. And so back to the wandering and the fear – a different inn – cold and desperation and how stupid can a tired man be? – the pushing and the begging and the suspicion worse – and the watchful man again and then the sentries.

Capture – and sleep – and bitterness – and anger – and determination again – and here he was, dangling halfway down the curtain wall of York Castle.

A last scalding clutch of strength in his arms to hold himself at the end of the rope – *I am a man yet and all my years will be worth something to me in this moment* – toes kicking against the smooth stone and eyes scrambling for some steady glimpse of the ground beneath – flat? grass? – and now he was falling, the stupid infantile bewilderment of the fall, and then the thump, somehow heard before felt, and then felt in elbows and shoulders and aching leg-bones.

Old bones. Old joints, and fraying old muscles, pulling the body together and up against the wall, to gasp for breath and count its blessings and bruises. *I am a man yet.*

What next can fate bring me?

Fate could next bring him Cornet Michael Blackburn – a younger man, fitter, lither, but not as experienced in these little feats – Blackburn scrabbling down after him, frantic clutching at the rope, feet slipping desperately on the stone, shoulders spasmodically stopping him on the descent but not controlling him, and now – dropping down the wall and jostling Morrice as he came and landing hard, some click or crack of stone on stone. But no, not stone. In the grey huddle of Blackburn, collapsed at the base of the wall, a single sharp beam of whiteness lances up into the night towards the moon: his shin-bone.

Morrice swallowing his revulsion, while his instinct started to test and comfort and work at the body beneath him. The young man was moaning miserably. Head held, cushioned, arms moved, back – the moaning of other aches coming as descant – other leg, and now the mess of the broken leg.

'Colonel...'

My mistake.

'Leave – leave me he—' It swung into a cry as Morrice straightened the leg out.

Fate wants me here after all.

'Don't worry, lad, couldn't get far without you anyway.' Somewhere there were shouts and boots in the night.

'Colonel, you must... I'm so cold...'

'All's right, lad. We'll stick here together for now.'

―――~―――

Politics and religion: at dawn, a man stands alone beside St Paul's Cathedral. The first of the sun is far above him, trying to kindle something from the broken stump of the cathedral spire. The man's hands are tied behind him. Beside him, the buttresses jag thin into the sky like so many impassive pikemen.

The city has been edgy for several days now. There have been wild stories; rumours and portents. There has been a toing and froing of soldiers, angry and afraid. Sometimes a shouting, and the animal and metallic sounds of skirmish, half-heard among the warren of lanes like a fishwife's tale, and doubted. London's citizens are quieter these days. Riots are an eternal feature of city life, and the Army coming to crush them; but it's becoming hard to distinguish the Army from the riot. People stay at home. Business is down.

A volley of musket fire crackles across the morning; the bound man staggers as if trying to stay upright in the wind, and drops.

Another church, soft honey stone in the heart of the little market town. It's Thursday in Burford – market day – but only a few wary traders are setting up stalls and carts. It's been heard that the Army has hundreds of mutineers locked in the church. The lanes around have become forbidden places, places of mysterious danger like the nights, with noises heard distant and strange. As the sun starts to warm the stone, and a few valiant cries come from the marketplace, three men are stood up against the thickest yew in the churchyard and shot to death with muskets, one after the other, shivering and wild, slumping onto the body of the man before and then all dragged away.

Cromwell's Army is at war with itself.

─ ~

The deaths of Leveller leaders in London and Oxfordshire had become papers in Mortimer Shay's pocket by the time he trotted through a warm afternoon to Astbury. The brick frontage glowed in the sun, and something of the grandeur of the house – the ranks of mullions and the high gables – caught his mood.

He held back his question until after supper, when Anthony Astbury was flighty with wine and warm by a fire in his study.

'A book? George was too much in books, and not enough.'

'This would be a particular book: goodly size. It's. . . an account book – from the King's household; you might have seen him marking it very occasionally.'

'He was a great reader, and he thought too much, when it were better that he were out hunting. Then when the time came for prudence, and restraint, when he might sensibly have buried himself in his books, he must be off like some empty-headed knight on a quest.' Astbury stood, and picked up a dark volume lying on its side on his desk. 'The only book we ever shared a concern for was this, the family Bible.' He brandished it, two-handed, at Shay and then placed it carefully in a chest next to the desk. 'The word of God and not too much of it, and the chronology of our family and our times.' He locked the chest and stood, pocketing the key. 'You are probably mentioned yourself, once or twice – my wife would have put you in.'

It certainly wasn't what Shay was after – not with Astbury checking it every other minute – but he'd break into the chest later just in case George had done something clever.

'Quite right. Nice to keep up these traditions.' Neither of them thought Shay believed it. 'No matter. Probably destroyed or lost in the chaos after Preston.'

In a dim corridor between the back of the house and the front, Shay found Rachel. But she hadn't seen the book either.

'If he had it, and wanted it to himself, it would have been in that study room. Your room. And you obviously haven't found it.'

'Obviously.'

'But I never saw him with the like outside. Even near the end – when he was more. . . frantic. It's important – or you wouldn't be after it so hard.'

'Royal accounts.' It wasn't a bad lie, and he decided to stick to it. 'These things are best kept together. Hardly means much now, does it?'

He walked with her a few steps, his bulk next to her slender glide, and she stopped at a window in the corridor. Outside, the evening was making an early experiment with summer, the last dusty light encouraging the birds.

'You said he was more frantic. You meant just before Preston – before his death.'

She was watching the lilac-green-greys of dusk through the window. 'It was almost as though he knew he would die. As if he had to tidy up his life – do all the moving, and the thinking, and the worrying that he wouldn't otherwise have time for. Bustling around, striding to and fro in the garden – sometimes with Jacob; usually on his own. Riding off for an hour or a day.'

Surely I don't have to search the whole bloody garden. 'Did he talk much? Did he say what he worried at?'

Rachel looked up at him for a moment, as if for inspiration. 'No. But I remember him discussing the – the Levellers – these men in the Army. More than once he started a conversation with my father about them. Their principles. Whether they couldn't be somehow loyal to the Crown.' She looked up at him again. 'Father told me of the fighting between Cromwell and the Levellers. Is that what George wanted? Was he. . . aiming at this?'

'I can't imagine what George wanted. The idea of some compact between the royal interest and these radical egalitarians seems lunatic. But. . .' – Rachel watched Shay's face as he spoke, now gazing into the evening and momentarily less sure – 'George was foolish, but not stupid. This obviously meant something to him.' He shook his head. 'What else?'

She shrugged, the pale shoulders held up for a second in a girl's imitation of the gesture. 'That was – oh, and there was Pontefract.'

Pontefract again?

'He referred to it two or three times. There was fighting there – the siege. And then, of course, the soldier came.'

'What soldier?'

Rachel glanced up, and back to the window. Then she raised the fingers of one hand and ran them deliberately down the window, watching them bump over the lead veins. 'That was a. . . a terrible evening.' Her fingertips were cold now, and she pressed them against her bodice. 'A storm, and then when we were at supper, John coming in to say that there was a messenger for George. A soldier, it turned out, from Doncaster; but it was to do with Pontefract, he said. And badly wounded. George sat with him a while – Mary tried to help nurse him, but George would only take advice, not help – and then the soldier died, during the night. We barely saw him. Anyway, that was George's last night here. The next day he went off to the war. To die.'

She leaned forward, until her forehead touched the window. 'And we remain here.'

Another low scream from the next room, and Thurloe winced.

I have followed, like a dumb puppy in my enthusiasm, and this is the price I pay.

There had been screams for – what – twenty minutes now? Was that so very long?

Another, an animal protest, a man losing control of voice and breath in his agony. Again he winced. *Why have I not learned? Should I not be inured now?* How many screams in those twenty minutes?

An angry voice through the wall, a desperate babbling murmur after it, and then a scream, and Thurloe gasped. *My little discomfort is nothing to that man's. My little discomfort may be the last piece of humanity in this evil building; in this world.*

In the adjacent room, lying on a table, was Cornet Michael Blackburn, who had escaped from Pontefract and been recaptured and had tried to escape from York. Blackburn with a broken leg, and Tarrant standing over him, working at the unhealed break with all his bitterness.

And whose side am I on?

Another scream cut through the stones, and Thurloe leapt up, hands clenching and unclenching. Then he spun and strode from the room.

Tarrant was lost in his interrogation: the latest bout of his struggle with the world was this competition of will with a wrecked youth. 'Who helped you? You were destitute, you were lost, and then you had horses and food and all very comfy. All I want is a name, Blackburn.' Blackburn's breaths were desperate gasps. 'A name!' and Tarrant's hand twisted at the leg and the breath was wrenched into another shriek.

'Tch— Tchay—'

'James?' Louder, as if to compete with the scream. 'James, is that the name?' Another vicious twist of his hand and Blackburn's scream scoured the walls.

'Tarrant!' Tarrant spun round to find Thurloe in the doorway. Tarrant was sweating, and frustrated; an animal. ''Fore God, this is enough! Men like you have suffered a generation or more to change these mediæval habits.'

'He's gone again, sir.' This from another man, Tarrant's assistant. Tarrant glanced back and then, hot and sneering, to Thurloe again.

'Besides. . . look – he'll tell you anything to make you stop, and we've no way of knowing if it's true.'

Tarrant glanced back at the unconscious man on the table, and strode out, shouldering Thurloe aside as he went.

Thurloe forced himself to look at the man on the table: his white sweat-greased face, his battered leg.

This is what I have become.

Oliver Cromwell had come to mistrust papers. Once, paper had told only one truth. It had told God's truth, and Cromwell had prayed and fought that all might read that truth for themselves. The spread of print had promised to bring every man closer to God's word. But now papers were become mere voices, just flimsy, rustling tongues. Each one had its insistent story.

He scanned the spread of pages on the desk in front of him, more reports from Thomas Scot's world of spies and correspondents, every one with some alarm or warning from Ireland.

Each tongue had its own particular claim to truth. Each, no doubt, had its deceits.

A knocking and a rustling, a rodent on the edge of his attention. He looked up: there was Scot, crept into the room and scrutinizing him.

Cromwell gave him no welcome or greeting. 'What have we fought for, Master Scot?' The rhetoric fell heavy. 'That we find no end of woes? Is this the eternal trial that God offers us on the corrupted earth? By squashing the latest boil of your Levellers I have brought a temporary peace inside our Army' – things flinched in Scot's face – 'but that division is raw and grieves me. And you bring me nothing but new dangers.'

'Ireland is an old and lasting danger, Master Cromwell. It will remain a danger until the ungodliness is wiped out.' The big eyes watched him. 'Until the last of the brute, disbelieving, heathen peasants is driven into the sea.'

Cromwell chewed on this.

Scot had another paper in his hand. Cromwell's eyes narrowed. 'And what's that? More ill from Dublin, no doubt.'

A pained smile from Scot. 'No, this is. . . from another quarter.'

A PROCLAMATION

Be it Known

That His Sovereign Majesty

King Charles Stuart

King *of* Scotland, *of* England,
of Ireland *and of* Wales *and* lesser dominions,

is pleased to proclaim his own well-beloved

James Graham

Earl of Montrose, Earl of Kincardine,
Lord Graham and Mugdock, and
Marquess of Montrose,

as His Majesty's avowed *Lord Lieutenant*
in the said Kingdom of *Scotland*, which do lie
nearest His Majesty's Heart.

'Nearest his heart?' Cromwell looked up at Thomas Scot, bleak and angry. 'That disinherited puppy has his father's politics and more, doesn't he?'

'Names the Kingdom of Scotland before England, too. A nice touch, that.' Scot's thin vinegar smile. 'It will please in the slums of Edinburgh.'

'You have me hopping like a flea over Ireland, and now you bring me Scotland! The Lord has been most generous to us, but he will not grant me victory in two places at the same time.'

'Montrose is still a divisive figure in Scotland. Unless the pretender

Charles can make his peace with the Church there, there will be no general support.'

'You presume too much!' Cromwell was simmering, a great brown pot of ill-suppressed heat, and Scot took an instinctive little step sidewards. 'Montrose has raised armies before, has he not? And the smallest of his armies has won great victories, has it not? And I cannot make a new peace with the Scottish Church without splitting the English Parliament and the English Army!'

Scot made a sad little shake of the head. 'Then Montrose must be def—'

'I say you presume too much! I am not some hound that you may unchain as you please! The Army is not a witch's charm with which you may be assured your every victory.'

Scot's eyes bulged among his sharp features. 'Then we must trust to providence. And to Scottish factiousness. For we have nothing else.'

Cromwell gazed at him grimly for a moment longer, and then the heavy eyes dropped again to the reports from Ireland on the desk.

— ⁓ —

After York, Thurloe had been in Nottingham on legal business again, settling the cases of Royalists and their fines: loyalty rehearsed as moot debate; battles being waged in accountants' ledgers. It felt sordid, and petty, and he was uncomfortable that this clerk's sweeping up was all his portion of the great conflict. Nottingham Castle squatted over his perception of the city, with its memories of Langdale's escape last autumn, a shadow from some other world which he could not grasp.

Business done, he continued northward rather than turning for London. Oliver Cromwell was still angry at the Leveller risings in the Army, hurt that the weapon he had forged had become two-edged, bitter at the self-destructiveness of it all; he was fretful, even he, apparently trapped in an eternity of threats and battles. St John too was become nervy.

So Thurloe headed for Doncaster, telling himself that it was the logical response to his chief's concern, knowing that it was his own unfinished business that was kicking at the horse's flanks.

Colonel Thomas Rainsborough had been a prominent figure in

the Leveller movement. Thomas Scot might be Parliament's chief of intelligence and someone Cromwell was obliged to rely on, but he too was a man of prominent Leveller sympathy. This apparently held true for some of those he employed: Tarrant, and Lyle in Doncaster. Rainsborough had been killed, and the prominent Leveller sympathizers had wanted revenge, but Cromwell hadn't wanted to unleash Scot to hunt witches throughout the Army and Government. So Cromwell had chosen him, Thurloe, a reliable neutral clerk, to do enough to assuage Leveller anger without frightening the horses.

But Thurloe wasn't comfortable with his own conclusions, not comfortable with the strange melodrama of that Doncaster morning. And he itched at the thought of Tarrant, a stupider man, and Lyle, with mere cunning, overmastering him.

Now the Levellers had gone from radicalism to rebellion; men had been hanged and shot. But still their sympathy was everywhere.

Was there something else to discover about Rainsborough, something that a hungrier man like Tarrant might have discovered? Or were Tarrant and his kind the mystery?

It was late morning when Thurloe made Doncaster, and Lyle was away from his base above the dairy. Thurloe went to find lodging. The town was dramatically quieter than when he'd last been here. With the fall of Pontefract up the road, the army quartered here had largely dispersed. Doncaster was feeling its way slowly back into normality, like something emerging from a long winter. It made a good bed easy to find and cheap.

'It's Thurloe, isn't it?'

A soldier, slowing from a natural stride and hesitating. Thurloe recognized the Adjutant who'd looked after him when he'd been here in the autumn. Polite greetings from careful men; an indifferent exchange of information about London and the garrison here packing up.

'What brings you back?'

Thurloe murmured something about his legal work, and an acquaintance in the town, wondering about the Adjutant. He'd had his own sympathy for the Levellers, hadn't he? An affiliation of reason, perhaps, not of the heart, and he'd kept his head down in recent months no doubt.

Courteous preparations to go their separate ways, and then Thurloe hesitated. 'I say—' The Adjutant turned back. 'I was wondering. . .' The Adjutant seemed relaxed enough; his days too were easier now. 'Your men gave me a full understanding of Colonel Rainsborough's death, but. . . was there – had there been anything. . . unusual, in the period before his death?' The Adjutant was frowning now. *Careful. What battle is this, and what side am I on?* 'Any non-military business involving the Colonel?'

The Adjutant shrugged, shook his head emptily. Thurloe shrugged back at him, diminishing the business.

'He had a visitor – from London – the week or two before.' Thurloe's face opened in interest. 'I only mention it because – visitors hardly unusual, I mean to say – they had an almighty row. The London man was asking questions around the place. Seemed quite close to Rainsborough; intimate – private meetings and so on – but I was at Rainsborough's lodging once and they were at it like lions. The Colonel, mainly – he had the devil's temper in him – then the London man left, looking pretty grim.'

'You wouldn't know him? I presume not.'

Again the shrug, the shake of the head. 'No – but – you know him, surely.'

'I?'

'When you were here last time, when Pontefract fell. I thought I saw him with you then. I assumed him for some colleague.'

Tarrant?

Back at the dairy, Thurloe learned that Lyle had returned and left again, but this time they knew where. Thurloe followed him, to the house of the late Reverend George Beaumont.

From the outside the house was normal, anonymous. Inside it was madness. Every room had been devastated: floorboards ripped up, plaster chipped away, furnishings slashed, cupboards hanging open or roughly dismantled. In his first bewilderment, wandering uneasily through the ground-floor rooms, skirting holes and stepping over debris, Thurloe imagined that Lyle had just done this in some bizarre berserker frenzy.

Then he realized the chaos for what it was: this was an investigation; this was the Government – or that fraction of it led by Thomas Scot – trying to discover, trying to understand. Thurloe thought of the confusion in his own head, and saw it embodied in this mayhem.

In a first-floor room he found Lyle, pensively running his fingers down a window pane, as if it was this most transparent thing that hid the answer he had not found elsewhere.

'Miss a piece?'

Lyle turned fast, alert. His face was dark against the window, and Thurloe couldn't see the expression. Lyle grunted. 'It's easier when you don't let 'em blow it up first.'

'Seems to have the same effect.'

Lyle looked around the room. 'Careful man. He hadn't left much to find. Good habits.'

'This was Beaumont, wasn't it? The priest they – we – hanged for communicating with the Royalists in Pontefract.'

'Mm.' He began to come closer, stepping carefully and intermittently looking around at the destruction he'd created. 'He was their channel in and out. We've had the place ever since. Giving it up now.'

'You knew for a while – before you arrested him, I mean?'

Lyle paused by a table and, perversely, righted a mug that was lying on its side. He looked up. 'A little while.'

Thurloe was somehow both committed to the game and tired of it. 'But you didn't find anything more about their system?'

He could see the face clearly now. Lyle was watching him; then shrugged. *Does he not tell me because he assumes I know, or because he does not want me to know?* 'We spotted a courier once. Suppose he was a courier – it was odd – didn't fit the normal pattern. Anyway, our soldiers tracked him west a day or two but lost him.'

He watched Thurloe a moment more, then lost interest and started forwards.

A courier? 'I assume that any reports – anything you intercepted, anything you found – were all passed to Scot, in London. It would be recorded there.'

Lyle stopped, not in front of Thurloe but to his side, and smiled. 'Yes, Thurloe. It would.'

He brushed past, and disappeared into the next room.

Thurloe left.

As he opened the front door and stepped into the daylight, there was a boy suddenly in front of him.

The boy was even more startled than he was. He hesitated, held out a tightly folded paper, then pulled it back again.

Thurloe waited.

'I've a letter, sir. For the Reverend Beaumont. But I didn't know what to. . .' He looked down at the paper, then up. 'Him being hanged. And that was months back. I didn't. . .'

'All's right, boy. I'll take it.' Thurloe gave him a penny.

Thurloe turned and stepped back into the house, then stopped. Paper in hand, he looked up towards the sounds of Lyle making his farewell round of the wrecked building.

Then he turned again, slipped the paper into his coat, and re-entered the daylight, closing the door quietly behind him.

$\sim$

To The Reverend George Beaumont, Doncaster

Dear Reverend,

I have been a wanderer these four months, since despair at what was becoming of Doncaster and Pontefract sent me into the bitterest roads of winter, and only now that I am, by the great kindness and mercy of God himself only, come unto some new station of rest and relative permanence, do I find the time to communicate with him who was most often in my thoughts as I roamed the land.

You were ever my guide in those dark evenings — and there have been many lonely rootless moments since that I have wished for your excellent mixture of principle with pragmatism.

And what has become of our young friend with the 'Levelling' tendencies? You know that I was ever uneasy at the dallying between the partisans of the King's interest and those most restless spirits in the Army, however tempting the possibilities for the Royal cause. But I confess a fondness for that lad; so handsome, and so earnest. Has his great scheme come to anything yet?

I continue to move, of course, in the same circles as I was used to; the followers of the Royal interest are a little forlorn in these days, but in any gathering there is always at least one with the blood and the heart for a scheme or a dare, and it keeps one's spirits alive. I mention it because only last week I listened to a man still very convinced that the Crown's dutiful obligations to all of its people equally, and the desire of those Levelling men for a society more flat and more free and without the traditional gradations, were principles in natural harmony, and he hinted that there were still those of both persuasions pursuing such an alliance most heartily. I confessed myself openly both weary and wary of such schemes, but it brought to my mind our young friend and our many conversations in strange furtive Doncaster, with soldiers at every window.

I do not wish to put you to extra burden, but it would please me much to hear just a line of the town. You may write to me as J. H., at the Sign of the Bear in York, and through my friends your words will surely find me, as they were ever wont to do, wherever I may have strayed.

Your friend.

May, 1649

[SS C/T/49/18]

Thurloe read it three times straight. To discipline his mind, he tried to hold his focus on the character of the writer – his doubts, his loneliness, his melancholy – but kept returning to the alarming implications of the middle paragraphs.

And what could he do with this? He was not the intended reader. Nor was he the proper man to receive and interpret the letter on behalf of Parliament. Through irritation and impetuousness he had in effect become the Reverend Beaumont. A dead man.

To admit his false status in either direction seemed difficult now. While his heart burned a little at the ambiguity of this strange position, Thurloe's head was wondering at its possibilities.

Sir, this day the royal [assume crown(s), from context] have been found in the Palace of [assume Westminster, from context], and transported

179

under guard east of the city to the Tower. No more is known of what is planned thereafter.

[SS C/S/49/40 (LATER DECYPHERING)]

Shay never considered landscape as other than terrain: barriers, weaknesses, avenues of attack or escape. So he was watching Jacob, rather than the flower beds in which the old man bobbed and prodded. People were terrain too: obstacles or advantages, vulnerabilities or strengths.

But Shay's consideration moved naturally from Jacob to his task, and from the task to the garden, and for a moment he tried to see the fascination or the attraction in the geometric plots, the regimental divisions of plants, the games with space and colour.

Jacob was walking towards him, carrying a small cloth bag, leaves and a stalk protruding from the top of it. Some new exotic curiosity for the garden. Shay wondered what the arrangement was between Anthony Astbury and old Jacob. Astbury was the sort of man who would want one of the modern gardens, but he probably left Jacob to get on with the details. The old man was more than just gnarled hands and strong shoulders; lettered too, presumably.

'Good soil is it, Jacob?'

Jacob made a noise which Shay took for agreement.

'A few generations of Astburys adding to the mix, eh?'

Jacob liked this. 'Aye, sir. 'Tween them and the dung he's nice and rich.' A watchful smile. 'Family are mostly up at the church. But there's a dozen or more dogs hereabouts; couple of servants maybe. And, uh. . .' He scratched his nose.

'That soldier. Came to see George last autumn and died.'

Jacob looked at him again. 'Aye, sir. 'Sright. Out in the orchard.'

'We'll all get there, eh Jacob?' The agreement noise. 'Jacob, you helped George burn some papers. Just before he left for the war – that last time.'

Nothing from Jacob.

'Was there a book among them? Large book – like a ledger?'

The old eyes were pale and sharp, and they watched Shay a moment. *Not remembering, but deciding.* 'No, sir. Th'weren't.'

Shay grunted, indifferent. 'Well. I'll go and pick out a plot for myself, eh?' But Jacob was off, his latest protégé cradled carefully in his hand.

Jacob the phlegmatic. Jacob the lettered. Shay turned and watched him go. *Jacob ruling the garden, collecting rare deliveries from across Europe.*

Next to the Jug Inn in Stoke, where Astbury received his correspondence: an apothecary's shop.

Jacob the gardener: another glimpse of how George Astbury had run his affairs?

— ⁓ ⁓

> *Sir, the [assume crowns, from context] of the Kings of England having previously been found inside the Palace of [assume Westminster, from context], and taken privily and securely to the Tower, [presumably Oliver Cromwell] now begins to think that they should be destroyed utterly, that they offer henceforth no temptation nor possibility of a re-crowning of any King in England. [Presumably Cromwell] is also jealous of the money that may be gained for his cause by the mere value of the gold. The timing of this destruction may not be long hence, although [presumably Cromwell] will seek to have his view endorsed by his confederates, such is its magnitude.*
>
> [SS C/S/49/56 (LATER DECYPHERING)]

— ⁓ ⁓

At this time, the Widow Carroll kept a house in St Mary's Gate, in Derby, with her nieces. St Mary's Gate was one of the unmarked borders of the town, between the affluent centre and the slums beyond. It was a street of trade, of bustle, of the ebb and flow of rich and poor, fine clothes brightening the mud and every kind of accent to be heard haggling; so the Widow Carroll and her nieces lived unremarked, although the nieces might fetch a second glance in their regular visits to church.

Derby neither knew nor cared whether there had ever been a Mr Carroll, or the exact link between widow and nieces. A set of women living alone must find some convenient tale or other and, after all, the establishment was intended precisely for the temporary escape from family bonds. At the Widow's, reached by any of a number of alleys and then a discreet side door, a man might find exultation, inspiration or obliteration, a memory or a forgetting, or just a few minutes of warmth in the night-time of the world.

Michael Manders was an occasional guest. In visits to the Widow's he had passed from ill-disguised ignorance to a confident pose of bravado, and he would tell select acquaintances that it allowed him to pursue his more appropriate romances without unseemly urges complicating them. The Widow's had been one of his first destinations on his return from the dream-like rescue of the two strange old men at Nottingham Castle, a chance to recapture his certainty and his poise, and several months later it had more than done its work.

Coming downstairs into the under-lit parlour, groin aching cosily and the last of a goblet of wine in his hand, he found the Widow waiting for him as always. As always the suggestion of a curtsey, and then she was passing him his cloak. After the cloak, the hat, and as he took it Manders noticed a fragment of paper protruding from under the ribbon that circled the crown.

A little stab of confusion; an innocuous paper snake in this paradise.

His eyes shifted up to the small impassive face of the Widow, but hers were down. Why would she—? Who would know—? Instinctively he started to speak, but she had turned away, and what would he have said anyway?

Manders was suddenly uneasy in the place, a flush of innocence or piety lurching in him, and he hurried out and away. He got well clear, the hat still clutched in his two hands, before he pulled the paper from under the ribbon and held it up under a lantern.

A small square of paper, folded once. On it a single word: 'Shenley', with the number 1 below it.

The arcane message made the discomfort worse. Manders stared at the mad puzzle a moment longer, then crumpled and thrust it into a pocket and hurried from the alleys into the more familiar part of town.

A life: John Blakiston was born in Sedgefield, in County Durham, and baptized in Durham Cathedral, where his father held a post. But from that bewildering splash onwards, Blakiston and his father would only move apart on matters of faith. Blakiston senior's resistance to the newer religious teachings put him in harmony with his King, but in growing disagreement with his son. John Blakiston's success as a young man of business – in textiles and then in coal – made him increasingly impatient with the conservatism and hierarchism of his father and the other men of influence in the locality. Puritanism started as a practical and psychological comfort to Blakiston, and became a growing conviction. The influence of his relationship with his father on this trend is only speculation, as is the influence of his wife, an older widow who brought into the relationship a merchant's fortune and a strong reforming belief.

Increasingly influential in his region, and opposed to the tendencies of the King, Blakiston was a Member of Parliament in the early 1640s and then Mayor of Newcastle in 1645: a man of wealth, a man of prominence, and a man in accord with the times. It was a surprise to no one when he was one of the first to sign the King's death warrant.

By June of 1649 he was in his mid-forties, a man of stately reputation but still fit and active. It was accordingly more of a surprise when, having eaten his usual hearty midday meal and set out for his usual walk afterwards, John Blakiston was found under a tree, his face locked in a torment, dead.

His death was ascribed variously to a heart attack, to shock, and to the work of demons peculiarly active in the north-east that summer. Such are the times.

The times are also of rumour, and suspicion, and such a chatter of papers as no human society has known before. Thomas Scot held a paper in each hand, and he presented the first to Thurloe and Tarrant.

A crumpled page – read, crushed in anger, and then re-smoothed.

Those who followed Blakiston's pen into infamy, shall follow his soul into damnation.

[SS C/T/49/22]

'The surgeon said it was natural.' Tarrant didn't offer it as contradiction, merely the only related fact he could find.

'Cut off a man's head, he dies,' Scot said sharply; 'that's natural. Cut his throat and he bleeds to death, naturally. Poison him and he dies, and that's natural too.'

He handed over the second paper.

To all Gentle-men who have shared BLAKISTONE's deeds and dreams: this levelling is not that for which we fought a war, nor is it that for which we killed a King. More shall fall as he. Signed, Mark Anthony.

[SS C/T/49/23]

'This one hardly makes sense,' Thurloe said.

'Royalist assassins make sense,' Scot snapped back. 'We have trifled with these traitors for too long.'

Tarrant produced a noise from his throat, of agreement.

'One of these can't be true,' Thurloe said quietly. 'And since it's unlikely that they'd be circulating at the same time by accident, I'm somehow less convinced by both. Perhaps Tarrant's surgeon was right after all.'

Scot's head dropped closer, the nose and jaw jutting forward. 'You do concede that Blakiston is dead, do you, Thurloe? You do concede that there is someone out there circulating these threats?' He stood again, as if suddenly repulsed. 'And you know what effect these will be having around the town.' He turned and stalked away, Thurloe nodding thoughtfully and watching him go.

'Old man's unhappy.' Tarrant said it with a strange pride of knowledge, and an expression that made it then an accusation. He leaned closer. 'Because he doesn't like these conspiracies.'

'Mm.' Thurloe was deliberately avoiding Tarrant's face, and comparing the two papers. 'Also, presumably, because he too signed the King's death warrant.'

Thomas Balfour at dice: a compact and silent rock at the table, hands moving minimally and mechanically, eyes flicking around the faces of the others, then down to the dice. Ivory eyes that jump and then settle, the pupils hard and fixed: aces.

He felt the stiffness in his neck, and the first drifts of wine-fog at the edge of his brain. He'd been here long enough, now. Not too much longer. He was up, but hard-fought and barely, and soon he'd get reckless.

Patter and rattle and click across the table. Good to be a dicing man: a game of mental stamina, an experience of intensity, a world for serious men only. A fellowship of lonely concentrating men. Vyse, he knew, was scared by the dark disreputability, and the cheerless focus made Manders uneasy; they would never accompany him here.

Patter and rattle and click across the table, his eyes jumped after the dice, and he reached for his wine. Some unnatural catch in the movement, an extra touch of confusion on the margin of his brain – enough; he set down the goblet without drinking – and then felt, distinctly, the pull of a hand reaching into his pocket.

Eyes momentarily wide and hard, and then calculation: *How well do I know this place? How well do I know these men?*

He sat back; resisted the urge to reach for the violated pocket. The wall was close behind him – unwindowed; he could visualize it – and the only two spectators were across the room. The dice chattered again, but he was oblivious. The only movement in his widened vision was a servant, leaving with a tray.

Patter and rattle and click across the table, and he stood, gave an empty gesture of reassurance to the few eyes that had watched him, and followed the man out. The door gave onto a muddy yard, the servant trudging across it towards an outhouse with the tray ill-balanced. Come at him from the side? More chance of being seen. How to follow? Balfour set off across the yard after his man, trying to match the timing of the paces but making his own longer. At the outhouse, at the door, with that tray, he'll be more distracted.

Across the yard, a fierce clutch at a shoulder and the servant wrenched round and the tray slewing against the wall and clattering and squelching into the mud and Balfour's forearm slamming the man back against the wall and a knife-point at his throat.

'I'm a charitable man,' he hissed, 'but at my own choosing. I'll take it back or I'll take your tongue.'

A high choke: 'What— I took – I took nothing!' The blade-point pricking the skin, and a yelp: 'Before God! Check – check!'

What had been in the pocket, after all?

'A stranger – paid me a shilling – if I put a paper in your pocket!'

Balfour switched hands on the knife, felt for the pocket, felt the paper inside. Eased back half a pace, and pulled it out. The man took his chance and bolted, stumbling and sliding across the yard and away into the darkness.

Back on the edge of the dice room, unwatched, Balfour unfolded the paper next to a lantern. A single word: 'Cross', with the number 3 written below it.

He collected his cloak and his meagre winnings, and left, confusion and then half a smile.

———

Henry Vyse was early for his customary rendezvous with Manders and Balfour, and he was pacing and impatient in the church porch when they arrived one after the other.

'You're late!'

'I was exact to time.' Balfour. 'You were hasty, Hal. What sport today, gentlemen?'

'Wait!' Vyse again. 'I have to tell you – the strangest incident. . .' The others turned back to the porch, studying the pale excited face in its gloom. 'Yesterday evening, I went to St John's folly, for – well—'

Balfour: 'For a liaison. We know.'

Manders, face full and hearty: 'Ah, sweet Charlotte! It is still sweet Charlotte, is it not? The fairy princess of Rounceby Hall?'

'Well, I don't—'

'Charlotte Adair. We know.'

'Great Gods, Vyse, if I'd been at her this long I'd have—'

Vyse lurching forward, hot and hand on dagger: 'If you even think that thought Manders, I'll cut your throat.'

'Steady, old fellow. A thousand pardons if I've sullied the dream.'

'She didn't come, anyway.'

'Ah. Sorry for you there, old lad. Her sister, now—'

'Listen, damn you! Time by time she is unable to come, and she – well, she leaves a small note – in a place known only to us.' A jovial Manders opening to speak, then Balfour's hand on his arm. 'There was a note. And a damned sweet one it was too. But inside it – slipped inside it – there was another paper.'

Balfour, colder now: 'For an old sovereign, Hal: a single word, and a number.'

Manders suddenly on edge: 'You too?'

Vyse was wide-eyed. 'You both had notes?' Two nods, and Vyse took a breath. 'But I'll take your sovereign, Tom. Mine has two words.'

Balfour nodded once. 'Very well then, gentlemen.' He shrugged. 'We match notes, I propose.' A glance at each. 'I give you "Cross 3".'

'"Dusk July".'

Finally Manders, with one cautious lick of the lips. '"Shenley 1".'

'But it makes no sense!' Vyse was disappointed.

Balfour shook his head. 'Neither singly nor together.'

Manders held up a ponderous hand. 'Seems likely enough.' The hand was still poised, as if to sanctify the moment. 'The month presupposes a day, and the numbers give it to us; dusk reinforces the idea of rendezvous. You're sure this isn't from the Adair sisters, Hal? The date would be the 13th or the 31st.'

'We'd need a place. And Shenley Cross is more likely than Cross Shenley.'

Vyse: 'Had your notes torn edges? One, at least?'

Three crumpled scraps, smoothed and held neatly together.

'There it is, then.'

'Pretty enough.'

Balfour looked up. 'I think we know from whom this comes, gentlemen, do we not? A message would come to us, and we'd not know how or from whom.' A glance at each again. 'But we're obliged not to hesitate.'

Thurloe found Thomas Scot in his cubicle, gaunt and angular and surrounded by the shelves of papers and books that were his world, a desiccated insect tapping around a dead trunk. As usual the large ledger was open in front of him, among the papers on the desk.

'Master Scot.' Scot looked up, high eyebrows sharpening the expression. 'Master Scot, I'm trying to understand our enemies.'

Scot sat back in the chair, and nodded. 'Very good, Master Thurloe. Quite right.' For a moment he looked rather forlorn, and then the energy flashed back into his face. 'Do not underestimate them; do not weaken for a moment. We must – we must – eradicate them.'

He nodded, agreeing with himself. More softly again: 'Understand them. Yes, that's good, Thurloe.' The old face screwed up. 'But – my counsel to you – do not try to understand too much.' His eyes dropped away. 'Too much understanding creates. . .' – he waved a brittle hand vaguely near his head – 'an overburdening. . .'

Thurloe waited. Eventually he said, 'Who are they? How do they work? At Nottingham I saw recklessness turned into brilliance, a man who could make a whole garrison conform to his design. At Pontefract I saw a man prepared to die for a paper.'

'They have their networks. They have their mercenaries – debased men prepared to sell the ruthlessness they learned in the European wars.'

It was a crude simplification, and they both knew it. Thurloe just looked at Scot, almost sadly. Scot pursed his lips, and glanced down at his ledger.

Thurloe pressed on. 'And the man whom we chased from Doncaster? The man who escaped?'

'A courier.' Thurloe breathed out silently. *I am becoming a little adept at these lures.* 'A sprat. Of no consequence, but he might have told us a thing or two.'

'Part of a chain of communication between the Pontefract garrison and the outside.'

'Yes.'

'I would like to read our reports on Pontefract, please.'

Scot's face pulled back over his teeth, and on an instinct his two spread hands covered the pages in front of him. 'I understand, Thurloe. I do. But too much information. . . in too many hands. . . it creates misunderstandings. Tensions. I would not want any mistaken assumptions, which you might make in all innocence, to further trouble my relationship with Master Cromwell, who has my fullest support, as a favoured instrument of the Creator himself.'

Thurloe watched him, and looked again at the double page under the fingers. Columns: short references to the left, text to the right. A summary of reports?

'You will have to rely, Master Thurloe' – Scot was sharp again, in eye and tone – 'on your own considerable talents, won't you? You will bring us something fresh, perhaps.'

Thurloe nodded. 'I'll try, Master Scot.'

Shenley Cross, dusk on the 13th of July, three shadows sheltering under a tree, hunched in cloaks and silent. An insidious apprehension – of wrongdoing, of unworthiness, of the cold.

'We're exposed here.'

'Mm. But we can see if anyone approaches. And we can be seen as three and no more. We are not here by chance.'

A grunt.

From the east, a wind was coming from the distant sea, unsettling the leaves and playing with the horses' manes. Hands adjusted cloaks on shoulders, shifted on reins, stroked a restive animal.

Then, out of the west and the last glow of the sun, a rider came at a canter, a shuddering shadow against the light and a pounding on the ground.

The horses' ears pricked up, and the men shifted too: peering, stretching, glancing at each other's murky faces. The rider loomed quickly, the noise growing and the shadow shading into horse and man, arms on reins and a high broad body. At last the horse juddered to a halt in front of the three, and in the twilight they saw the ghost of Nottingham Castle, the memory of the mill.

He looked at them individually, a brief but intent scrutiny. Balfour had got rid of the moustache.

A nod to each, as if accounting their good order. 'Vyse. Balfour. Manders.' They nodded back, uncertainly.

'My name is Mortimer Shay.' The confidence bespoke a new beginning. 'I'm glad to find you here, truly.'

He sat up on the horse, stretching his shoulders. 'You are crossing the bounds, gentlemen. I give you fair warning, and I urge you to heed me close, and make your choice with no boy's bravado, for those days are gone from you for ever.' Their eyes were fixed on him. 'Ride with me now, and I promise you no protection of law or grace. I fight for what we know to be worthy and pure, but I fight in the shadows, and in those shadows I have lost sight of the scruples of justice and the little details of Christ's morality.'

Again the scrutiny of the darkling faces. 'Ride with me now, and we shall try the mettle of this new world of theirs.' He pulled at his reins in the gloom, and the horse jumped and spun and carried him away. A moment, a glancing and a swallowing, and then the shadows – three of them – hurried after him into the west.

***

By the beginning of the third week in July, Thurloe was among the last ripples of the English Midlands before the terrain bunches up into the peaks and moors of the north. The road moved slow and listless through the humid morning, pulling itself up valleys and falling away invisible behind turns in the hills. He remembered from before the feeling of a place lost to the rest of the country.

There were no signs or markers to show the road, and few other humans to guide him. The road drifted among the folds in the landscape, edged with scrubby hedge or nothing. Then the oak, as he remembered it, and an opening in the hedge and a track disappearing into woods. Buried within the hedge end a fallen stone marker, with the name of the house smoothed away.

The track only turned past the woods – another trick of the gentle slopes – took him out of sight of the main road, then straightened. Thurloe and his horse were at the mouth of a perfect avenue of beech trees, not yet fully mature, but healthy and exactly aligned and spaced and drawing the eye instantly to a house at the end, its details blurred by the summer foliage.

He'd come via Doncaster. The Adjutant was still there, glad to take a drink with another quiet, intelligent man and talk a little. He had told Thurloe of the chasing of the courier. The government man in Doncaster – that would be Lyle – demanding three soldiers for an errand one morning, follow a man and tell where he went – always these little errands, and the Adjutant had learned not to ask questions – a sordid side to a war that was already sordid enough, wouldn't you say? Yes, Thurloe would say. The soldiers had followed their man as ordered, throughout the day; then, near Leek, as evening brought tiredness and gloom, a mistake and a scuffle and an exchange of shots, the man they were following escaping into the gathering night. Wounded, they'd said. For sure.

Leek: the courier had been heading towards the line of march of the Scottish army that had been invading for King Charles. Thurloe had checked the dates: the courier had been tracked and lost just a day or two before the battle at Preston had destroyed that army and the King's last hope. Was that significant?

And was any of this connected to the strange suggestion in J. H.'s letter to the Reverend Beaumont? An association between Royalists and Levellers was surely improbable. But the suggestion was troubling enough. And – he'd checked – the suggestion had been made elsewhere, too; publicly. Border in *The Kingdom's Weekly Intelligencer* had proposed it, and there had been hints elsewhere. *What path is there through this?*

Alone as he was this time, the strict discipline of the beech avenue struck him uneasily. Out of the casual chaos of the English landscape, hidden in the heart of the country, someone had forced precision. It made the house at the end of the avenue somehow ominous. The brick and the yellow stone window frames glowed in the morning, but the windows were blank and dull. The beauty of the place, the harmony of the building within the scented silence, reinforced the idea of something illicit concealed among the hills, far from the dirty dangers of England at war. Thurloe stood under the warm frontage, watching the creeper as it started to explore the window sills and the moss blotching the flagstones, and trying to place it all in the same world as London, and Doncaster, and skirmishes in the twilight. Three shallow steps up to the door.

An afternoon in an inn, with a map and a mug of wine. And memories. He'd been in the district himself, hadn't he, not so long afterwards? His seedy work of scrabbling money from compounding Royalists. The Astburys. Astbury House was near Leek. A rattling of memories in his mind. Something in the records he'd had back then: one of the Astburys was somehow very close to the King; that's why he'd been given particular instructions to press the family. The reference had been vague, but somehow – had it been copied from somewhere else? – taking for granted an understanding that it no longer gave.

And flashing among the rest, another memory: the young woman. An Astbury daughter, he'd guessed. In memory, there were golden streaks among the waves of her hair, but it had certainly been long and waving, emphasizing the slender body. Burning hottest of all was the memory of her anger – had she even said anything to him, though? – something raw and human within the world of careful compromises and little deceits. Thurloe tried to see himself wryly – the healthy joke of a married man looking twice at a lovely girl – and tried telling himself that the memory of the lithe body and the face hadn't distorted his logic.

In the present again: the front door, large panels of cracked and fading grey wood, opened.

It wasn't her.

A maid, pretty enough, but not her. Not as far as Thurloe could remember. He introduced himself in general terms, and asked for Sir Anthony Astbury.

Sir Anthony Astbury had gone early to a neighbour. Perhaps the mistress would see him. *Mistress? Astbury was a widower, surely.* The door closed again.

The blank panels of the door. The warmth of the morning across his shoulders. The distant bleating of sheep.

The door opened, and Thurloe was ushered in, and up a flight of stairs to an open landing. 'The mistress will see you, sir.' The maid nodded towards a door. 'She's just in there.'

The maid trotted down the stairs again, leaving Thurloe adrift on the landing. After a minute, he sat on one of two dark oak chairs that guarded a table under a portrait of a man in court dress from the previous century.

After several minutes, he was still there, occasionally straining his head up to the portrait above him, more often glancing towards the door. *Am I forgotten? Am I being tested?*

He walked to the door, and knocked.

He knocked again, and from inside heard words, indistinct.

He opened the door.

It was her.

Thurloe was cataloguing the details of the young woman against his memory – the hair – couldn't see any gold in it – slender body – a face somehow passionate – before he realized that she was only wearing a nightshirt – or some kind of undershirt. Loose, translucent white, billowing with her body as she'd turned. He hurried an apology and retreated, pulling the door closed softly, as if she might not have noticed, while her eyes still burned at him.

Rachel Astbury let out a breath, and sat down on a stool. Then she stood again, and watched the door.

What am I doing?

She ran her hands down her flanks, clenched them, and released them.

Some kind of Government man visiting the house. Some threat legal or financial, perhaps. How should she receive him?

Should I have received him at all?

She had no memory of her mother in the role. *How would my father receive him?* But she could not make his fussy politenesses hers.

How would Shay do it?

Shay the rationalist; the manipulator; the fighter.

To receive him formally is respectful. But I do not wish to respect him. To put him at his ease is appropriate, but I wish him uneasy. The parlour has too much of women's humility about it. My father's study is a man's room – it would be his more than mine.

Joanna's swallowed surprise as she'd instructed her to send the man up. Another of Miss Rachel's peculiars.

It is theoretically dangerous to be alone with this man. But the chances that he has come here to do me harm are slight. It is improper to be alone with this man. But I know what I do, and my family cannot think me any more wilful than they already do; so only he can feel uncomfortable.

Thurloe, outside, heard this time a clearly articulated invitation to enter. Again he lifted the latch and stepped in.

She was still undressed. The light through the window made the nightshirt glow white.

Rachel saw the effect she had on the man, and it gave her a moment to look at him. Not a soldier; no uniform, no obvious weapon. Dark clothes, and simple, but the hair worn long – not the austere styling of the puritans. The face: open, no cheekbones but strong nose and jaw, and a high forehead. Something about the eyes: a depth, a melancholy.

'Who are you?' she asked.

'My name is John Thurloe.'

'What are you?'

'I work for the Government.' *What am I, indeed?* 'I am charged with. . . protecting the sec—'

'Which Government? The usurpers and regicides and demagogues in London?'

'If you wish.'

'I did not think I had any choice.'

'It is the Government. You may choose to accommodate yourself to it or not. You would prefer an absence of government?'

'You people killed my uncle.'

'I am truly sorry. I would gladly wish that there had been any milder way of settling the differences of this country.'

Rachel watched him carefully, looking for a hint of superiority or insincerity, but she could find none. His eyes seemed even sadder.

Did she remember him?

'I am Rachel Astbury,' she said. She stepped forward to offer her hand. He could see her thighs moving against the dress and, faintly, the suggestion of her breasts. 'You are welcome to the house.'

He took the hand, cautiously. 'Sir Anthony Astbury's. . .?'

'Sir Anthony Astbury's out visiting.'

'I mean to say, what are you to Sir Anthony Astbury?'

She smiled, and was lovely. The smile brought an extra spark into the large brown eyes. He remembered her anger; it was a face for life, for emotions. 'How silly of me. I am his daughter.'

She was toying with him, childishly. He made an instinctive 'ah' of acknowledgement, but doubt had made him thoughtful again. *Is this girl some fantastical dream? Some natural naïf?* The probability was low. *So this is performance, and I am chosen as audience. Why?*

'Miss Astbury, I apologize for disturbing you. I was in the district and I had one or two questions for your father – perhaps for you.'

'And if I refuse to answer?'

'That is your choice.'

'Are you going to torture me?'

'Probably not. You might answer the question, though, just in case that I—'

'We know all about it: the savageries of your Army; your prisons; the kidnapping of children for ransom.'

Flirtation was becoming frustration. 'Of course. How do you know all about it?'

'Your practices are no secret. You are the shame of Europe. I'm not afraid to say it.'

'Obviously not.' *Is this ignorance or spitefulness or both?* 'But whatever you say of the Government, as an intelligent woman you should consider basing your private opinions on directly experienced facts and testimonies, and not the mummery play lies of your penny news-sheets.'

'You can without any difficulty contradict me, but it is truth which you cannot contradict.'

'I don't mind you keeping your pride up with fantastical propaganda at my expense, Miss Astbury. But I don't like to hear Plato wholly misapplied to justify it.'

Rachel's chin lifted for the next defiant spurt, but she caught herself. Her attempted superiority was becoming silliness. She frowned, and Thurloe watched the thought in her eyes. 'Well then,' she said, and it was a quieter Rachel Astbury now. 'Between your prison and your Plato you seem to have me. What is your question?'

'You mentioned an uncle, killed. That would be Sir George Astbury? Who died in the battle at Preston last autumn?'

'It would.'

'Once again, I offer my condolences.'

'I'd prefer my uncle, or your defeat.'

'I'll bear that in mind. Your uncle was very close to the late King, I think.'

'I believe so.'

'He served him in some. . . official capacity? Military?'

'I don't know. He wasn't a soldier, particularly.'

'What title did he have? In the royal household, I mean.'

Back in the world of politics and family and men, Rachel found part of herself outside the conversation. 'None that I know of.' Why was everyone so interested in George Astbury? Shay too—

The thought of Shay made her cautious. What would Shay think of her in this conversation? *Will he be proud of my boldness and my cleverness?* What if he heard her discussing Uncle George like this? Was there anything wrong in it?

'As I said, Miss Astbury, I have to involve myself with little administrative details of the Army and security. I'm trying to clarify one incident from that time – last autumn – just before Preston.' She was frowning again. 'A day or so before, a soldier came here I think.'

Why should he care about the soldier?

'Wounded, perhaps.'

Why should I care?

'One evening. Perhaps you remember.'

Why these games of mind and word? Suddenly Rachel wanted to be out of the conversation, to strip off the veils of meaning and posture.

'Yes. What of it?'

Thurloe's heart kicked at him. 'What do you remember of the incident?'

'There was nothing to remember.' She was colder now, indifferent. 'He arrived in the storm, badly wounded. During the night he died.'

'Who was he?'

'Don't you know?' Too distracted now even to care about the point.

'What did he say? Had he any message?'

'Nothing. Only my uncle spoke to him. Then he died.' She shrugged, and it made her seem younger. 'Now you must excuse me, Mr Thurloe.

I – I probably shouldn't have received you like this.'

'I'm very grateful that you did. Thank you, Miss Astbury.'

She offered her hand again – it brought Thurloe close to the top of her breasts in the open collar of the nightshirt, and close again to those eyes – but the life had gone from them, and the hand was withdrawn quickly and she had turned away.

Sir Anthony Astbury walked in through the front door as Thurloe was coming down the stairs. The old man insisted on receiving him – by turns suspicious and scared and hostile and ingratiating. Thurloe contrived some trivium left over from his previous visit, which successfully unsettled Astbury and then relaxed him when it was not immediately threatening, and presented himself as a respectful clerk anxious merely to keep all in order, which he knew was exactly what suited Astbury. The old man chattered of his desire to be co-operative, pressed wine on the deferential young official, and became quite lax in his tolerance of the new ways. Thurloe assured him that his host's absence had been no trouble, that Miss Rachel Astbury had offered him a very correct welcome, and repeated his condolences at the regrettable loss of Sir Anthony's brother the previous autumn. Miss Rachel had told him a curious story of a soldier coming out of the night just before Preston, and he hoped it might clarify some little detail for the Army: soldiers – a moment of shared superiority – seemed to care about such things.

Sir Anthony Astbury confirmed his daughter's story exactly but, even over a second glass of wine, could add no more. Nor could he be tempted into any indiscretion on the exact role his brother George had played in the royal administration.

The grey front door closed behind Thurloe, and he trotted back between the beech ranks, glancing over his shoulder at the house and wondering at its histories.

❦

Josiah Talbot was later home, to his damp two rooms in Shadwell, than he had planned. But what had he to do at this home, anyway, and what sort of home was it, anyway, close enough to the river and London for the stench and the mould, but just far enough away to remind him of his distance from success? Was there wrong in a man taking a drink of an afternoon?

He did not see the two men as they saw him, nor as they followed him, nor as they closed in once he was into the little house. These days he never saw the mighty Tower of London looming over his house. But while he stood for a moment in the centre of the first room, searching for a reason to have come home, the back room produced a masked figure and behind him he heard the door and spun to see a second.

These are the incidental perils of a life on the edge of politics and the edge of poverty; these are the expectations of his fate. Josiah Talbot had in him drink and despair enough for an edge of nasal defiance in his voice. 'What from Satan are you, then, eh? What—'

'Josiah Talbot.' The voice was flat and heavy. Two men standing close in front of him now. Not so tall, to speak of. But solid. Was the voice a young man's?

His name fell like a verdict of guilt.

Again: 'Josiah Talbot: time by time you have been wont to take a shilling for producing a reforming letter. You have been silent of late.'

'I haven't—'

'We fear you may have strayed. We fear you have grown sentimental for the King.'

'I never—'

'You took a shilling or two from the King's friends, too, Talbot.'

'Why shouldn't a man—'

'Tonight you pay, Talbot.'

Was this it? Was this death? Two masked devils in his shitty den, booming bland treasons at him?

'Tonight you leave this place, Talbot, or tonight you die in it.'

⌁

By this time the great fortress of London had been standing guard at the eastern approach to the city – the direction from which all evils had come – for almost six full centuries. Time and prosperity had allowed other, finer buildings to rise, and fall, and rise yet finer within the city walls.

The great grey sentry grew only wider and more solid, as the fears and fancies of England's Kings gave birth to new walls and new towers, so that generation by generation the fortress seemed to spread like a family, each new crenellated offspring adding the fashions of its time to the old inherited outlines. Its features and its functions were innumerable and ever-changing, and so history has found it impossible to know the Kings' vast and rambling fortress-palace as anything more than simply 'the Tower'.

On this night, at its darkest hour, there were three men huddling against the eastern wall of the Tower. Time and some long-forgotten mason's hastiness had produced a flaw at the foot of the wall at this point, which had become a crumbling of mortar and a loosening of stone, and then over the years a low opening in the wall. Now the opening was a gap three feet high and as many wide, and a rough cascade of stones slumped into the moat which slept still and stagnant a couple of feet below. Tonight a small rowing boat had been tied to one of those stones, and the three men had climbed slowly and awkwardly out of it, hissing curses behind covered mouths and clambering on hands and feet like primitive scavengers over the heap of stones and bones and last week's vegetables.

The stench was foul, a mocking acid reek, and the first man's face was clenched and his throat torturing him with rank retches as he neared the top of the stones and extended a hand towards the opening at the base of the wall. Feet planted rigid. Must be silent, must try to breathe. To reach the top is to reach a flat place, a forgotten courtyard of grass, fresh grass and the fresh night air. The hand found a firm hold in the opening and the muscles started to tighten and the body moved forward into the opening – and then flung back, a gangling twist of limbs as he pressed himself against the wall and tried not to breathe.

Movement inside the opening. There was supposed to be no one in this courtyard. But he'd seen movement, a flickering shadow, a pair of legs. Of course the courtyard was used! The kitchen waste wasn't rowing across the moat, was it? Must be silent. Must be still. Three black insects pressed against the grey wall.

The legs stopped in the opening. Then a pair of hands, a fumbling, and a long arc of piss soared over the stones and splashed noisily at the moat edge.

The performance lasted for no more than twenty seconds, but the first man held his rigid tortured pose for a full minute before relaxing, and moving his head forwards again to check that they were alone. Then he turned back, and extended a slow arm down the slope and grabbed the collar of the man below.

His face dropped slowly after the arm, and the words were spat individually in the softest murmur. 'This – was not – how – the name – of – Manders – was – born.'

The reply was softer still. 'Mm. Might be how it dies though, eh? Move, damn you.'

The yard was but thinly grassed, and the stench still carried from the moat in the cold night air, but it was flat and it was dark and, pressed against an inner wall, the three were glad enough. They had to wait a quarter-hour or more in silence, and their minds and their lurching stomachs peopled the black void of the yard with memories and fears and parallel worlds of what might happen or what could be happening instead.

They were waiting for a signal, and when it came it so shattered the utter emptiness of their waiting as to paralyse them for one awful terrified moment. An explosion to the west, from the direction of the city, but directions and civilizations were meaningless in the sudden thump across their night.

Hearts plunging up and hammering and muscles clenching and lurching for control in cramped limbs. Vyse was supposed to be counting, only realized he'd forgotten to start after one second, spent another second in a shock of failure, then gasped a desperate 'three' into the scrabbling confusion. Manders pushing a small barrel against a door, Balfour behind him with a tinderbox, and Vyse hissing the numbers out with new-found restraint. 'Nine. Ten.' No one should come out this way, the old man had said, but what if the old man was wrong? No spark. 'Twelve. Thirteen.' Manders with the short fuse ready, other hand on his sword hilt, Vyse swallowing and hissing. 'Fifteen.' No spark. 'Sixteen.' No spark. 'Seventeen.' The door blank in front of them and all their fears crowding mad and formless over their shoulders. 'Eighteen,' and Balfour had the taper lit. 'Nineteen.' Manders holding the fuse up from the barrel with precise fingers. 'Twenty!' and it was lit and now the hiss was coming from the fuse and they scrambled away behind the nearest buttress.

A fuse is an inexact device, and so are two men counting to twenty on opposite sides of a fortress, and a few of the bewildered inhabitants of the Tower – the men who were now waking and wondering and hurrying to the western walls and shouting orders into the darkness and peering out from the arrow-slits of the gatehouse – found their ears and brains playing an extra trick on them: the nagging impression of a second small explosion, this time from the east of the fortress, a kind of strange pre-echo appropriate to this night of demonry and confusion, before the vast roar that blasted into the sky to the west again.

A vast roar, a torrent of sound that shattered the open ground between the city and the fortress and hung heavy in the night sky, and the fickle tricks of the mind were erased in the assault on sense. Then, as the Tower's sentries stared from the turrets and walls and gaped and prayed, they found something new to wonder at: a great blaze had started up on the open ground between their defences and the first buildings of the city, burning in fierce unearthly yellows and blues. There was nothing there to burn, surely, no structure or waste, at least there hadn't been before night. Thinking their faces hidden in the darkness, despite the weird glow that flickered over the walls, the men in the fortress worried at their forgotten sins.

By chance, the Deputy Constable of the Tower was in residence that night. Once he had wrestled his way to the walls, and once he had passed a few moments in yellow-faced awe and unease staring at the fire, he gathered himself enough to order a detachment of sentries to sally out and investigate. By the time they approached the fire, edging closer with public bravado and private fears, the flames were already dying down. As the soldiers watched, the last ghostly veils of yellow and blue danced and waved in front of them and then vanished into the night, and the soldiers were left alone again in the void.

It was fully half an hour before – hurrying and shame-faced and bewildered – the reverberation of that smaller explosion to the east reached Deputy Constable Tichborne: on the other side of the fortress, masked men had battered their way into the outbuilding under the Salt Tower that had become the temporary home of the Mint; surprising the man left on duty there, they had escaped with the ceremonial crown and jewels of the Stuart Kings, which had been taken there for destruction.

⌐ ⌐

In the silent hours of the early morning, another explosion near the Tower – among the slum houses to the east – and then a fire. Buckets were hurried from the river. But the house of Josiah Talbot, sometime pamphleteer and now known for a drunk and a nuisance, was badly damaged.

A detachment of soldiers from the Tower was hastily at the scene: another blaze coming out of this bewitched night, burning in angry brains and flickering in fearful hearts. They stood and watched while the civilians flirted with the flames with their buckets, then scuffed aimlessly through the smoking ruin, replying intermittently to the scornful comments from the crowd who now watched them.

Of Josiah Talbot himself there was no sign.

⌐ ⌐

TO THE LORD PRESIDENT OF THE COUNCIL OF STATE,
BEING A REPORT ON THE EVENTS AT THE FORTRESS OF LONDON,
AND THE SEIZURE OF THE LATE KING'S JEWELS THEREFROM.

Sir,
the facts of these events may be given briefly. Shortly after midnight, on the night of 23rd–24th July, an explosion was made to the west of the Tower. Residue of a small powder barrel in this place supports this. At around the same time, a small group of men had gained entry to the fortress precincts by taking a small boat across the moat at its quietest area and climbing through a point where the wall was age-worn. These men used a small powder charge to gain access through a locked door to the Mint, which has of late been situated in outbuildings between the walls at the east of the fortress. This detonation was covered by a much larger charge set simultaneously on that same ground to the west, where scorching and

displacement of the ground may easily be discerned. This distraction of the inhabitants of the Tower was extended by use of a cart of straw nearby which was set afire immediately afterwards. Residue in the cart suggests that sulphur or some like mineral was employed to make the blaze more terrible. Under these confusions, the raiders, numbering at least three or four, entered the Mint, overmanned the guard who is used to pass the night on the premises but was much stupefied by the explosion, and, threatening violence to the guard if he would not reveal all to them, collected such of the regalia and jewels of the late Charles Stuart that had not yet been destroyed and melted according to the orders of the Council. These valuables were removed out of the fortress, it may be assumed by the same route that their removers gained entrance, and there is no more track of them.

A paper was left in the Mint, and one of the disguised raiders was heard to term it a receipt, declaring that 'Tichborne [Lieutenant Constable here, whose confirmed views against the King and name on the death warrant are widely known] shall not long enjoy the spoils of his crime.' The half-destruction of the house in Shadwell, nearby the scene of the exploit, of one Talbot, known for a pamphleteer inclined by turns to monarchy and more lately to radical ideas, is susceptible to suspicion but not clear link to these events.

It is not the purpose nor proper business of this report to speculate on the identities of the men without more fact, nor to comment on the management of the defences of the Tower. The news of the loss of the jewels, which in truth were already mostly destroyed, are known only to very few, and I have recommended to the Lieutenant Constable that this remain so; the embarrassment of those who know the truth will buy their silence and, should the Council agree, for the rest it might be put out that the royal relics have been destroyed according to the Council's original instruction, and so these events might never be widely known.

24th July 1649

[SS C/T/49/28]

Thurloe had walked a full circuit of the Tower three times, like a carrion crow circling a carcase. His report to the Committee had been clear in his head after one circuit and twenty minutes inside the fortress, examining the Mint and the moat and the forgotten yard and tolerating ten minutes of shame-faced outrage from Tichborne, invoking the Pope and the King and unpurged Royalists and unpurged Parliamentarians for the simple ignominy that someone had lifted his cloak and tickled his purse while he was looking the wrong way.

The reflections of his subsequent circuits of this battleground – from the shadowed corner of the moat, to the blackened earth near the city to the west, up round to Shadwell in the east, and back to the moat again – were not for a report. Not yet.

An explosion of sound and light masks the explosion of a vital doorway, and a whole castle looks the wrong way. *I have been here before.* Nottingham, a man on a horse; a letter. *There is cunning here as well as daring.* The dark, dank end of the moat; the hole in the wall. *There is knowledge here, knowledge as old as these stones.* The message to Tichborne; the abandoned house of a man of fluid loyalty. *How may these be parsed? How do they fit the sentence?* They do not fit. Yet. *These are but hanging prepositions.*

And yet they serve a purpose. Every minute of diffuse speculation moves the crown further off. While Thurloe and his thoughts go in circles, the men on horseback ride straight and away. *These men are creatures of the fog, creatures of the shadows.* Angry stupid Tichborne, who killed a King and now rattles in his emptier fortress; a pamphleteer, whose loyalties all have bought, and whose house may be stolen for a mere device. *These creatures feed on our confusions.*

~ ~

To the Lord President of the Council of State, London

Sir, the Scotchman Montrose has been lately here seeking to beg money and buy soldiers. He has secured one interview at Court, pleading the affinity of thrones in support of the cause of Prince Charles Stuart. So far he has for lack of coin secured few followers, but these few hardy *soldiers and tested, and he tells them he already has men from Sweden too.*

Copenhagen, August 1649.

❧

Sir Mortimer Shay had described precisely the location of the stable, on the edge of the lands of Cheshunt House and within sight of Waltham Abbey, and Henry Vyse found it exactly according to the description. Alone, he pushed open the door and slipped inside. The sun was lancing in white through a hundred gaps in the timbers, but his eyes still took a moment to adjust.

The stable was empty. A thin spread of straw on the earth floor, and two shambling posts holding the roof. Then Shay appeared from the shadow of the far corner.

He looked the question, and Vyse started to speak, then held up an uncertain hand to ask for pause, and returned to the doorway.

A minute later the three of them were standing together in front of Shay: Vyse, Balfour and Manders. Balfour carried a small sack. He stepped forward, crouched, and placed the sack on the floor. Shay found his lips dry. Then Balfour looked up uneasily at the older man.

Vyse said, 'We were too late.'

Balfour pulled the sack open, and there was a frail gleaming in the dust. The ceremonial riches of the Kings of England, one of the greatest collections of historical treasure in Europe, now consisted of half a dozen jewels, a golden spoon and a small golden bowl shaped like an eagle – and one misshapen apple-sized lump that glowed dull. Molten and resolidified, a clumsy golden ball, the ancient crown of the Saxons would be worn no more.

❧

A world away from London, Rachel was walking alone in the garden at Astbury. The garden was a fat luxury of nature, shocking colours in the flowers and plump drowsy bees and, in another quarter of the grounds, pendulous vegetables flaunting themselves among the leaves.

She wanted the paler shades of spring, the sadnesses of autumn. She wanted to be too cold to think.

She wanted Mary to scold her, Mary to laugh at for her prudence, Mary because an older sister was reassurance. Without Mary, her father had no one to act as intermediary to his younger daughter. He worried about her, worried about his inability to communicate adequately to her, and so withdrew into his study and his visits to neighbours who would say to him what he said to them. He was getting thinner.

She spent what time she could with Jacob. It made her feel small again, and away from war and politics and change, to follow him around the gardens and listen to him murmuring softly to his charges, occasionally noticing her and pretending he'd been talking to her. But she was restless, fretted, and it unsettled him.

She hadn't seen Shay for some while, and she wasn't sure she wanted to. He seemed to know her too well, to know the world too well; and he didn't seem to care about any of it.

She kept thinking of John Thurloe: the Government man; the clever, careful man, with sad eyes. She was supposed to hate the Government and its triumph and its oppression; she was supposed to know them all short-lived. Shay would defeat Thurloe and all the men like him. That seemed likely. But for now the only voice for the old world was her father's, peevish and distant.

She wondered about the clever, careful mind, and the sad eyes.

———

Oliver St John was eating when Cromwell entered – he always seemed to be eating when Cromwell entered – and dropped Thurloe's report onto the tablecloth in front of him.

St John took two further bites, scanning the paper dubiously from over the end of the ravaged chicken leg. Then he dropped the leg to the plate, cleared the last lumps of flesh from his teeth with one bulging rotation of his tongue, and wiped his hands on a napkin.

'My man Thurloe grows a little presumptuous, I fear.'

A grunt from Cromwell above him. 'I disagree. He grows more useful and shrewd. Enlightenment is all that we may seek of God, and this young man may be an instrument of it.' Cromwell picked up the paper again, and turned and left. Over his shoulder: 'I think that he may be my man now.'

To Mr J. H., at the Sign of the Bear

Sir,

your letter to the Reverend Beaumont came into my hands, but not immediately, and so I fear you have waited a more than reasonable time for a reply, and perhaps begun to cherish doubts about your correspondent.

I must immediately, and with the greatest regret, tell you the Reverend Beaumont is gone from us, into that greater Kingdom of which he spoke and of which he was so worthy a representative. We must hope that his rewards in that place are brighter than his end in this one, for I must also admit to you that it was ignominious, hanged for having secret communications with Pontefract garrison. I suppose we may say that he died honourably for he died for his principles, whatever those principles, and since I learn that his end was speedy, we may say that he died with God's mercy.

I feel it amiss that I had to read the privy correspondence of two gentlemen, and I hope you will excuse this in the sad circumstances, and yet through your words I inferred that you shared my high opinion of the excellent Beaumont. We met but a few times, and I confess that we did not always agree on politics or principle, yet in those few meetings I could only admire his clarity of intellect and sincerity of belief, and felt ever respected and on my mettle.

I understand from you that the work of the community of active minds of which he was a part goes on. I must confess that I am concerned at the idea of more causes for strife in these beggared islands, yet I am sympathetic with the desire of some men to remove so many false and vain degrees of difference between free Englishmen and their rulers. Do you think that this chatter of a combination between some of the King's friends and the so-called Levellers is more than mere tap-room muttering?

Sir, it would please me much to think that in these hard times there are yet men whose intellects may lift their gazes above those things which divide us, and who may accordingly maintain that kind of civilised relation between educated souls which, among many false and little ideals loose in these times, is surely something worth defending. If you would write to I. S. at the Angel in Doncaster, it will be passed to me. In any case, I hope that I have, by giving you the last sad news of an apparently mutual friend, rendered you some little service, though no more than that due to a true spirit.

[SS C/S/49/100]

$\sim$

By the first hours of August, Shay was through Cumbria and into the Scottish borderlands. He kept to the west, away from the centres of population and the concentrations of the Army. Here he was prey more to local scavengers than to Parliament's militia. The peasants would cut a throat for a shilling, and the decade of war grinding back and forth had left them raw and brutalized.

Hamilton's army had come south across these barrens the year before, with the usual indifferent excesses of troops on the march; it didn't take a foraging soldier long to work through the Ten Commandments, and the seventh and the eighth were usually broken well before the sixth was forgotten in battle. Those who'd survived Preston and straggled back again towards Scotland a month or two later – those who'd avoided capture and a slit nose and the hell of transportation to the Americas – would have paid the price for their earlier boisterous sins. Shay in his light-shy journey north had come across two corpses, bone and scraps of leathered flesh, and many more no doubt rested in the gullies and ditches and marshes of the wild landscape.

The sad, twinkling residue of English monarchy had been easily hidden; hopefully it would form the heart of the new regalia of the new King soon enough. The exploit at the fortress of London had been an incidental, a necessary obligation. If the new King was ever to benefit from it, Shay must continue to test his ground, and to prepare it.

And that meant Scotland. Ireland might prove a handy way to distract Parliament's Army, to swallow its men and its enthusiasm. But the political and military support for a restored Stuart King would come from Scotland.

Probably not this year. It would take more than one winter to forget Preston, for the clans to recover their strength and their heart, and for the politics to resettle towards the young Prince Charles. But next year. . .

For now, Shay's meetings and his observations were hidden things: lonely rendezvous with trusted men; distant scrutiny of fortifications and unobtrusive testing of roads; casual conversations with strangers; a chapel in a village near Glasgow; a doctor's house on the outskirts of Edinburgh. Shay needed to be momentarily remembered and then rapidly forgotten, to learn without asking, to impress without being felt, to happen and then to vanish.

Only once, eager for warmth and humanity and a glimpse of those whose wavering might become loyalty again, did he risk company. There was a supper and a dance at the house of a successful cloth-merchant outside Falkirk, a man who discreetly funded every cause that promised success, and Shay felt his way into it in the shadows and busyness. Head bowed under the harsh glare of the torches in the porch, he stepped into the front hall and disaster. A heavy figure suddenly looming in front of him – no time to move – the jarring of two large bodies clumsy together, the clutching, two faces inches apart and staring, and Shay knew that he knew the face and some surprise in the face suggested the feeling was mutual. Shay immediately in the skirmish, driving the man back into a dark corner of the hall, arm across the man's throat and trying to remember who he was and his other hand reaching into his pocket.

A moment of hesitation, a risky second to try to remember who the man was. The big face grinned stupidly, and sagged, and an ineffectual hand brushed at Shay as if at a fly.

The man was blind drunk, clearly incapable of thought or recollection, and it saved his life. Shay stepped aside and replaced his knife, and stalked onward down the corridor. The main hall was a chatter and a bustle, faces and clothes that had survived the upheavals serenely enough. The centre of the space glittered under the light of tall candelabra, but the edges were gloom and Shay eased into it comfortably.

A woman's face across the room – older, surely, and handsome still. And eyes that seemed suddenly to catch his, to frown, to widen in surprise, and then look away and around in confusion.

Immediately Shay was back against the wall, watching the room, and then slipping along the panels to the door and out.

In the passage, comfortable in the gloom, time to re-focus.

'No man ever liked the darkness so much.' A low female murmur, then a soft chuckle.

He heard himself breathing, felt the crowding years around his shoulders.

'Hello, Con.'

There was gentle wonder in the voice. 'Mighty Shay. You came back to us.' And a little mockery.

'Don't say it. You thought me dead. Everyone seems to.'

'Not you. You never really lived in our world; how could you die?'

He turned.

'Constance Blythe. Great God, it must be—'

'No! It mustn't.' Her murmur lightened. 'Why must everyone talk about time?'

He took her two hands in his and kissed them once, hard, searching her face. Caught in the faint light slipping through a window, its every crease and flaw was shadow. The flesh was thicker on the bones and tired, but he knew it as beauty.

'Are you hunted, or hunting?' She pulled her hands away. 'Ah, what mightn't be possible, now you're here?' She moved to stand beside him, and they stood in the gloom as if watching the sound coming through the closed door. She remembered a decorum, like a piece of the catechism. 'How is Margaret?'

'Well enough. I don't—'

'Of course you don't. That poor girl.'

'Meg's hardly lucky in me, I grant. You of all people—'

'Your embraces were marvellous, Mortimer. Thrilling. Rather terrifying. But we knew they were the things of an idle hour for you. For you, as pleasant an exercise as a morning's hunt.' He had started to protest, and then frowned, and then was silent. 'But to be the woman whom Mortimer Shay committed himself to, swore to protect for ever.' She shook her head. 'A hundred female souls died a little when it happened. And in that moment, darling lucky Meg became a kind of queen; we never looked at her so casually again.'

'Little old Meg? Surely—'

'Mortimer.' It was spat. 'Even you are not so much of a fool.'

He shifted uncomfortably, grunted. 'You were married too, I think.'

'I was married. And then I was widowed. In the end it was just another affair. Not as short and not as sweet. When a wife I was expected to make as much effort as when a mistress, for none of the little fondnesses or pretty offerings in return. Do you men know how boring it is to have to flatter, Mortimer? Especially when you know there are no pearls in it.'

Shay chuckled, deep in his throat, and glanced down at her.

She lifted a hand and ran the fingers intently down his sleeve, feeling the old muscle inside. 'But that was never your insecurity, was it?' Her hand clutched around his arm, and then released it. 'Sometimes, when I touched you, I was surprised to find you any softer than stone. And sometimes I was surprised to find you had any physical presence at all.'

'You flatter well enough still.' He said it indifferent. 'You always did.'

'No.' She was colder, firmer. 'You did not care enough for flattery. You would not trust enough.'

A voice suddenly in the hall, a clattering approach that disappeared up a flight of stairs.

Shay had pulled back into the shadows. Constance Blythe saw the movement, and laughed quietly.

He scowled. 'Have you children?'

She shook her head, without looking at him. 'Not any more.'

'I'm sorry.'

'I did not love them enough, and so the Lord took them back to him.' The sentiment was empty, and he said nothing. 'Not meant for a family, perhaps. Neither of us.'

Shay considered this. 'And what shall remain, then?' There was silence. He stirred himself with a grunt. 'I must—'

'Of course. And once again we shall wonder if you ever truly were, or whether we just dreamed you.' He laughed quietly. 'Shay, the world seems to move a little faster now you're back. I hope you've life enough for all of us.'

Again the laugh, soft and harsh in the throat. 'Plenty.' The echo of the laugh hung as whispers in the air, but the man was gone, and Lady Constance Blythe was left alone in the darkened hallway.

It had been the frustration at the Tower that had finally prompted Thurloe to contrive the letter in reply to the Reverend Beaumont's friend – the sense that he was nowhere in understanding his enemies, that they were somehow laughing at him. It only compounded his frustration with Thomas Scot, the conspiratorial old crow deliberately blocking him; Scot and Tarrant, the insecure bully. He was surely a cleverer man than them. The world – and in particular the tricks of his enemies – could teach him ways to prove himself.

Writing the letter had been a tussle between the instinct that he was doing wrong – wrong by a man and wrong by the interests he himself was supposed to uphold – and the intellectual satisfaction.

How did one write such a letter? *How would one capture the spirit of the poet when translating his Greek?* He'd not been at all sure how to refer to the Reverend's hanging, and it didn't help that he didn't really know what the reader would think. He'd started with strong interest and hearty support for Beaumont and the Royalists, but it looked ludicrous under his pen and he realized – *who am I myself supposed to be in this performance?* – that prudent doubt might be more credible. It might also provoke more discussion. He hoped the interest in the possibility of a Royalist-Leveller combination wasn't overdone. Likewise the flattery at the end – he rather warmed to his idea of a network of intelligent men corresponding regardless of the little differences of politics – but perhaps he'd been too strong in presuming the character of his reader.

And Doncaster sounded right. Better than London. In any case, it had to be plausible that he was being given Beaumont's letters. He knew the Angel Inn for a reliable place, and could easily arrange the forwarding. Strange to think of these deceptions moving between the inns of England.

TO THE LORD PRESIDENT OF THE COUNCIL OF STATE

Sir, the renegade Ormonde, perhaps contrary to expectation, contrives to continue to hold together his mongrel army in Ireland. The Confederacy can have no love for the Marquis or his cause, but they will take advantage of Royal gold, and the chance of this further support in their effort to rid Ireland entirely of the Godly. This ill-born Royalist-Catholic force is in the field and marching upon Dublin. Should Dublin fall — and sheer numbers may overmaster the stoutest hearts — we would have no garrison but Derry in this whole island, and no easy port for our traffic.

[NALSON COLLECTION 24, BODLEIAN LIBRARY]

The 2nd of August opened slow over Dublin, turgid with summer. The Royalist soldiers grew more lethargic with each hour of its heat. Dublin Castle, Parliament-held, was only a mile away, but through the bright haze it seemed distant and insubstantial.

The world was a heavy light, and buzzing insects, and the thick head that follows a disrupted night.

They'd been sent on a march through the darkness, fully one thousand of them, to secure an outpost near the city. But the guides had been half-asleep, or incompetent, or more likely treacherous, and the swift operation had collapsed into a weary weird dream of confused comings and goings in the lanes, stoppings and startings, cursing and drowsing and the stamp and the clank of uniforms and weapons. Only an hour before dawn they'd reached their objective, the little castle that would form another anchor point for their implacable march on Dublin, last but one of Parliament's strongholds in Ireland.

But the little castle that had seemed so solid, on the map and on the horizon at dusk, was found in the first dusty glow of morning to be a crumbling ruin. The Marquess himself had ridden up – after a good night's sleep, no doubt, and a like breakfast – to sneer and frown at their progress in fortifying the ruin. His horse had pranced him around it, as if trying to find an angle from which it might look impressive, and instead only finding fault. They'd stood sweating in their shirts, passing rocks man to man, indifferent and slow under their commander's scrutiny. Eventually, cross and impotent, he'd cantered away with curses and promises, back to camp. A comfortable camp, the Marquis of Ormonde's; comfortable and lively.

Apparently the Parliamentarians were moving near Dublin Castle. Someone had heard someone discussing it with the Marquis. Parliamentarians must be wondering how to hold out, with the whole country against them. The Marquis was going to bring up some reinforcements, and put some guns on the high ground just over there. That sounded like warm work, too – pushing cannon up a slope. Just to scare off some people who if they'd any sense would be staying inside their own walls.

The soldiers continued to swing the heavy stones man to man, a loping sweating rhythm and gasps of breath in the heat. They were fortifying the little ruined castle, that was the theory. But all they were really doing was moving stones from one pile to another.

Then, from some strange, half-grasped place in the back of their hearing, a foggy place in their heads that might be behind them in space or behind them in time, a drumming.

The drumming was a collective frowning of uncertainty, stones swinging to a stop in tired arms. The drumming was shouts of concern, and then alarm. At last the drumming was hooves, exploding from behind the little hill and thundering over the ground at them, first nothing, then dust, then a shadow of horses that grew and loomed and rushed towards the futile ruin, death coming unstoppable with swords outstretched, and the soldiers tired and slow and armed with heavy stones. The stones thumped dull to the ground, and there was a scrambling for coats and muskets, stumbling and snatching and swearing at each other, and the treacly lethargic dream became a frenzy of violence and flight, scrabbling and screaming across the suddenly sharp day.

VERITAS BRITANNICA
Liberty under God in a Kingdom under God

THE ALMIGHTY hath bleſſed the arms of the Godly with new TRIUMPH, even in the very heart of the pit of the BEAST. As is well-known, the thrice-forſaken Land of IRELAND is the moſt abject, the moſt pitiable, the moſt deſart place on this earth, a domain where the LIGHTS of learning and reaſon and mercy do not ſhine. In this dark waſte Satan himſelf do walk, and he hath the baſe and Godleſs natives to do his bidding, they being nothing but brute and vicious animals.

We ſhould not expect any grain of hope in ſuch a vile wilderneſs, and ſure the cauſe of the true RELIGION has ſuffered ſorely in that place, through defeats and diſaſters and trials, and with much barbarity and cruelty practiſed upon CHRISTIAN women and children, yet the LORD GOD doth ever ſhow his greatness even in the uttermoſt extremity.

There be but few outpoſts of GODLY men and brave in Ireland, yet DUBLIN CASTLE is one ſuch, and from this place a band of theſe men, though ſore beſet by a rampaging hoſte of the murderous Catholick adherents of the late CHARLES STUART and his cauſe, finding the horde diſtracted by their idolatries and vices did ſally forth and rout them quite, at the place called RATHMINES. The treacherous ORMONDE has paid the price of his many twiſts of loyalty theſe years paſt, and is now hunted through Ireland, and his rabble were purſued ten miles with the ſword and all deſtroyed, and ſo doth ALMIGHTY GOD ſhine his light in the darkneſs.

───～　～───

Sir,

   as you will have heard, Colonel Jones out of Dublin routed Ormonde's army as it approached the city. The army is quite scatterd. Idle preparation and ill-disciplind flight reflected the licence of Ormonde's camp and ill-quality of subordinate commanders. Jones was less than us in number, but much the greater in command and dareing. Our fugitive rabbel cut down or captured by hundreds. The Marquiss was bruised by a musquet-ball that struck his armour, but in truth is worse hurt in his pride, having lost artilery and amunition and plate all, and too the hope of takeing Dublin. For Cromwell is landed at that place the 15. August, with ten or twenty thousands, and so the city is saved for Parliament. He will now hunt the Royal caus town by town, there being no army in the field to hold him.
   T. M.

[SS C/S/49/131]

───～　～───

Sir Mortimer Shay in the shade of a tree, at a roadside somewhere in England, chewing on an apple and the words in front of him. *Thank you, Teach.* He saw the map of Ireland in his head. *Parliament shall have it easier than we might have hoped.* He placed the main fortified towns on the map. *But Oliver Cromwell is in the snare now, and the more he wriggles the bloodier he shall be.*

───～　～───

THE BALLAD OF MICHÆL BLACKBURN
Noted faithfully at the occafion of his execution,
befide Colonel John MORRICE
by a Loyal Chriftian Englifhman
Auguft 23. 1649

Grieve not for me, my love fo fair,
When **CROMWELL** comes I'll be elfewhere.
When he favagely attacked
Poor defencelefs **PONTEFRACT**
I was not there.

Grieve not for me, my love fo fair,
For I do fly upon the air.
When that pox'd unGodly rafcal
Thought he'd lock'd me in his caftle
I was not there.

Grieve not for me, my love fo fair,
With love I may all evils bear.
Tho' they laid for me fuch horrors
And for noble Colonel **MORRICE**
I was not there.

Grieve not for me, my love fo fair,
I do not fear the devil's fnare.
When **CROMWELL** at the laft is fent
To his eternal punifhment
I'll not be there.

Rejoice for me, my love fo fair,
For I'll be in the good **LORD**'s care.
When the heav'nly army mufters
Bringing **ENGLAND** His true juftice
I fhall be there.

Sir,

Cromwell has marched north from Dublin to Drogheda and now has that place in siege, most impatient and hasty to secure another harbour for his supplies and to quit the open field before winter comes on. Drogheda is well–held under old Aston, known for a good stubborn man and of course a veteran of all of the wars in Poland and Sweden and Germany and not easily frit. Cromwell is said to have offered terms for surrender, seeking speedy resolution before the weather full turns, and no dout desirous of husbanding his force for the long conquest to come, but Drogheda may put him off a while yet, knowing that Ormonde is coming up to their relief.

T. M.

[SS C/S/49/133]

The great hall which the Government had commandeered for Thomas Scot and his platoon of clerks looked out, from the windows of one of its long sides, on Cornhill. In the morning the sun from the great thoroughfare would bleach the men hunched at their papers. In the evening, torches would flicker weird through the glass. And always the smells of the city creeping in. The other three sides of the building were marked by the back alleyways of London: at one end, inaccessible from Cornhill, a closed courtyard where the rubbish of decades of building work had collected and where animals slunk to die. This was the exterior of the blank, fireplace end of the hall. At the other end, under a minstrels' gallery, Scot had his cubicle and other storerooms and offices huddled together, with rarely used windows opening onto the warren that spread from Cornhill away into the darker districts of the city.

After his experiences at Nottingham Castle, and Pontefract, and London fortress Thurloe had found that he was in the habit of exploring and understanding the obscurer details of his surroundings. After his experiences at Doncaster and here in London, rattling between the evasions of Scot and Tarrant and Lyle, he had found himself increasingly frustrated.

This morning was passing as had become routine, the subdued murmuring and careful bustle of the young men at their work, the scratching of pens and papers, the transit of the sun across the benches, until a blast of thunder hammered at the blank end of the hall and had the young men leaping startled to their feet and gaping in surprise. Thomas Scot hurried in a moment later, staring anxious at his shaken world. Everyone was watching the other end of the hall, where the explosion – had it been an explosion? – had happened. There were cracks in the plasterwork over the fireplace, and plaster dust drifting down, and shards of glass on the floor where one small window high in the corner had shattered.

Scot gasped, hoarse: 'Assassins!' and stared around himself.

Tarrant had grabbed his arm. 'Out – now!' Scot hesitated, resisted on instinct. 'We must get you to safety, Master Scot!'

'Fire! There's a fire!' Now, from a room against the back wall of the building, under the gallery and next to Scot's cubicle, thick smoke was beginning to drift. One intrepid spirit pushed at the door, and flames were visible.

'Move, sir!' Scot let himself be pulled towards the main door, then began flapping an arm towards his cubicle. 'You must away, Master Scot!' And Tarrant was still pulling him out into Cornhill, leading the way with knife drawn.

Scot was still gaping around as he left. 'Papers!' he called, shrill, to anyone. 'You must be careful!' But it wasn't clear to anyone whether the papers should be taken with them as they fled or left where they were; or perhaps Scot had been addressing his beloved papers directly. With the smoke still gusting in, the hall emptied with coughs and hurrying feet.

The empty hall, and the smoke, and then solitary movement. From the room of flames, John Thurloe emerged, a cloth held over his face and eyes straining for sight. Three steps took him to Scot's cubicle. A breath, hissed in through teeth and the muffling cloth, a final glance to see that he was alone, and in.

Who am I become? The ledger was on the desk, as always, exactly centred and open. *How many minutes?* He was around the desk and clutching at the ledger with both hands. *How many minutes? Surely not many.* Five. He'd allowed five. Once it was clear that there was no more threat and no more fire, they would – his hands were still clamped at the two sides of the ledger – *Concentrate!*

'1038. Dublin (Army) – 29th August 1649 – summary of attitudes and practices among soldiers during. . .' As he'd thought, each page was a summary of an intelligence report. '1039. Cicero – 29th August 1649 – the reformed Parliament is not minded to. . .' *Looking for August 1648. Preston. 17th August.* He had to focus on two narrow windows only. There was no time. Hands scrabbling at the pages, pulling them over in clumps. 1648 – April – the King believes – June – in Scotland it is – threats – the Army wants – July – the King is – *surely a minute gone already* – August – brushing at the pages with his palm, one at a time and clutching for meaning – Scottish – army – south – rumours of – direction of march will – a courier was – it is certain that. . . He snapped back – the courier – and dashed through Scot's meticulous script. '427. Doncaster – 15th August 1648 – presumed Royalist agent or courier, contrary to their usual routines, observed and pursued as far as Leek, where lost, believed wounded.' *Contrary to their usual routines?* There was nothing here. He knew all this. *Another minute gone – concentrate!* Again his hands gliding over the pages. *Rainsborough: Rainsborough died on 30th October.* Scottish stragglers seen – acts of revenge by – Duke of – In Newport it is – captured today – Rainsborough – He clutched at the page. '582. Doncaster – 30th October –' the report of Rainsborough's assassination. But nothing new in this. Lyle's immediate investigation of the death, presumably. Had a copy of his own report come here to be summarized? *Another minute: two minutes left.* Thurloe's head lifted instinctively and he strained to hear. *What am I even looking for now?* His fingers began to turn the pages into November. *No – not after – the history of that incident is in what came before.* Now his left hand brushing wildly at the pages, back into October, eyes staring for references to Pontefract and Doncaster. *What was going on in those towns in those strange weeks? What was going between them?*

In Cornhill, a crowd had gathered around Scot and his clerks, inflating and elaborating the story with every question and suggestion, and making the old man increasingly uncomfortable. 'That'll teach you to ban the lads' games!' a voice called, and Tarrant turned and glared at the crowd. 'Damn your taxes!' someone else added.

'Powder – it was powder.' A clerk emerging from an alley and hurrying up to Tarrant and Scot. 'You can see by the scorching on the wall.'

Tarrant: 'Is there any more?'

'I didn't – I didn't see any.'

'Check, man! You two as well.'

'Tarrant, may we not re-enter? There is surely no more danger.'

'In a moment, Master Scot.'

550 was a report on conditions inside Pontefract. 551 recorded the progress of the siege and Cromwell's intentions. 554 summarized attitudes in Doncaster. 559 reported a forthcoming sally by Pontefract's defenders against a forward battery. 561 was Doncaster again – news reaching Pontefract of Cromwell's army – not the usual – presumably Reverend Beaumont at work, 562 – *One minute. I must leave in one minute.* 562 – *Something unusual?* Eyes hurrying down the lines of 561 again. Military details being sent to the Royalist garrison in Pontefract, from Doncaster, and not by the usual hands. *What does any of this mean?* 562 was from the Scilly Isles, 563 was from Scotland. 564 gossip from Parliament, 567 progress of the siege and Cromwell's intentions again, 568— And suddenly the sound of voices and boots. *Move!*

567? Surely – checking the sequence of numbers, fingers scrabbling in the crease, finding the faint ridge, all that was left of the absent page. *Move!*

Tarrant led the way back into the building, ready for a new threat but certain that there was no other door by which it could come. Thomas Scot was quickly pushing past him and hurrying back into his cubicle, hands stretching to touch and check papers and heart sighing as it saw the ledger, open and unmoved, in its proper place on the table. 1039. Cicero.

Tarrant had moved on to explore the adjacent room, and was quickly out, as the first of the clerks began to drift in from the street. 'Remains of a powder barrel in there,' he said, to no one in particular. 'Misfired, maybe.' Scot was in front of him now, and anxious. 'Burned a few papers. Not much. I can't see how it made all that smoke.'

Nor would he. A bucket had been abandoned in the slime of the back alleys, showing little trace of the wet straw that had burned in it. Among the crowd of returning clerks came John Thurloe, curious like the rest.

———～———

To Mr I. S., at the Angel, in Doncaster

Sir,

I find on reflection that I am right grateful for your letter, however evil were the tidings therein. My instinct on learning of the low death of that high mind, the Reverend, made me almost to throw the letter into the fire with the rest unread. And I do confess that the hints that you yourself are closer in affinity to the Parliamentary interest made you in my eyes no better than he who put the rope around the Reverend's neck, and like to be damned for it equally, for there was never so base a deed, whatever the cause.

But Beaumont himself taught me to understand that honesty may be more worthy than rightness. Your words betray a thoughtful, questing intellect, and for that I honour you. If his death were somehow to move us closer to the point when men of character should be brought in closer connexion regardless of their politics, then it would be a blessing indeed out of that crime. So I must repent me of some of my early curses, and again give you thanks for your discretion and human feeling.

You will I think know as much as I about the events of these days. My more excitable friends of the King's interest are much seized of the prospects for Ormonde's campaign in Ireland. But in truth I think they see Ireland as a mere distraction and temptation for Master Cromwell and his armies, for what good will success in Ireland do for the King without there is a change in the arrangements of power in England? I suspect accordingly that their real hope is with a splitting of the Army itself. There are agitators at work among the soldiers, and one man at least of my acquaintance is spending large sums in attempts to corrupt them. Meanwhile emissaries are sent to certain officers to find those who would lead their men in a direction more congenial to the Royal interest than to the present leadership in Army and Parliament.

I wish I could remember the name of my young Levelling acquaintance in the Army in Doncaster. His given name was certainly Ralph, but I realise that you will make little of that. He had been also in Colchester, at the siege of that place — I recall he spoke with distaste that his work was all sieges. I cannot say that I wish all of his schemes well, but I hope that somewhere the lad is living and learning wisdom.

And you, sir, I trust that you are well. Knowing nothing of you or your inclinations, I do not know to wish you success, but I wish you peace and the knowledge of God, and tender you my respects.

[SS C/T/49/46]

＊＊＊

In the monstrous madness of battle, there is no difference between a shout and a scream.

By 11th September the artillery of the English Parliamentary Army had knocked breaches in the south and east walls of Drogheda, and late in the afternoon Cromwell sent his regiments thundering in to seize them. The gut-lurching moment of doubt, the treacherous jolt of sense that questions the stupidity of what you're about to do, the sick glances to left and right for sympathy, the ominous inevitable shoulders immediately in front, muscle-knotted and shuddering and denying the reassurance or release that a face could, denying the humanity. Around you the sobbing breaths, the muttering and the silly boasts and the pissing, and the loneliness that creeps insidious into the crowd, and then from another world the whistle or the trumpet of command, and then one shout and then everyone is shouting and if you shout your body must explode with the same energy and so if the implacable back in front of you starts forward you must go with it, shouting like a madman because only by madness can you justify what you are doing.

A scream is the body's complaint at the breaching of nature, an animal's futile protest that something has gone grotesquely wrong. So is the shout of the men in the charge.

Your head rings with pure empty noise, and this is what madness must sound like, and so the madness around you is normal. The head-clanging shouting and screaming, and the world is the jostle of arms and shoulders and pikes around you, metal and leather and wood and hats and straps and coats in the scrum, the thumping of boots on the earth and the lurching trot over ground that rises and drops step by clumsy step and still you scream because if you take even the smallest breath the spell might be broken and all this might be real. Ahead the smoke, the cannon mouths, the muskets of the defenders, the pikes, the violence and it doesn't matter because all sensation is a storm where nothing is felt normally any more, and the smoke billows and roars and swallows you in and the noise rises and soars and you are gone.

Wars belong to politicians and planners. Fighting is this: that there is no limit of soul or sense to the stupid destructive bravado of young men gathered together. And it is no more than this. To the south the attackers pushed enough men into the breach that they created a defensive position of their own, holding the defenders with pike and sword among the rubble before the defenders summoned a new charge and threw them back, until more men could be flung forward and again the breach was captured. To the east a futile battering against the defenders, lines of red and brown coats clambering up the stones and flung back down by musket balls and the vicious scything of chain-shot artillery, falling and dying by tens and twenties, and Cromwell sent more regiments into the furnace.

In the storm of smoke, bodies begin to float and tumble, collapsing forward and rearing up and cartwheeling, and the storm is colours and coats and the stumbling is now a slippery clamber over leather backs and a tripping on fallen pikes, and now the bodies are part of the rubble of the wall and you climb the backs and boulders into the roaring black cloud of the breach and, such is the all-swallowing numbing trancing chaos of the world of shouts and screams, that for an extra second you do not feel the pain.

Finally there is Cromwell, dismounting at the edge of the carnage, horse and man dusty and muddy and sweating with the day's fury. The battle is won now; Drogheda's defenders have broken and flee through the streets, or barricade themselves in strongpoints, or scrabble panicked through ditches and bushes in the hope of a way out of the ruined town. Cromwell stands still and fierce at the eastern breach, staring grim at the bodies of his men around him. He walks towards the breach, and the scattered bodies become a carpet, and then a wall. Up the slope of rubble the dead have piled two or three thick, broken sprawling bodies tangled among each other. His men have died in heaps, and as he stands among them his unblinking stare absorbs the great volume of destruction and also its little details: broken pikes and scattered clothing and shot-severed limbs.

Part of his mind is accounting the strategic: winter hurrying nearer, and Ormonde as well, a town that refused a fairly given invitation to surrender, precious days lost, towns unconquered and defiant and pagan ahead of him. Another part is gazing at the white faces of the men on the ground, battered or shocked or contorted or mewing fitfully, his Godly Englishmen, pious and well-drilled and far from home, come from counties like his own to die in this heretic island in this unnecessary war. The whole ground seems to writhe at him, red and brown and slicked with gore and moaning its wounds, as if the earth itself were in pain.

A man is near him now, a Colonel – he thinks he recognizes him. 'General, we—'

'No quarter.'

'Sir?'

Oliver Cromwell is a solid man, a rock strapped and wrapped in leather and armour, and the heaviest darkest thing about him as he turns are his eyes. The two words rumble low and hard again. 'No. Quarter.'

And so it begins.

Cavalrymen guard the outskirts of the town to prevent escapes. Men are executed at close range with muskets. Men are stabbed to death with swords by other men, or hacked. Priests are treated as soldiers and killed. Throats are cut. St Peter's Church is burned, and more die in the flames. The heads of sixteen Royalist officers are cut off and will be stuck up on spikes outside Dublin. Many men are beaten to death.

The beating of a man to death: the first blow from club or musket butt does not kill – it stupefies, and knocks only the fortunate ones unconscious; the second blow, to the man crawling and shuddering spasmodically on the ground, is sure to crack the skull if the first has not, and will begin to savage the flesh and organs of the face; even the third will probably not kill, but the recipient will no longer know it, the brain and its awareness being delicate and easily dulled; it takes four or five goodly blows with a club or other stout weapon to kill a man.

Drogheda rings with shouts and screams. In the monstrous madness of battle, there is no difference between exultation and anger and pain.

— ⁓ —

Sir, this day in a different part of the Palace was found the royal [assume crown, from context and consistency] of King Henry [assume Tudor], the Seventh of that name, having for some cause unknown been kept apart from those others previously discovered here. We expect imminently an order for its transfer to the Tower.

[SS C/S/49/158 (LATER DECYPHERING)]

— ⁓ —

The town of Wexford: notorious stronghold of Catholics and Royalists; the haven for a fleet of pirates who plunder English ships and thereby fund the royal alliance in Ireland.

Cromwell and his Army have had the town surrounded for more than a week: thousands of men, and among them mighty siege guns that will shatter masonry. Already fresh food is impossible to find. The flow of supplies into the city has shrivelled. There are uneasy fears about the water; people are falling sick. The daily thunderstorm of artillery was first terrifying, then the rallying call for a fragile pride, and only now do people start to see, in staring sleeplessness and silly habits and quarrels and tears, the permanent damage it has done to their nerves. The artillery has smashed two holes in the castle walls.

What has been happening to captured towns is well-known now. The news has travelled on horseback and running feet; repeated and magnified, it has travelled on the wind and the water. It can be read in scratched frantic letters; it can be read in the staggered faces of refugees; it can be read in the severed heads outside Dublin.

In the town, there is bitterness and muttering. Anonymous papers of protest are appearing. Soldiers are spat on. Seditious words are heard against the commanders who refuse to surrender. Food is being hoarded. Ships carrying coin and papers and children are sneaking into the pre-dawn mist. More people are going to church. More people are being robbed in the streets.

In his commandery in the town, the Royalist Colonel in charge of Wexford reads for the fourth time the short letter from Cromwell. His hands won't keep still; his heart is beating hard – that seems to happen a lot now. Cromwell offers terms for the protection of life and property if the town is surrendered.

It is 11th October. It is exactly one month since the slaughter of Drogheda.

In the town, rumours of the letter have spread helter-skelter; hungry mouths will find food quickest. Cromwell has offered generous terms. There have been other stories spreading, stories of towns that surrendered honourably and were spared. Cromwell will not want to cause outrage unless he is forced. Perhaps the stories of Cromwell's monstrosities are exaggerated. Surely a man of God is a man of peace. Imagine the relief of the siege ending, this frozen anguished existence changed instantly.

The Colonel's heart continues to hammer at his head. Pride. Pain. Honour. Escape. Duty. Fear. Ormonde's relieving forces coming nearer. Disease spreading in Cromwell's camp. Negotiation. Cleverness. One more exchange of letters. An extra concession for his people.

Then there is sound, sound outside his head, outside the room. From beyond the city a shrillness rises like angry birds; not birds – men, screaming in the charge and cheered on by artillery that applauds against his walls. Cromwell is attacking, and in his shock the Colonel knows that it cannot be, *because I am holding this piece of paper and the paper is real.* Then the world crumbles in explosions and wooden hammerings and faces and reports and impressions. The castle is surrendered. The castle is falling. Confusion. The walls have been abandoned. Shrieking panic in the streets. Fear.

Something has gone wrong. The laws, the conventions, the agreement have been forgotten. The assault is under way, with shouts and swords, and no arrangements have been made for mercy.

And so it begins again.

The crown of Henry Tudor, the seventh of that name, was twenty-two jewelled inches in circumference: seven across and as many high, from its padded brow-furrowing base to the tip of the flat cross at its summit. A little gleaming Golgotha, the last surviving crown to have touched the head of a King of England, the sacred relic now huddled in darkness in a mean unvelveted wooden chest. As the chest swayed in the hands of the man carrying it, the crown could be heard sliding across its base, a rat in a dungeon, or a usurped King.

To those who revered it and to those who despised it, it had become an embarrassing and uncomfortable demonstration of the obvious absence of a head to wear it. To forestall the dangerous enthusiasms of the former, the latter had decided that this last hostage should be destroyed.

There had been some discussion about the appropriate handling of the chest. It was obviously valuable, and to be closely guarded. As the object of this evening's activity and of so much concern, it was of great importance – but importance should not be allowed to attach to the object itself. The chest was sturdy, but unornamented. The guard was substantial – six men in two files of three escorting the bearer, a walking 'H' bunching and distorting at the frequent corridor turns – but not ceremonial. Nevertheless, the carriage of the crown through the palace to the water had something of the procession about it, something ritual. A captive was being escorted to execution, a victim to sacrifice. The boots fell naturally into rhythm as they tramped over the tiles and flagstones, the uncertainties in the faces seeming like gravity.

At the water's edge, confusion. The chest was carried down the three steps to the side of the boat, and handed to the man standing waiting inside, legs braced against the little restless bobbing of the river. His balance shifted as he reached for the chest, and shifted again as he swung it in close, and he waited to find stability again. And then stood looking around in uncertainty.

'On the thwart, sir, here.'

'Between those two pikemen, perhaps.'

'Shuffle along a bit.'

'Should I hold it, maybe, would that be right?'

'The thwart's the proper place.'

'Don't know. It seems too. . . you know.'

'On your head, then?' and a collective frown.

Eventually the small chest was stowed under its bearer's bench, and he settled himself over it, clumsy against the water's rocking. Immediately, automatically, he checked that it was still there, saw it not quite square to the line of the boat, and eased it straight with his boot in some buried instinct of propriety. Thus the crown of the Tudors, and of the Stuarts after them, was set on the river at last, to be rowed away for destruction by fire like the pagan Kings who had ruled this land a millennium before.

Two miles down the river, a pair of bulky shadows pressed into a stone wall and murmuring.

'You see the scene, Manders? You see your role?'

'I do, sir. And when I'm done? I should come to you – to aid you, in case. . .'

'When you're done you get away from here, and we can have no risk that you'll lead them to us. If you see a threat to us from the land and you can do aught about it, we'll be thankful, but otherwise get you well away into the night. Do not meet your friends until tomorrow. All being well, I should be good and clear by then. It's a part for a man prepared to stand alone, Manders, not just a man with strong arms to him.'

A grunt, and then silence.

'This is – this is when one finds out, sir, isn't it? I mean. . .'

A heavy nod, but it was unseen in the darkness. 'This is that time.'

A firm hand on a shoulder, and then Sir Mortimer Shay was gone into the gloom.

Approaching them along the Thames came the crown of the Tudors, gliding in furtive majesty. The boat was a broad and steady gig, eight rowers bending and heaving at the oars. Among them, squashed and awkward on the benches and struggling for dignity and balance, were as many pikemen, weapons high and wavering over the water. The blades flashed above them, collecting little freaks of light from the city and glittering in the growing gloom. The boat shoved itself smoothly over the river, a strange water porcupine bristling with its oars and pikes.

A coxswain sat in the stern at the tiller, to keep order among the rowers and negotiate the tricksy eddies of the river and its chaotic traffic, and one bench ahead of him was the courier.

The courier was the only man not holding anything, and he felt it in restless adjustments of his hands – now clasped, now held straight out on his knees. He tried to carry himself upright against the rocking of the boat, tried to manage a pose of dignity, gazing out into the evening of the city through the thicket of oarsmen and soldiers and trying not to catch any eyes.

'Pikes!' from the stern, and there was a shifting and a rustling and the soldiers looked around and saw the mighty bridge looming nearer behind them and understood, and the pikes wavered and dropped with thumps and jostling among the irritated oarsmen. One didn't quite make it and the pike-point scratched harsh against the underside of the bridge, the noise picked up by the hissing, cursing teeth of the soldiers.

The bridge made evening suddenly night, the city lights were fewer and farther through the arches, and the smooth progress over the water became somehow a more hidden thing, a whispered echoing scurrying in a tunnel, a rat in a sewer. By the time that the boat emerged moments later, the bridge buildings looking down blankly on this strange emanation from their skirts, the last light had gone and the sky was black, so that the few-second journey under the little city that was London Bridge seemed to have been a transit of hours, a journey to a different realm, and they had been cheated of the wistful fading of the evening.

The courier watched the rhythm of the rowers as they bent and heaved and sprawled back and lurched forward again, and swapped blank faces with the two nearest soldiers. There were bigger boats this side of the bridge, masts bustling against both sides of the river; but there were fewer lights, and ahead the east and the sea were empty darkness. To his left he could see the Tower now, a foggy white over the black invisible sins of the city, lurching closer with every sweep of the oars.

The chest rested on the bottom of the boat, peeping out from under the man above, uncomfortable as if a mouse had appeared under his cloak.

In the ebony shadow of the wharf, hidden by its height from the monstrous ghost of the Tower of London floating overhead, another boat bobbed and chattered on the oily water of the night.

Three men sat in it. Two bulky shapes, an older man and a younger, waited over the oars. A third man, slender and trying not to shiver in the shirt and close breeches that were all he wore, crouched in the bow.

Haunted voices came over the water at them, calls and cackles bouncing and echoing oddly in the darkness, suddenly shrill or eternally far away. Mighty creaks and whispers swooped nearby, as if the night itself were a shifting restless machine. Through the damp walls of the wharf they felt the spirits of traitors past, seeking company.

In the gloom, Balfour saw for the first time a small barrel in the corner of the stern, and turned to the comfortable bulk beside him. 'Powder again?'

A grunt.

'We foresaw no need.'

A reflective breath. 'Emergencies.'

Balfour shook his head. 'Sir Mortimer, you surely are a man for a revel.'

Somewhere above them, Michael Manders waited in his own darkness, and found his lips muttering forgotten entreaties.

The wharf stretched the length of the waterfront of the Tower of London, and the prickly boat was heading for its centre, the coxswain steering her in a slow curve from the middle of the Thames in towards the cold waiting fortress.

Huddled over the waterline at the centre of the wharf waited the barred mouth of Traitors' Gate. Queen Anne Boleyn, all the dancing and ambition behind her; Lady Jane Grey, used and terrified; Saint Thomas More, grim-faced and pale as he went to test his compact with God: all had been rowed through the sloshing, weed-greased archway, all of them on their way to death.

'Pikes!' again, this time well enough in advance, and the pikes wavered and bristled and fell slowly, the oarsmen ducking aside in irritation and the courier in alarm; then: 'Ahoy at the gate!'

High above, on the wharf, a shadow moved against the Tower.

A creaking of ropes, and the wooden gates began to swing open, the black water rushing and chattering through the lattices. Traitors' Gate showed the way to a fetid unlit tunnel beneath St Thomas's Tower and, beyond it, the moat running between the wharf and the fortress.

'Oars!' The coxswain skew-mouthed and staring as he tried to gauge the movement of the bow in the current, and the rowers looking around and pulling their blades in a foot and instinctively hunching as Traitors' Gate opened black to receive them, the slaps of the water echoing tinny in the stone purgatory, and then the bow was in, nicely in under the very centre of the arch.

Then a blur to trick the panicked brain and a roar of shattered wood and the centre of the boat disappeared and water was gushing up through the blasted planks. 'Now, fast and hard!' from somewhere in the darkness, and the prow of another rowing boat was racing in from the side. The assaulted boat was chaos, a screaming of shattered men and the wild mournful shouts of their confused and sinking comrades. 'Now, look for it! See it! Swim for it!' Again the words came from outside, from the nightmare of confusion, and the water was everywhere and so cold. The men who'd been in the way of the first plunging shock, a shattered arm and a smashed leg between them, were already drowned. The courier and the coxswain were sprawled back against the stern, askew and bewildered and alarmed – something had dropped, surely, something had smashed through the bottom of the boat and the boat's back was broken and now there was no stability any more, just wrenched portions of boat that rolled away under frantic arms and legs and kept on rolling and then they were floundering and retching in the thick clutching river.

In the attacking boat Shay had dropped his oars and spun round and was scrambling forwards. Behind him Balfour's oars kept the boat steady, and as Shay clambered along the boat Vyse disappeared in front of him, a pale flash of shirt that rolled over the bow and into the freezing water, a movement and a sound lost in the madness.

By the time Shay was leaning over the bow, the water in front of him was a maelstrom. The remains of the shattered boat, the flailing shouting men and the log-jam of oars and pikes, seethed and splashed up at him. He had a sword raised in his right hand and a pistol in his left, but for a moment he couldn't see Vyse and he couldn't see the crown. In the gloom and the chaos all the movement was a rolling whirlpool of black and white against grey. 'Forward a stroke!' and Balfour pulled them so, the bow nudging its way through the water and one bobbing body. An arm reached up at him and Shay hacked down at it. Then he saw Vyse, a purposeful white torso pushing through the water a few yards ahead – 'Again!' – two more swooping cuts of the blade at the churning of men and river – nearer now – and then what had seemed a shattered fragment of hull became a wooden chest.

'There!' Shay shouted to no one and no purpose, and 'Forward!' and still Balfour was pushing them forward. Vyse had seen the chest, had seen it before he jumped, was pulling himself furiously towards it, and as Shay watched with face clamped teeth-tight in intensity one long pale hand reached for it – but too far. 'Come on!'

Another man was reaching for the chest now, a clumsy stupid arm that clutched at it and slipped and pushed it away and lunged and clutched again; then Vyse had two hands on it and was trying to kick himself backwards in the water, but the flailing arm had slipped off the chest again and grabbed him by the shirt. Shay switched weapons between hands, braced his knees against the insides of the bow and found a precious moment of steadiness in his rigid right arm and fired. The face exploded black and away into the water, and Vyse was free and splashing his way back towards safety, kicking clumsily while clutching the chest to him.

A hand clutched at his shoulder, at his shirt, and he writhed and tried to pull away, and then the boat prow was over them and Shay drove his sword into the face of the pursuer and reached down for pale spluttering Vyse. 'Now away!' and Balfour instantly reversed the pull of the oars, and the momentum checked and changed and gradually they began to back away from the mêlée. Vyse was hard against the side of the boat, coughing, with the chest in both hands, and Shay had him by the neck of his shirt, but there were two soldiers clutching at his back and legs; overreaching dangerously, Shay hacked at them both, the sword in his right hand again and swooping mad and vicious. The men fell away, blooded and screaming, and he checked again but there was a moment's peace.

Over the bow, the shouting and the splashing and the drowning were receding into the darkness. There were figures on the wharf now, and shouts, and for a second Shay wondered about Manders. Then he bent again to Vyse, a hand under each shoulder, and hauled him bodily upwards out of the water until Vyse got one hand over the side and clutched tight.

Shay grappled the chest away from him, and Vyse got his other forearm wedged over the side. Shay turned to put down the chest, and as he did he saw at the other end of the boat a hand, then an arm and a shoulder and finally a head appearing over the stern.

Balfour saw it too, turned back for a moment to Shay, and then they both watched for one dumb moment as a soldier pulled himself over the stern and into the boat, to lie there spluttering and staring at them and instinctively reaching for sword or knife. Again Balfour looked over his shoulder, and his eyes widened: Shay's face, inhuman and black, the words dropping ominous like drumbeats: 'Kill him.'

And Thomas Balfour killed him. As the soldier flapped clumsily at the sides of the boat and tried to lever and kick himself up, Balfour had a knife from his belt and threw himself forwards. His right arm landed on the man's shoulder and neck and drove him down uncomfortably into the stern, and his left hand pushed the knife into the man's chest. Hasty and wide-eyed, Balfour pushed himself awkwardly up from the mass beneath him, and stared. He'd not heard the cry begin, but he heard it now, a high moan of agony and outrage, accompanied by a feeble flapping of hands towards the knife. He'd stabbed the man but the man wasn't dead, the man was still moaning and flapping for the knife and now his eyes flickered open and gaped at Balfour pitiably and hurt. Gasping incoherent words, Balfour fell forwards onto him again, scrabbled the knife free and stabbed and stabbed, hacking through coat and shirt and cutting at the thin feeble meat of the chest. The face stared and twisted at him, tortured and stupid and surely, surely dead now. His hand clutched for the man's face, stifling the moan and trying to cover the gazing sad eyes.

Revolted, futile, Balfour pushed himself up again and began trying to heave the man up by his armpits. Slumped like sacks in the boat, the man would not come. A shoulder – an arm – eventually Balfour had him by one leg and pulled the body up and against the side of the boat and then rolled it over the side into the Thames. He lay collapsed for a moment, chest crushed against the hard wood and face swaying over the water, aware that the body was still rolling and moving nearby. Then, as he watched balefully, it rolled upwards one last time and sank.

A hand grabbed his shoulder and wrenched him round and up, a pair of hands at his collar and Shay was shifting him back and down and he found himself on the bench. Legs wide and re-finding the balance, fists still clenched on the collar, Shay brought his face down close.

'You don't have to enjoy it. You don't have to exult in it. But sometimes you have to do it.' He released Balfour's collar at last, and gave the slightest nod. 'You did it. Now row. We must get away from here, and you must row.'

Behind him as he took the first heavy pull at the oars, Balfour could hear Vyse's gasping breaths starting to ease. Shay stepped to the pale shivering figure slumped in the bow, took off his jacket and pressed it down over the torso. Then he pulled away and bent to check the small wooden chest that now sat innocuous in the bottom of this other boat.

Oliver Cromwell scowled at the page, and let it thump to the table in his hand. He picked up a second page and moved it over and on top of the first. The scanning of his eyes back and forth over it became an irritated shake of the head.

'And I suppose, Master Thurloe' – Cromwell's heavy face staring up at him, no clue as to sympathy or irony, only the Lord's justice waiting to be done – 'you will have me denying this fiasco like the first.'

Thurloe took a breath. 'We have no proof that the crown is not at the bottom of the Thames.'

Cromwell's eyes widened a fraction. 'These men, whoever they are: they may have that proof – and thereby power to shame us.'

'Then they would only prove their guilt. None may use this story without revealing himself to us.'

Cromwell's jowls chewed at this for a moment. Then he nodded heavily.

The big head came forward, the eyes hard on Thurloe. 'Young man, I had you marked for a man of will. A man of resolve. A man ready for all the trials that God may send us.'

Thurloe waited.

'Ready to prove himself against such outrages as these. To overcome.' Still the implacable eyes.

Thurloe nodded slightly.

'Well then.'

To Mr J. H., at the Sign of the Bear

Sir,

I received with humble pleasure your last letter. I dare say that your willingness to look beyond the little divisions of present days is a fit commemoration of the broad-mindedness of Beaumont, who has brought us into contact in such sad circumstances. I may add that I am no strong adherent of any cause, and certainly not of the killing of good priests, and I think that such an event should cause us not to cower more cravenly between this or that wall of principle, but instead to begin to wonder whether we have not as a country lost something more important than both causes. We have not sage good hearts enough to waste them scatter-wise, and when we are so careless of men like Beaumont we should all I think pause a while and examine our causes and our consciences.

As you expected, there is little I can do to find a soldier knowing no more than his Christian name. If you could remember the Regiment in which he served — perhaps the name of his Colonel, or some identifying ribbon or device on the uniform or hat — I might have more success. There was a Colonel — Rainsborough was his name — who came from Colchester to Doncaster — could that have been the Regiment?

Or perhaps we may trace him from the other direction. Perhaps you will not wish to name your active friends in the Royal interest who are so enthusiastic for further strife, but perhaps you have heard the name of a man or men in the Army with whom they are in contact.

What do you do yourself in these days? I imagine these must be difficult times — as they are for all of our people, but I am not insensible to your difficulties, and I hope that partisanship does not stop me sympathising with the discomforts of a fellow man.

If you should ever choose to meet in person, at any time or place of mutual convenience, it would please me much. We might more easily identify your friend, and in any case a fresh conversation with a fresh mind would hearten me much. I sense that we share a belief in the common humanity of man, and I would be most glad to help you explore and come to terms with the world as it moves today, with all its errors and flaws.

[SS C/S/49/170]

⌁

What game do I play here? Shay in shadow, fingers tapping on a letter, trying to conjure the spirit out of it. *A little agitation, yes. And my odd hunger for more of Pontefract.* Blackburn's intriguing report of the death of Colonel Thomas Rainsborough, by raiders from Pontefract. *William Paulden has a plan, and William Paulden dies. Four men lead it, three go into the inn, just two bring out Rainsborough.*

George Astbury's obsession. The soldier had come from Pontefract, on George's last night at Astbury. Had the soldier brought with him the letter that George would have on his body? *George's obsession becoming my own.*

With bulldog persistence, Balfour had coaxed Manders and Vyse into a game of dice, and they were hunched over the table when Shay entered. Vyse stood immediately, glad of the chance to distance himself and somehow embarrassed.

But Shay said: 'Balfour. Manders. I'll have an errand for you, if you'd oblige me.'

There was the lurking sense that an errand for Mortimer Shay could involve anything from delivering a letter to assassinating Oliver Cromwell, but they could only nod.

Vyse was shaping to speak. 'Sorry, lad. Fair hair. Too distinctive. Next time.' And Shay was gone again.

∼

Thurloe, watching: *I am always looking now for the scene within the scene; the other reality; the plot.*

There were two horses being walked in a circle, skittering nervily and avoiding each other's glance, and around them the sporting men shuffled and muttered, affecting insouciance but watchful and posing like truebreeds themselves.

Today, a secret meeting.

There was money here; Thurloe could see it – in the boots, in the occasional feather, in purses passed casually out of cloaks to waiting lackeys and tipsters. There was more money in these twenty-odd men than in. . . in any twenty men he'd ever met, probably than in any two hundred men of his sort. Mr Garvey's Ajax would race Sir Thomas Tovey's Conqueror over one mile and a half – in recent days the ground had been first muddy, and then frosted, and he wondered how it would be under those rampaging hooves – and the prize, in silver no less, was a year's fees to a lawyer. As much again would pass around in private wagers.

Would these tend to be royal sympathizers, these twenty self-assured men, with their lolling glances and easy-given purses? Thurloe felt a flicker of isolation. Then rationality. There were dandies enough among Parliament men, and sober-dressed men enough among this group. *False premises, false observation.* But race meetings were a well-known cover for Royalist gatherings. Again the flicker of isolation, and Thurloe trying to hold to his logic.

There was a shout, incoherent. A shifting among the rich men – *rich men? See the faces, Master Thurloe, and the boots, see some worn leather and some hungry glances* – and then the two horses were being pulled and led away, and the little crowd began to tramp after them. Thurloe watched the cloaks swaying away, the rich blues and clarets, the feathers bouncing in the crisp air.

The reply had come from Mr J. H.: after reflection, he thought he would like to meet Mr I. S., for might two men not prove that there was a limit to suspicion in this uneasy world? Which noble sentiment Mr J. H. then undermined rather: Mr I. S. should be at the course at Newmarket on this day; at the start of the second race he should leave the ring and walk to the Bushel; Mr J. H. would meet him there.

Leaving at the start of the second race was a neat arrangement to set a time without setting a time – that he understood. Fifty yards away from the track the sound disappeared completely, and the town as he entered the main street was silent. It would do its trade in the evening.

He felt the cold in his ears, his nose. Autumn had conceded defeat.

The arrangement also meant that he could be watched. If his contact chose to have a friend or friends with him, Thurloe could be tracked. But his destination was known, so that hardly mattered. His contact – his contact's friends – could see if he was alone.

Thurloe had the odd sense of being in some way an object of what was happening. He was no longer an agent – *ago, I act* – in the situation, but instead that which was being acted upon.

Am I somehow vulnerable? Surely, I am on the side of the Government. *Can what I'm doing be wrong?* The private correspondence; the deliberate deception of Scot.

What if this is a trap?

Thurloe stopped immediately in the street, and reconsidered his progression to this minute and to this particular patch of dirt next to this particular tailor's.

If the situation is as promised, then I need not worry. If this is a trap, then I could have been taken already, or could yet be taken, and nothing I may do will change that. He started to walk again, with long steady steps. *Besides, I am in the game now. I must face the—*

He slowed.

Am I now a man who runs risks?

He tasted the idea cautiously, an unfamiliar fruit, or something about to sour. *Life has its risks. But I have never sought them out. I have never chosen risk over safety.* Pontefract; the red-headed man with the gunpowder. Doncaster; the letter. And his assault on Thomas Scot's ledger: an explosion of impetuousness against the attempts to obstruct him; a borrowed Royalist trick and his own true logic.

But risk surely didn't inhabit this quiet English street, merchants and slumped thatches, and a horse scratching its neck against a post.

He tried a pose of cheeriness, and knew it wasn't his, tried to kindle the excitement. *There is a stranger England now, always on the edge of my vision.*

This time the long steady steps took him to the Bushel.

The inn was a new building – trim, with straight timbers and clean bricks. Inside was as quiet as out. Just one other customer, hunched over a mug on the counter. Thurloe grunted for wine, and picked a chair sheltered by the chimney.

This meeting itself, the conversation, was a risk. He had not lied, but he had dissembled, about who he was, about Doncaster and the Reverend Beaumont, and conversation would more easily reveal it. But there were truths out there – the strange link between Royalists and Levellers – that he had to find.

My contact would prefer this chair, shielded by the chimney. Thurloe felt his legs readying to change places. But the wine came, and he waited.

Should he try to become someone else for the conversation; should he invent some other man and inhabit him? Or should he be as much himself as possible?

If I change places, put my back to the door, he will not see that I am waiting. Thurloe felt his legs relax again. *Or should I not seem—* He finally caught hold of himself, took a mouthful of wine.

The door opened, and a man stepped into the inn. Boots and a cloak and a hat and a face obscured by a scarf up to the eyes.

Is it? Thurloe watched him, fixed. *How will he—* The man glanced around the room, and back at Thurloe. *How do I—* Something shifted around the man's eyes, the suggestion of a question. Thurloe felt his own eyebrows lifting, openness, acknowledgement. *I am now a man who runs risks*, and his heart was thumping.

The man stepped forward towards Thurloe. He'd taken three steps, halved the distance between them, when a glance to the side froze him. He stopped still, stared for a second – towards the counter, towards the other customer – then turned and hurried out.

Thurloe half-rose – *follow? shout?* – and then half-turned towards the other customer. But the other customer was still hunched over his drink, a blank back denying Thurloe's hope for clarity. Thurloe subsided from his awkward posture, frustrated and angry. He knocked the rest of the wine back in one, and left, with a malevolent glance towards the shadow at the counter.

❦

The rain came down forever – as if there were no alternative to the steady hissing on hat and shoulders, the water sluicing down his back; as if God had decreed the flood for eternity. And Shay continued to stare at the weird scene, a little rustic hell, men and women on the margin of existence.

Two or three figures lurked on the edge of the tree line, watching like him, confused and suspicious. Further off, a man on horseback. They didn't stay long.

He shifted his body gingerly within the jacket, trying to make a friend of the rain: to believe it was a bath, to believe it was warm, to believe that a fireside awaited – the tricks of a lifetime of sieges and delayed attacks.

This was Surrey; even within England, a place of more than usual familiarity and comfort; London, a great city of the world, of art, of civilization, was less than half a day's easy riding.

Across two or three acres of common wasteland, a vagabond settlement had grown: wooden shelters and makeshift tents, of blankets and branches. Around them the inhabitants had started to till the land: the scrabbly undergrowth had been pulled aside, the earth turned until the weeds and roots had become uniform lines of rich brown clod, and in this earth they had planted what they needed.

A grumpy pig trudged closer and began to forage at Shay's boot. He looked down at it, a fellow creature in the storm.

They'd called themselves the True Levellers, whatever that meant. Their opponents – the scornful, the alarmed – called them Diggers. Which made more sense.

There'd been speeches; pamphlets, of course; demonstrations in the local church. The earth was a common resource for all. Property – the having of land, of wealth – was an offence to this. If all the unused land were put to use, all men would have enough.

Just more of the idle words and ideas that had filled the heads of unhappy, unsettled men in the last years of destruction and ruined harvests. Shay watched the people. A scarecrow band, crude sodden clothes and empty faces, ankle-deep in their precious earth and wrestling it with simple tools and hands that shivered white in the rain.

One man moved among them – an older man, his own age or more, amply built but with clothes that hung loose – a figure of authority, though did they have such a thing? – offering encouragement and support. As Shay watched, he pulled a hoe from a ghost-pale young woman, raised one open palm to heaven in a moment of damp rapture, flicked the collected water out of his palm and began to work the soil with the pedantic rigour of a man who hadn't been doing the same for the last hour.

Shay had come across the Weald, through the very fringes of mankind. Through furnace-settlements of a dozen inhabitants, where the charcoal smoke made a permanent dusk over the glistening smeared faces, a way of life for a thousand years or more. Through groups of outcasts – deserters from armies, deserters from life – that had reformed themselves as new communities in clearings in the endless forest, barbarian lives lived in the undergrowth: tinkers, tramps, and pedlars; itinerant smiths hammering at brute tools; crazed preachers watched by a scattering of world-shocked faces; the most desperate whores he'd ever seen. All the habits of humanity rehearsed as if by animals; as if, in its decay, English society were retreating, regressing.

Watching the cultivators through the curtain of water, he felt somehow uneasy.

It wasn't the poverty, or the politics. He'd seen extremes enough of both in the German lands, across three decades of chaos, and now all the upheavals in this island.

He looked again – at the woman thirty paces off, lost utterly in the misery of rain and desperation and still crouched over the mud, hands as trowels, scraping holes for the seeds and refilling them; at the man nearest him, driving a shovel down into the world with inhuman determination.

It was something unfamiliar and untouchable in these people. Mortimer Shay had spent his life moving among other men and women; never dependent, but always able to find some tie of companionship, to however remote a fellow – through duty, or through drink, through loyalty or masculinity or passion. Through all his life, Shay had counted on being able to join a stranger or group of strangers, of any quality or faith, and within an hour make himself comrade enough to be able to bed down next to them without fear.

Is this become my England?

Now, in the heart of the kingdom, he felt uneasy.

It was Oliver St John at his most typical: a glass of wine in his hand when Thurloe was shown in, a glass of wine thrust into Thurloe's hand before he was halfway across the room – 'You'll take a little food as well, of course?' – and every surface and object shining or plush; gorgeous fabrics and twinkling, probably foreign, glass. At first it increased the discomfort in Thurloe's mind, but gradually it relaxed him.

'Thought I'd lost you, Thurloe. Cromwell's man now. Greater things.' St John had settled back on a couch, shoulders sinking level with his knees. 'You've missed the wine, I suppose. You're sure we won't eat a little something? You're properly among the Spartans there, aren't you?'

'It's a change from Lincoln's Inn.'

'Cromwell rarely eats, and the drink is foul stuff. Fair sacrifices for your career, I suppose. Have you a fancy for a royal title?'

'I beg your pardon?'

'Some of them – most of them – we can abolish as worthy defenders of the public good. But there are serious administrative titles still; the Lord knows what they actually do, but they sound important. Vice-Admiral of the Shipyards, Master of the Forests, that sort of thing. I've a bagful of Lieutenancies to give away, and umpteen Secretaryships of various kinds.

We've our own men to reward as much as the King ever did, and folk like a little continuity. Do you suppose Cromwell wants a Groom of the Stool?' And they laughed, Thurloe easing into the atmosphere and St John boisterous. 'You look a little pale.'

'It's – it's an interesting mix of people.'

'It's the new world, John. If we let open the door to liberty, as we must, it's remarkable the people and the ideas that slip in.' He was watching Thurloe out of languid eyes, and then the slumped head came forward. 'How do you find Thomas Scot?'

'He's committed. He's sincere. A little—'

'He's a dried-up old lizard! And vicious. God save us, John, don't say you've gone fully puritan in six months.'

Thurloe smiled, and resumed. 'He is committed. He is sincere.' He hesitated, looked up at St John again. *Is conviviality making me indiscreet?* 'But about what? That. . . worries me.'

'Most men who signed the King's death warrant were rather afraid of what they were doing. Surprised. Scot was. . . like a stoat with a chicken; ferociously satisfied.'

'He's sympathetic to the Levellers.' St John was suddenly watching more carefully. 'He has men around him who are sympathetic. That's why you wanted me to investigate the death of Rainsborough.' A faint nod from the couch. 'I still don't quite know what was going on at Doncaster then; there's intelligence that Scot's keeping to himself. And now I have. . . indications – faint indications, from elsewhere – that there might have been – might still be – some possible link between the Levellers and the Royalists.'

St John sat up. 'But that's insanity, surely.'

'Quite. Some of the news-sheets suggested it, though, didn't they? And Lilburne and Sexby said as much.'

'We'd thought the Levellers a spent force.'

'But if they weren't. If their defeat in the spring had made them more ready for alternatives.'

'Lord, if that were even half likely we'd have to go so careful we'd come to a stop. We wouldn't know which way to turn.'

'Will you mention it – to Cromwell?'

St John chewed the idea. 'Lot on his mind, that man. The Army. Parliament. All of our souls.' He smiled. 'I'll slip it in.'

Thurloe took a mouthful of wine, and watched the light playing in the glass. 'Master St John; there's something else.' St John's eyebrows went up. 'The Royalist plotting; their intelligencing. I don't think we have the first idea about it.'

A great sniff. 'Probably true.'

'I've the feeling we're dealing with something that's – that's decades old.' Nottingham Castle, London fortress. 'Ancient. And our people, they're...'

'They're not ten days out of the shires. No, you're right.'

'But there must be someone who knows how the royal systems worked – not last year, not just during the war, but ten and twenty years ago. Someone who'd talk to us. I need to find such a man.'

St John's cheeks puffed out, and then he released the breath slowly. 'Yes,' he said, and the head swung round to Thurloe. 'Yes, there's a man who might do. If he's still alive.'

Winter again, and again Rachel walked among the spare bones of the trees and shrubs, charcoal against the silver landscape.

And what has another year brought us?

A dead King. The little exactions of the County Committee and their reforms – she saw and felt little of this – her father's business, and his complaints – but it was the only change she was made aware of. Her father more withdrawn, as if practising for his absence from the world. Sometimes in the evening he would take out the family Bible, and she'd see him running a solitary finger down the inscriptions on the flyleaves, muttering the details of the Astburys to himself. He could only look backwards, check his proper place in history, ready to give a full and correct pedigree when the time came for final justification. And she too was shrinking away from the world; or the world was shrinking away from her, like the plants.

Nearby now, Jacob's shoulders rose and fell over the spade; his perennial labours.

Then there was Shay. Shay's presence had grown in her life: mysterious, bleak despite his aggressive vitality, and somehow dangerous. All things that Astbury and the Astburys were not. Where Anthony and George Astbury had fussed and feared at the changes and the defeats, and stepped backwards and bent in the face of them, Shay was questioning, testing, challenging.

'I'm not going anywhere, Jacob.'

Jacob straightened, frowning. Then he got it, sniffed, and wiped his nose on his sleeve.

He bent to the spade again, guiding it deftly around the hibernating plants.

'Right you are, miss.'

Her tongue clicked in exasperation, and she turned and tramped back to the house.

———

Curving away into the last of the winter sun, the Thames was a dull silver against the fringing grey landscape. To the west, England was gloomy and pagan and mysterious. As Thurloe stepped up onto the bank, the boatman behind him looked surly and vulnerable, unhappy despite the exorbitant fare he'd bid for waiting.

The house – a broad frontage of red brick like its surrounding wall, a garden, and somewhere a forlorn bird – felt like the last outpost of civilization.

The dying evening made the house seem dilapidated, and the garden had darkened and shrunk for winter, but as Thurloe walked through it he could see the order and industry in it. The plots were trimmed and logically arranged, and even the most unpromising runts of plants had labels.

The ghost of a servant flickered in front of him behind the door, and drifted away down a passage, and Thurloe followed.

The house was an overstuffed chaos of things and colours and smells. The walls were packed with pictures and tapestries, part-obscured by darkwood furniture that lined the passage with little apparent thought for logic or utility, except that every surface was necessary to support something: astrological instruments, a death mask, stuffed animals, plates of half-eaten meals, a skull, a lute, racks of glass jars, a dead bird, erratic piles of books and papers. There was no straight path down the passage, only a track to be plotted among the debris. Occasional candles guttered and flashed, and the gloom made everything a weird soup of oranges and browns. The smell, meanwhile, was everywhere and overpowering and indistinct: an apothecary's shop, a perfumery, a kitchen, as if the world of senses had been distilled into one cloying spoonful of taste.

The servant had disappeared and, in following him, Thurloe found himself alone in a large study. It was as gloomy and diverse as the passage, but it was more clearly a place focused on learning. Bookshelves rose from floor to ceiling, except on one wall completely filled with a rack of hundreds of jars and pots of powders and leaves and liquids. Beside the rack a large table was covered in trays and glass beakers and apparatus. A fire glowed in the grate, and near it there was an enormous chair piled with cushions and fabrics.

Thurloe looked at the table and the rack warily, and moved towards the nearest bookshelf. Astrology, Botany, Alchemy, History, Medicine: all were represented here in heavy bindings and half a dozen languages.

In the pile of cushions and fabrics on the chair, two eyes opened, and a voice began to speak.

Startled, Thurloe couldn't make out the words, and even when he'd overcome the surprise and peered, and distinguished a great pink potato of a head, fringed with white bristles top and bottom and crowning an immense body, he still couldn't make out the words.

Something familiar in the rhythm and the sound and. . . Greek. The vast man in the chair was speaking Greek – with a foreign accent. Thurloe replayed the words, also somehow familiar. 'Who are ye? Is it on some business, or do ye wander at random over the sea, even as pirates, who wander, hazarding their lives and bringing evil to men of other lands?' Pirates? Evil to men of other lands?

Homer, of course. Polyphemus the one-eyed giant, to Odysseus.

Thurloe thought for a moment. 'We have come by another way, by other paths – as suppliants to thy knees, in the hope that thou wilt give us entertainment.' He stepped forward. 'My name is John Thurloe, Sir

Theodore.' He extended a hand. The pile of fabric in the chair didn't seem to have any hands, and he withdrew it again. Too late, a set of pudgy pink fingers emerged from among the fabric and flapped vaguely towards him. 'I was advised to seek your guidance.'

'Oh-ho, you wish to consult Mayerne.' In the accent – it wasn't quite French – the second syllable of his name was both swallowed and elaborate. 'Kings and Queens have found relief in these hands. For Princes and Princesses these hands were the first touch of the world.' The tiny eyes opened wide, perhaps surprised to find themselves in such an unlikely face. 'But such credentials do not serve in these days, I think.'

'Not your skills as physician, sir. But as a. . . a man of affairs.'

'Affairs?' A fleshy smile. 'A pretty word, that. Can you procure for me some gold leaf?'

'Gold leaf?'

'And ten ounces of the seeds of the *Tulipa Aleppensis*. I think it may prove beneficial to a certain palliative decoction of my devising. Your Parliament has become most insular in its habits, and restricts the trade in such things, which are the essence of my simple work here. They fear I would smuggle messages among my seeds, and commit heresies in my alembic with the gold.'

'Tiresome for you.'

There was a rumbling from the mountain of fabric. Sir Theodore de Mayerne was chuckling. 'They're right, of course. I would do those things. But tiresome all the same.'

'The more quickly enemies may converse with one another, the more quickly they will be friends.'

A great heave, and Mayerne's face pushed forward. 'That is rather good.' He relapsed into the chair. 'Quid pro quo.'

'I'll. . . do what I can.'

A cluck from the great face. 'That's what I miss about the servants of the King. They lied with such charm, such panache.' The eyes narrowed. 'Your so-solid honesties do not inspire joy, young man. Your pages will not flow with poetry. Your bed will not swell with luxuriant mistresses. But what is the quo that you seek?'

'I was told you were the most knowledgeable diplomat in England.'

'In Europe, young man. Europe. I knew no little boundaries of country. I served the free movement of knowledge.' The lips pushed out sulkily. 'Until your late King forbade me to travel. A logical calculation, but so pedantic, so narrow-minded.' The jowls juddered. 'Such a fragile man. Now Mayerne is little more than a prisoner, tolerated by your Parliament because of my serv—'

'You travelled back and forth across Europe. Switzerland. France. Here. On diplomatic business. Sometimes on secret diplomatic business.'

A little smile in the flesh. 'I travelled as a physician. As a scholar. I and my brother physicians, we speak in the universal language of learning, and we trade in our roots and seeds and minerals. As an adjunct, Mayerne learns things here and there; is able to pass useful counsel backward and forward; soothe the fevers of diplomacy. When once you have cured Richelieu of *lues venerea*, touched the offended member, what is a protocol or a fortress or a royal confidence?'

'You were trusted by both Stuart Kings, before—'

'I was used by both. I should say: ill-used.'

'Who were your intermediaries in the Stuart Court? Was there some. . . office, within the Court, responsible for these things?'

'Mayerne is not a clerk, to deal with officers. I whisper in the ears of Kings, and they whisper to me. Certain senior counsellors are my companions. . .'

'Which counsellors?'

The old man looked sulky.

'This was Thomas More's house, Sir Theodore, wasn't it?' The little eyes opened wider, waiting. 'A good man perhaps, but not a worldly one. You on the other hand are not a man to rot here in isolation. You thrive on contact, on influence. Things only the Parliament can give you; men like me.' The eyes narrowed again, buried in the slabs of the face. 'You thrive on tulip seeds.'

The little smile again.

'At the Court of Charles Stuart, for example.'

Mayerne's face rippled in thought. For such an old man – what had St John said? Nearly eighty – the face was amazingly unlined. 'For the diplomatic business, I would present it as gossip among the King's closest companions. First the man Buckingham, of course, though he was little more than a peacock. Later that pinched Archbishop. That was a trial, believe me. But I realized that for more secret business – very occasionally – I would be visited by someone of lower profile. Someone in the second rank at the Court; someone less noticed, someone less susceptible to the fashions of royal favour. The last of these that I met was a man named. . .' The eyes closed, though it was hard to notice it. 'Ass. . . something.'

Thurloe said slowly, 'Astbury?'

'Astbury.'

'Sir George Astbury?'

'There was another man before him. A different sort of man. Harder. Less civilized, less. . . less noble than Astbury. I allowed myself to see him less.' *Or perhaps he trusted you less.* 'I suspected him of pushing the King to restrict my travelling. But then he disappeared from the Court. Some loss of favour, some scandal perhaps; some excess. Young man, you have if I may say a too monarchical conception. You think of the individual man. Which is surprising in a product of the new liberties. In such a business, one man is vulnerable – to the assassin's blade, or the too-impertinent dose of the pox. And what can one man do?'

'Meaning that there was a. . . a group, an organization? A network?'

The face rippled again: Mayerne was frowning. 'I never knew for certain. And that, to be very sincere with you, was the most significant point. I was aware of – I could feel, you understand? – the existence of some group of men. Merely a reference now and then, you understand? The men behind the man. Men with great resources. Men who looked back and forward with great perspective. Men who dealt in centuries, not in Kings.'

'Was there a name for the group? Did you know any of the names?'

'The names, no. This group does not seem to exist, you understand? One does not meet them, correspond with them, hear from them. There are. . . like in the dance – but you would not know the French Court, I think? Ah, that was a place – there are veils. Veils behind veils. A Court office; a chamber of the royal administration. A man like this Astbury was a kind of veil, I think. And there was. . .' Thurloe waited. 'A bureau – a department of the administration – just a reference once, and it seemed as merely another veil.' A shudder of the face. 'No. I forget it.'

Thurloe watched the pudgy face, almost a baby's. Sir Theodore de Mayerne didn't seem forgetful.

'A man once visited me here because he said he was troubled by a distemper of the leg; by the end of the conversation I had helped to set an agent in the Court of Bohemia. Earlier, when first I began to travel to England from France, King Henri's advisers thought I would be their spy. Their intermediary was a Dutch spice merchant in London named Witt. He was murdered -- apparently by thieves – within a month. He was replaced by a Frenchman. Two years later I realized that this man was in regular contact with someone at the English Court. Two years after that, Henri was assassinated and this man quickly gained a good position in the administration of Louis, the new King of France.'

Again the shuddering in the body, and the head came forward.

'You must learn to see as I have learned. Not a battle, not a country, not a King. But the great currents of European politics and history. I urge you, do not be too confident with your Cromwell and your Parliament and your victories and your laws. The man Astbury, he died. His place will have been taken by another. Perhaps that man dies, but he will be replaced. There is much more than them. If England becomes uncomfortable, there is Scotland, or the Continent, or maybe England again while your back is turned. Always, in the shadows beyond, there will be a power that watches you, and manipulates. The men who rule in London today, do not be sure that there are not some among them playing this game. And it is a greater game than you can possibly imagine. The death of the King, the new power of your Parliament: for these men it is not a defeat, merely an adjustment.'

The room was silent. The thick mixture of scents, food and books and potions, hung heavy.

Thurloe nodded, slowly. 'Sir Theodore, thank you. You represent a – a more civilized world of learning and life. I wish you well in your studies. Perhaps – if I can lay hand on some tulips, say – I may call on you again.'

Mayerne considered this. 'Yes,' he said eventually. 'Perhaps you may. Good evening, young man. Next time, bring me news of Scotland. I am interested in the possibilities of the coal there.'

Thurloe nodded and left, wondering as he began the cumbersome journey back down the gloomy passage what other aspects of Scotland

Sir Theodore de Mayerne might be interested in.

A bell rang behind him – for a servant, presumably – but then a voice blustered out from the study, 'Young man! Master. . . Zur–lo!'

Thurloe walked back into the study. Mayerne seemed to scrutinize him, and he waited in silence.

'I remember now – You won't forget my little requests, no?' Mayerne was red from the exertion of raising his voice. 'This bureau of intelligence. The veil: I once heard it named as the' – he prepared his lips for the words – 'Comptrollerate-General. Comptrollerate-General. . . for Scrutiny and Survey.'

It was a bureaucratic name, empty of meaning, and Thurloe wasn't even sure he'd caught the words aright.

1650

The Islands of Blood

James Graham, Marquess of Montrose, came like a second adolescence among the Scottish Royalists refuged in the Netherlands. He was an ill-defined sense of hope, and a constant lurking embarrassment. Early worn by battle and flight, his age was a mask that didn't quite fit – tired, leathery face and straggling long hair – through which his enthusiastic eyes still gleamed real. Ladies were charmed, realized themselves smiling, found themselves checking how breasts and waists appeared in old dresses, wished they had money to give him as he discreetly asked, wondered if their current desperate circumstances might justify some brief act of abandon. Men took a glass of wine too many with him, felt that they shared his bravery and virility, made empty promises of funds. All saw the door close after him and felt uncomfortable: felt their fallen looks, their shrunken pockets, their fugitive ease.

Then they remembered that Montrose had always unsettled them, and this brought a kind of comfort. Montrose, with his passions and his quests, had always been trouble.

Montrose: the quickest to seize a cause by the throat and drag it out to battle, while other men – wiser men – waited for the season to ripen and turn, as it invariably did against Montrose in the end. But always somehow the hour's darling, a hero regardless. And now the seasons had come full circle, and it appeared after all that he had been right to stand out against them. In the places in the Netherlands where the Scots gathered together, news of Montrose's coming was heard with silence and shifting eyes. His youthful follies now seemed like their crimes.

William, Duke of Hamilton knew all this, and knew the queasy mix of feelings in himself as he waited to receive Montrose. He chose to do so alone, standing, in the centre of a bare room, a stag at bay.

He looked back further than this last decade of troubles: these two families had been rival centres of power before the name Montrose, before the Hamiltons had been Dukes; before the Stuarts had overstretched themselves and brought English politics to Scotland. It came in the life of every Hamilton, and sometimes more than once, that he must face one of these turbulent reivers over a council table or some marshy skirmish field. This uncomfortable meeting with Montrose was itself a point of duty – of family tradition.

Hamilton's dark pugnacious face hung fixed, dour. The receiving room had been new-scrubbed, and a blanched acrid reek of soap still sat sterile in the air.

'Your Grace, I come for your greeting and your blessing.' An open door and an open mouth and Montrose was off at a canter. 'The extended hand of Hamilton would be more honour than my cause deserves.'

Hamilton watched this, lugubrious. He seemed to consider the words. Eventually he said quietly, 'Hullo, Jamie.' Then, with the same steady sincerity, 'The cause of Montrose has never needed blessing from me, and I can add you no honour you do not already own.'

Montrose's face opened further: it was true enough, but pleasant to hear. 'You are the leader of His Majesty's interest here, Willie, and it's my duty as well as my pleasure.' The smile dwindled. 'On which account' – for once, he waited for the words – 'I offer you my formal condolence for your brother's murder and my personal. . . I was so very very sorry, Willie. He was so – so very dignified, and he carried it through like a lion, and – and the meanness of their execution of him only showed how much greater a man he was than they.'

Hamilton closed his eyes a moment. 'Thank you, Montrose. That was. . . nobly said.'

Montrose leaned in suddenly, and the smile escaped its restraints. 'Shall we now avenge him a little?'

Hamilton smiled slow and a little sad. 'You're as hot-headed fighting for the King as you once were hot-headed against him.'

'But I've stayed true since, Willie. And there's many here, and some back in Edinburgh, who now find my cause and the King's a little more congenial.' It was said without offence, and Hamilton merely nodded very slightly. Montrose was hurrying on, the words interrupted only by a flashed smile. 'If they'd a' come round a little sooner, maybe, we wouldn't be skulking and scurrying as we are.'

The words rushed around Hamilton like bees with a bear. He nodded again, accepting the point and indifferent to the style. The royal fortunes would ebb and flow – the tides were a little quicker these last years – but there would always be Hamiltons steady in the flood. And always Montroses splashing around them.

'Edinburgh begins to remember that its natural loyalty is to the King. And maybe we shall give them a little prod of it first, eh?'

Hamilton frowned, and still the words came steady. 'Are you sure that you're not being a little previous, Jamie? Are you sure Edinburgh will fall in as quick as you say?'

'The King's advisers have their spurs in me. I go in his name, and that will carry me well enough, I fancy.' Hamilton's face started to darken with worry. 'Oh, don't waste your time warning me of the politics.'

'There's not—'

'I'm sure you've tales of tricks and factions, and I'm sure you're right. I know your Edinburgh men well enough, Willie; they'll all have swapped sides again by supper time, and they'll have their eyes on the spoons.' Hamilton's mouth had no time to become a smile or a word. 'We can wait till Dumgoyne floods and there'll be no right time. If we wait we lose.'

'I've seen too many good Scots wasted.'

'And your brother will be one more such, if we do not pick up his flag!' The Duke flinched. The boyishness was suddenly absent in Montrose and Hamilton stepped back. 'God's sake, I am right done with this politics and these plodding two-faced men.' His head made an irritated shudder, and the long hair swung wild.

But as he re-focused on Hamilton, the impishness sprouted again. ''45, wasn't it?' The uncertainty was affected, and the sharp smile was fixed on the gloomy face opposite. 'I think you were a mile or so short of being able to join your friends at Kilsyth, eh, Willie? I missed the chance to defeat you with them.'

Something like life flickered in Hamilton's face. 'Had I been there, Jamie, you might have defeated no one.'

Shay's departure from the rusty manor lost in the west was like so many others before it: hurried, he not wanting to open himself to the possibility of staying a moment longer and Meg trying to make it easy for him; unemotional and unceremonial. He was a stranger to most of those on the farms around: a spirit glimpsed at certain seasons, or in certain star-stricken years; a grim threat told by mothers to errant children. By the time he was striding out to his horse, on the morning of his departure, Margaret Shay was already the centre of a little whirl of local visitors seeking her help or her wisdom or her judgement. Not for the first time, Shay felt an odd discomfort – even a jealousy: *for all my decades of service, am I failing in duty?* Braver men caught his eye: a grunted word of respect. Women curtseyed, eyes down.

And in the middle of the bustle, a single accidental moment: Meg hurrying out of the parlour with a purse of coins, Shay turning back to some word from Gareth, a collision. The unexpectedness of the intimacy felt like novelty. He looked down into her upturned face, as it moved from surprise to appraisal. He saw again the strong tight lines of jaw and cheek and forehead, saw the grey eyes watching him, considering him. She glanced towards where her visitors were, then back. She kissed a finger, and placed it carefully on his lips. 'Be wise as well as brave, Shay,' she said, and patted him on the shoulder and moved past him.

He was an early harbinger of spring to Astbury, a hundred miles nearer the sunrise. The earth thawed under his boots. Politicians and armies were waking from their enforced hibernation, and he must set to work among them. Shay's arrival foretold the strangest shoots and blooms among the devices of men.

For the moment, Astbury's ordered, segregated gardens were so many varieties of barrenness: skeleton regiments of stakes and stalks on the dark earth. But as he rode he could see Jacob moving among the trunks and beds, and soon enough Jacob would conjure life there again.

And I, meanwhile, will conjure death again.

At Astbury, closer to the world, he found news.

Sir,

    the Council are pleased with Cromwell's work in Ireland. His campaign has had enough speed to serve their stability, and enough blood to serve their politics. His popularity among them is untouchable, and they will bid him only continue his efforts as promptly and quickly as possible, for money and soldiers are scarce. Although the Parliament failed to persuade Cromwell to leave Ireland and turn his eyes to Scotland immediately, it is thought that he considers his work in the former nearly done and that it will not be long before he moves on to the latter.

    Admiral Blake is commissioned to sail against His Highness the Prince Rupert, thought to be in Portugal. Anthony Ascham is made Ambassador of the so-called Commonwealth of England to the Court of Madrid, an important thrust of the new attempts at diplomatic respectability by this administration. Charles Vane is likewise made Ambassador to Lisbon.

    S. V.

[SS C/S/50/6]

And I too must plan my spring campaign. The tug of home, and the secluded peace of Astbury garden, made it seem rather wearisome.

The house touched him with unease, too. The book was lost to him, and he could only hope that it was destroyed. Its destruction was a little disaster for the history of England and her Kings, but still better than its discovery. Even George Astbury would not have been so mad as to have the thing with him on Preston field, or to leave it to be ransacked in Hamilton's train. He had lived here more than anywhere, and there was nowhere else he could safely have kept it. He had left no key to it. It was not to be found. In which case, destruction and loss was much the best hope.

Anthony Ascham is made Ambassador to Madrid. Shay tried to remember if he'd ever met the man. So many anonymous silly courtiers. He should have been more diligent. *George Astbury would have been more diligent.*

Regardless, Ascham would serve.

Miles Teach in the skirmish, eyes narrow and all-seeing, body poised in the crouch for defence or attack or flight.

What forgotten town is it today? What country even? Just a bridge, a tower, and an enemy.

The enemy was filling the bridge now, surrounding the tower, with the stupid jostling of men whose blood is up and who have run out of uses for their energy. The tower would fall soon, and Teach had got well out of it an hour past.

Now he was in the trees, a shadow among the trunks, and the English soldiers were closer and beginning to fringe around the edges. Time to pull back further; no good prospects for a fox in a spinney.

Who is trying to kill me today?

But now another fugitive had bolted into the trees, desperate and stumbling in the undergrowth, and Teach's whole face swore. Immediately shouts and pursuit, a stray musket shot hustling through the leaves, and soldiers feeling their way into the green gloom in twos and threes.

The English knew they'd won; their voices and movements had the confident cruelty of those who no longer fear resistance. Teach was slipping backwards among the trees as fast as he could manage with discretion and the occasional glance around him.

My God, what have I not deserved from all this chaos?

Then shouts nearer, another stray shot thumping into a trunk, and suddenly two soldiers exploded out of the bracken at him from different directions. One sword, one musket; musket hesitant and skittering to a halt in the undergrowth, sword livelier and hungrier and dancing towards him. Musket starting to swing up level – *what idiot tries to use a musket in a forest?* – and Teach swerved towards the bewildered soldier with sword swinging, dashed the musket barrel down with a backward sweep of his blade from his left arm and swung his other shoulder into the man's face; down he went, flailing and stunned, and Teach had already turned towards the other, and swung his pistol up in his right hand, held low, held for the impossible breath that was the difference between a professional's life and a levy's hasty waste, and fired at the swordsman's upper body, now open in the swing, from all of three feet away.

The ball caught the man somewhere in chest or shoulder, and Teach knew it for mortal even as he turned again to the musketeer. The man was pulling himself up out of the undergrowth, angry for the fight, but he was thinking too much, much too much, wondering how the certain victory of two men against one had turned so, wondering whether he should reach for his musket, just there among the leaves like another fallen branch, and Teach had switched hands and sent him staggering back with one wild sweep of his sword and then driven the blade hard and sure into his chest. He kicked the body off the blade and swung round again. The other man was dying, sure enough, but dying noisily. Teach scrambled over and finished him, hand over mouth and knife into heart. Then up on his haunches with knife and sword and looking all around. Now he had the silence he needed. Another glance full around, the narrow eyes searching the trees for threat. Then he checked the ground, checked that he had all his weapons, and drifted quickly away into the darker heart of the wood.

These are the lives of Miles Teach.

— ⌒ —

TO THE LORD PRESIDENT OF THE COUNCIL OF STATE,

Sir, by horse couriers from the north of Scotland we learn of rumours and reports, diverse enough to be credited, that the Marquess of Montrose is landed in the Orknie Islands and bound for the mainland, here to take up his proclaimed Lieutenancy and raise an army in the Royal interest.

Edinburgh,
March.

— ⌒ —

'I confess that I perceive the Orkney Islands much as I do Turkey, or the moon.' Oliver St John, a walrus of decadence slumped in an ornate chair.

Thomas Scot, hovering: 'They are wild and primitive peoples in those islands. He may do much mischief among them, with their tribalisms and superstitions.'

'He may make himself a private kingdom for all I care.'

Cromwell, eyes lost in the Highland landscape of northern Scotland, visualizing a man's rain-blasted journey by goat track and cattle drove, the God-questioning wildernesses of forest and mountain: 'He might have made the mainland by the time these words were written. By the time we read them today, he might already be at work among the Catholic peasants of the far north.'

'As yet the Church in Scotland is against him.' Scot, feeling his way through the sentence cautiously.

But Cromwell wasn't listening. Hurriedly and briefly back from Ireland, his mind was between kingdoms. A slab of a hand rose and the fingers rummaged in his forehead. 'I fear we must soon turn again to Scotland.'

Sir,

from the fishermen of the far north it is heard that a man of great note has arrived in the Orkney Islands with many soldiers, joining a force already there; the host is reputed vast, and the effect on food prices prodigious. We may safely take this to be Montrose, joining the advance force he sent thither in the autumn to secure the place as base. The reports of the size of his force are inflated by mere peasant wonder and the benefit for sellers of fish; by other indications such as number of boats etc we know that his force remains slight, but a few hundred paid men of the German states and a horde of untrained men of the islands. Meanwhile, the clansmen of Ross and Munro, who might have been likely volunteers, are held comfortable for the rival interest, and it seems that this quarter of the Kingdom will be something of a wilderness to Montrose.

U. J.

[SS C/S/50/28]

'The world looks like a puzzle to you today, Uncle Shay.' She'd been sitting silently near him, as had become her habit in the mornings when he was in the house and eating or reading. It had started as a provocation, and he had been duly provoked, but now they both found a kind of satisfaction in it.

He was semi-resident at the house now. Sometimes he used a tavern in the district, not too far off on the Ashbourne road, for affairs that he did not wish to link to Astbury. Rachel knew the place, and grasped something of his motives.

Shay was still trying to decide whether he liked the 'Uncle' business. 'The world is a battlefield to me, always.' *I'm not Uncle enough to ignore the pleasure of a pretty young woman nearby.*

The fresh face darkened. 'That's a terrible way to go through life.'

He was half in a paper. 'And yet I have found that it serves.' He looked up. 'And I think that somewhere you agree with me. Marauding militia men. Gentlemen being stolen and ransomed. And a regime exacting taxes merely for old loyalties. This is not a world that you find comfortable, surely.'

'But there must be hope.' Her own voice sounded dead to her.

'Yes, there must.' He set the paper down on his lap, and looked at her with an old bear's discomfort. 'You – you and people like you – are the hope, Rachel. You are the inheritors of a world that I care about – a world that I inherited – and you will carry it forward, beyond these present upsets. This is the battlefield where I find myself. First I must survive. Then I must win.'

She ran her eyes from the heavy boots crossed on the flagstones, up the legs and the trunk to his iron head. 'And you have done – you would do. . . evil things, to win?'

He shifted on the hard chair, pulled himself straighter in it. 'Evil things will always happen. I had rather they were in my control, and not some other man's. I had rather they served a purpose that I care about, and not a purpose that I oppose.'

She affected lightness in her voice, to mask embarrassment. 'I had thought there might be a chance for. . . for morality.'

'And so there will be, for you.'

She smiled slowly. 'But not for you. Too much of a luxury for Uncle Shay the warrior.'

His face opened, and he looked at her with more of a smile. 'Too much of a limitation, Rachel.'

She looked down at her hands, folded on her thighs. 'They say you have led a. . . a very bad life.'

'They don't know the half of it.' His face hardened again. 'My life has been in the service of other lives, Rachel. In the service of a world in which I'll never be comfortable. Allow me at least to enjoy it.'

Rachel closed her eyes, and let her head back against the window. 'Enjoyment,' she said. 'I would like that. It seems like. . . like some silly game of childhood, now put aside.'

'Very well,' Shay said, and slumped further down in the chair again. 'We shall fight for enjoyment.'

He read distracted, and she watched him.

Eventually she said, quietly, 'Uncle George vexes you for some reason.'

He looked up, considering whether to accept the engagement on this terrain. A great breath, and then: 'Surface-wise, I admit I always thought George a fool. Too concerned to be the gentleman. Too concerned to be the courtier. Some of his habits with. . .' – he waved the paper – 'with the King's business were like. . . schoolboy games.' She looked sad, and Shay wondered if George Astbury had caught up his niece in some of his enthusiasms. 'He did not leave these affairs as he should. But he was not a stupid man. No, he was an intelligent, thoughtful man. And that's why I wish I understood what preoccupied him at the end.'

'The siege of Pontefract? The possibility of using the Levellers? You were scornful, I think.'

'It seems nonsense. The fancy of a simpleton. I've taken it as useful inspiration, nothing more – just a provocation to unsettle our enemies. But again, George was not a simpleton. So I want to know what he was planning – or what he feared.'

His head swung round to her. 'You tell me about him.'

It surprised her, and she sat up straighter. 'I think he cared about his duty very much. He worried that he was not the man he was supposed to be, and he worked diligently to compensate for this.' Shay nodded, reflectively. 'There's more. He could be very stubborn – very proud. At the end, he wasn't just worried about. . . about whatever he was worried about.

He was convinced by something – determined to prove himself against those who doubted him.'

He considered this. Then he nodded, and returned to the paper in his lap. He put it aside, and picked up another, and immediately the heavy face rumpled.

Rachel saw it. 'A reversal on the battlefield?'

'A printer has died.' He looked at her; had George slipped so gently into these confidences? 'And yes. An inconvenience. An additional journey for me. New arrangements.'

'How did he die?'

'He jumped from a battlement. Killed himself.'

The shock flared blatant on her face. 'What must have been in his mind, to want to do that?'

But Shay was lost in the paper, and Rachel could only watch his grim absorbed face, and wonder at his world.

—◆—

> . . . *Allgood Haseldine, Printer, died in custody at the Castle, of his own doing. Haseldine was well-known for a compromiser and sometimes a pen for hire, and his printing had oftentimes trod close to sedition. Finally there were found proofs enough that he was printing secretly the Royalist news-sheet called Mercurius Fidelis, and he was arrested on that charge. On his first night of confinement, let to walk one hour, he jumped from the Castle walls unto immediate death. It is said he had a wife.*

[SS C/T/50/7]

It was a curiosity at the end of a list of administrative trivia from Oxford, a sorry little tragedy buried in a commonwealth of broken families and broken minds, and Thurloe wondered at it.

First he wondered because this was now his world: the bureaucratic routines of the state; reports from adjutants and magistrates and village constables; little facts and little deaths; interrogations.

Then he wondered at Haseldine the printer, and why he would throw himself to his death rather than face the next hours or minutes of his life. Buried in his reckoning was an assumption of brutality in interrogations at Oxford, presumably well-known or at least well-rumoured among men like this printer. Did he simply fear pain – fear the humiliations of weakness and the collapse of his body in the presence of other men? Or was there something he was so determined not to reveal, some cause to which he was so committed, that he would chose death rather than risk it?

Underground printers weren't uncommon: some were truly unknown; some known and tolerated, monitored. In the last year such men had turned out edition after edition of the late King's *Eikon*, his book of self-justification and reflection. Those who were tracked were questioned, fined, perhaps imprisoned. But this?

'Matthew!' Thurloe now had a subordinate clerk to assist him and do his bidding, and earnest Matthew was at his side in seconds. Each time Thurloe used and relished his new little authority, it as quickly embarrassed him. He stood, trying vaguely to blunt the hierarchy.

What must it be like to launch yourself into space, knowing it means destruction? To want that destruction?

'Matthew, there's a Royalist news-sheet – *Mercurius Fidelis*. Can we get copies of it?'

———

There was lily of the valley starting to bloom at the edge of the wood now, the little white caps bobbing demurely as if ashamed of their poison. Our Lady's Tears, old Mrs Jacob had used to called it and, stiff-fingered and shooing the Astbury girls away, she'd gathered it for the herbalist every spring until she died. The symbol of Christ's coming; the symbol of the possibility of hope.

There were crocuses out too, clustering around Rachel's feet as she walked back towards the house, and dusty blue like the sky.

Mortimer Shay was gone again, southward first and then northward, he had said. With him went her connection with the world of war and politics beyond Astbury; with him went the darker shadows of life, leaving it a paler, blander thing.

Shay is fighting for my future. What is my future – if I am not to be the spinster of this forgotten green island adrift from the world?

Mary wrote regularly. Mary was comfortable and content. Mary had the life she wanted. Mary sounded deader and a little trapped.

I want to live.

Marriage – or men, at least, for a start.

She conjured again a picture of her father's generation at her age, a tableau drawn from memories of comments by her father, Uncle George and before that her mother. A dancing world of wildness, of sex, of pleasure. She tried to insert Mortimer Shay – tried to imagine a younger, leaner, lither Shay – the wild Shay of her father's fears, not the ominous, implacable hulk who now haunted Astbury.

Will Shay re-create that world for me?

His wife was still alive somewhere. The cleverest woman of her age, Father had said. It wasn't clear whether the tone of disapproval was at her having married Shay, or having been clever. Rachel wanted to meet Lady Shay.

Rachel wanted to be the brilliant centre of a brilliant Court.

Is that what Shay fights for? For his own youth again?

Shay fights; and that is all.

⌐ ⌐

To Mr I. S., at the Angel, in Doncaster

Sir,

It has taken me these months to overcome my alarm at our attempted meeting, and in truth that alarm has often times persuaded me that I must not continue this correspondence. I mean no disrespect to you, Sir, but this world of shadows and threats has wearied me quite to my core and I would abandon all things that speak to me of it.

But it is a world to which I am bound, and since we have but one life we are bound to live it as we find it, and, sensible of my discourtesy in so abruptly breaking off our meeting, and sensible too of the gap in our correspondence, I have found it meet that I should write again.

My apologies to you therefore, good Sir, and my hopes that you will understand my trials and that this finds you no worse than when I saw you.

First, a word about that unfortunate incident at Newmarket. By way of background I should say there are — as I think I have indicated — some men among the partisans of the Royal interest who believe that any alliance, even were it with the Levellers, would be a good alliance if it would advance the cause. Indeed they believe that they have found among the Levelling men some who reciprocate their belief that a mutual accord might somehow be possible. It seems so improbable to me, and yet they are in earnest, and the attacks by the Army last year on the Levellers in its ranks, and the consequent weakening of the Leveller interest, have only made them more determined to be proved right. They are become most heated about this plot, as they are about any scheme that seems to offer the hope of advancing the cause by sudden and surprising means, and those of us who are doubtful, or, as we would say, more prudent, are often cursed for faint-hearts and waverers. These are the men who were in contact with one or more individuals of the Leveller persuasion among the Army in Doncaster — around the Colonel Rainsborowe of whom you wrote.

One of these is a most hot-tempered fellow, and suspicious, and you must understand my shock when, on walking into the inn at Newmarket, I saw his face across the room. His volatility of character extends, I regret, into a predisposition to gamble, and with hindsight I apprehend that this alone may have placed him there on that day, but in my state of mind I could only guess at the most bewildering and alarming explanations, of great suspicion of me personally, and so I confess that my spirit failed me and I fled.

Meantimes, the life that I try to lead as a dutiful Christian takes me northwards, into Scotland. The Royal cause is rallying there — every sympathetic house from Oxford to the border is alive with enthusiasm for what the year may bring — and I have found some little responsibilities on the fringes of those who serve it, and so trudge thither with a heart not blithe but as faithful as I may stir it.

[SS C/T/50/8]

Thurloe found that he was being passed any documents relating to religious or political radicalism – though none of them to do with the Levellers themselves. He strongly suspected that Scot was trying to distract him.

A Declaration of the Grounds and Reasons why we the Poor Inhabitants of the Town of Wellingborrow, in the County of Northampton, have begun and give consent to dig up, manure and sow Corn upon the Common. . .

A collection of malcontents and enthusiasts and indigent peasants had occupied common land in Surrey, and started to plant it for their own subsistence. There had been scenes in the church. After initial amusement, the local landowners had grown unhappy. They didn't like the idea that people could start growing things on unused ground, and they didn't like their servants wandering into the camp of an evening: politics and the pox. There had been unexplained fires at the camp; anonymous beatings at night. The radicals had moved on.

Is this the freedom that was fought for, or must this be fought to preserve that freedom?

Another encampment nearby, through the winter months – *and how miserable was that?* – and enduring into spring; but now reportedly driven out.

In the beginning of Time, the great Creator Reason, made the Earth to be a Common Treasury, to preserve Beasts, Birds, Fishes, and Man, the lord that was to govern this Creation; for Man had Domination given to him, over the Beasts, Birds, and Fishes; but not one word was spoken in the beginning, That one branch of mankind should rule over another.

This was more than mere beggary and immorality.

O thou Powers of England, though thou hast promised to make this People a Free People, yet thou hast so handled the matter, through thy self-seeking humour, That thou hast wrapped us up more in bondage, and oppression lies heavier upon us; not only bringing thy fellow Creatures, the Commoners, to a morsel of Bread, but by confounding all sorts of people by thy Government, of doing and undoing.

More reports on his desk, covering the latest letter from J. H.; more pamphlets. There was a camp in Northamptonshire now. The local Justice had been ordered to prosecute the inhabitants. And Hertfordshire; and Gloucestershire. Enthusiasm and desperation, breaking out like sores across the land.

For truly the Kinglie power reigns strongly in the Lords of Mannors over the Poor; for my own particular, I have in other Writings as well as in this, Declared my Reasons, That the common Land is the poor Peoples Proprietie; and I have Digged upon the Commons, and I hope in time to obtain the Freedom, to get Food and Raiment therefrom by righteous labour, which is all I desire.

To most men it was madness, of course, and chaos. This upheaving of society was not what the war had been fought for.

But it was what the war had brought. Make it legitimate to challenge one form of authority; make it possible for all to speak their own truth; and it became harder to claim any one truth unimpeachably right. Thomas Scot and his ideals; Tarrant and his vengeance; *I with my ambition.* And Cromwell trying to hold the world together. *Is a society of vegetable-tillers theoretically any less legitimate than a society of clever clerks like me?*

John Thurloe frowned at the mess of papers, queasy at the implications of his logic.

That every one that is born in the Land, may be fed by the Earth his Mother that brought him forth, according to the Reason that rules in the Creation.

And where, in any of this, were his Royalist ghosts?

———

A town house on the outskirts of Edinburgh, discreet grey stone blending into the sky; the servants away, the door locked, and Sir Mortimer Shay settled in a large chair in the study.

'I had not looked to see you, sir. You favour Scotland with much attention.' The voice was low: measured and almost monotonous; but there was enough in the vowels and the eyes above them to show concern.

Shay smiled. 'In this decade, most that has been truly troublesome for these kingdoms has come out of Scotland; I have the hope we may tempt something good out of it, for once at least.'

The eyes were down. 'Montrose?' The eyes flicked up.

Shay said nothing.

'He is landed; that much is known among the men of influence here – and no doubt by you also, sir.'

'And?'

The other man looked away as if considering, then back at Shay; and he shook his head slowly. 'He's jumped too soon.' The side of Shay's mouth twisted as he listened. 'The Church party are not ready to treat with the King, and they'll never trust Montrose.'

'He may attract a following regardless. Then they shall be forced to come to terms.'

Again the slow, regretful shake of the head. 'They have the clans well satisfied for now. And they're ready for Montrose.'

Shay watched him bleakly, and took in and released a slow disgruntled breath.

During supper there was a knock at the door, and then a servant whispering in his master's ear, and a note passed to him. He glanced at it and, having checked that the servant had left, looked at Shay. 'If I may suggest, we might finish in haste.' He looked to the door again, wary. 'You might wish to accompany me on a short errand.'

In a church on the other side of the city, their horses tethered outside and shifting discontented in a wind that came with a sting from the nearby sea, they found a young man at prayer.

They sat in the shadows at the back of the church, and waited.

After a few minutes the young man stood, turned, and walked up the aisle towards them.

'Have you come far, pilgrim?'

The young man stopped, checked that the church was empty, and they completed the little liturgy. Shadowed Shay, glanced at warily by the young man, was introduced as a trusted friend.

The young man sat, sleek but obviously tired, and pulled a substantial Bible from a cloth pouch that hung round his neck. Having looked again around the church, he opened the Bible by the back cover and began to pull at the endpaper; it came away from the leather with difficulty but without tearing. From behind it, the young man extracted four or five sheets of unusually thin paper, which he passed to the Edinburgh man.

'Letters to you from the Court, and via you to certain of our friends.' The Edinburgh man nodded, and as a courtesy passed them immediately to Shay. The young man's eyes followed the movement. 'I landed less than an hour ago,' he said quickly; then, uncertain: 'I stopped only to give tha—'

'You were right to do so, boy.' Shay's voice was the shadows, the old stones. 'Surviving any day is miracle enough.'

The young man hesitated, glanced down at the Bible, and started to close it.

'What else?' Shay said, strong.

Another hesitation, then he reopened the Bible. 'I have two letters. . . addressed to the Parliament here in Scotland.' He leaned closer. 'From His Majesty.'

'Two?'

'But one only to be delivered.' Shay let out a growled sigh in understanding. 'Contingent. On. . . on—'

Shay finished it for him: 'On whether Montrose wins his battle. Should he win, one letter decrying the faction who've led the Church party against him. One letter disowning him should he fail.'

The young man nodded, at first unhappy but then trying to recover some poise.

When he was gone towards the centre of the city with his Bible, Shay slumped back in the pew. After a few moments he said, 'Montrose may fail. Indeed, I fear the Crown uses him only as a threat. But we must give him every chance. And we must ensure the cause does not fail with him. I may have to send a report to London.'

'To London?'

'Mm.' He grunted rough amusement. 'Lots of reports going to London. Very hard to know where they all come from, I imagine.'

To the Lord President of the Council of State,

Sir, this town is in a babel of ferment over the approach of Montrose. Every clan and interest has his partisan here, and they do scheme and watch one another like jealous vultures in a desert. For every man who loves peace and thinks our relations quite settled, there is another who fears us and hungers for a stricter religious settlement in London, and a third who hates both others for some forgotten pagan quarrel that none may remember including he. Montrose, for his former miraculous exploits in these same highlands, is quickly beloved again of the simple souls. Argyll and the other leaders here have offended too many with their preferments and their pride to be full sure that they have the control they claim. We have hopes and assurances that Montrose is weak and soon to be defeated. But a moment's ill-luck in some distant valley would turn Scotland quite about, and there are many in this town who would greet such a misfortune right heartily.

Edinburgh,

April.

'Signs of too much latitude of thinking among our Scottish friends, I fear.'

Cromwell – another hasty visit – took the paper without speaking, scanned it, and shook his head like an uncomfortable sheepdog. 'Lord, I am right weary of these Scots and their squabbles. They would burn this whole island for a flea.'

'Our other reports from Scotland show them more phlegmatic about Montrose. They have their consciences and their tribes under control.'

'There is too much of a risk. I am not ready for another war on Scotland.'

'I doubt it necessary.'

Cromwell's eyes were lost in the distance a moment, and then clear on St John. 'A message to Scotland, if you agree. From me, to the leaders in Edinburgh. Tell them this: that I believe that God has made these islands large enough for a diversity of true consciences; that I offer them all humility and respect and love as men of Godly belief and sincerity; that I wish them and their Church and their land no harm; that I will not suffer a Scottish apostate and outlaw to kindle malice against England and threaten our north; that I will root out such malice with fire and sword if I must go to the farthest end of these islands to find it.' A single heavy nod of self-approval. 'And Thomas Scot may have one of his tame preachers write a sermon to the same end.'

St John watched the performance sadly. 'Oliver, this smells of over-passion. We risk setting afire the very threat we wish to avoid. The Scots are that stubborn.'

'So am I.'

'Yes,' St John said with feeling. 'They will not like this trifling with their inward disputes.'

'Then they should not let their inward disputes become ours.'

John Thurloe had never troubled to look inside a hive of bees – in general a man who liked to prove things for himself, he nevertheless accepted some that could in safety be taken for granted – but he knew that it would look much like the mediæval hall in front of him now. One hundred feet from where he stood to the platform at the far end, at least half as many from the centurion stones under his boots up to the hammer-beams duelling far above his head, the hall was barricaded with long wooden desks, rank after rank of them stretching away. Each was lined with sober, mostly young men – men much his own age and type – each bent to his work in his own particular place at a desk, so that what Thurloe saw was in fact a bobbing pool of tops of heads, coloured and styled with such diversity as the Lord had offered. Among the dark coats moved other men – mostly brown-coated – taking and passing papers and instructions to the men at the desks.

It was some mighty impish conceit: to take one of the fuggy dining halls of his Cambridge, and fill it with these bent black-coated insects, and then set the whole to work in the heart of unsuspecting, complacent, commercial London.

This, in literal truth, was the British Government working.

'Master Thurloe!' Thomas Scot, standing at the first rank of desks, had seen him before he had seen Scot. 'What think you of this?'

Thurloe moved to him. Scot was given to waspish intensity, but rarely enthusiasm, and Thurloe was intrigued. Scot thrust a handwritten page at him.

The page was laid out in the form that, printed, it might shortly have. *Of the Right Diversity of Fruits in the Garden of Eden*, ran the title, and under it: *Or, How the* Lord *doth Nurture and Encourage a Fitting and Natural Variety of Spirits within His Kingdom.* The text opened with the variety of beautiful and God-created specimens that were to be found in Eden, and the rightness of each despite their difference, such was their overall conformity to his design; it then noted the poisonous and destructive effect of the introduction of that which God had not intended. So by turns the text moved through a general comparison of cultivation with the political world, to a warm celebration of the distinct but similarly faithful settlements that currently dominated London and Edinburgh, with a warning of the divisive and disastrous outcome that might be anticipated should Edinburgh fail to treat the Marquess of Montrose like the serpent he surely was.

'Do we use the word "kingdom"?' Thurloe said mildly, and Scot's face sharpened. 'Master Scot – forgive an indiscretion – but your own views are not usually so. . .'

A squawk of scorn. 'So damned lax! Master Thurloe, for myself I consider this opinion treason.' The lips recoiled from a pained feral smile. 'The Scotchmen in Edinburgh think themselves Godly, and we suffer them to sustain that delusion; they are Bishop-loving Stuart sentimentalists to a man, and I would see them purged. But for now it suits our purposes to divide Scotland, and this pretty paper will fuel the nauseating conceit that they have more in common with us than with that troublesome renegade Montrose.'

To his distaste, Thurloe found Scot's rare enthusiasm a little appealing, whatever the content. The old man pulled the paper back from him, and waved it in front of him happily.

Another uncomfortable smile. 'This,' he said, waving the paper again and then gesturing with it expansively at the hall behind him, 'is the world that you younger men will inherit. This is the world you are creating with us. Your talents – your minds – your voices – these are freer than they might have been these two thousand years past.'

I have been exalted in these mists.

James Graham, Marquess of Montrose, perched on a rock above the river and gritted his teeth into the wind, as it whipped his hair into his face and plucked spray from among the stones.

I have seen the palaces and fineries of many lands, and they have been but grey lifeless places to me, painted masques. My glories have been all in these wild Scottish landscapes: mad charges through the heather, brilliant coups from bracken-built villages with mean-mouthed hard-choked names known only to their inhabitants, nights snatched on patches of moor and riverbank that belong more to the spirits than to men. In these places only have I truly lived.

He blinked into the north-west, from where they had come, and then round towards his men, sheltering in the trees. Perhaps a thousand, Danes and Germans and Orcadians and such Scots as had, like in his previous campaigns, emerged silent from the mountains and the winds to follow him. *Wild men for a wild place.*

From among them, a single man was striding towards him.

And now, another nameless burn, another forgotten glen.

He watched the man approach, waited with open face.

'No sign?'

Montrose shook his head vigorously. 'No sign. Neither pursuit nor support.'

'We go on?'

'That we do. There'll be more to join us there. That's where the battle must be, besides.' He smiled down from the rock. 'His Majesty means to be King of more than merely Ross-shire, I think.'

'And if there is none more to join us?'

Montrose was jumping down from his rock, and his boots landed soft in the mossy ground, his face close to his lieutenant's. He scraped strands of hair out of his face, and again the smile stretched over him. 'Why, Johnnie, I beat you well enough in '45 with as few.'

❦

Thurloe had to travel to Liverpool in the third week of April. A printer named Peter Dupuy had been arrested for forging passes for those wanting to take ship abroad. At the same time a man named Potter was accused of seditious talk and plotting a rising in support of Charles Stuart. Gangs of the destitute, starving and hopeless after another bad harvest and another hard winter, were capturing food-wagons heading for the town; Liverpool was feeling uncomfortable.

Dupuy – it was probably Pierre rather than Peter – was a refugee from France. By the time Thurloe got to Liverpool, he'd been beaten through a phase of babbling suggestibility into incoherence. The ill-spelled testimony scrawled on the page suggested that Dupuy was rather better educated than the parish clerk, but none of it indicated any knowledge of wider Royalist organization. Thurloe was interested in the men who would know of Dupuy, but Dupuy clearly didn't know of them. A lonely exile using his one talent to earn his bread.

Rowland Potter, meanwhile, was a merchant who had done well selling shovels and pikes to the Army, and decided to branch into foodstuffs. As far as Thurloe could gather, this had offended those who'd previously enjoyed a local monopoly for this, and dark stories about Potter's allegiance and activities had begun circulating immediately. Half a dozen soldiers had been produced and persuaded, either by vanity or sixpence, to testify that the funny taste of their biscuit might be poison rather than the normal quality of supplies to the Army. The magistrate dealing with the case was a new man trying to meet the expectations of his sponsors and disprove the fears of the community, and succeeding in neither. Thurloe left him to it.

As he started for London again, the hills rose up to the east.

Behind: Liverpool, and the regime's rough justice. Ahead: London, and the duplicities of Scot and Tarrant.

Astbury House was close; it made sense to stop there. Thurloe had questions to ask, didn't he?

The beech avenue was a corridor into a quieter world. The brick and the stone glowed soft against the fertility of the hills behind. When Thurloe breathed, it seemed to reach forgotten corners of his body.

This time, Thurloe was asked to wait in the study. It was a room to make him feel comfortable: learning; books; titles – even editions – that he recognized. He stepped closer, trying to gauge whether Astbury was still buying books or was living in the scholarship of earlier decades.

This is not why I'm here. And yet – *This should not be why I am here.*

George Astbury had dealt in secret work for the late King. George Astbury had spent much time here, in his brother's house. What secrets had been talked here? What secrets had been kept here? *The soldier from Pontefract.*

Now nearer the shelves, he could see an alcove to the right, a portrait hanging in it. A woman, perhaps forty; the clothes rich, a fur neckline on a silvery gown, the style not so old. A handsome woman: strength in the bones, at forehead, cheek and jaw; large dark eyes.

Something about the face. Something in the glance; something to him. A promise? A warning?

Somewhere before, he'd—

'My mother.'

Thurloe swallowed the feeling that he'd been intruding, and turned. 'I see her in you,' he said, honestly. 'A compliment to you both.'

Rachel Astbury was dressed this time, and dressed well. A gown in deep grey-green, like heather, brimming with lace that drew attention to her bare collarbones and the top of her breasts; the hair pulled up at the back of her head, but still dropping to her shoulders.

The eyelids dropped for a moment, ignoring the comment or embarrassed by it.

Rachel's eyes, and the eyes of the portrait. Thurloe nodded towards it. 'Who was she?'

'She was born Isabelle Shay. Her family were from the western borders – the old marches.'

Shay?

'We'll talk in the garden, please.' She turned and led the way out.

As she opened the front door, a shawl over her shoulders now, the sun burned in her hair, and Thurloe remembered his first uncertain memories of her. *Concentrate.*

'My father must not be disturbed. He... he sleeps a great deal these days.'

Thurloe said quietly, 'It's a difficult world to have to live in.'

Rachel glanced back sharply, but the eyes were sincere – big and sad, as she'd remembered them. She nodded, and walked on.

Thurloe moved beside her and said, 'Your uncle – George Astbury – was a very intimate adviser to the late King. For intelligence. Secret dealing.'

She stopped. 'Question or statement?'

'It's true. I want to understand. . . what it was like. It brought danger here.' His voice dropped. 'It still could.'

She walked on again. 'You say secret. You mean he didn't tell you and your friends about it? Hardly surprising.'

Thurloe smiled uncomfortably. 'That's true.'

'What if he was? My uncle, like many men, served his King as best he could.' She slowed, and turned, and stood and looked into his face. 'In fact: yes, he did. Secret work. I don't know what: he never talked about it, never showed me anything. But I helped him burn his papers, before he died. I repeat: what of it?'

Papers. A system of correspondence. *And where is it now, this system?* 'It's all history now, of course.'

'So why are you interested in it?'

'There is a new world being born. Your generation – *our* generation – has the chance to be born in it anew.'

'But you're still fighting an old battle!'

'I'm trying to escape it.' There was real frustration in his voice. 'I'm stuck in. . . in the battles and schemes of old men. The deceits, the vindictive-ness. . . the loyalties of men whose time has passed.'

She walked on. She was. . . more subdued, somehow. Or perhaps just more thoughtful: age and life starting to hang on her. She pulled at the shawl, and it rode up revealing a patch of skin at the back of her neck.

They were walking along a path between two elaborate fences of trees. The trunks – Thurloe didn't recognize the breed of tree – were slender and precisely spaced, and only at waist height and head height had branches been allowed to sprout to right and left, the single limbs reaching out to the next tree. Something confused him, and he looked more closely: where the limbs met, they had somehow been grafted into each other. It made him uncomfortable.

Rachel Astbury had walked on a few paces, and now she turned into a path between two yew hedges. Thurloe followed.

She had disappeared. In front of him, the path stretched dead straight towards a distant opening, between the dark green walls, empty. He took two uneasy steps forward.

'Your new world is the upsetting of everything.' She said it dully. 'Destruction merely.'

There were openings to left and right in the hedges, dark in the darkness, further alleys leading to other junctions. She was a short distance down one of the alleys, waiting for him.

'It is the restoration of laws and liberties that governed this country fairly. Traditions that made places like this – the little society of Astbury – possible. Traditions that were twisted and destroyed as the old King got more desperate. It is the protection of those laws and liberties in a system of government that properly represents the real interests and quality of the country.'

She watched him, unblinking, then turned again and crunched away down the path.

Tarrant the torturer. The trivial oppressions of justice in Liverpool. *I wish I believed in what I said.*

The yew alley opened out onto a raised area of ground, paths to left and right and a section of the garden laid out in front below: neat blocks of shrubs and flowers, symmetries of shape and colour arranged by a scholar rather than a God; further out, beyond a low brick wall, lines of vegetable plants and frames. From somewhere far off, a faint heartbeat of metal on metal.

'We have our own forge here,' Rachel said to the garden. 'We grow our own food. We bake our own bread. We churn butter, and milk, gather honey, slaughter and salt meat, brew beer.'

'And still you've never offered me a drink.'

She moved off again, alongside a willow hedge that led to an arbour, a sheltering trelliswork of leaves and flowers. Buried among the leaves, part of the remains of a wall, was a worn stone: crudely carved figures, letters or numbers beside them; something pagan, older than all of the world's antipathies; something ancient being marked or worshipped here.

Thurloe murmured, 'Society is all but rude, to this delicious solitude'; he looked up in time to see her expression, and grunted. 'An acquaintance. The lines have stayed with me. Can you truly isolate yourself here? Cut yourself off, live on your bread and your beer? Pretend that the world does not exist?'

'What else is there? What is that world to me? It's death and division and questions and soldiers in the trees. It's men like you, strange creatures who are so damned sure of everything, going to rule the world with your Cromwell and your Greek. It's an alien world, it's far away, and I can't reach it even if I wanted to.'

The dress blended into the greenery of the arbour, and the hair was willow fronds. Rachel Astbury was a sunlit face and bust, and two vast eyes searching him.

'I believe in the same God as you, Rachel, in the same way. I believe in the same country as you, for the same benefit of the same people. I believe in my own ability to shape my own life, and on that basis I will accept God's judgement on me for good or ill. I believe in the beauty of Greek grammar as well as Greek poetry. I believe in the marshes at Maldon when the sun rises out of the mist and all I can hear is the invisible sea. I believe—'

She leaned forward and up and kissed him, her lips and breath warm on his. Thurloe's hand had come up instinctively as she moved, had touched her side, and now held her. When she pulled away, eyes somehow alarmed at what she'd done, his hand stayed on her a moment longer.

'You'd better—'

'Yes. I should—'

Thurloe trotted away down the beech alley, the sunlight flashing at him between the trunks, head flushed with the memory of Rachel Astbury's breath on his mouth. Foolishness, of course: an aberration, an impossibility, a misconjugation. But something warm, and live, and natural.

Something was nagging at him, knocking at his brain with each bump of the horse beneath him.

Rachel Astbury: truly lovely, and something real in the world of deceits.

Blackburn. Cornet Michael Blackburn under torture, pressed to tell who had helped him.

A syllable he could not suppress, a syllable his tormentors could not catch.

Shay?

Sir,

   Montrose was routed not far from this place, before he could even emerge from the northern forests, and those of his meagre force who did not perish in the field are prisoners, or prey to the wild clansmen of these parts. The Marquess himself escaped the slaughter but was shortly betrayed, and is now in the hands of the Church party in Edinburgh. The swift efficacy of their victory has left these men the unchallenged masters of Scotland — and the unavoidable partners of any cause that desires success here. For the great Montrose himself there will be no more miraculous scapes and triumphs: his enemies have him at last and, whatever their future policy, they will see him swing a traitor first.

   U. J.

[SS C/S/50/61]

AN OPEN LETTER:
FROM THE PRECINCTS OF ST PAUL'S
AN EPISTLE TO THE SCOTTISH

Gentlemen,

   good neighbourlinefs does lie in a proper concern for the interefts of the neighbour as much as a difcreet indifference to his privy bufinefs, and fo too does it lie in an honeft fincere advifing as much as a prudent filence. For furely it is only Chriftian charity to help a man to his beft interefts, to fhow him to the right road. To correct a man before he err in policy or prayer, fuch as to fave him from peril to his perfon and morefo to his foul, is no more than to cry 'beware' fhould his foot be about to tread on a fnake. The Samaritan would have done no lefs a fervice, and deferved no lefs a renown, by croffing the way to help a man ftricken by falfe doctrine as one ftricken bodily.

   Not lefs is it the right bufinefs of a neighbour to warn, when fome accident or mif-dealing in the houfe befide his does threaten him *directly, ſuch that if we ſee our neighbour's fire rage unchecked in the grate we muſt fear leſt it do bring deſtruction on our houſe as well as his, no leſs than if he let ſome diſtemper to ſpread among the pigs that graze next ours, or ſuffer ſomeone afflicted of a plague to move among us.*

In this honeſt ſpirit are we bold, in fraternity and humanity and Godly fellowſhip, to ſay to our neighbours that there is ſuch an outcaſt among them, ſent from other lands by a pretender to ſpread evil, we ſay that there is ſuch a diſtemper among them, compoſed mongrel-wiſe of parts royaliſt and parts crypto-catholick howſoever it may diſguiſe itſelf with other names, and we ſay that a fire does rage in their houſe, of pride and vainglorious bombaſt againſt their neighbour, and we ſay that there lies peril in their path ſhould they take another ſtep.

And the peril of our Scottiſh brethren is this, that if they ſuffer theſe errors to ſpread among them, and do perſiſt in theſe miſ-deeds, then it may be conſidered that, not only in Chriſtian duty but alſo in the mere ſpirit of ſelf-preservation common to all conſcious beings, England would be full-juſtified in intervening precipitately, with a ſtrength that has become too-well known in theſe iſlands, to correct the wrongs of Scotland, for the good of all of us.

To Edinburgh from London we ſend hope that wiſer counſels ſhall prevail, that the men of Scotland ſhall ſhow that prudence of mind and greatneſs of ſpirit that has ever been their quality, and love.

[SS C/T/50/13]

'Master Scot!' and there was a thumping of boots and some military clatter from the entrance passage, and as Oliver Cromwell appeared in the doorway of the great hall of Government scribes every head lifted in concern – a strange reverse bow to greet the most powerful man in the country. Cromwell hesitated only a moment, a shadow among the wooden panels, and then strode towards his man.

Thomas Scot had taken an instinctive step back, but contrived one forwards again as Cromwell closed fast. Still the boots thumped, and now there was a crumpled paper in the outstretched fist.

'Master Scot.' It had become a growl. The heads had all dropped as quickly as they had surfaced. 'What devil's foolishness is this?'

Scot had breathed himself to defiant height, and returned the glare while his mind raced for comprehension; then he took the paper, uncrumpled and scanned it. He frowned.

Three steps away, John Thurloe watched discreetly.

Cromwell's voice was lower still. 'I give you latitude enough, the Lord knows it, and every credit. But this is nigh treason.' Scot's eyes flicked up and as hastily away. The worst of curses might be endured, but that word brought a unique peril. 'There are no prouder more stubborn men on this earth than those that preside in Edinburgh, and those who preach. This. . . toy will touch them at their tenderest. Are you and your. . . coven of clerks quite deaf to political sense? Epistle – St Paul's: it's blasphemy even.'

Scot had managed to raise one hand; it quavered between them.

'This is not our work, Master Cromwell.' There was something of relief in the words. Disbelief began to bubble on Cromwell's face. 'Sincerely. You know me for a proud and honest man, whatever other failings you may ascribe.'

Cromwell blinked. 'Then who?'

'Perhaps some over-passionate partisan, of our interest but not of our controlling.' Thurloe was only a step away now, and silently took the page, and stepped away again. 'It may be impolitic' – there was a renewed edge of defiance in the old voice – 'but the reactionary precepts of the Scottish are mistrusted by many of your dearest supporters.'

Cromwell swallowed his irritation, but the words were growled again. 'Is there not licensing of papers in this country?'

'Of course. But the over-enthusiastic might somehow circumvent it. Or the unscrupulous. This may have been a ruse intended to bring us difficulty.'

'It will succeed, very like.'

Thurloe was still working instinctively at the creases of the paper, as he read and reread the text.

Since it is not idiotic loyalty, it is brilliant treachery.

Shay had two papers in front of him on the desk, two reports from Scotland. His eyes kept being distracted by the brightness of colour from the Astbury garden, shining its whites and yellows and weird vivid green through the window. Then he would drag them down to the desk again.

To the left, the report of Montrose's utter defeat, written in a great house on the edge of the Highlands, of necessity more a castle than a home, an outpost of learning and relative civility in the wilderness.

To the right, a report written in the discreet solidity of an Edinburgh town house.

> Sir,
>
> I have this day been ill-received wherever I have called, and we may perhaps rejoice in the fact. Each of my visits has been met with the merest courtesy required of the host and no warmth besides, and to this cold fare sometimes has been added a pointed remark and once a veritable sermon. The infamous public letter from London lately circulating in the town has roused the taciturn Scots to a rare heat, of affronted pride and dignity and religious principle.
>
> We may only speculate if this has contributed to the most recent adjustments of view among the leadership here. They have let go of some last more extreme demands, and sent to their representatives treating with His Majesty's representatives in the Netherlands to conclude an arrangement as speedily as possible. Neither confirmation nor exact terms have yet been received here in Edinburgh, but I may declare with comfort that there will shortly be such an arrangement, and that accordingly His Majesty will once more have the political, financial and, we may thereby hope, military support of a substantial party in these islands.
>
> W. J.

[SS C/S/50/64]

Again the colours glistened at him through the window, and again he dragged himself down to the affairs of the real world. There would be a King once more, in Scotland at least. *And once more we shall try our luck against Cromwell.*

Anthony Ascham, Ambassador-designate of the Commonwealth of England to the Court of the Kings of Spain at Madrid, passed his last night, before formally presenting his credentials for that office, in an inn on the edge of the city.

The month-long journey had felt like a wild, adventurous interval between the dignified civilized pillars of London and Madrid. A rest day. A festival of misrule. A period in the wilderness to sharpen his faith. London, where they knew him as the bold theorist of the new regime – Ascham took another mouthful of the rich Spanish wine – the sober thinker. To Madrid – capital of perhaps the most cultured and powerful royal Court in Europe – *surely our very antithesis. And yet I have been sent, and tomorrow I will be accepted* – where he would be the austere diplomat. *And in the evenings we shall debate a little, I imagine. I shall learn Spanish.* The messenger arriving just an hour ago – such formalities, such obsequiousness. *I shall publish in Spanish. 'On the friendship and advice of the Commonwealth of England, to His Majesty the King of Spain'. That would sound well.* The serving girl was hovering, and he brandished his goblet – a warm superior smile.

Two men with their backs to him, nearer the door. Once glanced towards him. *What must they think of me?*

Between the two capitals of power and politics, the sea and the hundreds of rocky miles of northern Spain. The colours so sharp and strong: dark greens and browns and orange. One didn't see orange like that in England. And so much rock, and scattered sparse across it in terrifying isolation the mountain taverns, straw and stink and hugger-mugger bedding, and those dark, raven-haired women. A wildness to the place and to the people. A danger. It seemed so very far from the green horse-churned fields of England, and London's brilliant bustling.

He felt rather young again. Another mouthful of wine. *Not yet forty, after all. I could be back in London before I'm forty, with this fine appointment already a glorious success behind me.* Young because rather nervous. Young because the Spanish women seemed to watch him voraciously, to want to mother him and then possibly to swallow him whole.

It would surely be unseemly. 'A Discourse on the effects of Absolutism on Public Morality'?

The door to some other room opened an inch, and an eye appeared in the gap. It seemed to stare at him for one dark moment, and then the door closed. *The Englishman in Spain. The official Englishman. Do women automatically find foreigners more interesting? 'On the allure of the exotic'.*

The serving girl was back beside him, a full scarlet skirt, a loose blouse, the suggestion of brown breasts free inside it, big dark eyes and that long, long hair. She reached the bottle towards him but, on a whim of dignity, Ascham held up his hand. She frowned a little, and her wrist dropped to the table with the bottle. He tried to pat it in avuncular fashion. *Enigmatic. Faintly austere. She will wonder.*

Later, on the edge of a dream of bronzed glory and voluptuousness, a thundering of feet and a slam and black ghosts and a panicky stifling, and one half-real moment feeling the hand over his mouth and seeing metal flickering in the night above him, and then the cold burn of pain, and nothing.

———

Sir,

I judge Irelande largely lost to your purposes now. Cork has been surrenderd to the soldiers of Parliament, and as we lately hear they soon after defeated the Irish in the field close by. Now we learn that Clonmel, despite a valiant resistance, has likewise been given over to the invaders as its defence could no longer be sustained. Waterford holds, but only by the hardest and is like to fall at any hour. The Irish — those as are still ready to bear arms — have retreated into the hilly fastnesses of the west. There they will not be easy caught, but nor will they do Cromwell any harm. Clearest of all, the man himself thinks the business done, as we understand that he is leaving at last for England to resume duties there, bidding others to complete the conquest here. Proud of the discretion you gave me to judge my activities for myself, I believe that I will now be better used in England again, and in truth I

shall not be sorry to leave this place, for it shall be like escaping from
the pit itself.

    T. M.

[SS C/S/50/71]

Shay only skimmed the report, with just a smile at the flash of Teach at
the end. He had expected nothing more of Ireland. The compromise with
the more Protestant Scots made the compromise with the Catholic Irish
unsustainable, anyway. *Come on then, Teach. You and Ireland have served
your turn; the game is now elsewhere.*

Teach and the old hearts of the royal cause would begin to converge on
Scotland now, to hope to be there to welcome the young King and seek
his favour, perhaps to strap on a sword again. Shay's road there would be
longer: it would lead south to Oxfordshire, and east, to Norfolk, before
it turned again northward. *Two weeks in the saddle?* His backside shifted
instinctively on the oak chair. *I seem to have been riding to war these thirty
years.*

TO MR J. H., AT THE SIGN OF THE BEAR

Sir,

    *I was much heartened at your note about the incident at New
Market, though saddened by your distraught circumstances, for
I had feared some indiscretion or ill aspect of mine had deterred
you. Truly the climate of bitterness around you must try your soul,
and I likewise am troubled by the belligerence of those around me.
Cromwell is much vexed at the thought of war, and at the hot-
headedness of the pamphleteers who have brought it on, and at the
posturing of Charles Stuart, but he is entirely determined to come to
Scotland and defeat the Scots again if he needs to. The military plans
and preparations are well in hand, and the General himself eager
to be on the march. Is there no road by which men of the prudent
middling sort might lead their sundered countrymen to safety again?*

Even our concerns about the Levellers do make men here more
angry than cautious, and I must say that I am concerned indeed. It
seems that Colonel Rainsborough or those around him had indeed at
some time and in some way had some correspondence with Royalist
elements, and at the same time that Levellers in the Government had
communication from Royalists. Can you imagine who that might
have been? For it seems fantastical to me, and leaves me grieving for
the right balance of this distracted land.

[SS C/S/50/74]

⚊ ⚊

'I can't believe that you dared come to London. Uxbridge was bad enough, but here!'

Shay gripped the man's arm, as much to stop him fidgeting. 'Then we may hope that no one else will believe it.'

'I often have visitors from Parliament; the Army even. To see my books. Or on business.'

'Perfect. My reputation can only benefit.'

'I wasn't thinking of you.' It was said with deliberate bitterness.

Shay ran one finger along a line of books, enjoying its rhythmic bumping over the spines. The room was hardly big enough for the two of them, and all four walls were solid leather, rank after rank of buff-coloured boots on parade, broken by the rare gleam of calfskin. A table was piled with letters, news-sheets and pamphlets.

He felt somehow clumsy in this temple. 'Did you bring it?' he asked sharply.

A startled glance from the other, and then a little nod. He lifted a copy of the *Veritas Britannica* to show another pile of papers, and Shay dropped onto a stool in front of it.

'*Being a strict record of the Debates held within the Army, at Putneye, during October of the year of our Lord 1647*'.

In his ear, insistent: 'Cromwell ordered these suppressed.'

'But you have rather more respect for our history.' He looked up.

The man flushed slightly. 'To have lost them. . . It would have been – I thought it—'

'I understand.' Shay watched the strained figure as it straightened the top paper unnecessarily. Not for the first time, he marvelled at the little braveries that flickered in men. 'Our history will need these details. We're all servants of the future.'

The man looked at him, examining the idea. 'Yes. That's rather good. Yes, we are.'

Shay began to turn over the pages, skimming and occasionally slowing. Cromwell and the other senior commanders trying to take the heat out of the radical men in the Army by giving them a hearing. Wild ideas, and the uneasy balancing of discipline and release. Votes for all men; fundamental rights; equality before the law; freedom of conscience.

Shay said, 'Tell me about Thomas Rainsborough.'

'The most eloquent of the radical men, and the most forward. A devil in his manner, but—'

'A politician? A rabble-rouser?'

The man hesitated. 'No. No, I should say not. Passionate, yes, but when he spoke he was most earnest and most sober.'

'Trouble for Cromwell, though.'

'They shared a mistrust of the King. But Cromwell thought the Levellers meant chaos in the Army, and anarchy in England. He worried about the King being captured by the Leveller faction.'

Shay had found Rainsborough in the record.

> *Col. Rainsborowe: For really I think that the poorest he that is in England has a life to live, as the greatest he; and therefore truly, sir, I think it's clear, that every man that is to live under a government ought first by his own consent to put himself under that government; and I do think that the poorest man in England is not at all bound in a strict sense to that government that he has not had a voice to put himself under.*
>
> [SS C/T/47/7 & WORCESTER COLLEGE MS 65]

One finger thumped at the page, slowly. *This, surely, cannot be reconciled with Royalism.*

How should a King behave before his people?

These are the decades of Charles Stuart, the second King of that name: a satin sheltered childhood, lace and loneliness and the strange tensions of his father's retreat from his own Government; an adolescence at war, an uncomfortable, precocious presence on the battlefield, just another ridiculous extravagance in the tent like the gold dinner service and the bust of Aurelius, his pudgy insecurities being played out across a whole nation, and then the forced adulthood turned back to childhood games again, hiding and disguise and catch me if you can, and then the courtiers, with their endless matronly obeisances and scoldings, coming to tell him that his father, so cold and so painful, had been murdered by his own people. *This is not what I was promised.*

I've never met this people. Perhaps some forgotten ceremonial unveiling of the infant to the world, and the soldiers plodding nearby like cattle when he stood in the tent doorway in defiance of his father's hasty murmured pleas. Then fear and poverty and exile kept the company small, and of his own class. *Shall they think me handsome?*

At the start of his third decade, Charles II was invited by his people to join them, and he came to Edinburgh by ship and by a plodding ride through endless wet hills, stopping at houses of surpassing meanness and gloom. Finally the entry to Edinburgh, his first conscious introduction to his people, a present for his twentieth birthday.

And shall these people, too, think me tall and handsome? They seemed an emotionless, stubborn set of faces, these Scots gathered to greet him from their doorways and from their windows like raised eyebrows. Not to greet him; to consider him. *This is not what I was promised in the paintings; this is not like the dreams.*

Used and forgotten, the Marquess of Montrose was there to greet his master too. From a spike protruding high out of the tolbooth his head gazed down on the procession, blackened and shrivelling and most indifferent of all.

Shay adjusted his bulk on the bench, resettling his shoulders against the damp plaster wall. Unsuccessful. He remembered the conversation in London; stared down again at the letter in his fist.

This is supposed to be a mere device. Levellers in communication with Royalists. Royalists in communication with Levellers. *What wasps' nest have I kicked?*

'Teach, I'm bored of the politicians. I've a fancy for a yarn.' Teach, crammed into a wooden chair across the fireplace, waited. He was leaner since his time in Ireland. 'What happened in Doncaster? With that man Rainsborough? I heard you had a hand.'

Shay's second hearing of the death of Colonel Thomas Rainsborough was in a slumped excuse for a tavern, in an unnamed Scottish hamlet.

'That?' Miles Teach shifted uncomfortably, and then shrugged, dismissive. 'Wholly reckless, and it hardly changed the war, did it? Something for the young bloods to feel better about themselves – siege eats at a man, d'you know? – and it rattled the enemy.'

'I heard you helped to plan it.'

Again the uncomfortable shrug. Then a deliberate shake of the head. 'One of the Pauldens thought of it. William. Clever man.'

'You said two or three of you had the secret channel to the outside. Him?'

A nod. 'Yes. The other Paulden – Thomas – he knew enough of things too. He got away, I think? Abroad?' Shay nodded. 'William Paulden's idea and plan. Kidnap Rainsborough and—'

'Kidnap him?' Shay was forward, startled. 'Not kill?'

'No. It wasn't intended, anyway.'

'I'd not thought. I'd just assumed it was a sortie, a revenging.'

'Lot of the men in Pontefract had been Marmaduke Langdale's troops, and they'd heard he'd been taken after Preston. Someone – don't know – had the wild idea of doing something to force Parliament to release him. This became kidnapping Rainsborough.' Teach watched the effect of his words. 'A nonsense, I guess. Doubt politics works like that. And men don't kidnap easily.'

'As you found.' A grunt from Teach. 'What happened?'

Teach shrugged. 'Like the Swedes used to say. "Reality happened."' Shay smiled instinctively. 'We rode in. Surprised the pickets and the gate. Got to his billet – an inn—'

'Wait – who did what?'

'We'd split up. We were four at the inn – William Paulden was scouting around – and Thomas Paulden went on immediately to spy the road. That left myself, and. . . Austwick – he was the regular military man in the thing, commanding type – and a lad.'

'Blackburn. Cornet Blackburn.'

'Mm. I'd a ruse about having a message for this Rainsborough, and that got us in. The lad held the horses, Austwick took me upstairs and we rooted out Rainsborough. His Adjutant too. Got them into the yard again and out into the street.' *Just two men.* 'Then it got out of hand.'

'How?'

Teach scowled. 'Shay, you know the skirmish better than most men living. Frightened men happened. Angry men, excited men. Everyone's blood up. Hot words. Rainsborough resisted. Or perhaps it was his man. One or both of them lashed out. Then there was a pistol – not Rainsborough, the other, his Lieutenant – he had a pistol suddenly – a regular scuffle and . . .' He shrugged. 'No choice. Middle of an enemy camp. No time for a brawl or a parley.'

'You killed them both?'

It wasn't a question one asked, and they both knew it. Teach looked faintly bitter. 'I don't think I did for Rainsborough; I make no boast either way. That was Austwick, I think. The other? I don't know. Perhaps.'

Shay knew he'd gone too far, and felt uneasy at his own strange obsession with the story. 'As you say,' he murmured. 'A bit of recklessness. But we've few enough heroics. Folk'll take them where they find them.'

Teach grunted and looked away. Shay was amused for an instant, and then lost again. *I have learned nothing of this. These facts, the men and the deaths, are nothing.*

Four men came to the inn, and were still alive: Thomas Paulden, Teach, Austwick and Blackburn. He'd found two so far.

The letter was still in his pocket. Astbury's strange interest in Pontefract, and the Levellers and Rainsborough. Rainsborough is to be kidnapped. Rainsborough is killed. *Where is the truth in this?*

The garden at Chelsea had exploded into colour. When Thurloe stepped up from the river, the silvered black of shrivelled winter had become yellows and reds and mysterious gradations of purple, with an undergrowth of all the greens. Sir Theodore de Mayerne's garden was an encyclopedia of herbs and shrubs, and now that it was fully awake Thurloe saw more clearly the meticulous ordering. It seemed too that the rich smells, crammed together in the corridor in his previous visit, had now been taken out and spread over the garden, fresher now and in their proper places.

The old man was sitting in a chair on the path, well-wrapped despite the July heat, head slumped, silent and staring into his horticultural world. For a moment Thurloe wondered if he might be dead. Then the two eyebrows rose slowly up the dome, and the eyes fixed Thurloe and waited.

Thurloe said, 'A man named Duncan Campbell will visit you. He is troubled by irregularities and excitements in his heart rhythm. Duncan Campbell is factor in London for Archibald Campbell.'

Silence. Then Mayerne's mouth flickered. 'The Marquess of Argyll?'

'He.'

'The Campbell land is. . . in the west of Scotland, I think.'

'Yes. I don't know about mining there, but I understand that also you have an interest in oysters; Argyll has substantial estates on the Clyde.'

The heavy face bulged up in a smile, and Mayerne's eyes disappeared for a moment. 'That,' he said, 'is most thoughtful of you, young man.' The eyes reappeared, sharp and shrewd. 'How may I oblige you today?'

Thurloe was caught in a deep breath. 'This garden is a miraculous place.'

'No, Master Thurloe; quite the opposite.' A shudder, and the head shifted forward. 'It is a supremely rational place. While men like you burn Europe with your hysterias of religion and politics, men like me are creating places like this together. Did you come here to debate which of us will leave more to future centuries?'

'In your secret diplomacy in the Stuart Court, did you meet a man named Shay?'

The eyebrows rode up again. 'Shay.' And dropped. 'No. I do not. . .' The eyes closed. 'The name, though. . .'

Thurloe waited.

'Somehow in connection with. . . Wallenstein. His murder in 163. . . 3 was it? 1634? Bohemia. Somehow I remember the name Shay in that connection.'

'This Shay was – one of the killers? He would have been on the side of—'

'The side?' The great body heaved. 'Young man, you have the silliest idea of European politics.' Mayerne's head slumped. Thurloe waited, uncomfortable. 'But no. . . No. . . Shay though.' The faint eyebrow bristles, slowly up again. 'I remember a Shay. A woman.'

'A woman?'

'In the 1630s I was guest on three occasions with a young man in Oxfordshire. A troubled soul; a very worthy *chevalier* of the intellect. He attracted to that place many very civilized, open minds. Scholars. Poets. Churchmen. Travellers. Natural philosophers. Devotees of Erasmus and sympathizers of Grotius.' Thurloe was struggling. *Always there is a world behind the world.* 'I met once – twice – a woman named Shay there. A careful, piercing intellect, and quite the better of any of the men. You should speak to. . . but my so ancient brain will not. . .'

Thurloe waited. *Beyond the walls of this garden is a world of battles and tortures and conspiracies.*

'Another. She was less interested in the debates, but she knew everyone. But everyone. Most charming, and apparently in the company of every faction of the Court. If you could ever meet her. . .' The eyes had disappeared again. 'But I have it! Constance Blythe. Constance Blythe.' The repetition was slow; the first name emerged as if French, the surname as a squawked attempt at the vowel.

'Constance Blythe. Thank you, Sir Theodore.'

'I'm obliged to you for your Scotchman, young man. Let us continue in correspondence.' And Thurloe left him, slumped in his carefully ordered paradise.

~◆~

Sir Mortimer Shay and Lady Constance Blythe stood on the edge of an Edinburgh hall, silent, and watching the cautious courtesies of the men and women around them as they felt their way into conversations.

It was a tentative time: new loyalties being tested and doubted; old enmities being swallowed, bitter and uneasy. The English Royalists who had come back from exile wore their fineries to impress, light laces and bright colours, and felt cold and uncomfortable among the more staid formal clothes of the Scots. Laughs came hesitant, and every glance was reviewed for meaning. Shay watched it all bleakly.

Lady Constance said, 'Tell me you're busy, Shay. Tell me you gallop through the night on quests of passion and revenge. Tell me this cause is worth something.'

'As it happens, I have some instructions to send tonight. Whatever success the King has with the Scots, he will need his supporters in England to rise. Will that do?'

She was watching him, and smiling. 'Actually, it might.' She turned to face the hall again. 'You remember Jasper Fylde? I was thinking of him just now.'

Shay shook his head, indifferent. 'No.'

'Of course you don't. Dead these twenty years. And Tom Blayne, about the same time. And John Egerton, who died at – which battle was it? And Hoxton, who was killed with you in Germany. Can you imagine what it's like to know that all the men you've bedded are dead? I longed to be sweetness, and I find I am disease.'

'There are men enough left, Con; and you're as handsome as ever.'

She glanced at him with something like pity. 'Bless you for that, Shay. Shall we grow ancient together? A great boar and a fat sow in the corner of the farmyard, sustaining ourselves on turnips and some unconscious memory of pleasure? Idle shrivelled brains, and idle shrivelled privates. But no. You'll be away to some meadow, where Meg is always spring.'

She looked out into the drifting figures. 'And what of me now? Am I supposed to be their memorial? Here lieth. . . none any more, because they're all dead.'

A snicker of laughter near them. She glanced at it, and gave a little frown of distaste. 'Think of it. Life was fruit, and jewels, and music, and a generation of beautiful men. I danced and sang whole years away. We were golden and glorious, all of us.'

'We were rancid, petty and foolish.' He smiled roughly. 'We lived our every hour, though.'

'Like gilded cattle before the slaughter.'

'You were too wise for that, Con.'

'Not wise. Never wise. But I had brain enough to be useful to you and your predecessors.'

Shay nodded into the room. 'This is the field where I must fight my battle. Tell me of it.'

She sniffed. 'A marsh. Little firm ground to be had. There are some who are sincere in their religion, but they know that the King's adherence to that cause is political only, and so they will use him politically. The old soldiers are true enough. Leslie. Leven. They're obliged to play at politics but they are not political. Don't let your sympathy over-account their influence. You cannot trust Argyll too little. A heart so shrunken by thirst, and by betrayal, that he is become ambition only. A beast of survival. His mother was a Douglas, royal blood on both sides though not always the right side of the blanket. For Argyll, and for Hamilton, even though he's a solider man than his dead brother, the little difficulties of the Stuarts are just a distraction from older squabbles.'

'And the English here?'

'Fisher. Booth.' A little shrug. 'Wilmot's true. Apt to try to be cleverer than his brain would stand, and to drink more than his manhood would stand. He tried to make a peace with the Parliamentarians in '43. No, '44, of course. Taylor. Percy... Percy thought he was going to marry Lady Margaret Soane, but Fisher beat him to it. 163... 8.'

Shay watched the hard lost eyes. 'Good. Something else. Last year, Parliament sold all of the royal pictures. Vast amount of money. There were a handful of men doing most of the buying. Huygens. Javach. Le Blon – I think he was fronting for Swed—'

'For Golden Christina, yes, he would have been.'

'And Kenyon. Martin Kenyon.'

'Kenyon.' The eyes flickered, and were still. Shay waited. 'Helped to arrange the King's visit to Madrid in 1623.'

'So buying for Spain.'

'Perhaps. Not the one to worry about. Javach – Jabach, actually – he'll have had the private suppers with the Parliament men, if they've sense. Lives in France, works for Mazarin. If there was politics among the pictures, it was him.' Again she focused on the people in front of them. 'Look at us!' She shivered for effect. 'Such desperate, wheedling men now. Ralph Fortescue once hid a pearl in his cuff and let it drop into my hand, and the next day sent the most elaborately dirty poem on the theme. Last night a man took my hand to kiss it and he actually left crumbs in my palm. Desperate.'

Shay grunted. 'I grant, I look at some of these political men and wonder why I bother.'

Constance Blythe's surprise was genuine, though the voice stayed low. 'But you don't do it for any of us, surely. Truly, Mortimer, I would die of ecstasy if I thought that I was in your mind as you fought your wars across Europe, or as you carved your way through this island doing. . . whatever you do. But you're no Lancelot. It's not for one sad old whore, or for any of these painted relics. Not even for Meg. You do it because it is you.'

Shay was staring bleak across the room. 'And what do you offer me at the end, Con? What is my rest or reward? Is that all I am ever to be – an eternal destruction?'

'We must live what we are, Shay. There is nothing else.'

TO MR I. S., AT THE ANGEL, IN DONCASTER

Sir,

I was heartily glad to hear from you, and relieved that you yet endure these turbulent times in fair health. I know not what to make of the goings between Leveller and Royalist: it is plain that the men trapped in Pontefract had contact with the world outside by divers privy means, but with whom I cannot say.

I am now established in Edinburgh, which is a very pit of politics, with every man jostling for his interest and his private advantage, so that I do

think myself glad when most solitary, or in the company of the meanest
servant rather than one of the Court men. No doubt, though, the Royal
party is in the ascendant, and the more belligerent of the King's interest
are become very cocksure accordingly. There is still some hedging and
cavilling by the leaders of the Scottish Church, but all know it for mere
posture and performance, intended to get the best bargain they may.
All know that they will come round to public support of the young King
Charles, and with the levies, who already perform prodigiously under
the guidance of veteran sergeants of our own late conflicts and those in
the Continent, looking most warlike, there is such a general enthusiasm
for battle that it does quite chill me. The defences of this place are vast,
with many unchristian tricks and traps laid for those who would attack.

You will understand that communication with me in Edinburgh may
be difficult. But there is a lad who goes to and fro Galashiels, and if you
were to write to me at Macrae's at that place your words may chance to
reach me, and would bring pleasure if they did.

[SS C/T/50/63]

'It looks too hard a nut, gentlemen.' Cromwell, hot and hard-breathing like
the horse from which he'd just descended, thick hair plastered to his head
from the steady drizzle, was already talking as he approached. Lambert,
his second-in-command, and Scot and Thurloe turned and gathered as he
joined them under the tent awning. 'We went as close to the city as respect
for providence would allow, and the lines are well-made. I won't risk good
men against them.' He ran a hand through his sodden hair, and looked
at the three of them.

Scot, obviously disappointed at the possibility of withdrawal, said, 'I
regret that I have not better information to offer from inside the city.'

Thurloe said, quietly, 'I hear that the lines are strong, and the men
enthusiastic to fight.'

Cromwell's face twisted in a silent growl at him, and then he nodded.
'One last demonstration to try to tempt them out. If that fails, we must

withdraw for a spell. The men are drowning in this rain to no purpose, and the Scots left us a desert to feed on. Lambert?'

'I agree, General.'

'Well then. Colonels to me in one half-hour.' Lambert grunted acknowledgement and stamped off into the rain. 'Thurloe: you have a friend inside the walls?'

Thurloe nodded slightly. 'A correspondent.'

'I cannot find cracks in their barricades, but their alliance is loose enough. Can't we play on that a little? Can't the more reasonable men be helped to understand that we are not their enemy?'

              ◆—~

To Mr J. H., at Macrae's in Galashiels

Sir,

I was obliged on an errand to ride to be with the Army, so we may temporarily have been closer than you imagined when you wrote. I shall be spending time at Newcastle, and you might write to me at the George, in that place.

You will have seen and, perhaps, as I did, been contented at the more pacific posture of General Cromwell these last days. It seems he does not wish to spend the lives of men in fighting other men so close in nature and sympathy. He is wont to talk of the Godliness of many of the leaders of the Scottish Church party, and I think he truly regrets that they came close to battle. We must hope that events give breath and nourishment to this side of his nature, and thereby give us all hope for some kind of reconciliation. It is well known here how suspicious the Church leaders are of the young Charles Stuart — many of the preachers in the camps are Edinburgh men, and their language is most unchristian on the subject of the prince and his friends.

I do not wonder at your discomforts, caught up among these divided and fratricidal factions, and wish only that you may come through with your spirit unaffected.

[SS C/S/50/104]

Sir Mortimer Shay in the kitchen: an iron-grey head among the hanging joints of meat, steam and the thick smell of stew gusting around him, the alehouse serving girl brushing past him and back and wondering at the games of men, an eye in a doorway watching the bustle beyond.

And what do you, Scoutmaster?

Like all good scouts, Francis Ruce was an elusive, insubstantial presence: hardly seen, hard to track. Shay had done two days' scouting of his own – watching and casual enquiries and mental games on the map – and it had brought him to this alehouse kitchen five minutes before Scoutmaster Ruce had slipped into the alehouse and sat opposite another man. The other had scanned the room, then exchanged words with Ruce, and Ruce had dropped his hat on the bench between them and settled back in his chair.

Not good. The scout should wait, the source visit. *Are you scout tonight or source, Mr Ruce?*

The scouts were the eyes of the army in the field, the ears. Sharp eyes and ears meant timely readiness to face the enemy; they meant winning the race to the good ground; they meant a powerful line of march and a robust deployment. Dim eyes and dull ears meant surprise, weakness and vulnerability.

At Naseby in '45 the royal cause had suffered badly. Some said it was the scouting. Francis Ruce had been Scoutmaster. At Preston in '48, Cromwell had surprised the royal army by the unlikely expedient of staying north of the river.

It was natural for Ruce, as Scoutmaster, to come to such a place in such a manner. If he is to be a good scout, a scout must have his sources, to learn what he must of the enemy's movements and condition.

A scout who becomes himself a source, is the best possible source.

Are you scout tonight or source?

One of a dozen murmured conversations in the alehouse, Ruce and the other talked on, heads bent, eyes unmeeting, and Shay tried to read the currents of the exchange, to gauge where the power lay in a glance, an expression of watchfulness, a clenched hand.

'A trumpet call for free Englishmen!' Every head swung round, and Shay adjusted his glance a moment from the doorway. A young man was standing on a chair at the other end of the room, a paper clutched tight in two hands. Shay's eyes, no threat seen, flicked back and tried to read the two faces. Had Ruce reacted more quickly?

A scout is naturally alert. A source is naturally uneasy. *The blade always has two edges.*

After some initial jeers, friendly or indifferent, the young man pressed on defiantly, reading the pamphlet in a voice a little high and unmodulated, and his audience settled. Ruce and the other had returned to their murmuring, and Shay resumed his study of their expressions and postures, only half-hearing the occasional shouts of agreement from the crowd at the reading.

The reading ended, with cheerful jeers and applause and stamping, and then someone started on a ballad, and Ruce's companion was standing.

Was it imagined? The companion crushing something in his fist and pocketing it as he stood? A scrap of paper? *These are suspicions only. Scout or source? Without – there:* as he picked up his hat in his right hand, Ruce's left hand went underneath it to support some heavier thing clutched in it.

Information is insubstantial; payment is substantial.

I think I have you, little man.

<hr />

MERCURIUS FIDELIS

or

The honeſt truth written for every Engliſhman
that cares to read it

From MONDAY, JULY **25**. *to* MONDAY, AUGUST **1**. **1650**.

MONDAAY, JULY **25**.

ROMWELL'S army having invaded thrice-wronged SCOTLAND, that vainglorious ſoldier has roamed the countryſide viſiting DEVASTATION upon poor honeſt ſouls and quite failing to ſecure any military purpoſe. As much as he has ſhown himſelf ready to fall upon the innocent and the weak in the homes, ſo he has been ſtrangely behindhand in facing the military ſtrength of the proud SCOTS and the perſon of HIS MAJESTY. Vainly has he tried to tempt the wiſe ROYAL commanders to imprudence, and fruſtration do only increaſe his cruelty.

TUESDAY, JULY 26.

Even as HIS MAJESTY does defy the illegitimate armies of the illegitimate PARLIAMENT, ſo does HIS HIGHNESS the PRINCE RUPERT of the RHINE do the like to their bewildered ſhips. Now ſafely berthed with our many friends in Portugal, HIS HIGHNESS continues to torment his tormentors.

FRIDAY, JULY 29.

DUNBAR having fallen to the voracious Parliamentarian HORDE, and MUSSELBURGH too, Cromwell has found himſelt unable to gain anything by theſe hollow performances except the malicious ſatiſfaction of innocent ſuffering, and his bold ſhow of force towards the great walls of EDINBURGH on this day was met only with muſket balls and SCORN, and he was obliged to retire to nurſe his wounds.

SATURDAY, JULY 30.

Indeed, ſo great was his ſhame, and so little his ſucceſs, that this CROMWELL had on the next day following to retreat all the way to MUSSELBURGH, there to reconſider his hubris. SHAME upon ſhame was his only lot, for he found that he had loſt more in the RETREAT than mere hirelings and PRIDE and ravaged land. Having reached what he conſidered SAFETY, he diſcovered that he had careleſſly left behind him his ſecond abettor in theſe VIOLENT proceedings, General LAMBERT, captured by the quick-footed ROYAL ſoldiers.

SUNDAY, JULY 31.

HIS MAJESTY attended HOLY SERVICE, and was heard to remark on the greatnefs of GOD and on his many MERCIES to thofe who do truly and humbly LOVE him. A FISH being opened at a table in GLASGOW town, it was found to contain an other fifh whole infide it, and this was taken to PORTEND great developments from the prefent ftate of AFFAIRS. This day a gallant band of LANCERS under the excellent MONTGOMERY attacked CROMWELL even in his own camp, and he remains under conftant ftrife and prefs of events.

[SS C/T/50/71]

Another long day, and Francis Ruce felt it in his shoulders as he rode, felt it in the jolts of his equally tired horse as it tramped stiff-legged through the evening.

I have deserved more than this.

A burned-out cottage ahead, an unpleasant outline against the field.

I don't think I've slept easy these five years or more. Ten. Always between the lines. Always on the edge.

A shadow moving near the ruin? *Careful.* It was a lonely road. There had been attacks. Vicious locals; bitter starving peasants stunned by another lost harvest; scavenging deserters from any one of the armies that had crossed this land in the last few years. Everyone had a reason to steal these days, and no one had a reason not to kill.

I will survive, and I will survive with something to show for it.

The shadow broke from the edge of the building, and became a man. Ruce reached for his pistol.

'Ruce!' Ruce kept his hand on the pistol, pulled the horse up. 'I'd have hoped for no one better.' Ruce peered into the gloom. He knew the man, surely, by sight. 'Come in here, will you? Need your help.' A man of influence among the Generals. A man worth respecting, worth cultivating.

But in the waist-high remnant of a doorway a weight smashing on the back of his neck and Ruce was stumbling and then his legs were kicked away and he dropped into the rubble, felt a hand driving his face into the ground, felt through his panic a blade at his throat. 'Hands!' A squawk of confusion. 'Your hands behind you or I cut your throat!' Now a knee pressing his head down, and his hands were quickly tied behind him, and he was wrenched face-up again, shoulders and elbows and hips ungainly and sore.

The man stood upright, and watched him. Ruce shuffled backwards to a sitting position against the slumped wall. Then the man was looming down at him, squatting close by, a knife in his hand.

A moment more, of thought. Then, 'Ruce: you should know. You're probably going to die tonight. At my hand.' Ruce's eyes wide, mouth gaping to speak and a hand was thrust into it and his head slammed back against the stone. 'You should learn to speak when asked. Understand?' A nod, and the hand was pulled away. 'But know that when you speak, your life depends on it. Understand?'

Ruce nodded again, instinctive, but warier.

'You've sold us, Ruce. Time and again. Tonight you'll—'

'I never—' and the knife flashed forward and pierced his throat.

A prick merely, but Ruce froze in the shock.

Deliberately, the man pulled the knife back and shifted his grip, took Ruce's collar in two hands and ripped downwards, baring the chest. Then he adjusted the knife again and, with the same deliberation, carved a shallow cut across Ruce's breast, and Ruce gasped shrill and shocked.

'You've sold us, Ruce. Time and again.' This time the man stopped, and waited for the reaction. Ruce was gasping, cold, eyes wide. 'You tell me. Everything, yes. Who you told. What you told.' He flicked the knife up and caught the haft between finger and thumb and, casually, angled the blade forward and tapped Ruce on the nose.

And Ruce told him: a conversation in a brothel, years back, a man who knew everything about him, his needs, his weaknesses. Not a demand but a suggestion, a sharing of information to facilitate stalemate, fewer deaths. *How much did he offer to pay you?* Just expenses, and why shouldn't I? And still the heavy face bored into him. *Who? Describe him?* Different men, no names, but they all seemed to know him. His mother. His debts. And had anyone truly looked after him all these years?

Shay watched him, tired. An ideal weakling. Vulnerable on so many points, and someone had known it.

How were you summoned? How were you met?

Simple codes, simple alerts. Anonymous meetings in alehouses and woodland clearings. Anonymous men; masked men.

A name. Give me a name, or you may die this night.

But Francis Ruce, shivering and weak-bladdered, could give no name.

And Mortimer Shay, short of time and frustrated, leaned forward and clamped his hand over the gabbling mouth again and cut the throat.

It bulged crimson and he watched it, bored, and wondered.

~ ~

Rachel read the *Mercurius Fidelis* sitting in the arbour in the flower garden, as if it were some precious secret of romance.

Either I want to shelter in this garden for ever, like some vestal virgin of horticulture, or I want the world of this news-sheet. This was Shay's world: the politics, the plots, the armies and the sieges. This news-sheet was him talking to her. He would, presumably, want her to care about the defiance of Edinburgh against the English Army. He was working to bring the Scottish Church and the Scottish leaders around in support of his King.

My King. Those Scotsmen are the leaders of my cause now.

The news-sheet was ridiculous, of course. The portrait of Cromwell as some bewildered demon staggering around the Scottish countryside was presumably exaggerated. But then she remembered all the times soldiers had come to Astbury: the wilfulness, the damage, the feeling that there were no longer any limits to what might be about to happen; and she wondered about the women of Musselburgh and Dunbar.

She tried to imagine how Thurloe fitted in Cromwell's rampaging organism. He seemed far too careful, too cerebral, too... gentle, to be part of the chaos of horses and cannons and big men in uniform and shouting that was her image of an army. Perhaps Cromwell used decent men like Thurloe to soften the image of his rule. Or perhaps Thurloe was just a convenient tool of Cromwell's world – one who could write a letter, or pursue a case at law. Or put clever pressure on a family like the Astburys.

Or might it be the other way round? Might the Army be the tool of the clever men – a necessary tool to achieve the new kind of stability they desired? She wondered about a world ruled by Thurloes: thoughtful, surely. Principled, or merely indifferent?

He has a wife, I think. She wondered about Mrs Thurloe. A dowdy breeder of the offspring of a clever man; or his clever partner, trading Greek quips in the parlour?

If Shay and his Scotsmen do not win, is that the kind of man I am supposed to marry?

———

William Seymour, grey hair bobbing behind him as he walked stiffly over the flagstones, heard his name from the shadows and turned to see the outline of two men on a bench. One rose and stepped to the edge of the light.

'Shay. How do you?'

'Well enough. How is the young King?'

Seymour preferred to move as little as possible, and did not see why Shay should not do the walking, but discretion overcame him and he stepped closer to the shadows. Miles Teach stood, respectful, but stayed back against the wall. 'He is. . . a different sort of man to his father.'

'That's certainly true.' Shay managed a heavy smile. 'Poor Seymour. Your service has deserved more stability than this, I think.'

Seymour seemed to take it as licence to express his frustrations. 'These people, Shay!' His head came closer, and the cracked voice dropped further still. 'Such a hotpot of politicking and religion as you never saw. The man Cromwell has advanced again and sent envoys to the Church leaders here offering negotiations. He knows their suspicions of the King; he knows our divisions. Yesterday' – the voice was a shrill whisper – 'the Church leaders demanded – demanded! – that the King sign a paper disowning the religion of his parents and restating his own support to the Scottish religious settlement.'

'I heard as much. He'll sign, I hope.'

Seymour's eyes went wider still. 'No, Shay! He will not. Young Charles cares nothing for his father's beliefs, I think, but he has all of his father's pride.'

'He must be persuaded. Leslie's army would simply disappear. If the Scottish leaders withdraw their support, we are lost.'

'I know that!' Seymour was spitting his frustration. He caught himself, hissed in a deep breath, and stared at Shay.

Shay gripped his narrow arm. 'I understand. What a pit we're in, eh?' He stepped back. 'Tell me if – No, let me offer now. I have a young man – Vyse, Bernard Vyse's boy. A fine lad, and it's time he got acquainted with the Court and his duties there. May I send him to assist you?'

Seymour thought for a moment, nodded, and turned and stalked uncomfortably away.

Teach, closer now, said: 'Trouble?'

Shay, over his shoulder: 'Perhaps. Cromwell knows our cracks and is pulling at them. The King must bow his head to these miserable Scotch faith-pedlars, or we can all go and live in permanent exile.'

To Mr I. S., at the George, in Newcastle

Sir,

The hopes for peace, I fear, have taken their heaviest blow since your General Cromwell brought his army over the border. I learned from a man at breakfast today that yesterday night His Majesty, at last, under much persuasion from his friends, signed the paper demanded of him by the leaders of the Scottish Church party. He has disavowed the beliefs of his own parents, and repeated his support to the new Scottish settlement. The Scots are cock-a-hoop at this, which they see as confirmation of their power over the King, and as a reinforcement to the strength of their movement. The King's friends, meanwhile, are likewise delighted, knowing that the Scots are now full committed to fight against Cromwell in the King's interest. These squabbling fractions of men are for now united, in religion and in desire for war.

[SS C/T/50/79]

On the table in front of Cromwell, four papers showing the signs of having recently been in his unhappy fist. 'It has never been my habit to retreat, gentlemen. But I think this a false battle, and I do not think we can win it. These latest news from inside Edinburgh confirm what Thurloe's report told us a day ago: the royal whelp has put his neck in the Scottish leash. None of them will be negotiating with us now. None of them will be crossing the lines to join us.' He shook his head, great glum swings from shoulder to shoulder, discontented at the whole world. 'My palsied Army shrinks daily on this wasteland, and it will not do.'

Thurloe remembered uncomfortably yesterday's pride, hurrying in to Cromwell with his paper, the news that Charles Stuart had signed the declaration days earlier. Excitement at the clever arrangements that had got a paper from Edinburgh to Newcastle and near back again in less than two days. Excitement that he had the information that others did not. Excitement that the information was significant.

I did not care a penny for the significance itself. Now he saw the real significance, in the bitter faces of Scot, Lambert – swiftly rescued after his capture by the Royalists, but still smarting at the indignity – and most of all Oliver Cromwell.

'We must withdraw from this place, as best we may.'

———

'Shay.'

'Leslie.'

David Leslie's flowing curls were white now, the moustache likewise. 'What would Prince Maurice have made of us?'

Shay's mouth curled. 'Not much, I fear. He'd want another half a year with your levies, at the least. But then he always was a miserable old goat. Gustavus Adolphus, now. . .'

Leslie's eyes brightened. 'Would attack.' In the angular Scotch accent, the word snapped sharp.

'Spoken like his favourite lieutenant.' He glanced at the room around them. There was a briskness to the bustle of the Court men and the soldiers. 'You're ready to give open battle?' The words were lower.

Leslie's voiced dropped accordingly, but the hunger was still in the face. 'Cromwell knows he can't split us now. And he hasn't the supplies for a campaign, and his men get more miserable by the hour. The cavalry are chivvying him daily – wearing him down. The only decision is whether we wait for him to retreat – merely push him out of Scotland.'

'You want more, of course.'

'He retreats; he returns. He's weak, now, and we won't have a like chance again. And if we wait any longer the Church men hereabout will find some way to lose the opportunity.' The accent emphasized the irritation. He leaned forward. 'If I could somehow fix Cromwell – surround him – I would shatter the myth for ever.'

Shay nodded, slowly. Then he patted Leslie roughly on the arm. 'Let's see what comes, old horse. All these Godly prayerful men around, perhaps you'll get lucky.'

Leslie nodded brightly and strode off, bent-backed but spry.

Shay watched him go, then looked around. Balfour was sitting on a chair near the door, as ever quiet and watchful. 'Tom.' He was up and across in a moment. 'I'll have a little journey for you.'

To Mr I. S., at the George, in Newcastle

Sir,

Where previously there was great appetite for violence, I rejoice to say that the majority here now finds the pleasures of peace more seductive. The caprices of the Church leadership here do infuriate the young King's advisors, but such is their hold over the simple men who make up most of the army that there is nothing the Court men may do. The Church party are now most satisfied that General Cromwell is departing their land and, wanting in the final reckoning to be on terms with him as comfortable as the recent fluctuations do allow, are reluctant to press their military advantage and waste lives. I think they will do what they can ahorse to harry your forces away as fast as is possible, but happily the foot-men are mostly kept behind their stout defences in the city and should not be risked against Cromwell.

I write thus to you, in haste, in anticipation that you will soon be travelling southward again, and accordingly to wish you safe journey homeward, that we may continue to correspond, with our consciences untroubled by any clash of arms or further difference between us.

[SS C/T/50/89]

Oliver Cromwell on campaign was an even more volatile prospect than when in London, and Thomas Scot composed his brittle dignity before entering the inn-room that served as his headquarters.

Cromwell's big eyes rolled up ominously.

'General, I regret that I have no useful intelligence to offer you on the Scottish manoeuvrings or intentions. Our most promising channel has grown quite cold. I fear this must encourage a more precipit—'

'No matter.' The eyes had dropped again, and Cromwell was drifting back into the papers on the table in front of him. 'Thurloe has a report that the Scots don't want to fight. They want us away from Edinburgh, which I will gladly manage, for this month at least, but they'll not throw more than a few horsemen at us. We have time to move towards Berwick without abandoning our supplies or artillery. If the supplies keep coming in by sea we may even find a new safe base nearby.'

Scot left, unsure whether he was supposed to feel grateful or vengeful towards Thurloe.

Thurloe himself was woken early by the increasingly familiar sound of military urgency. The two men who'd been sharing his room were gone, and he dressed quickly and hurried downstairs into the dawn to find a riot of galloping and shouting. Weapons were being grabbed, papers were being burned, and a stream of white-faced couriers was emerging from Cromwell's room.

The Scottish army was advancing from Edinburgh. A detachment of its infantry had circled the English and blocked the road south. Cromwell and his Army were surrounded.

Thurloe first absorbed the news with his usual dogged grappling at military affairs. Then he reabsorbed it, with a growing queasiness in his belly, and hurried off to find Thomas Scot.

The sun rose feeble out of the sea and began to climb the Doon Hill. As it reached the top it picked out a line of men and then, breaking over them, began to hurry down the western slope in the footsteps of the Scottish army, tramping towards battle. But the light was losing against the clouds that were being chased in off the water by an angry wind, and growing heavy.

Among the small group on the crest, Sir Mortimer Shay: dark pride.

The letter to the Parliament man: reassurance, the Scots unlikely to bring out their infantry, no need for Cromwell to hurry. *I have created this.*

The landscape rolled out below him like a map. In the distance, the sea, a white blank margin to the world and to what was possible in it. Immediately in front of him, backs and boots dropping away down the hill, the army that he had helped to pull together and bring to this place, Scottish soldiers fighting for his King. At the foot of the Doon Hill, protecting the new Scottish position, the river wandered from outside his leftward vision across the scene to the sea. Between the advancing Scots and the empty sea was the English Army, smudges of men spread across the plain.

Teach said: 'Seems a pity to be abandoning this high ground.' He had to articulate the words with care to make them carry.

'I never generalled a battle. All my fighting was hand-to-hand.' Shay shrugged slightly. 'I never saw my enemy's plan, or his dispositions, or his regiments. Only his face.'

Teach grunted agreement. 'Leslie says that since there is no chance Cromwell will climb the hill to meet us, we must go down to him. And if we don't force him to battle, he'll have time to escape by sea.'

'Mm. And these Scots are miserable enough without spending another hour on this god-forsaken mountain.' As he said it, the wind blustered up again and this time it brought moisture, and they and the others on the hill hunched and looked instinctively for shelter.

The backs of the soldiers bent a little as the rain came on. Behind them, their commanders wrapped cloaks around themselves more tightly and began to follow them down out of the wind.

'We have him now, regardless.' Teach had to shout the words.

Shay nodded slowly, watching his world spread out in front of him like papers on a desk. 'So it seems.'

Somewhere below him across the river, one of the flags or clusters, was Oliver Cromwell, trapped.

—— ——

Oliver Cromwell's great thick-coated shoulders were bent over the table, carrying the world. The face, when it looked up to find Thurloe standing there, seemed as usual bigger and more strongly shaded than the things around it. Dark brown hair; the nose, the wart, the textured flesh hanging heavy on the cheeks; and the eyes, far away in a plan or a prayer. The lives of tens of thousands of men; his commission on behalf of the country; the future of an ideal that might reshape Europe – all depended on how shrewdly he read a crude sketch map, how keenly he saw into a landscape, and whether once more he could summon up enough genius to make God himself think his cause worthy of favour.

Thurloe felt his stomach kick again, and set his teeth hard. 'Master Cromwell' – the eyes focused on him – 'I must... admit failure. Apologize.'

The eyebrows rose a fraction.

'The letters I've been getting – insights on Royalist intentions and movements – I strongly believe they're... deliberate deceptions.'

The great nose wrinkled up.

'I've checked against Master Scot's sources. Charles Stuart actually signed his declaration to the Scottish Church on the 16th of August – at least two days after my correspondent wrote to say he had done so. My correspondent wanted to make us think the Scots and the Royalists were more united than they were – to make us hesitate – to buy time for their politics. The same when he wrote that the Edinburgh lines were strong, and the defenders eager to fight.' He winced, took a breath. 'The same when he wrote that the Scots would not pursue – making us relax – allowing them to surround us.' *Breathe.* 'I'm. . . sorry.'

Oliver Cromwell nodded. Then his head dropped to the papers on the table again.

One of the papers crackled as Cromwell unrolled it.

'What – what happens now?'

Cromwell looked up again, and the eyes re-focused. 'Now, Master Thurloe, we will fight a battle.' Fate itself was speaking, low and ominous. 'We will depend on God's mercy, as always, and nothing else. God is never deceived.'

The eyes and the shoulders dropped to the table again. Thurloe nodded, pointlessly, and turned to go.

'Thurloe.'

He turned back.

The big eyes focused sharp and narrow, and the words fell hard. 'Next time.'

- ~ -

Shay and Teach found a little shelter halfway down the hill, an outcrop of rock at their backs and a gorse reaching over them.

Teach pulled some biscuit from inside his jacket, and shared it. 'And today: another little slaughter.'

'Mm.' Shay's eyes were still on his trap. 'Tomorrow, I think.'

'A strange country we have become.'

'I was born in battle, Teach; in blood. I am a creature of fields like this. It served me well enough as an education. You too, I think.'

Teach nodded. 'And yet you keep your young terriers away from the field.'

Shay's glance was quick, the return slower. 'Their duties took them elsewhere.'

'You sent them. Vyse and Manders on the staff. Balfour another courier's errand. In their different ways, they'd each want to be on the field, but you' – the accusation came soft, jovial – 'you made sure they'd be elsewhere. I charge you for an old sentimentalist, in spite of yourself.'

Shay took in a vast slow breath, uncomfortably as if through a wound. 'Is it wrong to hope that this all might be worth something?' The voice was low, slow, heavy. 'Can't our ravaged generation leave something – anything – a little bit good?'

Teach nodded again. The waiting continued to eat at their guts, as the soldiers shifted and settled at the river, opposite the English soldiers caught between them and the sea.

—◆ ◆—

Shay had found a cottage where a pretty, scared, manless woman would give him a bed for a penny. He woke to darkness, a hand on his shoulder and then a candle offering hints of Thomas Balfour.

'Sir Mortimer.' Shay blinked away the glare and the momentary confusion. *Have I lived my life in these broken hours?*

'A man must find his own bed, Tom. This one's taken.'

'There's movement across the river – from Cromwell's lines.'

Shay forcing his old-feeling head into thought. 'He's resetting his regiments for the battle. Or he's preparing a rearguard to cover an evacuation by sea. Either way, our Scots won't move before morning.'

'Shouldn't—'

'They won't move because they can't yet know what to move against.' He smiled without warmth. 'Sorry, Tom: sometimes there's only waiting.'

Balfour nodded. 'I'm sorry I woke you.'

'Don't be. You did rightly, boy. It's better – it's always better – to sleep too little than sleep too long. Ask Master Cromwell.'

—◆ ◆—

In the darkness, the Scottish army slept like cows, bunched together in the fields, against hedges where they could, rolled in their cloths and padded with torn clumps of grass, quietly shrivelling in the rain.

A constant shivering, a shifting of the black uncomfortable lumps, soft bitter chatter and hunched curses, and always the rain and the cold.

Across the river, the English commanders dragged their men through the night, through hours of little shifts and stops that moved them only sideways and apparently no distance at all. And always the rain and the cold, sharp at the neck and insidious in the boots.

Shay slept ill after the interruption, Cromwell nagging at his shoulder whichever way he rolled. He was awake with the first faintness of dawn, set off by some odd crease in a dream or in the grey world outside. The inescapable first pang of uncertainty – *What place is this? What death am I trying to avoid today?* – and then he was up, buckling himself together like a groom with a dray horse, and plunging into his boots.

Then he was away into the grey flush of the morning, cold but alive, striding up the Doon Hill again, in time to watch Cromwell's miracle.

This then is his genius. He sees further and quicker than other men, and he acts faster.

The centre and left of the Scottish army slept tight between the hill and the river, and woke to sounds of battle and found itself with no space to manoeuvre. They stood uneasy or milled around, according to the temper of their regimental commanders, while the right wing of the army tried to hold back the torrent.

It is so obvious, but he sees it first, and to see it second is too late.

The English Army, rank after rank of them grim and shivering and stretching back out of the reach of morning, were concentrated in a single column, and Cromwell sent them in one continuous punch out of the gloom against the Scottish right. As one attack faltered against the desperate sodden Scottish defence, the next broke over it like the storm, and so over and over until the defence shrank and was washed away. From the hill, only the faintest trace of the English singing could be heard drifting up. *Oh praise ye the Lord, all ye nations.* From the hill, the Scottish ribbons and pennants flickered and fell into the drowning brown scrum of soldiers, and still the English ranks and the English colours kept coming.

Does this make him truly the angel of his God? That he sees the battle so entirely and so rightly?

The Scottish right broke. Lost now and individually alone, its soldiers died in the bloody mud, slipped, scrabbled away through the swamp, wrestled to freedom through the milling, chaotic shoulders of their former comrades, ran. Their regiments evaporated in fear and confusion and their remains were swallowed by the endless ordered flow of the English. And still the psalm rolling over the carnage: *Praise him, all ye people. For his merciful kindness is great toward us.*

As the Scottish right collapsed, its fugitives raced through the hesitating centre regiments like woodworm through timber, and through the mists of morning and artillery smoke the timber could be seen to brittle and creak, then it too was engulfed. As the English roared through the Scottish army at Dunbar, right to left – *The truth of the Lord endureth for ever* – from the Doon Hill its remnants could be seen drifting away over the river and the hillside in desperate, lonely hope of safety.

Shay watched it all from the remove of the hill and the months past. *The Crown has lost another year of striving, in one moment of ruthless clarity from that man.* Down from the overcast morning he scowled at all his meetings and manoeuvrings, all the uncovered truths and undiscovered lies that had led to this place.

Praise ye the Lord.

Angry and frustrated, Shay found himself stalking through the wreck of so many hopes looking for Vyse, Manders and Balfour, and uncomfortable about it. *Have my hopes become so contingent? Do I depend so little on myself these days?* The royal cause was a scattered threadbare thing now, huddled and hunted in cottages and ditches; he strode among torn uniforms and pale bewildered men, and the litter of weapons thrown aside in flight or shame.

He recognized the sick shock of defeat in the faces, though they were all unfamiliar. And they stayed unfamiliar and unreassuring: the men who might have seen the three young men, or should have seen them, had not and could not help him.

Shay walked the scattered remnants of the army increasingly grim, some instinct of undefeated self maintaining the high shoulders and long stride, while the unease grew in him. Eventually he got on the trail of rumours of the three, reports at two or three removes. They had been in the battle after all. Heroism. Where the battle was thickest. Charging in. Death or glory. He forced himself to mistrust the worst reports as much as the best. At least one was dead. They had died together, united as always.

Among the hearsay and the platitudes he felt his anger swelling. *You should not have been there. Do I control nothing now?*

Eventually the trail led to a low mean cottage, slumping stones among old bent trees. A figure was carrying in a bucket of water, and as Shay strode forwards the head turned, pale and golden, and he knew that Henry Vyse at least was alive and hope kicked in his belly. Vyse didn't break his step, distracted, and they reached the doorway together and Shay grabbed at the young man's shoulder but Vyse was pushing him away and handing over the bucket to another. At his second attempt Shay caught at him, pulled him closer: 'Why in hell's name—' and then he realized that the other man had been Balfour, and growing relief brought him closer to normality.

On a bench in the gloomy cottage room was Manders, paper-white and battered. He was mud-caked from hair to boots, varying black to grey as it dried patchily, and his left leg from the knee down was a blasted crimson mess, a silly patchwork of red-pink flesh and white bone and fragments of trouser and boot. Shay was beside him in two strides, staring down at the waxy feverish face. The eyes alternated wide in shock and tight shut in pain, and a surgeon was readying himself nearby.

Shay gripped the shuddering head in two great hands, and gazed down. 'You had no need to be there, Michael!'

Manders gulped and coughed at the air, and words hissed from his throat. 'This cause – Will. Not. Fail for.' A long shallow breath. 'Want. Of my. Hand.'

Shay smiled hard at the grim bravado. 'We might succeed after all, boy. If this is not the last King of England to know he has a Manders in his ranks.' And he continued to hold the pale shivering face clamped in his hands as the surgeon approached with his knife.

Edinburgh, new-captured by Cromwell's Army, was edgy. Every face was suspicion and a desire not to offend. Every back alley was furtive with fears and rumours and hurried departures. Thurloe tramped the great grey streets trying to feel like a conqueror, and constantly expecting a knife in his back.

The self-claimed King and his broken followers had retreated west and north, with the Firth of Forth on their flank as a shield. Cromwell was consolidating his troops, the city's docks were choked with supply ships up from London, and John Thurloe had leisure to pursue an untried thread.

Lady Constance Blythe had kept him waiting the fifteen minutes no doubt necessary to dress her age adequately for company, and then offered him her hand like an insignificant gift. A protracted ritual in which hostess and younger man refused to sit in the presence of, or certainly before, the other ended with the lady comfortable in the high, cushioned chair that seemed to be the centre of the first-floor room, and Thurloe in an oak chair pulled round in front of her.

Thurloe thanked her for her time, and introduced his task. He was come up from London on behalf of the Parliament. Parliament was most anxious to rebuild a peace between London and Edinburgh. Battles created divisions where there need not be divisions. He did not wish to be indiscreet, but no doubt Lady Constance would know that there was not always perfect harmony between Parliament and Army. . .

Something of scorn touched Lady Constance's face. *Good; let her think me weak.* Her face was a little more pink than was natural, but the painting was subtly done. If he looked closely, he could see the age of the skin, its looseness, but her cheekbones were strong and gave the face its character, and she held herself well. Still, no question, a handsome woman, and obviously knew every art of dress and posture to reinforce nature.

'Parliament is looking for men of character, in English and Scottish society, whose affinities and reason might help to restore harmony. It's so difficult to get sense and restraint from the men of this city at the moment, and you were recommended to me as someone who had moved in royal society and at the highest levels here in Scotland.'

Constance Blythe wondered if there was innuendo somewhere beneath this, but contented herself with the surface flattery.

'I'm hoping that you might advise me.'

'You expect me to—'

'Sir Peter Booth, for example. He I think has connections in Scotland.'

'He does, but none of significance.' *What a quaint, stubborn little deference. It may remain fun after all to glide around this city.*

'Or Sir Oliver Percy.'

'He'd talk to you, sure enough. You'd buy him for fifty pounds flat, but he'd repulse as many as he brought with him.' *Such a funny breed these Parliament men are. Dark dogged upstarts. Rather nice eyes.*

'Maurice Monroe?'

She considered. 'Much more intelligent man. With intelligent friends.'

'There was a circle around Sir George Astbury, I thought. He's dead now of course, sadly. But I thought—'

'George Astbury? He'd hardly have done for a turncoat!'

'I'm not seeking a—'

'He was pure, blind loyal, and King James and then King Charles loved him for it. He'd no more have thought of dallying with you than of ploughing one of the maids or stealing the royal plate.'

'I thought he had an acquaintance, who might – Shaw, was it? Shay?'

'Shay?'

'Yes.' Thurloe's heart thumping. 'I thought him of that circle.'

'With Astbury?' She was incredulous. 'Why, they were no more than cous—' She was overwhelmed by a sudden spatter of coughs, which hissed like a cat's out of her throat. 'No more th—' Another cough. 'I beg your pardon. Do you mind. . .?' She rang a little bell on the table beside her, waited until the maid hurried in, asked her for water, and held up a frail hand to Thurloe to plead for his forbearance. Thurloe smiled pleasantly, and waited in silence.

Constance Blythe huddled smaller over the hands folded in her lap, watching them through angry eyes. *You foolish old trollop.*

How would this clerk know of Shay? He is no clerk, and if he knows that name then he plays a much darker game. And I so proud and full of myself and talking. She felt the tears start to come, covered them with another bout of coughing. *They always would call me a dumb tart.*

She glared at the fat pink skin on the back of her hand, its minute painted scales. *Has the rot in your body started on your brain as well? So stupid! Lord, I might have been a desperate virgin flashing my paps at him.*

She felt herself pulling back from the pasty flesh that cloaked her, recoiling from her moment's complacency. *My family is older than my kingdom. My spirit is more than my skin.* She became again the mind, watching carefully through the mask of the face. *Kings and Courts have swooned for me.*

Restored by a cup of water. She began again. 'Excuse me, please. I tire so quickly these days, and it has been a time of great strain.' Thurloe nodded sympathetically, and opened his mouth to speak. 'You were asking about someone. Yes – George Astbury. A pleasant man, George. Something of a fool, but we all are as we age, you'll learn that one day. Even when younger, though, he was apt to be pudding-headed. His companions – vanity is not just a failing in the old, isn't that right? – his companions – that was his failing always, a kind of vanity. It's worse in the stupid, you know.' Thurloe no longer knew which generation he was in, let alone its qualities, and again tried to speak. 'But his companions, now. There was Simon Treves. And Oliver Baynes. Baynes was a most handsome man, and always at the heart of any little intrigues at Court. And Thomas Tryon. Tryhorn?'

'When was—'

'Tryon. There's a nephew. He'd be very susceptible to whatever nasty schemes you people have in mind. No doubt you've thought of him. I don't know if you people realize—' She started to cough again. She took another little mouthful of water, but it only made the coughing richer. 'I'm – I'm sorry. I'm – when I get excited, you know. I'm sorry.' Her frailty itself seemed to pain her. 'I wonder if we could continue this another day.'

Thurloe was frustrated, but in no place to force himself, and part of his frustration was at the possibility that Lady Constance Blythe might be a waste of his time and focus. Stepping into the street he checked the names in his head. Astbury and Treves and Baynes and Tryh—... Tryon. Astbury and this Shay were cousins of some kind. He'd wanted more about—

He stood still in the street, boots sinking slowly into the mud. Again he rehearsed the conversation.

She had changed course during the interview, completely. *Not tired, but extremely shrewd.* He stopped, and glanced back up at the first-floor window.

She was watching him. Thurloe smiled, knew that he'd caught her eye, and walked on. He would have the house watched, and he would return soon with a little more rigour in his thinking.

Constance Blythe watched him go. *Lovely big eyes. But I'm rather afraid that that might be a very clever young man.* She reached for the bell. *Such a pity, that the world is to be dominated by the clever men and not the glorious.*

'Marie, bring me paper and ink. You will go with a message to the doctor in ten minutes.'

A summons from Mortimer Shay was a commandment to Balfour and Vyse, and they enjoyed the thought of activity and usefulness in this time of confusion and regathering and politics. Twenty minutes after Shay had sent his message the two were standing in front of him in his lodging.

Shay held a small paper in his fingers, and waved it once. 'We have – how does Manders?'

'Well enough.' Balfour.

Vyse added, 'He now curses and complains with full heart, and his thoughts begin to turn to women again. One leg or no, recovery is nearly complete.'

Shay grunted, smiled in spite of himself, and waved the paper again. 'We have urgent and vital duty. There is a woman in Edinburgh. An old spirit and a great one, and dear to our cause. The man Thurloe has begun to take interest in her for what she may know.' He shook his head. 'She must be out of the city within the hour; she will need our help.' Firm nods from the two young men. 'Your help. I will be close by, but not at the wall; this is an exploit for younger, faster men.' Acceptance and subdued eagerness on the faces, and inside the knowledge that they were more expendable.

Vyse: 'And must we assume that this Thurloe may be watching her?'

'It's possible.' He glanced at each of them. 'There is a time for sport and a time for decision. If you have the opportunity, kill him.' The two young men nodded, Balfour once and simply, Vyse more uneasily. *Lord, I know not whether I love more the one for his determination, or the other because he gives us something worth fighting for.*

Shay's glance hardened, and he caught each pair of eyes again. 'You are gentlemen, and I need not say it; but forgive me if I emphasize her importance for our cause. Her life is worth vastly more than yours both.'

Thurloe was walking towards Lady Constance Blythe's house again at dusk, a soldier with him. Even the cobbled streets were thick with mud, and the two squelched in an uneven rhythm, the musket occasionally knocking into Thurloe's side as the soldier wrestled with it and a lantern. Through fifteen minutes of little sighs and huffs and asides, the soldier – a local man – had made clear his dissatisfaction with the extra duty.

The evening was clear-skied and warm, but the city's tall grey town houses, crowding impassive on either side made it seem more dreary.

Thurloe stopped them opposite the house, and behind him the soldier began to look around for a more sheltered spot to base himself and those who would come after him. Like all of its neighbours, the house was narrow – probably only one room and a stair or corridor wide – and four floors high. There was light glowing from the first-floor windows – where he'd been earlier in the day – and the suspicion of it from somewhere on the ground floor.

'That's the other snag with coming out at night, sir,' the soldier was saying, with the misleading implication that there had been only one other snag previously identified. In the Lowland Scots accent, selected vowels echoed the painfulness of the situation described. 'During the day, you see, these shops would be open, and we could ask if maybe there was a handy spot inside for our lookout.'

Irritation and amusement jostled in Thurloe, and the unworthy satisfaction of knowing that he would not himself be suffering outdoors tonight. Such a pleasant simplicity to the world of the soldiers. Inside better than outside. Dry better than wet. He wished his own head could find such certainties.

'Come with me a moment,' he said. 'I've an idea.'

He would draw Lady Constance's attention to the sentry; say the man was for her protection – such a brittle environment after the fall of the city, and her co-operation was much appreciated. She'd be grateful or she'd be intimidated, and either would serve. With the soldier huffing behind him, he knocked at the front door.

Silence, and half a minute passed. Listening closely, Thurloe convinced himself he could hear sporadic steps in the hall beyond. He knocked again.

This time the steps came clear, and quickly nearer, and the door opened without sound of a bolt. The maid – Marie, wasn't it? – peered out warily.

'Good evening,' Thurloe said, and stepped up into the hall. Really it was just a corridor, running from front door to back, broken halfway along by a step down that also marked the change from plaster walls and floor tiles to whitewash and flagstones. 'I'd like to see Lady Constance again.'

The maid took a breath. 'She's gone to bed. The house is locked up now. You must come again tomorrow.'

Thurloe had been pleased with his little idea, and he was irrationally annoyed to be thwarted. And this frustration kept him asking questions.

She has retired to bed. Yet the first-floor living room is illuminated, and not the second-floor bedroom.

He peered down the corridor. *The house is closed up for the night. But the doors are unbolted.*

'Soldier! Bring the lantern!' Back to the maid, with a soft smile. 'I'll trespass a few yards further, if I may.' And he was past her, with the heavy boots of the soldier tramping behind him.

Crouched over the mud just outside the back door, lantern held above him, Thurloe could see the track of a pair of small boots stepping off the back step and away. 'Quickly' – insistent to the soldier – 'if you had to get out of the city from here, as fast as possible and avoiding sentries, how would you go?'

There was a frustrating pause as the soldier warmed up to the urgency of the situation and then to full understanding. Then he was off and eager, proud of his local knowledge and something to do. He led off in the same direction as the boot tracks, Thurloe hurrying after with the lantern and trying to distinguish the trail in the mess of mud and his jolting, ill-lit view.

The alley opened onto a side street, but the soldier was unerringly across it and into another alley, a weird black world of looming, jerking, distorted shadows. He jinked right and then left again, and ten trotted paces later stopped at a fork. 'Either up here to the left, sir, curving more to the left as she goes and then taking the first right and so down some steps. Or down to the right and keep following down as she twists about. Used to run wild in these lanes as littlins, we did. Either way you get to the same place. Small gateway – not even a gate to it and it won't be guarded.'

Thurloe could make out no suggestion of the boot prints. 'Take your pick,' he said. 'I'll see you at the gate.'

Constance Blythe hesitated at the gateway, then stepped into it, a threshold between the town she knew but now feared, and the unknown land outside. *This is what we are come to.* She felt her vulnerability, exposed in the opening. *I have lived in lights and beauty, and now I huddle in darkness and the shit of vagrants, desperate and afraid.*

'Lady Constance?' As she heard the voice she heard other noises behind it – footsteps, and the stamping of horses – and then saw two shapes in the gloom, one of them mounted. 'Shay has come for you. I'm Vyse; this is Balfour. Will you get up on his horse, please?' Shay's name sparked a flicker of warmth in her, and for a moment she felt the old thrill of young men and an exploit.

Then, behind them, slippery steps from the darkness, and hasty breaths. Balfour hissed fierce: 'Into the wall, my lady. Vyse' –Vyse looked up grim – 'I will show myself.' Vyse nodded resolute and stepped away.

A figure appeared in the little gateway, heard and saw at the same time a man on a horse wheeling and splashing not ten paces away, and stepped forward and opened his mouth in the shout. He stepped forward onto Henry Vyse's knife and died, with a single breathless choke, and two pairs of wide white eyes stared in shock at each other, and the dead man slumped into the mud. Vyse gaped for a second, then heard the horse and the hissed command and was fumbling his knife away and grabbing at the old lady and dragging her out and pushing her up onto Balfour's horse and lunging for his own and they were away.

Moments later they pulled up in front of the vast mounted hulk of Sir

Mortimer Shay, a shadow in the darkness glistening with knife and sword and pistol. They helped the old lady over onto his larger horse, bundled side-saddle in front of him, and then they all hurried away into the deeper night of the countryside. For one last time Constance Blythe felt Mortimer Shay's great arms wrapped round her, felt a girl again, and safe.

Behind them, another figure came splashing through the mud to the gateway, tried to pull sense from the confusion of hoof-beats in the darkness, then saw the outline of the body slumped at his feet. He dropped instinctively, pulled the face upward, and knew it dead.

Once again, John Thurloe shook his head grim into the night, and wondered at his enemies.

◆～

Paris, October

Sir,

I fear the thanks I can offer are meagre fare against the grandeur of the generosity that is yours; more than them I have only my prayers, that you may live healthy and long, not from any unChristian preference, but that the world might benefit from your charity and greatness of spirit. For as much Verhovius may teach me in this new work, so humbly and gratefully received, of the right functioning of the state, so much do you teach me in your giving it.

If I may reinforce this little thanks with a token of esteem, allow me to report that I have entrusted to Eberhardt the delivery to you in The Hague of, firstly, some bulbs of the Turkey Daffodil that I had of Morison and which may please you a little, and, second, a sample of a new Cydonia that is commencing to settle in this climate. You are the wiser judge of these affairs, but I am sure that any man desirous to earn a little credit with Hartlib in London could do nothing better than make him a gift of the Cydonia, and if you were to do so and win advantage thereby, at last I might feel I had demonstrated adequately my gratitude.

I dined yesterday with Hobbs, de Bonnefons and de Roberval. De Bonnefons is completing his Jardinier, and Hobbs is much swollen with his own new treatise, like to be delivered within the year, but strangely cautious on it, for he is normally not slow to debate. From his manner, and certain of his remarks, I think that there shall be in this offspring humours that will not please all the stricter theorists of your English Royal cause, but which he is too strong in will and earnest in intellect to moderate. He told us that Cromwell continues to seek an accommodation with the Scottish Church, and that the hidden truths of Stirling are known by London before they are known by the young King himself who is in the very place, which proffered insight on the tendencies not merely of our friend's homeland, but also of his acquaintanceship, for I think he has not got these tales from Payne, and more probably from Dury or someone else in London. I conceive that our friend's experiments in human motion may yet lead him to jump the Channel once more.

Here all the talk is of Turenne, as is become habitual. Wilhelm, as you will know better than I, is turned quiet again, and Mazarin was feeling confident enough yesterday to be most ungenerous to three or four petitioners, and in truth he has the nobles by their ears; and yet he may never settle, and Turenne is undefeated, and each day of this unquiet costs the treasury livres beyond counting, and I fear that your Queen's hopes of assistance for the Royal campaigns will meet but cold courtesy.

'Philomelus'

[SS C/X/50/179]

Shay came into East Anglia by muddy lanes and silent failing inns. The nights were longer, and he filled them with plodding wet journeys and the occasional indifferent meeting. He needed to know what was happening in Norfolk, felt the old ache of displacement – *I am not where the battle is* – but the eastern counties stretched out in flat, cloud-pressed eternities, and their roads sucked heavily at his horse's hooves.

In the last week of November he came to a farmhouse, coat sodden and wet face glistening in the firelight.

'I sent word in September! Fully two months ago.' The voice was too heavy with tiredness to carry the anger.

The man perched on the chair opposite him was small and neat and feverish with nerves. 'These affairs – they may not be sparked like flint, sir. Surely you—'

'Two – months.' Shay growled the words with equal weight.

'I know, but. . .' – inspiration wild in the flickering face – 'Cromwell and his Army are still in the north. We are as much a distraction as ever!'

'What of it? He has beaten the Scottish army for this year. A platoon of militia could hold Edinburgh and the border right through to spring.'

But the local man was lost in his fantasy now, voice breathy and agitated. 'But surely – what of it, sir? What of it? Cromwell may try to bring his Army the length of England, but he'll not get to Norwich before me, will he?' He was nodding with a mad steady regularity. 'Our troops will gather, we will march on Norwich – three hours only – and our friends there are ready to open the gates. The greatest town of the east will be ours!'

Shay watched the eyes, thought of the endless boggy miles he had travelled. *What is Norwich? Cromwell could lose it whole and never notice.*

He was at the fireside again two nights later, dark and wet after another day's riding, as the news began to stagger in from the nearby villages. A few dozens of men at Easton, the same at Thetford. . . weavers, carpenters, farmers, rounded up like sheep. Not a gentleman, not a trained sword, among them.

As winter bit, the royal hopes for the year shrivelled and cowered as a huddle of terrified men in a village square, and Mortimer Shay watched it grim.

To Mr J. H., at Macrae's.

Sir, you will I hope excuse a delay in writing to you. The chaos of war and then certain administrative duties and continuous travelling have kept me much distracted. You, I imagine, will have been likewise greatly shifted about since the battle at Dunbar and the fall of Edinburgh to General Cromwell. Should this find you, I hope that it finds you well enough. Are you with the prince's remnants at Stirling? Is there much expectation of new war? They do say that the Royal position at Stirling is impregnable, and sure it is the key to the rest of Scotland, but I think that most here care little for the rest of Scotland.

My duties bring me sometimes northwards. I learn that Edinburgh Castle, which has stood out these several months against the Army now occupying the rest of the city, is like to fall soon, and that this will restore a further stability to a place that in truth has grown quickly used to the new politics. They say that Cromwell is speedily attracting support from Scots happier with a compromised peace than a principled war.

I pray that you keep safe, and will let me know something of how you fare.

[SS C/S/50/172]

～～～

John Thurloe likewise heard of the failed Norfolk risings at the fireside, but cosy in dry clothes and his family and a general feeling of content. With his new letter to J. H., he had overcome his frustration and set himself up against his man once more.

Anne was pregnant, pleased with his unexpected return, and inflating herself with quiet pride at his apparent importance, and so more inclined to keep the children out of his way and let him play master of the house. She was cosy-wrapped and pretty to him, and their days felt warm and well-fed.

Thanks to privy contacts in high Royalist circles, these risings were known of in advance, and we judge that they would have failed even were they to have formed not in these mean flocks but with credible strength. The Norwich authorities were aware of them fully, and ready to oppose and overwhelm them even had the misguided rebels reached to the town.

Thurloe mused on those privy contacts. The phrase could mean much. Nevertheless, it seemed that the Royalists could not plan—

But that is not the lesson, surely. That little complacency is not what we learn. The risings were not sympathetic manifestations of Royalist feeling, born of local grudge and nostalgia. *If they were betrayed at a high level, then they were known and planned at a high level.* Had these been intended to complement the campaign in the north?

How would I command risings from four hundred miles off?

John Thurloe by the fire, a snug and flexible intelligence at ease. He was still gazing pleasantly into the flames five minutes later, when the servant boy came in on some errand.

'Adam.' Adam was from the village, in awe of Thurloe's unimaginable learning and wealth and gravely aware of the precious chance he represented. 'In my study, on the table, there's a package of news-sheets. Bring them, would you?'

———— ~⁓

Margaret Shay watched her husband from the window. The stiff straight back, the big shoulders, the hair above his neck plucked up in the wind. She badly wanted to touch him, to pull at his sleeve, to lead him out of his chilly reverie and into the house. But he could not be disturbed when he was like this. And soon he would be off again, to some other war or quest. She knew the signs – the changed tone, the grumpiness, the fidgeting; she had polished his boots herself in readiness.

Shay's eyes were on the hills: his lungs, his ramparts. His mind was lost beyond them.

I have never thought of the ending. I have never thought of the aim.

Always the struggle merely. His life was the next challenge, the next feat, the next scheme, the next skirmish. *As if my world was an endless string of nameless German towns, with their blank horror-shocked faces and their mindless atrocities; as if my eternity was wading through blood and dreaming of treasons.*

Now the cause was in Scotland: packs of Scottish politicians jostling to use the young King, newly arrived among them from his exile, defeated once already at Dunbar, and forced to trust his future and his Crown to the temporary interest of their factions, to the commitment of their cheap-levied clansmen.

Shay took a deep breath. Bracing himself for the fray.

And always the ghost of George Astbury somewhere over his shoulder, a more elusive guardian of the secrets of the Comptrollerate-General than he would have imagined.

Astbury had been worried about Pontefract and Doncaster, and somehow with the Levellers. Shay himself had played with the idea of a compact between Levellers and Royalists to unsettle his correspondent, the Parliamentarian I. S.; but the idea of such a compact was surely fantastical. What, then, had been so fretting Astbury? Had it anything to do with the Levellers in the Army?

There had been a channel for communication between the Royalists besieged in Pontefract and the outside world; messages delivered via a church. Directly or indirectly the Reverend Beaumont had been the next link in the chain. Messages to Pontefract from George Astbury via the Comptrollerate-General network had gone through Beaumont. Messages coming out of Pontefract had entered the network through him.

What then of the soldier, who had come from Pontefract all the way to George Astbury the night before Preston, mortally wounded? Was he some kind of courier for Astbury? It was surely unlikely. The network didn't function with irregular couriers, and a soldier was the worst possible choice for one in any case. But surely he had brought that letter. And what, if anything, did any of this have to do with the killing of Colonel Rainsborough two or three months later?

And what of Preston? Astbury had been worried about the scouts, and he'd been right: Scoutmaster Ruce had turned traitor. *Ruce, whom Astbury didn't think much of.* Shay remembered the panicked face, the babbled details of being approached by Parliament's intelligencers. *Ruce didn't turn; he was turned.* They'd known Ruce, known his weaknesses. *George Astbury had been right; Ruce hadn't been the man to have contrived this himself.*

Behind all these fancies lurked a greater concern, lurching out at him when he dared to consider it. Had Astbury not destroyed the great book of the Comptrollerate-General after all, but hidden it? The possibility haunted Shay: a cataclysm of secrets, waiting somewhere to ambush England.

Later, in the parlour, Shay said: 'I have always known that I would conquer.' She watched him, hand frozen at the needle. 'Lately I have begun to doubt.' She laid down the needle and the work, and her eyes searched his face. 'They have. . . a different breed of men now, in the Parliamentary service. There's one man. A clerk. Rather clever, I suspect.'

Still she watched; loving, worrying. He shrugged himself out of the mood. 'I'll have them yet.'

'You are a great man, Mortimer. In your terrible way, you're a good one. But you may not always be right.'

He looked at her, absorbing this.

'On your own ground, in your own way, you have always been unstoppable. But a warhorse is little use at sea. With a rapier and pistol you can destroy a world, but you cannot rebuild one.'

He pondered it.

Too soon Margaret Shay was waiting to say goodbye again. He was striding over the stones, head turned towards Gareth and snapping orders as the silent steward trotted beside him with mumbles of agreement and acceptance. A momentary halt, and the strange ritual handshake between the two men, gauntlet gripping elbow, a familiarity reaching back into the decades. Then he was striding towards her again, as he always had been, striding down the corridor at Richmond Palace and through all the years at her. He stopped in front of her, suddenly uncertain.

She grabbed a fistful of his jacket, and rested her forehead on his chest. 'My little heart gallops with you, old wolf.' She looked up at the face. 'Where you are, there is life.'

Shay gasped, and pressed her head between his hands, and kissed her. 'You are my aim. You are my end. You are the one thing I have ever found that was worth living for.'

1651

The Fugitive Crown

On 1st January, the young Charles Stuart was crowned King of the Scots. But Scone, sober masks concealing self-congratulation or doubt from the uncomfortably poised young man, was unknown to Astbury. News of the ceremony would not come through the hills for weeks, and what would it mean anyway, that the pretender King of England had got himself crowned somewhere else? Rachel tried not to notice the turning months, under the snow that blurred everything. In the valley where Astbury huddled, the world had stopped. Nothing came or changed or went. The rhythm of the meagre meals, of encounters with her ghostly father, of a ritual daily exchange with Jacob, were the heartbeats of her existence. One afternoon, the house utterly silent, Rachel walked far out into the fields until she knew she could not be seen or heard, and screamed at the white encircling hills and threw herself down into the snow.

John Thurloe passed December and January among his family, trying poses of complacent fatherhood: stern, benign, patriarchal, playful. Anne – locally more influential than Parliament – had insisted that they go to church on 25th December, and he had glanced, like a drake patrolling his pond, down the descending line of Thurloes and thought, *Is this success? Is this stability?* Anne was grown large, and her stately, stiff-backed gait reinforced the little arrogances she was acquiring, and Thurloe smiled at it and teased her. In the evenings he read, to himself or to her, while the pile of *Mercurius Fidelis* news-sheets rested on his desk. Whenever he saw them he would touch one with a finger, glance at it, peer at the fat ramshackle letters, the smudges and the printing mistakes and the forced waspishness of wording and emphasis – and wonder at a code or cypher. Once he went as far as to underline all the words in one sheet that seemed unnatural, and then try to re-see the text as instruction or exhortation should those words have double meanings. But he could make nothing of it.

England's soldiers endured another winter in the field. Last year it had been Ireland, with its evil spirits, and the plagues that had eaten at besiegers as well as besieged. This year it was Scotland, tents and horses disappearing under snow, the constant search for warmth, for wood to burn, cramped fetid Edinburgh bunk rooms and petrifying weeks in camp before Stirling, a primitive struggle to survive the day, and all the time watching the tides of disease spreading through the regiments. Buried in and behind the fortified town, in this farthest corner of the land, Royalism mustered its strength in fireside bravados and little parlour intrigues, and waited for spring.

———

With the winter sun white on her face, Margaret Shay sat cloak-wrapped on the bench and reviewed her world.

She knew what waited underneath the soil of every one of the wide sweep of fields below her. She knew the condition and character of each tree. She knew who the distant trudging figures in the landscape should be, and could check her knowledge by how they walked and where they stopped and which other figures they tarried with.

It has been a long while since I wrote a verse.

The habit of a more naïve time, perhaps. A silly painted time, self-regarding and conceited. *So many rhyming vanities.* She did not feel now like a woman who wrote trifles.

Yet I fear this is not wisdom, but age only. It wasn't the times that had changed; only her. *A farmer's wife now, doughy and stupid.* A mind once open to the infinities of natural philosophy, now sceptical of over-reliance on parsnips.

Where is the world we promised ourselves, on those dewy golden mornings, the evenings of hungry intelligence?

The times had indeed changed, and changed the people. The handsome witty men were become clerks and controversialists and sentimental. Spiteful pamphlets and sickly laments for lost loves and lost causes.

I wish I had given Shay sons. He would have been a terrifying inspiration, a riotous guide to the world, *and I would have planted in them seeds he would not know.*

Perhaps he would have loved them more than me. And the wars would have killed them. *Shay's wars would have killed them.* In any case there had been no sons, and now Shay's voracious potential, which could out-stride the world, could not out-stride time, and he was rendered futile. *And I, who promised and was promised so much...*

No. *This is but lazy melancholy. These are the indulgent complaints of a silly girl, an unfocused mind.* It had been the lot of women in every age to take the roles neglected by men. Her generation of men had created a world first of speculation, and then of chaos; her duty accordingly had been to provide rationality and then stability.

These truths are only worthy if one has a daughter to teach them to. Women do not make the world; but there is none else to nourish and protect it. *I inspired men out of their dullness, and then I offered the scaffolds to their fancies. And now I manage an unruled estate, and decide justice in its disorder.* In the tumult, women had become poets, and prophesiers, the defenders of concepts and the defenders of castles. *I have tended to his wounds and tended to his lands and tended to his restive questing spirit.*

She had married Shay because – *partly I married Shay because when we danced his arms were hard and his shoulders were like crags, and I would not let my eyes smile and he wondered at it, and I saw him realize that for once he had a challenge for which he had no weapon or trick and never would, and in one heart-burst I saw all the sparkling charming girls shrink, and still his instinctive hand slipped down my bodice to my hip, for Shay is ancient and Shay is also a boy* – she had married Shay because he was the least bounded man in existence, nothing of convention or habit or morality, and accordingly offered the whole universe, corporeal and intellectual, for her to roam untrammelled. And her dominion was a valley in north Wales.

This had been her duty; this had been her world; this had been her life. *I wish I had had a daughter.*

Thurloe thought that he had been granted a personal epiphany one evening when, the family all asleep, he took a second glass of wine and tried considering *Mercurius Fidelis* by pure logic. *One: for the sake of argument, we shall assume that these sheets definitely contain messages. Two: if I wished to write to one or two men, I would write to them singly rather than hiding a message in a news-sheet, which is an elaborate means and might be risked unnecessarily. Three: ergo, if there are messages in these sheets then they are to be read by a number of men, which is the advantage of the news-sheet.* He looked for words that repeated between news-sheets, which might in code carry alternative meanings for politics or conspiracy. But it seemed perverse to look for encoded references to Oliver Cromwell and Charles Stuart in a news-sheet that talked incessantly of Oliver Cromwell and Charles Stuart. *Four: if words had hidden and alternative meanings, my collection of fellow conspirators across England would each need to know my list of secret meanings of words. Five: it would be the more elaborate and thereby more troublesome and more risky an arrangement for a relatively large number of men each to have a list, on paper or in brain, of concealed meanings. Six: ergo, it is more likely that this is not a code in which words are to be substituted for other words, and the meaning accordingly somewhere outside the paper, but a cypher in which the letters and words of a message are somehow concealed within the text, and to be found entirely within this paper.* He picked up the nearest paper, held it against the candle and wondered at the spots and holes in it. *No, again, such things could not be replicated.* He tried reading every other word of *Mercurius Fidelis* of October 26. to November 2. 1648. *Recent do show the.* Every third word. *Recent surely the.* Starting with the second word. Or the third. Backwards.

He put down the paper. *I am playing children's games in a world in flames.* He took a great mouthful of wine, holding it in his cheeks a moment so that it stung his tongue, and then swallowing it grossly. He picked up the sheet again and read the first letter of every word. *R.E.D.* Red? *R.E.D.S.S.T.T.* Hardly. He read the first letter of every sentence, and suddenly the room was cold and the wine was thumping in his head.

R.E.P.O.R.T.

Report. True, the letters after that became gibberish again, but wasn't that a word of potential significance? The noun. . . no, the imperative?

He picked up another sheet, winey blood thundering heavy through him, from earlier that same month – September 28. to October 5. 1648. *T.T.H.E.T.M.G.*

With great concentration, Thurloe crumpled the sheet two-handed into as compact a ball as he could make, and threw it into the fire. *In a large collection of random letters, thus ordered, it is likely that some shall by mere chance have some little meaning. Especially to a drunk man with dreams of glory.* The paper ball hit one of the fire dogs and bounced out into the room.

After a moment, Thurloe went to retrieve it. *The genius of the poets and the appreciation of the ages, Master Thurloe, I think we may take as more reliable than your stubbornness. If there is a mistake, it is likely in your Greek and not theirs.* He smoothed the paper out, replaced it in the pile and went to bed.

Anne Thurloe gave birth to another daughter on the coldest day of January, the midwife blustering out of a snowstorm with a babbling of little wisdoms, and the house was a bustling of maids and good women of the neighbourhood and messengers from London and unregulated children. Thurloe moved quietly among them, doggedly retrieving rogue infants when no female could be found, issuing instructions and judgements to the couriers, talking Greek to his earnest uncomprehending eldest boy.

At around this time, a solitary rider came by patient winding roads to the royal town of Stirling.

There was a great hall in Stirling that had become the centre of the Court-in-exile – in the mornings it jostled and flowed with gossip and plot and the business of politics and royalty and arms. Shay treated it with a caustic loathing, but was to be seen there most days, somewhere on the edge of the business, a hand on an arm, a word in an ear.

On this day there was a flicker of disruption on the margins of the Court, for the solitary rider was not recognized and had none of the routines for greeting or entry; his clothes were unfamiliar and rural, the weather-worn face under the greying curls likewise uncourtly, and the accent almost impenetrable to the sentry. Raised voices began to cut through the mundane chatter of the hall, and among the first to glance over was Shay, sensitive to the change of rhythm. The sentry, scornful and too casual with the primitive who was now trying to get past him, reached out an arm and grabbed at the stranger's shoulder. In a second: the arm flung up, a vicious head-butt, and the sentry was sprawling back over an outstretched leg, and in fairness how could he have known the history of blood and war, decades old, in this peasant?

It was Gareth, and it took Shay a moment to accept the fact – Gareth, his steward; Gareth who in the last twenty years had not been known to leave his home valley, let alone leave Wales; Gareth who had come alone through three restive kingdoms, across the lines of war. How was Gareth become part of this world? Gareth saw him, but strangely the only familiar face in the great bustling hall caused the leathered features to look even more lost than before. Through the cliques of curious men, oblivious, the little Welshman walked up to Shay, and then collapsed to his knees in front of him, and around Sir Mortimer Shay the whole world rotted and shrank and dimmed and he felt his blood curdling and writhing inside his emptying body in a sickening pain of cold, a great roar of impossibility for which he had no breath.

Lady Margaret Shay had walked out into a morning, and sat as was her habit on the seat overlooking the valley that had been her kingdom, with the beeches as dark winter sentinels either side of her, and had slept and never woken. In the heaving Scottish hall, surrounded by men confused and alarmed, the face of a lone old man whitened and perished.

— ~ —

Thurloe would, in the future, politely ascribe his revelation to an inspiration from God: a more proper authority to whom to give the credit, than an unhealthy interest in classical grammar and in long waving hair that seemed to burn in the sun.

A too-generous supper, and an unsettled night. A dream of Greek, of verbs in their tables, of poems on the page, verses in their lines; a dream of vegetable frames, or was it hedges, row after row, and a long dress and a rich cascade of hair flashing among them; but when to turn, which path to follow? How to mark the way through the maze? Theseus was given his clew, his thread, to guide him through the maze of the poem. And the poem could easily be recalled, because he could remember the layout on the page, recall the numbers indicating every tenth line of verse. Which path through the garden? The numbers mark the lines. The hedges, the lines of vegetables, fertile greens and flashes of colour; which path through the garden? Then glimpses of her again, or of some woman's body, shocking naked flesh glowing at him from around corners in the hedges, some paths but not others: an ankle, a bare ankle outrageous and exciting among exposed nature, and nothing, and nothing, just the endless avenues of green, and the flash of a thigh, and nothing, and a breast, looming out at him with a promising smile and opening lips and Thurloe awoke in a tangle of sheets and foolishness.

He got up, and went and splashed water on his face. As he stood bent over the bowl, he began a faintly embarrassed attempt to explain away the dream. A mystery, an attempt to find a path, the promise of reward: his child's games with *Mercurius Fidelis*, of course. Dull-headed, he began to rehearse the ideas of alternate letters, or words, tried to remember how many hedge paths there had been in the dream, caught himself trying to recapture the image of the breast.

He'd tried all that. Every second letter. Every second word. All the variations.

Some paths, but not others. How to tell which path?

He'd found one edition of the news-sheet with a word concealed in the initial letters. He'd found at least one other that did not have any word so concealed. He lit a candle, sat in front of the pile of news-sheets again. That of October 26. 1648 had a word. September 28. did not. He smoothed out September 28. again, still creased after its near-destruction in the fire, and checked. Definitely no word. Some but not others.

He pulled out another *Mercurius*, from May 1649, took a breath, held it, and started down the page.

Y. E.

Ye? A flicker of possibility, but inconclusive. T. Yet? D. T.

A snarl pushed through his teeth and dwindled to a sigh.

He pulled out another, and stared into it, the fat clumsy letters blurring under him and then clarifying. July 1650. A distracting vision of Rachel Astbury's naked thigh in his cloudy head. C. A. V. Not promising. Should be asleep. E. Cave? A word, but he couldn't think of a context. 'Cave' the Latin word, perhaps. N. D.

Thurloe sat back, gazing blearily at the page and feeling raddled and stupid.

Complete the exercise, Master Thurloe.

He leaned forward. I. S. Is? But the precursor was meaningless. H. There was no—

Cavendish.

A great thump in his chest, and cold blood flushing his head. There was no more, and he couldn't see what it meant, but surely that was more than chance.

Another sheet, snatched up at random by fumbling fingers: March 1649. T. H. E. The? Again the excitement. O. Theo? L. Doubt again. D. Theold.

The old?

C. A. U. S. E. L. I. V. E. S.

Thurloe sat back in his chair, chilled and gasping with the vulnerable secret. He thrilled to it, and then felt immediately alone and isolated, the sole possessor of the revelation in the vast night.

There was surely no possibility that this was chance. 'Report' on the news-sheet of October 26. might be a freakish coincidence. 'The old cause lives' – not long after the execution of the old King – inconceivable.

Some have messages, and some do not. But how were they distinguished?

Thurloe wrapped a cloak round himself and poured a mug of wine, and sat down at the desk again, and started into the pages.

I have looked at these for hours, and I have not seen it. But I am now certain that there is an 'it'.

Where is the error in your parsing, Master Thurloe?

The error.

He compared October 26. and providential September 28. again, and then others, some with messages and some without. Inside five minutes he had it.

Before he slept again, Thurloe offered a prayer: of thanks; of faint shame; of a glimpsed hope.

As the seasons turned again, bringing tentative spring sunlight to alleys and angles of Edinburgh that had not felt it in six months, the latest Duke of Hamilton found himself back in Scotland to lead the royal interest.

William Hamilton, pug-faced and darkly steady, strode the streets and halls that his brother had commanded two years before. Around him clustered the same men, or the sons or brothers of the same men, respectful or awestruck or obsequious, who had followed the ducal coronet when his brother had worn it.

He knew the men around him, of course, the wary calculating Edinburgh politicians who'd spent the last ten years tacking back and forth between the Crown and the English Parliament, and the threadbare old-style grandees who'd been in exile on the Continent. The men who'd banished him from Court last autumn, and welcomed him now in the spring. He knew them personally, or knew the type, or knew the names: names who had always been part of the world of the Hamiltons – particular names with particular roles.

One name was missing, of course. The face of the Marquess of Montrose still hung over Edinburgh's gate, more black and shrunken with another year; now the severed head on the tolbooth was like a devil's fist, clenched at those who dared to usurp his dream of glory. Montrose's limbs had been sent to the four corners of Scotland; his heart had been rescued from the grave by his family. Montrose's son was still a boy: this year there was no Montrose at the table.

You'll miss this battle, Jamie.

From the luxury of uninterruption that his status gave him, in the King's absence seated alone at the head of the Council table, Hamilton watched the stares and glances bickering between the Scots and the English, the soldiers and the civilians, the Royalists and the religious.

And I don't know which of us will feel the loss more.

The debate slunk on like a surly dog, occasionally snapping vicious. Should a new army be raised to fight for King Charles against the English? Who should command such an army? Should Royalists and their former sympathizers be allowed to participate in official debates in Scotland? Was

Oliver Cromwell's recent reported sickness the result of Scottish prayer or his own sin?

Hamilton's slow eye kept straying back to one man, seated away from the table and against the wall, in a shadowed corner of the great stone chamber. A large, older man, dark and watchful. The man they had told him, back in the Netherlands, to look to and to listen to. The man called Shay.

❦

The journey north was long, tedious and uncomfortable, a destructive combination of boredom, physical discomfort and the constant frustrations of dealing with local officials to get a change of horse or a bed. After a cosy winter, Thurloe was not looking forward to months of campaigning in Scotland – most of it no doubt in the rain – and he felt newly alienated from the strange world of soldiers.

Eventually he reached Glasgow – where it had indeed come on to drizzle – and growled his way through the necessary invocations to get a bed and a meal. The broth – whatever it was – and a fire restored him a little, and he reported to the commandery feeling readier if not enthusiastic.

General Lambert received him – cumbersome greetings – Cromwell still down with fever – polite enquiry about the journey. Then he began to search ponderously for a paper. He didn't find it, and clearly hadn't needed the prop anyway: 'It's the, er, it's the march-about for you, Master Thurloe.' Thurloe waited. 'Master Oliver St John is sent on an embassy to. . . to the Netherlands, I think. He and General Cromwell have agreed that you will accompany him. Take a month or so, I think.'

All Thurloe could imagine was the grim idea of getting on a horse again. Gradually the positive aspects began to trickle in: a promising recognition of his ability; diplomatic work clearly more interesting – and frankly more civilized – than trudging around behind the army. Perhaps a chance to run an errand or two for Sir Theodore de Mayerne, and get a little credit there. 'Any excitement here, General?'

Lambert shook his head. A fighting soldier, Thurloe knew, and he'd be hating the idleness and the administration and the extra work in

Cromwell's absence. 'Not much. Do you know of Birkenhead? Sir John Birkenhead?'

'Noisy Royalist. Gets arrested occasionally.'

'We've just arrested him again. Him and a few others. Seditious assembly. Why the Army gets stuck with these affairs I don't know.' A sympathetic tut from Thurloe. 'Only real complaint they have is that he was carrying a Royalist news-sheet. The *Fidelis*.' He leaned forward. 'I'd love to stamp them all out, Thurloe, but is that realistic? Stamp them all out. But the Army can't trouble every time someone reads one of these rags.'

'Did he get the *Fidelis* at the meeting? Or was he taking it there?'

A frown across the thick flesh of Lambert's forehead. 'Taking it, I think.'

'A courier?'

'Doesn't seem his style. Too grand, too high a profile for that.'

Thurloe nodded. 'You have a copy? The news-sheet?'

Lambert pawed at the papers on the desk a moment, and then bawled for his Adjutant. The Adjutant hurried in and retrieved the paper.

Thurloe snatched at it. First the day, the date: and yes! The error was there. Then quickly through the initials: M.A.C.K.A.Y. – and after that nonsense.

A distinct name, certainly. But it had no meaning.

A memory: *Cavendish*. Another name in *Mercurius Fidelis*. July 1650, when the Royalist army was preparing to go onto the offensive. A message to Royalists – to all of them – or perhaps only some who would recognize a meaning. A local relevance? A reassurance? A warning?

Or a trigger?

Thurloe looked up at the two soldiers. 'You'll forgive a busybody civilian, I hope.' Lambert looked wary. 'But I think this might be rather more important. One for the Army to take seriously. I'd recommend a closer look at Birkenhead and his friends.' He hesitated. 'A more persuasive look.'

＊＊＊

Mortimer Shay came to Astbury with the spring again. To Rachel it seemed paler, colder around him.

She found him first in the study, in front of the painting of his half-sister, turning around almost guilty as Rachel came into the room. Had he been touching the portrait?

She walked up to him, and reached her arms around him as best she could and laid her head on his chest a moment. Then she stepped back a pace.

'I wish I'd known Lady Margaret.'

'I wish you had. She'd have liked you very much.' Rachel flushed slightly. 'You're the two most. . . truly honest people I know.'

The voice was hoarse, the throat exhausted, the eyes likewise.

'And still you ride. And still you fight.'

'There is nothing else, girl. I fight. Eventually I'll die. That's all there is.' The words came dull, as if through fog.

'Won't you – can't you make your home here with us? Just a while? Even a few days.'

'Men are fighting and dying for you. You only want your faerie land.' There was no bite to the words. He wasn't really looking at her. 'Another rising has failed. A network of men captured around Glasgow. Maybe another leftover of George Astbury's schoolboy habits.'

'Or maybe you made the mistake!' The last of her comforts, her certainties, was fissuring. *Surely I cannot be wiser than he.* 'Or maybe there are people out there more persuasive than you. Better than you. Maybe this country wants a future, not an endless war.'

'These people have not understood me yet. They have not found the end of my vengeance.'

'That's all you offer? Vengeance? For ever? You don't even know what people you're talking about.'

'I know my enemies when I find them. And they shall know me well enough.'

She stared at him, scared and sad.

Anthony Astbury insisted on receiving his half-brother-in-law, and Shay and Rachel watched uncomfortably as the skeletal figure stepped gingerly down the staircase towards them, over-formal clothes hanging loose around him. Trying to shake hands, he stumbled into Shay, a reed against a rock, and for a moment the two clutched at each other. Astbury straightened, and his eyes closed for a moment of intense effort. Then he said, ponderously, 'She was the jewel of our age, Mor— Mortimer.' Shay nodded. 'She was – she was your redemption.' And at that Shay swallowed a breath with difficulty.

Then Astbury had to mark this newest change in his world in the family Bible, and Shay and Rachel sat stiff in chairs opposite him as he heaved open the cover as if it were the front door and brushed shakily at the flyleaves and scratched out the words with brittle formality. *Margaret Shay, d. January 1651.*

Rachel's eyes flickered empty between the two men: her ridiculous father, begging him to stop, to die, to end everyone's pain; and Shay, an empty hulk, a castle where no lights showed.

Oliver St John stepped onto Dutch soil on 17th March 1651, oblivious to a sorry-looking crowd of hecklers being jostled away behind cross-wise pikes, bellowing for a bath and a good meal. John Thurloe followed him onto the quay – more watchful of the hecklers, asking himself who had paid them – wondering at the smells and the quiet flat faces and the neatness of the place.

While St John restored himself after the trials of the sea passage, Thurloe chatted with the English Parliament's representative in The Hague.

'Will they receive us?'

'Oh they'll receive you well enough. They can see how the wind's blowing. They're merchants here, first, last and always, and they want to know about English maritime policy, not our domestic squabbles.'

'But the Royalists have been here as well.'

'They still are. Always on the hunt for support, or money, or a promising Princess.'

'They'll know about this embassy?'

'Oh yes. Before you got off the boat. We usually know what each other's about.' A bowl of fruit pushed towards Thurloe. 'They've an agent in the town – young chap – busybusy, you know? Escaped here after the siege of Pontefract, and been carrying on the fight ever since.'

'Pontefract?'

'A man called Thurloe has asked to meet me.'

'We know that name, surely.'

'We do. One of Cromwell's terrier-hounds. His wife is niece to Thomas Overbury, by the by.'

'Overbury – who was poisoned in the Tower? Lord, he'd better not start asking questions about that.'

'He has other cares now. He's here with St John's embassy to the Dutch.'

'He's not just any Roundhead clerk. He's Cromwell's most trusted agent. The rising man. You're going to arrange a little accident for him?'

'No. I'm going to meet him.'

'What can you possibly gain? There's too much risk in it.'

'I don't see that – unless you take me for an utter simpleton. I want to see this man. Besides, the Dutch wouldn't like us disappearing a visiting diplomat.'

'This is mere curiosity.'

'He is the new England. I want to know what we face.'

Thurloe had been kept more than an hour when a servant finally beckoned him out of the waiting room. It had been a cold room, unfurnished, and Thurloe catalogued it with his other observations of the house and what he had heard of the Royalists in this city. The fewest possible servants, and those badly dressed. The economies and the selling of jewels. No one invited to dine. The British royal cause in Holland was living a threadbare exile.

The room into which he was shown was also spartan, but there was a fire burning at least, a single log in the grate. The door closed behind him.

The room was empty. For a moment, he was uneasy. This was no longer a land in which he represented the prevailing authority. It was a borderland, a place of exchange, where he and his Royalist opponents met on equal terms. He looked around the room quickly, seeing windows and thinking of them as exits, feeling little flutters of doubt and foolishness.

What would happen if—? He was no fighter. St John and the rest of his party would – but he had told no one where he was going or what he was doing.

The latch clicked up, and Thurloe turned to face the door, bracing himself.

A single man stepped in and closed the door behind him, a man about his own age.

A man with bright red hair, and Thurloe saw his own surprise reflected in the other's face.

Pontefract, two years before. The man burning papers in the fire. The red hair, the strange smile, and the barrel of powder.

Red hair caught his breath. 'You,' he said with emphasis, 'I had not expected. My intrepid friend from Pontefract.' A more attentive scrutiny. 'You, then, are Thurloe. How do you? Did those papers mean so much to you that you've hunted me two years?'

Thurloe tried a bit of bravado. 'I had no need to hunt you, or your papers, Master Paulden.' Thomas Paulden smiled, and the memory of that strange morning in Pontefract flared brighter with it. 'I'm intrigued that you agreed to see me.'

'I was intrigued that you asked.'

Thurloe hesitated, tried to identify why he had wanted to come, thought again of his vulnerability.

'Lost your nerve, Master Thurloe?'

'Wondering about a conversation in which I assume you will lie consistently.'

'That's hardly civil, Thurloe, but I take your point. And yet a man may learn from a lie, don't you find?'

'What were you so desperate to destroy at Pontefract?'

Paulden smiled. 'A love letter. I'd been composing it for days; couldn't get it right.'

'It seemed rather bulky for a love letter.'

'That was the problem. One tries to get the precise word, and I was rambling.'

'But what I don't understand is why this outburst of. . . extreme discretion only came to you at the last possible moment – with someone like me at the door. You must have known – for hours, probably days – that the castle was going to surrender.'

'I'd had it on my person for two days – one didn't want to risk losing it in a sudden sortie or collapse. Had I found a chance to escape unsearched, I would have kept it with me. Once it was clear that that was impossible, I had to wait to find a few minutes' privacy with a fire and powder – which wasn't easy in the chaos of that day.'

'All that for love. You thought there was so much chance of escape?'

'There were ways in and out. There are always ways.'

'For messages too, I think.'

Paulden smiled. 'You have your spies in our camps, Master Thurloe. Allow us ours in yours.'

'You have a network, surely. Across the country. Ready to pass a message or give practical help.'

Still the smile. 'There are loyal Englishmen still, Thurloe, and more than you'd choose to acknowledge. You'll forgive me if I take your protest as frustration.'

'Loyalties shift damn' fast, Paulden, as you've found to your cost. And networks may be broken or turned.' Paulden held the smile on his lips, but his eyes were hard now. 'The currents and connections of affinity are known. The Astbury family – George Astbury in particular. His sister-in-law's family. Lady Constance Blythe. General Langdale.'

The smile had weakened on Paulden's face, and now spread again. 'Why, these are relics of thirty years past, Thurloe. I think most of those are dead, aren't they? Though you must, of course, hunt phantoms if it please you.' The tone was different, and the clear dismissal unusual, and Thurloe marked it. 'I'm pleased to reassure you that our cause is in fresher hands.'

'Old hands or new, they're hardly competent. The battle of Dunbar was a disaster for you, the stillborn offspring of your. . . cankered cause and your rotten, corrupted structures.' *Careful. In provoking him I must not overbalance myself.* 'What faith can you have in your networks now, if they're so easily abused?'

'And still you come scurrying to the Continent for support. Still Scotland waits to descend on England. You take us seriously enough, I think.'

'While we win the battles, and you are confined to mere spiteful schoolboy pettinesses, we'll tolerate you cheerfully enough.' Thurloe wondered an instant at his own bravado. 'The assassination of Ascham at Madrid. If backstair tuppenny cut-throats are your heroes, we may pity rather than fear you. The assassination of Rainsborough, too. Had you a hand in that?'

Paulden's smile was stretched thin. 'We heard that loss burned fierce. Bit uncomfortable for you, surely. The Army's darling, and Cromwell couldn't trust him. My brother's idea, since you ask. And yes, I rode in the party. Perhaps you owe us for doing you a favour.'

'Your idea of an alliance between Royalists and Levellers is fantasy.' *Is it fantasy?*

'You will learn in time.'

'Neither your scheming nor your raid gained you anything in Doncaster.'

'Perhaps not. But there are other Doncasters, Thurloe, where men you think yours have not forgotten where their true interest and loyalty are.'

'There was something else behind the raid, wasn't there? It was too elaborate, too risky, to be mere impetuousness.'

Paulden was suddenly back against his chair, watchful, and then forward as quickly with the old grin. It was the same wild face Thurloe had seen hovering over the powder barrel in defeated Pontefract. 'Wouldn't want you to have any false confidence, Thurloe. Wouldn't want you to go away without learning something.'

Thurloe held his expression; held his breath.

'Among the many friends we have in every town in England, among the men we have infesting your administration, there was. . . at least one, in Doncaster. Unhappy to find that the ideals you'd used to fire all those years of war had turned out to be deceits and vanities. A man who passed us, as so many do, useful information; in his case, time by time, the plans and tactics for the siege. My brother devised a plan to meet him. A plan to give himself the run of Doncaster and let the man reveal himself. The attempt to kidnap Rainsborough was an entertaining cover for all that.'

'Kidnap? Rainsborough was killed.'

A shrug.

'And if your aim was to contact your informant, you didn't succeed.'

Paulden sat back again. 'Perhaps we did not, Thurloe. Perhaps we did.'

'You did not. I have re-watched that morning as if from every window. You met no one. You gained nothing. Your source was just another ghost.'

The smile was fixed, grim. 'Perhaps, Thurloe. Perhaps you will learn otherwise.'

The life had gone out of the conversation. Paulden roused himself to his former alert consideration of his visitor, but the momentum was gone.

Thurloe stood, and turned to leave. Paulden went to open the door for him, but instead his outstretched arm held it closed an instant, blocking Thurloe's exit, the flare of red hair close to him.

Once again, the voice had the strange whimsy of the confrontation in Pontefract. 'Perhaps only my brother knows the truth. But he told me a little of his plan. And if ever a man should show a strange inclination to refer to the history of Doncaster, Thurloe, you will learn.'

Sir Mortimer Shay in other men's spring: a man slumped at the edge of a room, waiting; a man on a horse, crossing and re-crossing the endless moors of northern Britain.

In the councils, oblivious to the debate and watching the divisions. Watching Leslie, the grey professional soldier; Hamilton, the fatalistic bulldog; and the young King, a beautiful youth among the dull stones and plaster, by turns bored and baffled. *A young man after my own taste, I think; but this world of grim observances and earnest stratagems is not yours, is it, lad?*

Sport with his companions, watching the three lads and shooing away the grasps of nostalgia or regret. He and Teach would rehearse their sword and musket drill together, because even an old soldier must keep up to the mark, and because especially an old soldier likes to show off when he can. An occasional intimate conversation with Constance Blythe, allowing her to reminisce and telling himself it was for her benefit, feeling himself drifting into a comfortable unchangeable past. Meg's death had left him notionally freer – as if that had ever worried him – but sexless, as if that activity felt like a habit from a phase of life now closed.

In the mornings or the dark hours, the silly traffic of intelligencing work: the papers read, the papers written; the solitary journeys; the private signs on trees and windows; faces in scarves, and faces in shadows – always the shadows. And the meetings – in stairways, doorways, stables and taverns – exchanging the little intimacies of indiscretion: a flask of wine; a hand on a shoulder; a pose of incredulity; gold. Where necessary he used his companions: Vyse or Manders for a front; dispassionate, early-worn Balfour for the more patient work; Teach when it mattered. They knew the game they were playing, though Shay kept his plans his own.

In the afternoons, or the evenings, sitting with one or two others – Leslie, or ancient Leven, or Teach – and naming forgotten brutal German towns and eccentric European Princelings. Old soldiers' tales: ritual, reused, soiled. Shay had always hated the habit; it used to be a pose, to cultivate men of that sort for his purposes. Now it felt like duty: his obligation to his age.

Then he would haul himself up onto his horse again, and trot off into another dusk or another dawn, a half-glimpsed rider heavy-wrapped against the cold of the world.

His boots were smeared with the mud of a dozen different counties across the north and east of England. In April he plunged south through the heart of the country, as far down as Warwickshire and the sad escarpment at Edgehill, and crossed into south Wales. Thirty different beds for those thirty nights: in a grand house in Cheshire, a stubborn grey Yorkshire manor, cottages, inns, barns, mossy tree-roots, a church porch. He was checking his arrangements – the places to sleep, the places to hide, the places to leave a message or dress a wound or find a horse, the places to get a drink or a musket or a ship. He was rekindling the embers of rebellion – reminding men of duties, of loyalties, of friendships, of better times, of the attraction of a purse of money. Among the bruised and grieving loyalists of Norfolk he commiserated for last November's fiasco, and when like mewling puppies they produced noises of defiant determination, he would welcome and encourage them and wonder at his own weariness.

Sometimes he was at Astbury, once more the stranger coming out of the night, taking some heat from the fire, retiring to the room that was kept for him, wondering at the secrets the house still hid from him, unable to return Rachel's searching looks. Sometimes, even when in the district, he avoided the house, stuck to the tavern on the Ashbourne road.

In a wayside inn in Lancashire, ten hours in the saddle behind him and food a distant memory before that, he tramped heavily up the stairs to a private room. He stood on the threshold, but it was empty – a fire burning well, a chair beside it – and. . . no, a figure in darkness the other side of the hearth. He closed the door behind him, and stepped in.

He waited, but the figure was silent. After a moment, Shay said, 'Have you travelled far, pilgrim?'

The figure didn't move: between the boots and the wide-brimmed hat there was a heavy cloak, swept up over the figure's face and shoulder.

Shay stepped closer. 'Have you travelled far, pilgrim?'

The cloak swooped away from the face, a heavy bird flapping towards the warmth of the fire.

'Not worth mentioning, sir. No service too much.' The figure leaned forward, and the firelight picked out a heavy nose and a moustache to match. The jaw came forward under the moustache, and the voice said with stolid earnestness: 'God – save – the King.'

There were protocols for this contingency; Shay had devised some of them himself.

But he hesitated, shook his head, and sat down across the fire. 'Is the food edible here?' he asked.

'I don't – It should – That is, if you think it advisable – Not to draw attention, you know?'

Shay rubbed roughly at his face, seemed to feel its wind-stung crevasses. 'I think I'll manage a meal in an inn without rousing the county. Boy!' The last word was yelled, hoarse, towards the door. 'Sir Greville Marsh?'

Sir Greville Marsh glanced towards the door. Quietly: 'I am, sir, and I'm proud to meet you.'

Shay looked at the face: a fat man hollowed out by sickness and hunger, a wine-blasted nose busy with hairs and spots, the moustache shot with grey. Shay held out his hand. 'It is I who owe you honour, sir.' Marsh shook hands warily, as if over-honoured. 'Our cause depends on men like you, and those of us who live freer of Cromwell's rule should be humble before you.'

'Oh, it's not all that bad, really.' Marsh pulled at the chair and it scraped over the boards towards the fire. 'One lives; one lives.'

There was a clattering on the stairs and the boy stuck his head in. Shay commanded food and drink, and waited for the door to close again. 'Now—'

'What vexes me' – Marsh was leaning forward, conspiratorial – 'is the new men. Oh yes. Popping up all over the county. The new County Committee, now, take that. Very efficient it may be, and I'm not saying that a little improvement wasn't needed, but it's got everyone's backs up.'

'Of cou—'

'I know what you'll say! Be flexible, that's what they all say. Accommodate oneself. I'm a stubborn soul, I know it. Bend with the wind a little, I should. I do sir, believe me. I do try, I've tried to get on good terms with the Committee. Responsibility, d'you see? But all the changes, they upset the mood of the common folk.' He coughed, throat crackling. 'Rot set in under – no disrespect, sir, 'pon my word – to be honest it was in the time of His late Majesty. The old customs, you know? Now, some of the new men, the rabble-rousers, they made their names complaining at the royal taxes, but the new taxes: worse, sir, worse!' Another cough, and he swallowed uncomfortably. 'It trickles down, that's the trouble. Upset the administration at the county level, and it causes problems in the village: we've had some very nasty little problems with the election of the constable, and with the ale-conner. There's a. . . a tension, in the village.'

A stew came, miraculously thick and hot, and a flask of wine, and Shay ate absorbed in the tastes while Sir Greville Marsh described his land dispute with Mr Bailey of Crossgill – 'if you could see how he treats his oaks, sir!' – and the continued rancour arising from an opinion that he, Sir Greville, had been obliged to give – 'and honesty, sir, that's what a gentleman owes to the common folk, that's what I say' – in the case of Tetlow, the preacher, in 1641.

Shay finished the stew and put the wooden bowl and spoon down by the hearth with respectful care, and took a mouthful of wine, and gave a vast sigh of animal content, eyes closed and head slumped back.

Sir Greville broke mid-sentence for a moment, with something like concern at Shay's behaviour. Shay opened his eyes, and narrowed them and sat up. 'You're a good man, Marsh,' he said, and he meant it. 'If the young King could see you, it would give him heart.' Marsh bridled in embarrassment – *Strange,* Shay thought, *I reckoned him a mere inflated bladder, but I believe he truly cares for nothing more than the good of his little hamlet* – and made to speak, and Shay hurried on. 'But I must know – the crisis is coming – perhaps a couple of months, perhaps a little more – these discontents you speak of – will the country hereabouts rise?'

Marsh sucked in a long breath. 'It's diff—'

'Will – they – rise?'

Marsh sat back, frowned unhappily, a little cowed.

Shay managed a smile, trying to take the edge off his impatience. 'You know them, sir, what do you think?'

Marsh nodded, confidence warming once more, and leaned forwards. 'They're good simple souls in these parts, sir. Loyal. And with good men at their head, well. . .' He sat back, apparently getting momentum, and then plunged forwards again. 'Rivers, of Littledale, he has a scheme for a handful of us – just a handful, that's the way, you see? – a handful of us to arrest the Mayor of Lancaster on market day – Toulnson – one of the new men, and not popular – he's on the County Committee – arrest him, d'you see? for corruption, and put up Shuttleworth in his place, whom everyone respects, all sides – and the great thing is that Rivers's cousin is Captain of the militia in the town, and though Toulnson when he was Commissioner put a lot of his own people into the militia, at the moment John Rivers says they'll follow, there's been that much sharp practice with commissions recently. . .' He hesitated, as if hoping that Shay would reset the sentence for him. 'There we all are then: our man as Mayor; the militia loyal, and able to control the gates; we suspend all new taxes levied since the beginning of last year, pending a proper review, and freeze bread prices in the market at a penny lower than they are today.' The voice low and urgent: 'The old ways, d'you see? Make folk feel comfortable again – with their local habits, the prices, the preaching – declare for the King then.' He sat back, and nodded, satisfied, as if he'd just placed the crown on Charles Stuart's head in Westminster Abbey.

'It could work,' Shay said. *Staggeringly, there's a faint chance it actually could work.* And then he looked at Marsh again, at the life-beaten face.

'Couldn't it, though?' Marsh smiled, and looked into the fire. 'It would be something, wouldn't it? Something to tell the grandchildren.' He looked up apologetically. 'My son – well, he's gone – he – he. . .' He shook his head, lost in the fire again. Then tried again, more reflectively. 'It would be something, wouldn't it, sir?' He turned to Shay again and – perhaps it was just a trick of the fire – there was a new light in the eyes, a fat man's geniality hiding in a thin man. 'Something for the old ways.'

Shay watched him; watched them both, somehow distanced from the routine. *Are you the world I am offering Vyse, and Balfour, and Rachel? Why are you alive, and Meg not?*

He hungered to spend the night there, but couldn't risk it and couldn't stop so early. Soon he was pulling himself up onto the horse again, and man and beast weaved out of the inn gate into the gloom and began to tramp northwards.

TO MR I. S., AT THE GEORGE, NEWCASTLE

Sir,

I have been no kind of correspondent these many months. I am sorry for it. As I recollect you surmised when last you wrote, it has been an unsettled time for the Royal army. And I have had certain personal hurt that has distracted me quite. The army is well-established now at Stirling. But it is no longer a cheerful prospect, for souls are low as if winter has still not quitted this place, and the defences are left weak. There is fear that should Cromwell attack directly here it would cause a great crisis in the army and in the compact with the loyal Scots. I trust you are well.

[SS C/T/51/38]

Remembering his way through winding roads to Astbury, Thurloe tried to distinguish his motives in coming. But the effort only made him uneasy, first at the idea that he was acting on emotion as much as professional intent, and then at the tension implied by the increasingly apparent overlap – or was it now a conflict? – between the professional and the emotional.

Astbury and the Astbury family were a centre of Royalist plotting in England, and Paulden's distinct reaction in The Hague had only reinforced his impression. What then of Rachel Astbury's otherworldly innocence? Was it her attempts at manipulation, the games he'd taken for girlish whim, that he should take more seriously?

Paulden had also been spurred into the fuller story of Pontefract and Doncaster, and how should that be read? Should he read Paulden's deflection of the question about the link between Royalist and Leveller as confirmation that it was a confected fantasy, or confirmation that it was somehow real? And if there was some kind of truth in that strange link, and if there was truth in Paulden's story of the source in Doncaster sending messages to the Royalists in besieged Pontefract, then. . .

The raid had also been an attempt to contact the supposed agent in Doncaster. Somehow, the raid had gone wrong, and Colonel Thomas Rainsborough had—

Rainsborough?

Surely that was insanity.

Reports had come out of Pontefract. Lyle, the Leveller sympathizer, had passed them to Scot, the Leveller sympathizer. Scot – it would have to have been Scot himself – had decided that at least one of those reports had to be erased from the record, even from his own private ledger of reports. Tarrant, the Leveller sympathizer, had come to Doncaster and had an angry exchange with Rainsborough, the prominent Leveller. And soon after that, Rainsborough had died.

But Rainsborough had been killed by Royalists, surely?

Rachel Astbury received him in the parlour, alone, hair down. She felt herself relaxing, smiling as she saw him. His smile in response was slower, heavier, touched by thought.

He removed his hat, and dropped it onto the table beside him. 'Hallo, Rachel,' he said.

She looked at the hat on the table. This was somehow a new Thurloe:

more confident, more comfortable. She'd words prepared, but swallowed them; waited.

'You're an old family, aren't you? You have a family Bible, I hazard.' She nodded on instinct, uncertain. 'I'd like to see it please.'

Rachel stared at him a moment. *What is in there for him? What reason have I to refuse?* 'Why?'

I cannot stop him, regardless.

'A curiosity. Something I was trying to remember as I rode.' He smiled without humour. 'Perhaps we may prove that religion is no division between us.'

Several minutes later she brought in the fat volume. Thurloe placed it on the table and opened it, respectful. On the flyleaf, his finger ran back through the neat history of the Astburys. The children of a Mary Lowell – the sale of a piece of land – the marriage of Mary Astbury to Sir Henry Lowell – more land sold – the death of the King – the fine paid to recover the estate – and so back through the milestones of country and county and family, a troubling world controlled for once in the handwriting scratched on the crackling, yellowing pages. A pair of entries, the words written smaller and less sure, a little family sorrow: the death of Isabelle Astbury, wife of Anthony, in childbed; a day later the death of her newborn son. Then back to the birth of Rachel Astbury, and it made him think of her as a girl, and he glanced up at the anxious face and the woman's body – the birth of Mary Astbury, and back down to the foot of the preceding column, and there it was.

A year after the marriage of Sir Anthony Astbury to Isabelle Shay, of Chester in the County of Cheshire, was an entry in a different hand – Isabelle's?

21st March, 1624. Mortimer Shay, brother of Isabelle Astbury, m. Margaret Talbot.

Thurloe closed the Bible with care.

He looked into her face, and then down at his hand as he flexed it open and closed, then up to her again.

'Royalism isn't dead in this land, Rachel. There's life in it yet. Not in the silly fantasies of romantics and old men, but in a network of committed men and women controlled and functioning as a network. A network of support, of communication, of intrigue. Of action.'

She was frowning, trying to gauge his tone.

'Men are dying as a result. Idiots persuaded to rise in a futile rebellion. The tools of this network who are captured and left to swing. Inoffensive men who are found to be a useful symbol of the new regime, and assassinated to prove a point. A little piece of deception, a misleading letter, and thousands of men die in battle.' She had stepped back. 'This is treason, Rachel. Not a game between one faction and another, but a deliberately maintained underground campaign of sedition and insurrection and murder. This country could be settled now. At peace. It is not, and that is so solely because of the men who are the clockspring of it all – one man, perhaps.'

Her face had gone cold, and Thurloe found his own voice rising to try to make an impact. 'George Astbury was one of these men, and he surely made this house a centre of this work. He's dead, and his work has been taken on by others. Perhaps by one of his relatives through his sister-in-law, your mother. The Shays – there was one more at least, wasn't there? Mortimer Shay, I think.' Her eyes were wide, at the words and more at the tone.

She stayed silent.

'You must tell me, because I have to know where you stand. I have to know if – if you're part of the future of this country.'

'To hell with you!' The words were spat, cat-hissed, and Thurloe's eyes closed for a moment. 'With you, and your laws and your liberties.'

'Rachel—'

'Your soft words about the future are just pretence: for me – perhaps for yourself. Your world is constant struggle. It's violence. It's tyranny.'

He stepped towards her, and she pulled away.

'Each day that these men are left free to act is greater complicity for you. Greater danger.'

'How can you pretend to care?'

'But I—'

'I thought that. . . I thought that I might. . . But you have nothing for me. You are nothing to me.' Her chin came up, and her chest rose and swelled. 'Get out!' The face was wild, lost, vicious. 'All of you: go!'

The decade of war seemed to have fought itself in the weary body of Oliver Cromwell. Now emerging from months of intermittent fever, he was thinner and paler, the flesh hanging slack on his cheeks. Wide pinked eyes stared bleak at Thomas Scot, and John Thurloe and General Lambert.

He took in a laboured breath. 'How do our enemies? Lambert?'

'General, our scouts report no change in the strength of the lines, nor the attitude of the men behind them.' He shook his head to emphasize the point.

'Scot?'

'No change, Master Cromwell. There is no military frailty to strain their politics, and thus no political frailty to unsettle their military.' The reedy voice and the sharp rhetorician's mind picked out the words.

Cromwell swung round to Thurloe, and the eyebrows merely lifted.

Thurloe looked down at the letter in his hand – the few lines which were all he had from J. H. – doubts about the strength of the defences at Stirling, fears of what would happen should the English Army attack. *What hidden grammar is in these lines?*

A determined shake of the head. 'I have no reason to question Master Scot or General Lambert. They're comfortable behind their lines at Stirling. They're gathering men in Fife and the north-east at leisure, and I assume' – he glanced at Lambert – 'that the longer they have to do that the more comfortable they'll be.'

'Well that's just it, isn't it, Master Thurloe?' Cromwell's voice came hoarse out of the jowls. 'We're hundreds of miles from home, living off this impoverished and resistant land, and time is against us. Time is on the side of General Leslie and the Duke of Hamilton and their Princeling, impregnable at Stirling and husbanding their strength.'

The bloodshot eyes widened, and he looked at them each. 'I have a will to change this arrangement, gentlemen. We are over-extended, vulnerable, a house built upon sand, and we can but butt against them. I will see the Scots so vulnerable; I will see them exposed. We must be the ones in control of the manoeuvres; we must be the ones drawing them into our strength.'

Lambert's austere features had creased. 'But that would mean—'

'It would mean England.' The words fell deep, ominous. 'That's right, John. We must draw out the fox. We must have him loose, even in England, if we are to hunt him to destruction. Can we do it?'

Lambert, a little pale, nodded warily.

Cromwell's glare settled heavily on Scot and Thurloe. 'I must take them in the flank. I must chivvy them out of their snug burrow. And then I must harry them through the north of England, even to the heart of the country. It will risk many men; it will risk our firmest ground. I will do it if you can tell me that you have the measure of them. That you hear our enemies right – that you read them – that you whisper to them.'

The eyebrows rose. Oliver Cromwell's eyes were massive globes gazing out at the two of them.

Scot and Thurloe glanced quickly and uneasily at each other. Each breathed in. They too nodded.

To Mr J. H., at Macrae's in Galashiels

Sir,

Truly these men will run and run at the same stone wall until their heads are quite dulled — unless, that is, they should by some exceptional feat of strong-headedness crack through those stones, and find themselves in the pit. I am not privy to their planning, but I infer from much bustling and toing and froing, and from certain comments either ominous or belligerent from those better-informed, that Cromwell and Lambert do mean to focus all their strength on Stirling, and to continue to spend that strength until one or both sides are obliterated. I will not say that I would not be pleased were the English arms to have victory — I care enough for my beliefs that I will welcome a success for them, howsoever it may be — but, truly, have we seen in this whole century such a hot-blooded fever?

I must tell you that I am resolved to maintain as best I may an even-tempered intellectual life in the middle of the chaos: that I shall do my duty to the world: that I shall strive as much to do my duty to my mind.

I hope that this even-handed determination may make me a better servant to both. For these political eruptions will pass, and will I trust lead us to some better time and place. We should I think strive to render ourselves as fitted for that time and place as we may, and even if we do not ourselves survive to see it, our children should not thank us were we to have passed these years in mere frozen stagnation, rather than sustaining as best we may what progress God may see fit to show us in the arts and in the understanding of the world he has created for us.

I was in part prompted by the information that an old friend from the University is trying this year to publish, fifty years after that remarkable philosopher's death, Gilbert's private reflections on the relationship between the earth and the stars. I do not venture to presume that you are an enthusiast for natural philosophy, yet, even in this unruly summer, a man may rest his head upon a cannon, and stare up into the heavens!

[SS C/S/51/50]

～

North Queensferry early on a summer morning: mist hangs sleepy on the expanse of the Forth river, the barrier to Edinburgh and England. Far out in the estuary, towards the sea in the east, the gannets are starting to shriek and reel. The tide is low, and these first few yards of the unmeasurable, unknowable north of Scotland are dark mud, rising gently from the mist to the few cottages of the village. The cottages are silent. The ferry's oars haven't moved for months, for the Forth is now a frontier; the ferryman drinks more now, and sleeps in.

An early cormorant splashes on the mud, trying its thin pools for food.

From the mist a thumping and splashing, a weird heartbeat of the pre-dawn, and shapeless, consonantless voices. At night, drowned demons of men who died without God come from the firth to rot fish and steal away the souls of children. Thumping and splashing, then patches of mist darken and solidify and lunge forward towards the mudflats, a thousand men in new-built boats crossing the frontier of night and mist, Colonel Overton kneeling in the prow reciting the Lord's Prayer as the shore materializes.

The thumping and splashing of the oars, and now urgent voices of exhortation, strangely subdued out of instinctive respect for the mist-spirits, and the boats slew and squelch into the mud, and boots begin to tumble out and stamp ungainly towards the village.

Thy will be done; Thy will be done; Thy will be done.

—◦—

The news was in Stirling in hours, despite the winding miry roads it had to travel. Shay heard it first from Vyse and Manders, respectively hurrying and clumping into his room and insistent with rumours of an undefined English attack, until he hushed them both. Then Balfour arrived with a summons, and Shay heard the news a second time over the Council table.

'Cromwell has outflanked us, Your Majesty, gentlemen.' Leslie, voice reedy and pedantic. 'He's put men across the Forth, and we can't stop him reinforcing them. He's behind us.'

And heard it again. 'This smacks of bad generalship. We've let him baffle us: he kept us looking one way, and he went t'other. While we focused all of our effort on Stirling, waiting dumb as ducks for him to hit us there, he's leapt into the heart of our supplies and our recruits.'

'Will he reinforce them? Put himself entirely to our north?'

'Nothing to stop him.'

'Pardon me.' It was Hamilton, steady and austere. 'If he does move entirely across the Forth, behind us, isn't he trapped?'

Uncomfortable glances. Leslie took up the point warily. 'He commands the sea. Supply is no difficulty for him. It rather depends on whether we think we can face him in pitched battle, on open ground, and defeat him.'

Silence. Then, from somewhere down the table, 'He's left the door to England open, surely.'

A moment while it was absorbed, and then noise like a flood.

'Advance into England while he's across our supplies? It's madness.'

'What are we fighting for if not England?'

'Our priority must be to defend Scotland!'

'We'll gather supplies and recruits as we march. We'll be heading towards our heartland!'

'It's a betrayal of the Scots.'

'It's dangerous.'

At the head of the table, silent and watchful, slumping and then catching himself, King Charles Stuart. *Everything seems to happen around me, and sometimes to me. Am I not supposed to lead?* Occasional uncomfortable glances at him from the men at the table about to speak, sometimes a muttered token 'Y'r M'sty' as they begin. *What am I supposed to say?*

At the opposite end of the room, away from the table, Sir Mortimer Shay. His conversations were private, in corners, to single men – not in these circuses. Hamilton, Leslie, they had had such information as he could give them, and it was up to them to manage their dispositions as a result. He merely watched, half-listening.

Is this where George Astbury sat? Is this what he heard, what. . . exactly three years ago, before they marched down to die at Preston?

When Manders entered Shay's room, breaths coming hard and steady after the concentrated effort of getting up the stairs, he found Shay leaning against the edge of a table. Beside him were Lady Constance Blythe, silent on a chair, and a small wooden chest prominent on the table.

As usual Shay made no allowances for his incapacity, letting him clamber his way around the door and close it, and then starting into speech.

'Manders; good man. I have a duty for you.' Manders straightened on his single crutch. 'You escort Lady Constance to the Continent tonight; you'll start downriver at dusk.'

Manders fought for restraint as he spoke: 'But – sir, that's – the army could go south at any moment!'

'Con's days of hand-to-hand fighting are mostly done. You would likewise agree that she cannot be entrusted to some Scottish ferryman.'

Manders swallowed his frustration. 'Of course.'

Shay read his expression. 'Scotland will be left to Cromwell's grim mercies. We don't know what will happen in England. The expedition is a risk in itself. I will not compound that by risking you and in particular Lady Constance.'

Lady Constance said quietly, 'Women are an encumbrance to the army,

Michael. Even at the best of times, the men restrict their movements if they have to think about our safety.' She didn't sound as if she believed it, and Manders wondered at the conversation that had preceded his arrival and left her so subdued.

He grunted, and nodded to her as civilly as he could manage. His eyes strayed to the wooden chest at Shay's elbow.

'Yes. You'll take this with you.' Shay lifted the lid of the chest, and watched their widening eyes. 'I have spent the last two days visiting some of the greater men hereabouts, invoking their commitment to our cause.'

The coins and jewels glowed and smiled from the dull box, and then disappeared with the snap of the lid under Shay's hand.

Lady Constance seemed sad. 'Mortimer, do you trust the cause so little, that you think only of smuggling these small treasures out?'

Shay shook his head. 'Sad times, Con. There are men who would pay more attention to this box than to your face.'

Later, Shay and Manders standing together in a doorway, Balfour and Vyse waiting across the room. Shay's words were low and earnest.

'Whatever happens in England, men like you will preserve something of the old ways. That spirit will come home again – perhaps in a month, perhaps in a century. But it will survive in men like you.'

Manders just nodded heavily, his one leg shifting uneasily under the extra weight of Shay's hands on his shoulders.

'But first you must get safe out of here; more important, you must get her safe out of here.'

Again the nod.

Shay leaned closer. 'My affection for that woman is unrestrained. But listen well, boy: in the uttermost, it were better that she were dead than captured. Do you understand me?' Manders's eyes widened, and he nodded uncomfortably. 'Otherwise... Manders, at Dunbar you were reckless with your life; but Lady Constance – her freedom alone – is truly a cause to die for.'

'She is a lady, sir; I need no more.'

Again he felt the old man's hands holding his head, felt the great heavy eyes on him; then Shay had turned away into the night.

The three young men were left alone. For a moment they stood silent, in a circle, hands on each other's shoulders. Then Manders let his arms fall, and hopped back a pace, resettling the crutch against his side.

Vyse said: 'I hear the girls in France are very pretty, Manders. Try to behave as a gentleman, will you?'

'Gods, what a thought.' Balfour. 'The syphilis'll eat away his other leg and we'll just have to prop him against the chimney in the evenings.'

The smiles were routine. Manders looked at each of them.

'Hal. Tom. You fight for me, so do it well.' They nodded on instinct. 'And come safe through. We will hunt together again.'

It had become Thurloe's habit to ride to the Edinburgh docks once in every day. He was enjoying the city more than he pretended: for men represented variously as barbarian, over-religious, or merely dull, he found the Scots of the capital disproportionately rational and intelligent, civilized in their pleasures, discreet as to their beliefs and serious about their Greek. But despite a more pleasant social life than he was used to in London, he looked forward to his daily escape.

He claimed it gave him contact with the working end of the control of departures by sea, which tiresome part of exercising a closer stranglehold on the country seemed to have become part of his responsibility in Edinburgh. He claimed that a more immediate view of the tides of people and ships made him think more clearly about the secret currents he was trying to understand. In truth, he merely welcomed the open space and empty air of the sea, after the constricted, reeking city.

The tree branches held claims to spring this morning, but the air still felt like winter as he rode. The sky was white, and the cold bone-deep.

Where now was his Royalist network? Active out of Stirling, presumably. Infiltrating the front lines of the Parliamentary Army, perhaps – maybe deeper. Spreading sedition in England. *And what of Doncaster and Pontefract?* William Paulden in The Hague had tried to impress him with the mystery of what had been going on there. Still the suggestion of Leveller treachery. But, in truth, he had only heard of it through the J. H. letters; and those he now knew for deliberate deceptions.

The Army, typically, had taken over the front room of a sordid waterfront tavern to monitor arrivals and departures, and with little jealousies and rivalries tried to co-ordinate with the customs men next door. As Thurloe stepped down from the cobbles into the tavern, head bent under the beams and nose twisting at the ill mix of fish and filth, the two soldiers sitting at a table in the window hurriedly closed the lid of a small chest and began to inspect a pile of papers with elaborate focus.

Thurloe nodded to the tavern owner for a drink, and sat. The two soldiers looked up with wide-eyed attention. 'Gentlemen.' They nodded deferentially, which made him more suspicious. 'What have we?'

One of the soldiers pushed the pile of papers over, thin and greasy sheets, tickets of leave that they'd collected from people on the ships they'd searched. Thurloe counted them first; six today. 'What else?' He went through the sheaf again as he waited. His eyes flicked up to the two soldiers. He scanned the sheaf again, and something caught his attention. This time he held the soldiers' eyes. 'What else did you find?'

He deliberately didn't lower his eyes to the chest, unobtrusive on the bench beside them. He was learning to treat soldiers as he did his children. 'Any other little successes?' Their peccadilloes had to be wheedled out without shame.

Eventually one of them glanced at his companion, and said: 'We seized – this.' He nodded to the chest.

'Well done. What is it?'

The soldier looked around the tavern, hesitated as the owner put a mug of heated wine in front of Thurloe and turned away, and lifted the chest lid for a moment. 'We'll be handing it in to the Colonel.'

'Of course. I'll bet they didn't want you finding that, did they?'

At last a little pride began to glow in the two faces. 'That they did not, sir. Old lady it was. And her son.' Thurloe's mind was starting to turn, to wonder. 'Him with only one leg, and looking very sick. Near dead, she thought. Making a bit of a fuss, she was. Anyway, they were on deck, wrapped all very cosy, and she handed over their passes very quick and obliging – bit too quick, if you take my meaning, sir – and soon as she thinks we're inspecting the passes she's glancing all nervous at her son. So we checked them both. He was missing a leg – but through the blanket it looked like it was growing back, if you follow.' He grinned, and his companion grinned. They'd enjoyed developing that line. 'Chest was hidden under his dressings and wrappings.'

In their way they'd done well, unfortunately. 'Good for you. No wonder you were so absorbed.' They were dealing with someone who knew how they thought, how they behaved. 'These the two passes? Mathilda Beatty? Thomas Beatty?' Brow-racked scrutiny from the soldiers; they knew something was wrong now. 'With the seals smudged? Smudged so you don't see the fakery so well?' The two young faces were sullen, dumb. 'Tell me: the lady – fifties, perhaps sixty? Gold hair gone grey? Handsome?' Still the boyish discomfort. 'Tell me!'

'Sounds like it could be.'

'How long ago? Quickly!'

'Twenty minutes maybe?'

'Can they be stopped? The guard ship, can it catch them?' The soldiers started to ponder, which was always fatal. 'Move, man! Go now!'

From the rail of the brig *Verity*, pushing down the choppy Firth of Forth, Lady Constance Blythe watched her island for the first time. *I have always moved among people, not among countries.* Departure felt like death. She did not know where she was going, and would hardly know even once she was there. *Who shall I know, and who shall know me?*

Michael Manders sat against one of the masts, and she knew that he was watching the thinning land with his own regrets and shame.

Then a more anxious shout from one of the crewmen, and the Captain was staring around agitated, and it was immediately clear something was wrong.

'The guard ship!' He hurried to the rail, talking half to himself. Leaning out, he shaded his eyes and peered back towards the city. 'She's after us!' This now clearly addressed to Lady Constance. Fear and accusation as he spoke to her: 'She's signalling us to stop!'

And thus must all fairy stories end.

Manders was sitting up, attentive and calculating.

'Can't we – can't we outrun the ship?' she said feebly.

The Captain staring at her and back out to sea, shaking his head. 'What? If we fail. . .'

Manders was watching her now. She thought he might have been looking at the Captain, but it was unmistakably at her, and there was something hard and distant in the expression.

Then he was levering himself up against the mast with clumsy intent, and hopping doggedly towards her with something held close against his side, and with a sick sadness at her fragility, at the waste of it all, she knew what Shay must have ordered. *I am become like an old religion, better eradicated than spread, or like a contagion.*

Manders approached her, and smiled, and she tried to smile proudly back at him. His arm reached towards her, and then over her shoulder, and he gripped the rigging and began to hop along the deck using it for balance.

The Captain had turned away, mouth opening in the shout, when an arm came hard around his throat and choked the sound, and he felt metal in his back, and heard words intimate in his ear. 'We shall outrun her, Captain.'

'But. . .' – the words a constricted rasp – 'it's treason. . . If she catches up. . .'

The words were still quiet, almost playful. 'Perhaps she catches up, perhaps she doesn't. Perhaps we must fight her. What is certain, Captain, is that if we do not try to outrun her I will blow out your spine.' Manders was actually smiling now, enjoying the wind in his face. 'Come, let us see what sort of men we may be, eh?'

Lady Constance Blythe watched him with misted eyes and an old excitement kindling in her. There were still men. There was still hope. *Oh, my gallant gallant lads.*

❧ ❧

'We shall march into England!'

It came out more shrill than he'd hoped. *Why can't I have the gravity of these old dark men?* Two dozen heads swung round to the source of the sound, surprised and flustered and a little indignant. *Will they heed me will they heed me will they heed me?*

'Your Majesty—'

'That is my decision.'

That swung it. The doubters hadn't strength enough to overturn the clear wish of the King – *but wasn't the deal that we were supposed to control him?* – and the forward men were quick to pocket the advantage – *but that was unexpected, and it might become a dangerous habit.*

'Your Majesty's decision is most welcome.'

'We thank Your Majesty for your prudent consideration.'

'Perhaps we may present Your Majesty with the details tomorrow. Some trivial matters of logistics. For your approval.'

Charles Stuart wiped his palms on his velvet breeches, and breathed out very slowly.

What have I done?

Shay watched from the side, glances at the political men around the table and a close scrutiny of the young man at the top. *Given the chance, this exquisite boy might be a King more than his father.* Again he looked around the room, the meeting breaking up into clumps of grumbles and plots. *But is a Scottish army invading England really that chance?*

Three years on, another Duke of Hamilton was marching south, for another Charles Stuart. The previous Duke had had George Astbury worrying beside him. Now, another Comptroller-General must help prepare the way, stir risings in support, squeeze out the last insipid drops of Royalist feeling in the counties.

And so we try again, old George.

———

Thomas Scot came hurrying at a stiff-legged trot, his cloak flapping clumsily and papers held tight in one hand. 'South!' he said through breaths. 'They're marching, Master Cromwell. As you had hoped.' The last sentence emerged more hesitant, still doubting the wisdom of leaving England open. 'I have the news straight from the young Charles's Court. South – for England. The Duke of Hamilton commands.' He rattled the papers. 'It confirms what our scouts have been suggesting.'

Thurloe looked at Thomas Scot, excited and apprehensive, at Cromwell, granite, and at the sheaf clenched in Scot's hand. *Another sortie of papers. Another set of pages come to offer us truths.*

Cromwell, knowing that the uncomfortable world of waiting, of speculations, of reports, was again being superseded by his world of battle, was unexcited. 'There it is, gentlemen. The fox has broken cover. We must pray that God make our hounds keen.'

Fortified Stirling, defiant on its crag, had been a place of defence for a millennium, the iron buckle on the waist of Scotland. Now the Scottish army was streaming south from the town, through the cockpit of their history, across its bones.

The army is a whole society on the move, a whole economy: smiths and armourers and soldiers; foragers and butchers and cooks; pickpockets and royal accountants; whores and priests; a King. This little civilization moves at the pace of its slowest: the gorgeous coats poised on the warhorses must circle and wait, buzz out and back, to the trudge of the broken-soled pikeman and the women-of-all-trades with the wagons.

There were some Englishmen in the army, mostly in the gorgeous coats, and they rode impatient – wondering at strategy and Court politics, perhaps anxious to be away from the bogs and ditches where Wallace and the Bruce had humiliated their ancestors. They couldn't leave Scotland fast enough, and they couldn't leave the trudging rascally Scottish foot-soldiers, their foul grating grumbling accents and their stink, at all. The Scots tramped steadily in the herd, pennies in their pockets and something to do at last. England was rich, wasn't it? Plump cattle and plump girls; rich houses to liberate. These were the calculations of men, and the instincts of boys on a spree, and something tugging in blood that had been foraging southward since before time.

A summer evening, a few miles south of Carlisle, and Shay caught up with the rearguard of the royal army. He was supposed to press on, to get through the army; he needed to be thrusting ahead, to be off on some task which he could not immediately define. So at least some grim insistence inside was telling him, thudding stubborn through his weariness.

But it was so pleasant to fall in for a moment with the last riders of the rearguard, with the flat rays of the falling sun warming the yellow fields and sparkling the helmets and sword-points and bronzing the faces, to match pace with the gentle bounce of the uniforms and the rattle of their bridles. For a moment the world was peaceful and companionable, and Shay breathed in the landscape and listened to the quiet chat of the men. In that aching moment he was young and callow once more, and craving the assurance and competence of those beside him. In the moment his dreams were fresh again, unbloodied and still to be pursued.

Dry boots, fresh clothes thick and warm, belts and weapons and saddle comfortable, the promise of supper, the casual banter of good men, the gentle drumbeat of hooves on solid ground, the private pleasure of moving in rhythm with others, the soft light, the scent of some deep rightness coming off the fields and hedges.

The soldier trotting next to him – *a boy; really just a boy* – glanced cautiously over and mumbled his respects. Shay felt the heaviness of his age, tried to contrive some gruff pleasantry in return, and then heard the dull snap of a musket shot from somewhere behind and a clang as it hit a backplate and then wild shouts and hooves and on an instinct he'd kicked his horse into the gallop and was lurching forward; the boy had hesitated, wanting to look before he decided – *there is never time to decide* – and Shay tried to slap at the boy's horse as he passed to get it moving: 'Ride!'

Careering forward, the all-absorbing thunder of hooves and billowing dust, and Shay was snatching for opportunities and avenues of escape, but there was none through the hedges on either side, and now he risked a glance over his shoulder – *what is the threat? What is the opportunity?* – a detachment of Cromwell's English horsemen – were they dropping back now? – perhaps less than a dozen, but impossible to tell through the chaos of dust and his shuddering vision. Then into the vision lurched the boy, slowing dramatically and shrinking away from Shay on a horse that bucked and spun and the boy was teetering and scrabbling and falling backwards into the road.

Shay heaved at his reins and pulled viciously at his horse's neck and the beast veered under him and he felt his stomach plunging away and then he was lashing the horse into the charge. Forty yards off the boy was staggering to his feet, grappling clumsy for his horse, thirty yards off, but the horse was shying and skittering and there were two English horsemen looming beyond him. Twenty yards and the first horseman was on the boy with a wild windmill stroke of his sabre and the boy was staggering aside; ten yards and Shay's pistol was up and he fired and the rider disappeared backwards into the dust. Shay yanked hard on the reins again, pulling his horse around to protect the boy on the ground and colliding broadside with the second English rider. Confusion, Shay trying to punch the man off-balance backhanded while reaching for his sword, and the rider was pulling away, but then Shay's horse had shied and reared and he was slipping off it as best he could into the dust.

All sense was useless, the world a swirl of noise and dirt, and Shay was jumping between instincts: scrabbling for his sword, peering fierce through the dust for the enemy, trying to work out where the boy was. Through the haze he saw the English rider, a few yards off and pulling his horse around and coming back to the attack, and Shay had forgotten – what had happened to his sword? – then he tripped over the boy.

He pulled himself up onto his knees, sensed the dark onrush of the cavalryman, and tried to pull the boy up with him; but the boy was slumped and hard to grasp and the cavalryman was a vast shadow exploding over them and Shay could only try to shield the boy with his torso, then a fierce cry from behind and thunder and Shay dropped flat on the boy and over them both vaulted a miraculous second horse, a soaring arc of muscles and hooves through Shay's bewildered vision, and the attacking cavalryman slowed and hesitated and was transfixed by a rigid sword that exploded out of his back.

Silence.

No more of Cromwell's cavalry. The dust settling, and through it the world solidifying once more.

Shay pulled himself to his knees again, and checked the boy. Their rescuer trotted back, and dropped quickly to the ground; one of their companions from the rearguard. 'That was the bravest thing, sir,' he said. A quiet voice, unemotional; a large fit man, perhaps thirty. 'Coming back for the boy.'

Shay grunted. 'Yours was just as good a deed, lad. And more successful.' He glanced down at the boy in the dust, a young glare of shock and a vicious dirty crimson rip across the chest, then up, and shook his head.

The other man winced in frustration, and then his face evened again. Together they dragged the boy's body out of the road, and collected the three horses. There was no hedge here: scattered trees, and then uneven moorland spreading away, as much as they could see of it in the dying evening.

The horses tied, the boy covered, the two men dropped to the ground.

Shay thrust out his hand. 'Thank you. I'm very much obliged to you.'

The young man shook hands. 'Austwick, sir. Allen Austwick.' *Austwick?* 'Captain.'

'Shay.' Shay was still scrabbling at the surprise. *Austwick?*

'I know who you are, sir. Well – we weren't sure of the name. The Ghost, that's what the men call you.'

'They do, do they?' Momentarily, Shay felt his vanity warming pleasantly. *Of all the men to find in a ditch in a skirmish: Austwick indeed.*

'No one sees you come, no one sees you go. You're with the army, then you're not, then you're back. Murmuring in the Duke's ear. With the men around the King. You're listened to. Soldiers have an instinct for these things.' He caught himself. 'If that doesn't seem fanciful.'

Shay shook his head. 'I've lived among soldiers these thirty years. I have great respect for their instincts.' He looked around them in the gloom. 'Austwick, you said? We're better off here for the night, I fancy.'

'Agreed, sir. Good a spot as any.'

'Road's not as safe as it might be.'

'Agreed, sir.'

In the last of the light they found comfortable places for themselves among the easy undulations of the earth, and Shay glanced with approval at Austwick setting his sword close beside where he'd lie and checking his pistol while he could see. Darkness closed the world over them.

'Austwick. If you've no better distraction to suggest, I'd like to ask you for the tale of Doncaster, and the Leveller Colonel.'

Silence.

'I know you were there. I have a. . . professional interest in the matter. I've had the tale from Teach, and from the lad Blackburn before he died.'

Silence, as if Austwick had disappeared in the darkness.

Then: 'You spoke to Michael Blackburn?'

'I helped him and Morrice away. Not far enough away, unfortunately. I know how the sortie ran. I know that William Paulden planned it; he that died just after. I know that Thomas Paulden and Teach and you and Blackburn were close in it. It. . . helps if I see it from different perspectives.'

Again the darkness swallowed the last of his words, and gave nothing back. Teach had described Austwick as a commanding presence in the operation; this was a different man now. 'William Paulden was scouting around the town, yes? His brother, Captain Thomas, went off to the north gate. You and Teach and Blackburn got into Rainsborough's lodging by pretending to have a message.'

A grunt from the night, the quiet suggestion of a chuckle. Then, 'A simple trick, I guess, but they'd no reason to suspect.'

Shay's third hearing of the death of Colonel Thomas Rainsborough was in a Cumbria ditch, settling himself against a shoulder of earth and grass and listening to a disembodied voice in the night.

'Blackburn looked after the horses, I think.'

'Right. I went with Teach after the Colonel's Lieutenant. He'd let us in, swallowed our story. He took us up to Rainsborough's room.'

'The Lieutenant was up already?'

'I guess you know an Adjutant's job, sir. All the papers and logistics. First awake, last to bed. He was pretty distracted from the start – barely checked our papers – mind elsewhere, yes? I was proper wound up, sir, but I suppose visitors with a message was just routine business to him.'

'Mm. And Rainsborough?'

'His Lieutenant woke him, and he was out of his room half-dressed. We had sword and pistol on the two of them and pushed them down into the street.'

Just two men to bring down two men. 'You took a hell of a chance.'

'Maybe so. But they'd never have believed we were just messengers if we'd come with a platoon. And men will do what they're told if they're half-awake and well-threatened.'

'That changed in the street, though.'

'Chaos.' The darkness emptied again. Then: 'What we had in the roadway not half an hour back; like that.'

Shay grunted. He felt himself getting drowsy. A warm night; the ground soft. 'Try to see the individual actions. Who moved? Who spoke?'

'Mr Shay. . .'

'Tell me. Who was first in the street?'

'Me. Well, Blackburn led the horses forward and then came back to help. I went out; Teach and Blackburn were pushing Rainsborough and his man after. I mounted. Captain William Paulden coming up. Then Rainsborough muttered something, then—'

'What?'

'Cursing us. Whores – no, pimps. Pimps, and snakes. And cowards. And he used a strange phrase: working – no, festering in the innards – maybe it was guts – intestines, maybe – festering in the intestines of Satan.'

'Charming.'

'Then Rainsborough's Lieutenant was cursing us too, by St Nicholas and St James and everyone else, and it had all fallen apart. Rainsborough was in a fury by now, and Teach saw him reaching for a weapon or lunging and shouted a warning and then Blackburn was among them and it was a proper scramble. Rainsborough cursing again, and then somehow everyone was armed. I think maybe Blackburn had stumbled and dropped his weapons, or they were snatched. Rainsborough had a blade – he may even have grabbed it from one of the saddles. The Lieutenant had a pistol and that went off, but in the confusion he hit Rainsborough, and then Teach finished the Lieutenant with his sword and Rainsborough was still waving his blade around, even though he was already mortally wounded, and I swung at him once or twice – maybe Mr Paulden – and between the two of us that did for him.'

The scene shrank away into the darkness, and Shay could hear Austwick breathing.

'I think it was like that. Hard to be sure.'

'Doesn't normally matter how a man dies, does it? Thank you for indulging my curiosity.'

'I understand, sir. To—' He caught himself. Shay frowned; waited. 'To be honest, I knew there was some other business behind it.'

Careful. 'Right. What. . . what exactly had you learned?'

Austwick was shifting his weight, and Shay heard it in leather and grass. 'Well, naturally, the details of the skirmish would hardly matter. And the whole attack was a bit of bravado, I guess. But. . . I'm sure I wasn't listening when I shouldn't, sir, but I just overheard.' Shay was holding himself absolutely still. 'Captain William Paulden and Mr Teach – something about getting someone out – not a kidnap but a rescue.'

A rescue?

Austwick had stopped.

'Right. The rescue.' *Who on earth needed to be rescued?* 'Nothing else? It's not a crime, Captain – very natural – not as if there can be any doubt of your loyalty – but I like to be sure who knows what.'

'Of course, sir. Thank you. That was all. Someone to be rescued from Doncaster. They were looking out for this person during the raid. That was all.'

Shay waited, burning with frustration for the story he never seemed to hear: a sun that never emerged from scudding clouds; a glimpsed woman who never turned to face him. Austwick had disappeared into the silence again.

— ∼ —

MERCURIUS FIDELIS
or
The honeſt truth written for every Engliſhman
that cares to read it
From Monday, July 28. *to* Monday, Aaugust 4. 1651.

aving ſo precipitately and cauſeleſſly invaded yet more of SCOTLAND, laying waſte to the fertile plains of FIFE, the marauders of PARLIAMENT have paid the price due for reckleſſneſs and SIN. Even as the ſavage band

moved north, so HIS MAJESTY KING CHARLES shrewdly
has led his Army of LOYALISTS south, and the rebels have been
left holding the bag. CROMWELL continues his depredations,
having now captured the fair town of PERTH, of which we
wait to hear whether it has suffered the same HORRORS as so
many bore in poor IRELAND. Only this may we hope, that
having been so shamefully misled, he will not spend more time
in exercising his humiliation on more innocents.

Meantime HIS MAJESTY continues his serene progress
into the BOSOM of his own country, and the TRAITORS
do lay down their weapons. Every VILLAGE and TOWN
he enters does welcome him with prayers of thanks and
REJOICING, for HIS MAJESTY'S manner and bearing are
so comely and his people know that they are delivered at last.

So does the LORD GOD reveal his mercy and boundless
kindness to those who trust in HIM.

Recollect, among the deserved HYMNS of joy, the
TERRORS that have been inflicted by the illegitimate and savage
CLIQUE that have set loose their dogs, and that have been suffered
by so many diverse PEOPLE in this sore-tried land. In your
prayers remember poor COLCHESTER and PONTEFRACT,
and the many primitive villages of SCOTLAND and IRELAND
that grieve yet. So too remember the MARTYRS so foully and
lawlessly MURDERED in those places, and remember every
VILLAGE in ENGLAND your sons who are lost. Even as we
pray, we doubt not that GOD will hear us, for GOD hears all,
and every suffering that is borne with faith in HIM shall he return
with ten-fold mercy. PRAISE BE TO GOD.

[SS C/T/51/83 (EXTRACT)]

Mercurius Fidelis: the text received on a translucent paper folded
together and then glued and placed between two glued pages of a mouldy
chapbook, or by any of a dozen other ruses; prepared at night, by inky
fingers that sometimes shook and fumbled with the type, under eyes that

would not rest; printed in the first hours of light, alongside a pile of notices advertising the sale of stock of a bankrupt mercer; carried in satchels and furniture and hat-linings, under cloaks and saddles and heaps of straw, from Oxford across all the counties of England.

It was read in great manors and unhappy cottages, in rural markets and city counting houses, in parlours where old loyalties were whispered and halls where the new regime was being trumpeted. For some it was amusement; for some it was hope; for some it was a balm soothing the ache of a loss; for some it was the ache, the reminder of what they had used to be, or had failed to be.

It was read with excitement, for wasn't it natural that in the end dawn would follow night? It was read with trepidation, for the Committee men and the magistrates and the Clerks of Fines would be harder than ever on Royalists now, and new debts and hostaged sons would be held against those who might be tempted to remember their old loyalty too hastily. It was read by Sir Greville Marsh, with the boy's thrill at sport in his chest and then, thumping in his gut, the echoes of all the failures that life had made his, and it was read by dozens of other men like him, in dinner-table conversations, racecourse huddles, candlelit cellars, furtive market-stall exchanges and isolated oak-tree rendezvous.

It was read by John Thurloe, carefully, and he knew that the crisis – his crisis – had come.

─── ∼───

'Teach, you didn't tell me what was really happening at Doncaster.' A campfire at evening; the scene had used to relax Shay, but they were getting close to Preston, and he was becoming oddly fretful.

Teach's face, blank, turned to him. A flicker as he considered, then blank again. 'No,' he said, and turned forward. 'I didn't.'

'A rescue. A source.' Again the blank face studying him. 'Some affair of Astbury's?'

'You know the game.'

'Yes.' *I do. I would have done the same.* Teach of all men would only tell the minimum of his dealings with George Astbury – Astbury's instructions, his obsessions.

But at last, feeling in Teach's face. 'Look, Shay: Astbury was. . . he was wild. Everything was a plot. Everything was a brilliant scheme to turn the war. You know it. You've said as much.'

Shay nodded.

'Doncaster was a. . . a fool's errand. Astbury was mad about some business with the Parliament forces there: a contact, a scheme, I – I don't know. William Paulden knew more. His brother might have got something from him, too. There were messages coming from someone in Doncaster; someone who'd found a way to send in – not via Beaumont, but using that channel.' He shook his head in the gloom. 'Then a man was supposed to meet us in Doncaster – perhaps this man – meet at the bridge, I think. He never appeared. That was it. Whole thing was a nonsense.'

To Mr J. H., at Macrae's in Galashiels

Sir,

I know not if this will come to you, not knowing if you are with the Royal Army now that it is on the march south, and not knowing if you have arrangements still to receive such trivial correspondence as I must offer in this time of trial. I hope you survive yet and prosper.

I am sometimes with the caterpillar Army as it hurries south on its innumerable feet towards your King. Spirits seem well enough around me: I had thought that a decade of blood must have exhausted all, but I think that all do now perceive an imminent ending to their labours, and this gives the Army great heart. Scotland is safe-held behind us now, and as the Army marches south the men feel closer to their homes and this does truly raise their spirits. I have been lately in London, and it is strong for Cromwell, and in my latest journey northward I found generous garrisons at Derby and Sheffield, and a dozen places beside, up the full length of the country.

I am not a man of high politics and strategy, and yet I infer that we are near some final crisis of this protracted war, and I venture to hope that *in one means or another this land may soon have absorbed the last of the blood that has so unnecessarily drenched it. Perhaps we may yet meet as companions, in some England of peace and not of this voracious conflict.*

[SS C/S/51/80]

Shay read it dully, absorbing its messages, indifferent. *This, perhaps, is age, that I care now more for some trivial incident of the past than the strategy of tomorrow.*

Was Astbury's obsession just an amateur's over-concentration on a single source, some insignificant malcontent in the Doncaster garrison?

The raid on Doncaster; the rescue of a source. *But how to make contact?* The source in Doncaster was a stranger to the Pontefract men. *Surely they'd have arranged some word of recognition.* Some other memory. *Blackburn: according to Blackburn, William Paulden had said to listen for the signal. But what was the signal, and who knew it?* Teach didn't seem to know; Thomas Paulden was abroad; William Paulden was dead. William Paulden, who'd stayed out of the inn to patrol the streets.

And how did any of that connect with the courier, weeks earlier, hurrying through the night to Astbury?

He shook his head. *And who now is the obsessed?*

Garrisons at Derby and Sheffield, the key points on the eastern route. That was the meat of it.

Cromwell dropped from his horse like a leather-strapped, well-armed sack of potatoes, and sank to his ankles in the mud. Immediately he was tramping away through it, water and dirt splashing around him, and Thomas Scot was hurrying along beside him oblivious to the ruin of his cloak.

'They're turning, Master Cromwell!' Cromwell stopped, and the weary head snapped round. 'I have it from the royal Court. They're going southwest. Avoiding the direct route to the east.'

Cromwell's heavy features opened with life. 'Are they now? Making for the Welsh border, and Gloucester.' Scot nodded. Cromwell began to stride forward again through the mire. He shouldered his way into a tent and grabbed at a map and began tracing the veins of England on it with heavy fingers. 'Excellent.' He was talking to himself; Scot and Thurloe followed the meditation obediently. 'Wales; Gloucester; the Severn Valley. It's excellent.'

'The old heartland of Royalism. They're heading for their supporters.'

Cromwell snorted. 'Mere sentiment. Not strategy. They've let us shepherd them. They've abandoned the thought of London, and they're scrabbling for friends.' His heavy fist began to thump at the west of England, and Thurloe saw Cromwell the warrior beginning to glow and flare. 'We have them, gentlemen.'

~

MERCURIUS FIDELIS
or
The honeſt truth written for every Engliſhman
that cares to read it
From Mpnday, Auguſt 11. *to* Monday, Auguſt 18. 1651.

Having croſſed the border into his native KINGDOM after a long and lamented abſence, HIS MAJESTY has continued his march with the celerity fitting to his optimiſm, well aware of the forces hurrying cloſe behind in the chaſe. Oliver CROMWELL, having tired of his works in Scotland, is now haſtening ſouthward in purſuit of HIS MAJESTY, and all ENGLAND ſhall ſhortly ſee who ſhall win the race for London.

MONDAY, AUGUST 11.
Leaving CUMBRIA on this day, HIS MAJESTY with his impoſing force of SCOTTISH ſoldiers, continued generally SOUTHWARD, although it is not known what route he intends. Diſdaining to wait for mere feaſting among thoſe in northern diſtricts who have expreſſed warmth for him, or to wait for the purſuing ENGLISH Army, KING CHARLES hopes to find yet greater ſupport elſewhere. Doubting not in the ſkill of his SCOTS,

and the terror that they fhall fpread wherever they are feen, the
KING waits only on PROVIDENCE to reveal her defigns.
ENGLAND fhall quickly fee the refult, and the WILL of the
LORD GOD fhall be done.

WEDNESDAY, AUGUST 13.
Last Wednesday, a great fifh was feen af far up the River THAMES
as PUTNEY, being remarked by many failors and diverfe people,
and it is not known what this ftrange fign portends.

FRIDAY, AUGUST 15.
At DURHAM on this day, CROMWELL was heard to remark
that He hath ever trufted in the power of one PSALM over one
hundred MUSKETS. Yet such words are not needed for the will of
the LORD GOD to be feen and underftood, for HE fhall make all
things clear to thofe who patiently wait for his REVELATION.
We are all but SERVANTS of the will of GOD, and muft ftrive
ever to know his MERCY and his GRACE.

[SS C/S/51/91 (EXTRACT)]

Shay was surprised to see the *Mercurius*, and then uninterested – he
tended to forget that it was published regardless of his contribution – until
an instinctive second glance showed him the misprint in the date, and
then he was scrabbling at the page with fingers that would not grip, and
holding it crumpled in front of his face.

Standing in the middle of the hall at Astbury he growled an endless 'No'
– a refusal, a denial of the impossible – that stretched out hoarse across the
house and hung in the dust and searched the corners for clarity.

Alte Veste: a Bavarian musketeer a yard away, the barrel pointing at his
belly, the vast black muzzle that was the darkest, lastest thing he would
ever see, and the fat click that seemed to punch him as the hammer
snapped forward.

Rachel came quickly from the study, and circled him warily.

'Uncle Shay. . . Shay! What's wrong?' She caught at his arm. 'Tell me!'
His head swung down towards her, eyes staring wide. They blinked, and

re-focused on her. 'Yesterday – today – Shay, you're like. . . you're just like Uncle George. . . you're behaving just like him, when he came back – the last time, before Preston.'

Mortimer Shay's face and torso collapsed in the sigh.

And so we have come full round.

He looked at the beautiful, desperate eyes.

Was this it, George? Not just doubt in the cause, but certainty – the certainty that something was very badly wrong?

He swung away, moving with heavy stilted steps. The arrests in the spring. The I. S. letters that fixed the Scottish army at Stirling when Cromwell was preparing to attack the flank, and steered the army down through England, tracked by an enemy that seemed to anticipate every manoeuvre. And now the rogue, countermanding message in the news-sheet.

I. S.?

Memories lurching at him in the nightmare. *A man called Thurloe has been set to investigate the affair at Doncaster.* Edinburgh and the rescue of Con Blythe. The insistent visits here.

Is there anything I can touch now that is not immediately cankered?

'Shay!' He turned. Two pale soft palms reached up and held his leathery cheeks. 'What's happening to my world?'

Again he watched the eyes, the pupils large and all-absorbing, searching him.

Can I know defeat? Can I know loss?

Her hands fell to his chest, clutched at his jacket, and shook it.

Perhaps I must. He reached up a bent finger, and roughly stroked it down her child-soft cheek. *But I must do it as Shay.*

─── ∾───

'General Leslie is—' Henry Vyse had knocked and opened the door and started speaking, but the room was empty.

A room like so many in Worcester now. Bare – the owners had scrabbled away anything of value, so the floor was only boards, the mantelpiece looked uncomfortably empty, and there were dark squares on the wall where a mirror and a picture had been. And over-inhabited: Miles Teach had found himself a palliasse from somewhere, and it dominated what had been a small parlour, his blanket folded neatly on top; there was another set of rolled bedding on the other side of the room, and Teach had reserved much of the rest of the floor for Shay when he came. This counted for luxury; Vyse himself was in a room of six.

All the rooms had the same smell now: a ripe mix of wet cloth, of old leather boots, of mud, of long-marched men.

Teach kept his space tidy, Vyse saw that. He'd noticed it before – with Shay as well – and there was a flicker of awe at the ancient habits of the veterans. Boots orderly together by the palliasse; a shirt drying on the back of the single chair; the single bag strapped closed on the table; under it, a few papers in a pile, an odd pattern of holes or wear in one; next to the bag a knife; aligned next to the knife a pistol, cleaned or ready for cleaning.

'Help you, boy?' Vyse turned. Miles Teach was in the doorway, neutral, waiting.

'Pardon me, Mr Teach. General Leslie was asking – Manders said you were in here.'

'I was. Then I was taking a piss. Old man's weakness.'

'I wasn't – I hope you don't think—'

'Not much of me, is there?' He saw what Vyse had seen. 'Boots and a blade.'

'That's a curious paper.'

Teach looked a little sour. 'A device merely. A memento.' He managed a smile. 'These games that Shay makes us play. Secret meetings and hidden messages. Don't get too fond.'

'Have you heard from him lately?' A shake of the head. 'How do you judge our situation here? Are you hopeful? I mean, if you write—'

'I have never been hopeful, boy.' Miles Teach was grim; then an uncomfortable smile spread, and he began to recite. 'I've fought each day as I've found it, and counted it success if I've lived to tomorrow. My family never had enough money for its station, and my cause never had enough luck for its ends. I've been fighting thirty years or more, a dozen countries and a dozen Princes, defeats and victories and all it's brought me is what you see. A man, and a knapsack.'

'You and Sir Mortimer, you're like – you're men like no others. How do you become—?'

'You're born. Without fortune, without looks, without luck. And you survive.' The empty smiled flickered again. 'Something about General Leslie, was there?'

'Will we survive here?'

'Ask me tomorrow, boy.'

⌁

Rachel Astbury opened her mouth to speak again, jaw set and eyes insistent, but Shay held up a heavy finger.

To live we must first survive. He stared into the lovely face. *Where now is the essence of the cause?*

'Rachel,' he said, and there was a new lightness in the voice, 'would you take a glass of wine with me? I will need to be away quite soon, and I must get my affairs straight with you.'

Somewhere above them, Anthony Astbury dozed, in the bedroom where he spent most of his time now.

A flask between them, Shay smiled soberly at Rachel's uneasy face, and tried to align his thoughts.

'As you saw, today I suffered a. . . a great disappointment. Great frustration. A lot of my work is in jeopardy.' He smiled heavily. 'I shall fight on, because that is what I do. And I shall probably win. But whatever I do, whatever stratagems I contrive, whatever blood I spill, I cannot save England entirely unaided. The young King, the Scots, this man Cromwell and his troops – there is a chance they may thwart me somehow.'

She smiled. 'But you'll probably win.'

'Probably. But perhaps not immediately. Not for a while. Perhaps England is destined to take a different path, at least for a time.' One heavy eyebrow lifted. 'It is possible that your young friend Thurloe may represent my end, and your future.'

She leaned forward, cross. 'Uncle Shay' – the words came hard – 'I am quite sick of men telling me what my future shall be.'

He didn't smile; merely nodded. 'Well enough,' he said. 'But if you're to decide for yourself, you must know – you must be absolutely clear – what is essential to you. I had to remind myself of the point a few moments ago.'

He took a mouthful of wine. 'For example: to be you – to survive, to have a future possible – do you need to be ruled by a Stuart King?'

She frowned. 'But—'

'Yes or no?'

'I've survived without.'

'Yes, you have. Good. Do you need any King?'

She shrugged. 'No.'

'Bishops – a particular structure in state and Church – particular forms used in the pulpit?'

A little shake of the head. 'For me, no. But there must be something – something to believe in, surely?'

He drank again. 'Of course. But we start with the essential, and then you may develop such passions and loyalties as is your fancy.' His head came forward closer to hers. 'Do you need Astbury?'

She recoiled a little. 'It's – it's—'

'I know. It's all you've ever known. It's your family and it's your identity and it's a beautiful peace, which I – who have seen horror and foulness and sin and man at his basest, and who have been that man – which I hesitate to touch for fear it will vanish. But do you need it?'

She shook her head deliberately, but there was venom in her eyes.

'Well enough.' He sat back, and gestured airily with his goblet. 'Rachel, I fiercely hope that you will always have this place, and indeed I might wish to grow old here myself, and die here among your apple trees and your children.' The goblet rattled onto the table. 'But there may come a moment when all things are in the balance, and you must choose. It's useful to have confirmed to yourself what is truly essential.'

'This is not a pleasant game, Sha—'

'Humour me. I'm old and bitter and I see my plans collapsing to dust. Humour me.' He watched her. 'Could you leave, I wonder? Could you really do it? Just get on a horse and ride away?'

'Of course I could.'

His observation was more deliberate. 'Yes, I think you could.' Then, lighter again: 'What would you take?'

'What—'

'Yes – Cromwell is at the door – you jump on your horse – you have seconds to fill your saddle-bags, perhaps a satchel – what would you take?'

She continued to talk through a scowl. 'Food, perhaps. Money, I suppose.'

'Good. But you're not that ruthless. Leaving Astbury for the last time and you only think of money?'

'I have a locket – a miniature – of my mother.'

'Bless you for that.'

'A few family jewels.'

'That's good.' A sudden inspiration. 'Rachel, I have a handful of family trinkets of my own. When I leave here I'd like to put them in your care – just until I return from what may be a battle.'

Very uneasy now – the game more real – she nodded. *Is this what women are supposed to do? Indulge the caprices of their men before battle?*

'Thank you,' Shay said pleasantly. 'That's good. If you'll take an old soldier's advice, while the times are unsettled you'll keep your few precious things close by and ready.'

She continued to watch him, warily.

Shay stood suddenly. 'Very well.' He smiled broadly at her. 'Thank you for indulging an old man. There's little enough light in my life now, and I have to be reminded of why I care for what I still care for.'

Rachel stood too, slowly, and then blurted: 'The family Bible.'

'The Bible?'

'I'd take that. Father would like me to. Who we are. . . it's in there.'

Shay shook his head. 'You Astburys. So sentimental. But it's a charming idea, and your father would like it.'

'I think you're not so hard as you claim, Sir Mortimer Shay.' She pulled herself taller. 'Is this uncomfortable game over now?' Then she looked at him coyly. 'If it means anything to you, Uncle George did not behave half so distracted as you do, even at the very last.'

Shay considered this.

'Perhaps he didn't see as clearly as I do.' He stepped forward, and went to rest his hands on the lace at her shoulders, but stopped and let them drop. He searched her eyes. 'I once said that you were the world I was fighting for. I meant it. Your spirit is strong, and you will survive. And whether I die next week or in fifty years, things that I care about will survive in you.'

———~———

Mortimer Shay arrived at Worcester by old tracks marked not in maps but in the rhythms of man – the tracks taken by sheep drovers, by poachers, by rebels, for more than a thousand years.

As he dropped down off the horse, pulling a sack with him, there was movement past a series of windows, a hurrying face, and as Shay's glance reached a doorway Balfour was standing in it. He looked sick and somehow ashamed, and Shay's gut kicked.

Balfour hurried forward, gave a sort of nod of the head, and stared Shay in the eye bleak. 'Hal's dead,' he said. 'Fever. Not two hours ago.' He added, 'I'm sorry,' but Shay had barged past him and was striding towards the building.

Henry Vyse was laid out on a bed in the commandery, so conclusively pale that he seemed an extension of the rumpled sheets and battered pillow. Teach was sitting beside him, and turned as Shay stamped in and stood and moved aside. 'He didn't seem right two days ago,' he said, 'then yesterday. . .' – but Shay wasn't listening. They stepped past each other, Shay suddenly slow and unwilling to see the truth on the bed, and Teach got the same bleak stare of accusation that Balfour had. As their eyes met, Teach nodded sadly, and gently knocked Shay's arm with the back of his fist, a tiny nudge of humanity.

For a long time Shay stood staring down at Vyse's white face. The boy looked younger, and more beautiful, and utterly at peace. Shay could feel sentiment and suspicion of sentiment squabbling in him, and this twisting of reactions revolted him.

The beauty of Vyse's bones and fresh skin were his mother's, and as Shay looked down at Hester Carraway for one last and unexpected time, something died, a final door closing on a piece of his past, a particular intensity of life guttering and expiring.

Behind Balfour, Miles Teach stood in the doorway watching Shay with compassion. His hand dropped casually to his pocket, to the slender glass vial in there.

A short walk after supper, a grind of the heel, and any alternative truth would be destroyed: Henry Vyse would have died of fever, and there would be nothing left to tell the contrary.

A short walk after supper, a grind of the heel, and any alternative truth

Shay entered the Council meeting late and last, face grim and eyes distant, and everyone in the room turned, watched his dark striding progress over the flagstones. He stopped beside the young King's chair, gave a brief nod, then strode on to his customary place against the wall. Teach was nearby, and nodded as he sat. Shay ignored him.

The Duke of Hamilton kept his eyes on Shay a few moments longer. A good man, this Shay. The men in Holland had been right. A man of few words, and sensible ones. A quality of silence that appealed to Hamilton, in this court of peacocks and politicians. And each time somehow darker, as if fate itself were taking possession of Mortimer Shay and becoming him, or swallowing him.

It was only fate now, Hamilton realized that. The return to Scotland, the jostling there, and now this risky march into England: at no point could he remember taking a true decision, being given the choice of alternatives and ignoring them. It was the destiny of the Hamiltons in this generation that they would tie their fortunes to the Stuarts, and march with them against their own kingdom. His glance shifted to the young man beside him, at the head of the table.

The things we have suffered for Charles Stuart.

Charles Stuart had also watched the ominous man longer than was necessary. A strange man. Unsettling. Not one of his close advisers – *has he even been presented to me? Is this my world, of unknown shadow-men on the edge of my decisions?* – but always here. The man had an overpowering sense of the ominous to him, and age. The King's attention shifted to the mouths at the table, chattering at him and about him and over him, then back to the man at the edge of the room. *I am a latecomer to a play that I do not know and cannot fully understand.*

'The worst news: Derby and the men of Lancashire are beaten quite. No help from that quarter.'

'There may be worse yet.'

'Or better. Granted Derby would have helped, but—'

'Helped? We're outnumbered two-for-one.'

'But we can still attract men, and we can still fight and we can still win. This is the King's army.'

'It's a Scottish army – God save Your Majesty – and it repels as many as it attracts.'

Skittering feet on the stones, then a young courier, with awed and hasty bow to the King, was whispering frantically in Leslie's ear. Hamilton watched implacable; the young King with uncertainty.

Leslie said: 'They've crossed the Severn. Below us. Somewhere called Upton.' He reached for one of the maps on the table.

'That's not ten miles from here.'

'They're surrounding us.'

'Cromwell has brought his Army down at impossible speed.'

'Right. I don't credit the story.'

'If he's whipped them all the way from Scotland this fast, they'll be too whipped to fight.'

'If Massey here can bring his people over with him – give us Gloucestershire – we'll be stronger still.'

'But can you, Edward?'

'It's good sense.'

'It's good sense but it's brought no men. Chancers and hungry peasants. Pitchforks and broken nags. Cromwell is surrounding us while we wait.'

'We have no choice now.'

'No. No, we don't. We've staked all on gathering men. We gather what we can, ten or ten thousand, and soon, willy-nilly, we must fight Cromwell.'

The hall, Worcester's grandest, echoed on with the voices. The young King's eyes were wide. *Will no one explain this to me?*

The royal cause: hunted and trapped in the heart of its own domain.

I have done this.

John Thurloe looked down on Worcester from the hills to the east: a year to the day since his awakening and Cromwell's miracle at Dunbar; the fertile quilt of English countryside rippling away in front of him, with the city and its spiking cathedral and its fugitive army snug at the centre of the bowl of landscape; Royalism in the palm of his hand.

Stretching down the slope below him towards the city, the dark shadows of Cromwell's regiments, leather and metal and bristling pikes. Thomas Scot was on horseback near him, the animal scuttling and pacing back and forth while the old man kept his eyes fixed on the city, fervent for final victory.

I have helped to guide this Army. I have helped to track and influence our prey. This is my battle.

Somewhere out there, in front of him, the trap was closing.

I wish I understood what was happening.

To the south, one arm of Cromwell's pincer, a column of the Parliamentary Army was pushing up towards the city. To Thurloe they were distant dust, a cloud that appeared on the horizon, moved towards him, and stopped. He could not see the grim stalemate in the meadow, the press of men in the soft ground stabbing and hacking away at each other with pike and sword, the staged volleys of musket fire that thumped out of the mêlée in a wave of screams.

Miles Teach in the press: everywhere, a rearing horse and a bellowed encouragement, a hand on a shoulder and a sinewy arm pulling a man out of the mire, an inspiration among the stubborn, unyielding Scottish foot-soldiers as they absorbed surge after surge from the English pikemen and would not give. A yell from his side and a hurtling shadow and his pistol came up as the instinctive extension of his arm and exploded and the man went down, still the screaming, always the screaming, and he was hacking his way left and right out of the swamp of men, scrabbling for a hold of his bridle and up and wheeling and a final swing of his sword and a boot in a man's face and away.

Cromwell, up on the hill to the east, with Thurloe watching him. Cromwell lost in the view, staring into its dust, hearing its echoes on the wind, becoming somehow a corporeal part of the battlefield, feeling its every current and sensation in his blood and brain and fingers, willing its changes.

'General!' A rider hurrying towards him from the south-west. 'General Fleetwood's compliments, and the Scots aren't yielding. We cannot shift them. Our regiments have no strength left.'

'Fight!' Cromwell roaring up at him. 'Fight harder! God will determine your fittedness for glory or damnation. Prove yourself worthy of him! Ride!' The man, wide-eyed, nodded as if this made sense, and spun away.

Cromwell stared after him, granite and calculating. Then around with a mighty arm out-thrust: 'Three regiments: you, sir! You! And you! With me now!' And he was up on his horse and pulling it around and kicking the orderly away and galloping off down the slope, eyes as wide and wild as the beast beneath him, streams of his cavalry hurrying after him. Thurloe stared after them, awed, watched them lancing down towards the river and the Scottish flank, knew despite his ignorance that nothing surely could stop them.

Inside Worcester, the same incoherent scrambling for understanding, the scrummaging of messengers and throwing out of commands, the last futile clutching at the hope that rationality might triumph over mayhem.

'There's movement on the Red Hill!'

'The Red—'

'To the east!'

'Cromwell's attacking at last.'

'Your Grace, will you—'

'From Montgomery and his Scots in the meadow. They're attacked on the flank and they cannot hold!'

'From the flank?'

'That's where Cromwell's gone. He's taken his cavalry to reinforce his southern attack.'

'How many regiments?'

'He's stripped his troops on the hill?'

'If the south gives, the city is wide open.'

Boots hurrying down the steps of the cathedral tower. 'They've weakened themselves on the hill!'

'Majesty, we—'

'Half of their cavalry has gone south: we can strike them to the east now, can't we?'

'Majesty, our southern flank is in bad danger.'

'We'll have no better chance, surely! May we not attack them now?'

A breath of silence at last; uncertain faces, rapid calculations.

Hamilton, steady: 'Aye, Your Majesty. I think we may. My regiments will drive for the wood yonder. For the hill—'

'I shall lead the attack on the hill.'

'Majesty?'

'Majesty, it were better—'

'Follow, damn you!'

Shay snatched up a sack and stuffed it inside his jacket. Only Balfour saw the movement. 'What is that?'

Shay looked at him, glanced at the other men hurrying around them, then back. 'What we reacquired on the river.' Balfour's eyes widened. 'It cannot leave the kingdom. If we win today, I will see it placed where it rightly belongs. If not, it must disappear again for a time.'

Thurloe watched them come, two dark tentacles stretching out from the city in front of him and feeling their way across the plain towards his hill. Nearer, he saw the ranks of the Parliamentary infantry starting to shift uneasily as they too saw what was coming at them. Their apprehension and anticipation became his own, felt in shifting feet and clenched hands and a thumping heart. Still the tentacles pushed forward towards him, and now the line of backs just a few yards off was tramping away from him, down to meet the attack. He tried to gauge how long it would take for the two forces to meet, looked around him at the rigid faces all staring down the slope, realized suddenly his own vulnerability if the English ranks should break and allow the tentacle to creep up the hill and lunge for him, looked down again and saw that the armies were indistinguishable, the Scottish no longer visible beyond the ranks of his own side, felt his stomach muscles tensing instinctively, bracing himself for the moment of impact.

The tentacles out of Worcester hit the Parliamentary infantry with one vast rattle of metal, the shattering of a mirror across the land, and a monstrous bellow from thousands of chests something between a shout and a sigh.

The Parliamentary infantry gave ground, and held. Gave ground, and held. The structure was breaking up now, the regiments fragmenting and the line of backs becoming uneven and broken. A sudden scuffling, and the rear rank broke open in a whirl of swords and jostling horses and half a dozen Royalist riders were barging and hacking their way into the English foot-soldiers backing away around them. But one rider was pressing on, as if having broken through the encircling Army he was determined to keep riding all the way to London. He came thundering up the thick grass of the slope, straight at Thurloe, sword outstretched and the distance between them shrinking with terrifying speed. Thurloe gasped and felt his chest lurching and scrabbled for the pistol at his side and pulled it up, shaking and fumbling at the hammer, and still the vast horse and the sword were spearing towards him and at last the barrel came up and he pulled the trigger and the snap of the pistol was swallowed by the rearing shrieking horse. Had he hit it? There was no sign, but the horse was rearing and wheeling and the rider was trying to control it and then another rider swooped in from the side and cut him down.

Arm shuddering, Thurloe lowered the pistol and fought for breath. There was a new noise now, another shapeless roar of men and horses rising towards his peak. Looking left, Thurloe saw a new tentacle reaching up for him, a charge of cavalry, and he gazed frantically around for help and his own horse and the possibility of escape. But now the charge was veering down the slope again, and he saw that it was Cromwell – Cromwell, who had turned the tide and unlocked the Parliamentary attack to the south of the city, and had now returned to turn the tide against the Scottish sortie to the east. The column of horsemen poured into the side of the mêlée, and the line of Parliamentary shoulders began to reform and straighten, and then to push again down the hill towards the distant spire.

Exhausted, wounded and grim, the Royalist leaders pulled back into the commandery at the heart of the city. South and east the lines cracked, and collapsed, and Worcester's streets were quickly choked with the remnants of the King's Scottish army, shocked and panicked and scrambling futile for escape. The cannon in the outer defences had been turned inward by the English, and were reaching out of the sky to shatter plaster walls and set thatch aflame, the dust and smoke thickening the last of the light. As sheep heading blind for shearing or slaughter, the routed men jostled and stumbled through the channels of the city, a dumb riot of screams and smashed glass and snatched supplies and stupid scuffles. Behind them came the Parliamentary Army, convinced that victory must mean riches and bloody triumph, and hunting ravenously for both.

Somewhere in the gloom of the city, a cut throat and an instinctive pistol shot and a snatched horse, Miles Teach was scrambling his way to freedom.

Upstairs in the commandery, the Duke of Hamilton lay on a straw mattress with a shattered thigh, scarlet and darkening. The young King stared at mortality, his face as pale as the dying man's below him. Tentatively, he reached out his fingers and placed them on Hamilton's chest. 'I – I have no words. What your family has done for mine. . .'

A spasm of movement, and Hamilton had gripped the King's hand. Clumsily he pulled it to his lips, and released it. 'I pray – that we – may have – the chance' – the words were coming hoarse and hard – 'and the honour – to do so – again.' The eyes closed in the clenched pug face, exhausted, and the breath dropped into a shallow rasping.

Hands clutched at the King's arm, pulling him away, and he went. William, Duke of Hamilton, listened to the footsteps, tried to pull at the ring on his finger, felt the precious cool of a wet cloth on his forehead, in the hand of a clansman who would not leave him, and whispered words that the man could not hear.

Another Hamilton. Another Stuart. Another season turns.

The royal Court had become a handful of muddy, sweat-streaked men, clustered around the King in a wrecked parlour, toppled chairs and papers scuffing under boots and the roaring of a mob in their ears.

Mortimer Shay pulled at a loose stone at the front of the hearth, revealing a thin sheaf of paper. The door slammed open and a pike and a musket barrel and two wild alien faces were pushing in, and Balfour launched himself into the opening with sword level. One man recoiled and screamed and fell, another hesitated, a pistol roared in Balfour's ear and then Shay was heaving the door closed and slamming the bolt across. Immediately the door began to judder, musket butts clubbing furiously against it, the hinges and the bolt coughing dust and straining, and more arms were dragging the King away towards the back of the room. Shay and Balfour were backing away after them, and Shay was trying to reach the hearth and the half-revealed papers, but Balfour was grabbing at him and pulling, and with all sense distracted by the hammering at the door and the shouts the papers were just beyond Shay's fingers – *the Directory!* – and Balfour still wrenching him away and as the front door disintegrated in planks and pikes and boots they were closing the back door and pulling a cart against it and racing down the alley.

In a stable, a moment to regroup, the hunted men kicking impatiently in the straw while grooms held a dozen restive horses nearby. Another man hurried in; a murmured exchange and the King watching impatiently.

'Your Majesty, the road to the north may still be open.' Another unknown face addressing him. 'But we cannot at the moment reach it. And they will be looking for you.' A glance round the stable. 'I have a troop of men in the yard outside. If you'll wait ready here, I'll see if we can't draw the enemy fire and buy you a few minutes and a clear path.'

The Earl of Cleveland, sixty and dapper despite the chaos of the day, heaved himself up onto a horse. 'I am about ready to settle my account with Master Cromwell.' He nodded down. 'If Your Majesty will excuse me.' Two or three others reached for horses and followed him out of the stable towards the street.

Balfour grabbed at a saddle and pulled himself up; Shay clutched his wrist. 'Balfour, stay close by.'

'I am full done with running, Master Shay.'

'No!' *Vyse and Manders and all the future I will never own.*

The young man stared down sadly. 'I thank you for your kindnesses and your friendship. You are the man I would wish to be.' And he yanked at the reins and hurried out into the street, Shay staring after him.

The last charge of English Royalism thundered out of a stableyard and down Worcester High Street on the 3rd of September in the year 1651, the flame-torn evening sky above and the bellowing of cannon and the awestruck yells of soldiers engulfing it. The ragged troop filled the width of the street and launched itself into the noise, with no hope or goal, only the wild euphoric sense that now, after a decade of war and ultimate defeat, all that was possible was a defiant, exultant roar of the self. The riders hurled themselves into the smoke and were lost, and the English soldiers staggering amazed aside did not see the half-dozen men far behind in the dust, cantering from alley to shadow to smoke and so away towards the northern gate of the city.

In the chaos of Worcester, while the streets are still moans and blood and the echoes of Royalism's last charge still ring, while Cromwell's surgeon tuts mournfully over the semi-conscious Duke upstairs, a man stands in the parlour of the commandery considering the wreckage. Some instinct of memory makes him look first at the hearth, and he immediately sees the shifted stone, the edge of the thin sheaf of paper flirting with his hopes. Reverentially he holds the sheaf in his hands, feeling the texture with his fingertips and beginning to skim the strange columns of words: names, Royalist names surely, and other letters, and symbols.

North of the city the lost King disappears into the night, the horses hammering over the dry ground, carrying men too desperate to control or think. More men looming out of the gloom, the King's companions veering towards them with swords drawn, shouts of challenge, reassurance, recognition, and the group pulling up for a moment beside a copse. 'Whither away?'

Breathless sweating shadowed faces in the last of the light. Shay's voice came low and hard out of the grey: 'For now, north. Assume the first five miles are hostile ground. Ride as fast as the road allows. Kill anyone.'

'But—'

'You cannot risk time or challenge! Ride down anyone on foot. Kill anyone on horseback. After five miles, ease the pace: discretion will become more important than speed. Who knows this area?'

Hesitation. 'I, sir.'

'The life of the King, the future of the realm, depend on your judgement. Be sure of your trust. You will choose where he goes, where he stays. Choose well.'

'And you, sir?' It was the King.

'We must get you out of this island, Majesty. There are arrangements to make; paths to prepare.' Shay felt the bulk in his jacket. 'I have other affairs to finish. I will find you.'

He looked around the black shapes, peering at the faces until he recognized one. 'Musgrave, surely?' Acknowledgement. 'Will you wait with me? I have an errand for you; the King has bodyguards enough for tonight.' Wary agreement from the other.

The King again. 'How will you find me?'

'I have ways.' He held the young man's saddle, and looked into the fresh, worried eyes. 'Majesty, whatever befalls, you will never be as much a King as you were today. I honour you for it, and I hope that England has the chance to know it again.'

'Thank—'

'Now ride!' A moment's uncertainty, then they were gone into the night. Shay listened a moment to the hooves diminishing, then pulled the horse around to face Sir Ralph Musgrave, waiting anxious.

Shay reached out a hand, and gripped his shoulder. Musgrave flinched at the fierce grip and, dimly, his eyes were wide in concern. 'Musgrave, I hope to get the King away to the Continent. There's high chance he'll be captured. Either way, this cannot be with him.' He released the shoulder, reached into his jacket, and thrust the sack at the other man. 'This – this is England. I leave it in your charge. Hide it. Bury it. Guard its secret well. I pray we may live to see it restored to the King.'

＊

Midnight, and the wild lantern-lit faces of Cromwell and Thomas Scot, conspirators come at last to unquestioned power. 'The young Charles is out.' Cromwell, like a man at first fuelled and then doped by a feast, had lost his battle energy and seemed heavier. 'We've torn Worcester apart, checked every prisoner, and he's gone.'

'He can't be far. We control all the roads, we dominate every town.'

Thurloe, two paces away, glanced at Tarrant and Lyle beside him. Their eyes were wide and hungry, straining hounds, and he felt his own excitement. After today's victory, what might not be possible?

Cromwell continued to growl. 'He could be far enough. He has sympathizers yet in these parts.'

'Not after your triumph today, Master Cromwell.'

'Find him!' Cromwell leaned forward, and his face melted and reformed in the lantern light. 'This day must be Royalism's last.'

—◆—

The dreams of the young Charles II:

I'm become a dirty secret, a shit-stain on the boots of men who are inconvenienced and embarrassed but cannot be rid of me.

First the night ride out of the chaos of Worcester, the aching exhausted miles, the horses stumbling and rasping, the murmurs and fears and complaints of his few companions coming at him like phantoms out of the darkness. Hours later, lost in the middle of England, the shadow of a house looming in the black. Dropping down off the horses at last, arse sore and body desperate for rest, but someone had thrust a bundle of clothes at him with an urgent command. Clumsily wriggling out of his clothes and into the new, in the freezing night, and *why can't this wait until I am inside?* and then someone clutching at his arm and pulling him – away from the house, away from the promise of warmth and normality. Leaves and branches slapping at him, and still being pulled forward by his companion, and then a terse apology and a blanket, and the King of England spent the last hours of the night shivering and writhing among the leaves and soil of the copse.

Dawn in the copse, and then it had started to rain, and still they could not move – 'This'll dampen the searchers' enthusiasm' – but the King was lost in a permanent shivering cold. Later in the day they emerged, mounted up again and hurried away with talk of Wales. More pounding exhausted miles, legs and back a constant ache, avoiding human contact as much as possible, stopping to rest, a blissful moment of ease on solid ground in warm sunshine and then a challenge barked out of the shadows and they were up and away again, and all the Severn crossings were guarded. Words muttered to him; they dared not risk it. So back again as they had come, the hours and the miles passing as distant figures on the horizon, half glimpsed as he lived with the aches and the deep tiredness. They rode through the night, and came to some new destination at dawn; but it wasn't new, it was the place they'd left the day before. Familiarity made it a kind of comfort, but now there was talk of soldiers nearby. A day in hiding, and at last in the evening he was allowed into the house.

Sleep and wakefulness were no longer distinct states. Instead he lived in weary haze between them, emerging once to voices.

'. . . White Ladies here, and then to the border, but the crossings were guarded so we returned. We hid him today—'

'Where?' A voice he recognized, old and hoarse.

'In an oak on the—'

'In a tree?' It was the voice of the man called Shay. 'God's sake, this is no game!'

'We thought to make for Wales.'

'No.'

'Why not?'

But Shay could not be persuaded to explain why not Wales, and the military presence at the Severn crossings had spooked them all.

Finally, hustled into a secret room: a fumbling in the corner of panelling, the snap of a sprung catch releasing, and a section of the wood coming loose. A candle pressed into his hand, and some bread and a pot. The urgent voices, telling him to hide, hide quickly. Then stumbling forward into the hole, the panelling pushed close behind him and the candle guttering and threatening to go out.

This then is monarchy in England. A sordid past; a body to be buried. This is my inheritance, and I am the last relic of it.

❧

They were frustrating, tiring days of travel and waiting. Thomas Scot had been to London and come back again, a dogged old man determined not to lose clutch of possible victory over the Stuarts. Thurloe had made the same journey twice, and was feeling almost as old as Scot. Tarrant and Lyle came and went on searches and investigations and interrogations.

Tarrant was as tired as the rest of them, but movement was his instinctive demonstration of relevance. He stepped to the table where Thurloe was reading papers, and knocked on it. 'Military law. That's the answer.' He was looking at Scot.

Scot and Thurloe glanced at him warily. There was a young Army Captain with them, and he looked startled – as if, the only representative of the military present, they were offering him the Crown personally.

'Until now we've made no fuss. We must put the whole country on alert. Everyone must be looking for Charles Stuart.'

'I disagree,' Thurloe said. Tarrant's volume always made his own words instinctively quieter. 'We'll make his sympathizers as active as his detractors.'

'No time for half measures. Whole country must decide which side it's on.'

Scot said uneasily, 'But military law? The Army?'

'We just make a list of the most prominent Royalists and round them up. Make the pretender unpopular, too.'

Scot: 'Stuart's protectors won't use the obvious contacts, surely.'

'We put pressure on them regardless!'

Thurloe thought: *I have such a list.*

While the conversation continued, he pulled from an inside pocket the sheaf of paper retrieved from the hearth in Worcester, placed it inconspicuous on the other papers in front of him.

His closest examination of it had been the first, in the thrill of discovery. A list of names, presumably contacts for the Royalist network he'd been fighting. Names divided into groups, distinguished by letters or pairs of letters. Names followed by two or three letters, and then crude symbols – lines, circles, curves. But until he could decypher the symbols and letters, it was just a list of probable Royalists, and most of them would hardly be a surprise. He had put the sheaf away, looking forward to a quiet evening that had not yet come.

Now he began to scan the pages again, absently.

Lyle arrived, with reports of Royalist activity in the aftermath of the defeat at Worcester, and actions to suppress it. Scot listened without much interest. Thurloe glanced up at them. *I have such a list, and I do not think I shall share it.*

It was instinctive, and his conscious mind caught up with it only slowly. *The private correspondence with J. H. The investigation of Astbury, of Pontefract and Doncaster. The conversation with a Royalist agent in The Hague. The assault on Scot's private ledger in London.* And now he felt the pages under his fingers. *Somewhere I have crossed a line.*

Lyle finished, and Tarrant picked up his theme. 'This cannot be hard. They can only use the most trusted people, and we know who they are. Look, you – Captain – this is your part of the country – you too, Lyle – who are the most prominent Royalists ten miles around? As an example.'

The Captain hesitated, but no one had anything else to say. 'I – I don't know. Havisham at Lichfield. And Smythe. Palmer at Rugely. Sir James Bohun near Cannock. The Giffords at Boscobel. There's—'

'Boscobel?' Lyle said.

'Near Stafford. There's an old priory there; the White Ladies. But there's only servants looking after the estate now.' Tarrant started to speak, impatient, but now that he'd started the Captain was determined to carry on. 'Marley at Wolverhampton. Whitgreave at—'

'What name was that, Captain?' Thurloe had looked up.

'Whitgreave, sir. Thomas.'

'You know him, Thurloe?'

Thurloe shook his head, and buried himself in the paper again.

A little petulant, the Captain finished. 'Sir John Yates, and old Purvis, in Telford.'

Even Tarrant felt that his idea had lost momentum, but repeated his push for prominent Royalists to be arrested to make life more difficult for the escaping King. Scot agreed to suggest it to Cromwell.

The conversation petered out, and Scot left, followed quickly by Lyle and Tarrant.

Unemployed but keen to seem active, the Captain remained standing, and then began to pace back and forth in front of the window until Thurloe asked him to stop.

Thomas Whitgreave. There was a Whitgreave on his list. *Surely worth a little wager.* Thurloe looked again at the adjacent names. 'Captain: do you know anyone – potential Royalist sympathizers, that is – named Brownlow, Hogg or Wolfe?'

'There's a Brownlow in Wolverhampton, sir. I don't know the others.'

Two lines away there was an unusual entry. Not a name, like the others, but the single letters W.L.P. An abbreviated name? A place?

Some immediate memory of the conversation was calling to him.

～～

The dreams of the young Charles II:

'There are soldiers at Boscobel again; searching the house and the White Ladies Priory. We barely got him out in time.'

'They're striking at random.'

'So why come to a place twice?'

I am a burden on the world. I am a burden on life.

'You are more than these soldiers, surely.'

'We must assume that there are men of wit against us. We must assume that men's loyalties are known.'

'We're safe here with Whitgreave. He's not been active for years.'

Then a heavy hammering from below, and shouts, and swearing from the men near him, then one was lunging at him and pushing him into hiding and the noises from the world outside were muffled and all he had was darkness and the senses of his own body: heart, cold, bladder, his fingers in his hair.

Then a burst of light, blinking and confusion, and a word of reassurance, and somehow they had come through but now they had to move again. Another change of clothes, the King dressed as a servant, embarrassment and attempts at polite humour. Then riding again, a woman sharing his horse, plucky but dull-faced and her hand uneasily around his waist. Yellow Cotswold stone sickly sweet against the landscape, confinement again – another unfamiliar house with polite and wary strangers, a man and his very pregnant wife – and more consultations – talk of Bristol, of a ship – silence again, and more tedious waiting – and more consultations – no ship to be had in Bristol, and had the young King been recognized? – and soon they would have to move again – and through the thin wall the screams of the young wife, in some terrible pain.

Tarrant slammed through the door and jumped into speech and pushed a paper onto Thurloe's table. 'Council's had enough of these games. No more waiting and hoping. A public order for the apprehension of Charles Stuart. There it—'

'This is idiocy!'

A sly smile. 'This is the Council of State, Thurloe. In case you'd forgotten, you work—'

'This will put twice as many men against us as for us!' His fist clenched, and he dropped it in impotent frustration onto the table. 'I warned them. We have to—'

'Do what you like. Doesn't really matter.' And Tarrant turned and left, without closing the door.

Thurloe hissed out his anger, and dragged himself back into the map.

If I was wanting a boat from here, where would I look? His finger followed the jagged line of the coast on the map.

The young Captain had watched the exchange silently from a chair in the corner; an educated man, it transpired, who found working as Thurloe's go-between to the Army a gentler and more pleasant task than the alternatives. 'Can we try to guess where they're headed, sir?'

He looked up, irritable. 'That's what—' *We do not guess, Master Thurloe.* Another glance at the map. 'I'd rather do better than that.'

'But how?'

I have been trying merely to block this man: I am blindfolded, trying to get in front of him and flailing clumsily for his head.

I must get beside him. I must get inside his head. I must see.

Hypothesis: I have a network of loyalists. The purpose of this must be to give me practical support. I have spent years helping men like Langdale and Morrice and Blackburn escape; I know what contingencies may arise. I have this so arranged that if I find myself in, for example, Dorset needing a ship to the Continent, I have contacts who will help me.

He reached into his coat, and pulled out the sheaf of papers.

Do not try to break it. Try to understand how to use it.

A contingency will arise in a particular location, not in the abstract.

Potential supporters are relevant because of proximity. A list of supporters will most usefully be given geographically. So the individual or double letters dividing the list are most likely. . . *counties*.

More than one 'D'. Devon, Derbyshire. Dorset is Do.

More specificity is required for this to be useful. So the double or treble letters after each name are likely the towns or villages where they live. But what then are the strange symbols that follow?

Don't try to break it. Try to use it.

Hypothesis: I am in trouble. I need help. A blacksmith is no use to me if I need gold. An Earl is no use to me if I need a horse re-shod. So the list of my network tells me the practical benefit of each. What might a man in trouble need? Money. Food. A place to hide. A horse. A weapon. *Or, of course, a ship.*

Thurloe tried to make the crude symbols mean something. A short vertical line: the mast of a ship? Or a musket? Or a man to give protection? Did two vertical lines mean the same as one, but just with greater capacity, or were they something different?

'Sir?'

I cannot outrun the fox, but I may out-think him. Do not chase the answer; anticipate it.

I am in Dorset, and I seek a boat. I do not seek it in Yeovil or Dorchester, miles inland. He ran his finger across the map again. A boat would be sought at Weymouth, at Bridport, at Lyme, at Ware, at Sidmouth.

Then through the entries in the list for Dorset. Can 'Wy' be anything other than Weymouth? 'Ly' anything other than Lyme? There were five names followed by 'Wy', and they seemed between them to use all of the symbols. Two entries for 'Ly', one followed by a flat 'u', the other by a short horizontal line.

The short horizontal line featured frequently in the list. It featured after two names in 'Yv' – presumably Yeovil; inland. It was unlikely to be a boat.

The flat 'u'? He looked for entries offering only this symbol. One in Weymouth. One in Lyme. One in 'Sdm' – presumably Sidmouth. He checked through the rest. Only a handful, and all in places that seemed to be on the coast.

Thurloe started to copy names onto a separate paper. The soldier watched him. After two minutes, Thurloe looked up, and took a breath.

'Your instructions are these. See the names on this list. Higgins in Weymouth, Cobb in Abbotsbury, Marsden in Bridport, Limbry in Lyme, and so on and so on.' He handed over the paper. 'Each of these men is to be found, and watched.'

◆——◆

The dreams of the young Charles II:

A place called Trent, and the grim faces of his protectors, murmurs of a new order from Cromwell's Government. A soft bed, and then an explosion of bells and shouts, someone hurrying into his room: 'Your Majesty; thank God. The town's alive with the news that you're killed; someone claims they shot you.' *Am I so hated? Am I so invisible, that even alive I am dead?* An attempted witticism. Another figure in the room, an argument: stay, away from the confusion, or go, while no one thinks the King alive. Stay, and the tedious days stretch past, long hours of boredom, dull cold room and dull cold men. Talk of boats. Shay, the dark ghost, appears and disappears, making arrangements as usual.

Then they must move again. In the middle of the unreal, unresting, uneasy weeks, an insane fantasy of masquerade: disguise, a wedding party, 'Majesty, this is Juliana Coningsby' – a fresh pretty face shining out of the huddle of dour men, a flash of excited deference on her face – *I am a man after all, and something more* – and the suggestion of a curtsey and the pale warmth of her breasts over the lace – 'she'll be your bride for the day' – and for one wonderful moment the possibility of a normal emotion, *I will enjoy this because she is a pretty girl.* Then again the hustling and the worry, the pretences and the sidelong glances, and the furtive looking behind, but beside him the young female body and a coy smile, and at the end of the day when the game was over, the peach cheeks and the red lips still close beside him, and a smile and a thrill and a gasp and he kissed her, and her eyes went wide and she sighed a breath into him, and then she was gone, and there was another huddled arrival at the back door of an unknown house.

'Our priority is a boat. We must wait for him.'

'He's overdue, and badly. We can't risk it any more.'

'You said you trusted Limbry.'

Shay, dark, grim: 'Yes, I did. Perhaps he's dead. Perhaps he's frightened. Perhaps he thinks he's being watched. We can't risk waiting any more.'

So on again. Bridport, a tired arrival in twilight, turning the final corner with the promise of an inn and a bed, and suddenly their horses were swamped with soldiers, a troop of them milling around and joking and complaining in the darkness. A murmur in his ear – 'On, Sire, show no care' – and nudging their horses through the men – 'Way please, brave gentlemen, and leave some ale for us if you please' – and so into the yard. Slipping down off the horse, holding himself up against its heaving flank, and being ushered away in the darkness towards the inn door, movements and voices around him, eyes watching, a pair of eyes frowning and following and then he was inside.

Slumped in a chair by the fire. *Have I never slept?* And still the murmurs around him, the physicians with their patient.

'We can't stay in a place alive with soldiers.'

'We can't show that we care.'

'He was recognized! In the yard. I'm sure of it.'

'Shay's arranged a boat. The coast is only a mile off. We must wait.'

Another arrival, heavy boots, bringing Shay's voice: 'Ill news. My man was watched; followed. I'm sure of it. If they think we're here we can't trust to the bluff.'

So up again and out into the yard and out through a different gate, and behind them murmurs, and then a shout, and a hiss in his ear and the horse bucking and lurching and they were plunging into the night and someone had grabbed his rein and pulled them away into a lane and then eased them to a halt, and they waited in the darkness, begging the horses to breathe quietly and waiting for the sound of life coming into the lane that would mean capture and death. Then on again, another town, another arrival, more soldiers in the streets. A bed at last, and fitful sleep, and through the door and the light-chinked floorboards came the raucous jollity of the soldiers relaxing in the room beneath, the men hunting him.

'We found an ostler, Mr Thurloe. Former soldier. Swears he saw the King – the young Charles Stuart, that is – in the inn yard.'

So close.

'And there was someone who was desperate to get away from us, that's certain.'

Thurloe found himself oddly untroubled by the near miss. 'They know the net is closing on them, and that will make them more hasty. The man you were following – Marsden. Arrest him – now. He'll have something to tell us of this network, at least.'

'Yes, sir. I was going to. But he's. . . gone, sir.'

Instinctive frustration, but then Thurloe smiled at the Captain.

'Bad luck, Captain. Next time, eh?' The Captain smiled back, uncertainly.

I'm walking right beside you now.

The Royalist network worked as he thought it did. Now the better he understood it, the better he would be at manipulating it.

'Captain, would you come back in half an hour? I'll have a longer list of names, and they must all be followed. You'd better find some assistants. I'll have orders for every harbour along the south coast, and they'll need to report back to me regularly. Those orders must go out tonight.'

~

The dreams of the young Charles II:

They say these stones were here at the time of Christ himself.

I am tiny against them, and my life is tiny against theirs. I am a fieldmouse, hunted by scavenger birds, in the shadows of the history that these stones have seen.

They say the heathens used them for magic; for sacrifices. A perfect circle of pillars and lintels, vast altars.

Is that me? Another of their sacrifices?

A week's travelling, with its exhaustion and its muscle torture and its heart-battering encounters with the soldiers of his enemies, had brought him back to the house where it started. Two weeks there. Two weeks of rest, but longed-for rest became numbing boredom, and the steady pounding of his protectors' failures to find a way out. *Could I live the rest of my life like this? A fugitive, a non-person, an invisible being. The guilty conscience of my race, never seen but haunting them.* A sudden memory of the surgeons coming to his mother, when baby Anne was sick. Optimism and then regret. Optimism and then regret. Optimism – and eventually baby Anne had died. His protectors had arranged a boat at Southampton. But it was commandeered by the navy. Portsmouth, perhaps, but they could find no contact. There was a man in Chichester who could help, but then it became clear that he could not. Bognor. Worthing. Other places he'd never heard of, and the same outcome. Unknown names floated before him and then proved insubstantial. Every afternoon a possibility, an enthusiasm; every morning a disappointment. Now another haven, and the same rhythms. At night, the cramped and stifling hiding hole, generations of fugitive priests teaching him their devotion. During the day, the heathen stone circle, safely away from the house.

I wish I could become one with these stones.

The stones towered over him, impervious to history, ageless. By afternoon the stone against his back was warm, and the grass seemed more comfortable than most places he'd slept in the previous month.

I wish Juliana Coningsby were here.

─ ⌒ ⌒ ─

The face of Thomas Scot lowered itself into Thurloe's vision, and watched him uncertainly. Thurloe finished the note he was writing, and looked up.

Scot was perched on the edge of a chair. 'You are ploughing your own furrow, Master Thurloe.'

Thurloe shrugged. 'As Tarrant pointed out' – Tarrant shifted somewhere behind Scot – 'the Council of State's order overtook my little efforts. But I'll keep trying to do what I can to help. I've been collating reports from the south coast.'

'That's good, of course.' Scot's whine was uneasy. 'We all want to succeed.' The beak leaned forward. 'We all work together in this.'

Thurloe looked at him, and at Tarrant, and back again. 'Exactly as you have taught me, Master Scot.' He glanced down at the papers. 'I've identified some likely Royalist sympathizers – the ones they'd really trust – and—'

'How?'

'And I've had them watched. Tighter checks on ship movements, and I've got reports of attempts to charter ships. Nothing certain, of course.' Tarrant was still looking for a chance to interrupt, but Thurloe kept on. 'I think there may be a pattern. I think we chased them out of Dorset. There was a report of the King near Salisbury. I think they're moving eastward along the coast. Southampton and Portsmouth too big, too military – too much risk for them. I think they tried in Emsworth' – he touched a paper with one finger – 'but failed, around the end of the first week in October.' Another paper, another finger. 'I think they're into Sussex now. I think they failed again a day or two later, in Chichester.'

'What does this give us?' Tarrant. 'You're talking about miles of uninhabited coast. There must be dozens of coves; God knows how much empty beach. They'll wait for darkness or fog, and—'

'Brighton,' Thurloe said. 'Two or three men among hundreds, and one ship among many.'

<hr>

The George Inn in Brighton, freshly but badly whitewashed, and clean enough. The landlord was a young man already wearied by the struggle to survive. 'But that's—' and a hand clamped over his mouth and drove him back against his shelves, and half a dozen mugs juddered and fell, and a dagger was pricking his throat. The attacker glanced anxiously over his shoulder as the door opened, relaxed as he saw who it was, and turned again to the panicked face close in front of his own.

The new arrival saw the scene, saw the empty room, threw the bolt across the door and strode down the steps and across the room. 'What have we?'

'Our host thinks he's recognized someone.'

The landlord felt the heavy hand distorting his mouth, felt the sharp pain of the blade in his throat, and watched mesmerized as the new arrival came closer with eyes that stared at him and never blinked.

The face thrust in, so that there were three of them intimate around the blade and the muffled mouth. The landlord's eyes were wide and screaming.

'A lucky evening for you, landlord.' An old face, impossibly worn, with dark dark eyes that reached into him. 'My friend is going to take his knife and his hand away, and as long as you stay utterly silent he's not going to cut your throat. I'm not going to cut your throat either. Even if you breathe a word of who you think you've seen.' A flicker of a frown as the words registered. The hand and the blade dropped, hovered near him. 'You think you know your guest, don't you?' A panicked shake of the head. 'You know him, and that might earn you a purse of gold. But you don't know me, do you?' Frowning, desperate for sense and desperate for escape. 'You never will. I'm not the man who'll kill you. But if you breathe a word of who you think you've seen, I'm the man who'll hunt down every last member of your family, be they one or one hundred years, and gut them. I'm the man who'll burn every building you try to take a minute's rest in. I'm the man who'll tear your clothes from you and leave you alone on the beach, more alone than any man has ever been, and wait for the seagulls to pick you to death. And you'll never know who I was.' He stooped suddenly, and the landlord felt his stomach heaving.

The old man stood, with a mug in his hand, and replaced it on the shelf. 'Take a glass of wine with my friend here, landlord, to celebrate your luck.' He turned to the other: 'My contact's watched; this will have to do. I have final arrangements to make.' Then he was gone, and the landlord's knees began to buckle.

◦—◦

The dreams of the young Charles II:

Another bleary awakening, another hand across my mouth, another set of tired earnest eyes staring down into mine. I am so exhausted it will kill me, and that will be relief. The weariness crouches behind my eyes, the nausea; if they take me will this end?

'Again?'

'Yes Majesty. Quickly now.'

'There's a boat?'

'Not here. We have horses ready.'

'The King! They have him to earth!' Scot and Lyle and Thurloe up and staring at the soldier hurrying in.

Tarrant was shortly behind. 'Where?'

'In the town! At the Whale.'

Pulling on coats and boots – reaching for weapons – Thurloe snatching at a list of ships due to leave Brighton – jostling out into the street – even Thomas Scot trying to run – and hurrying through the midnight mud with torches held high. 'How was it reported?'

'It's everywhere!' There were more shouts now, more figures shifting in the gloom as they came near the Whale tavern.

Thurloe's blood was up, he could feel his heart drumming in him, wondered at seeing the King close up, wondered if somehow he might be the one to. . . and then something caught in his mind, and he slowed, dropped a pace behind the others. He felt the silliness of his excitement, and immediately afterwards there was doubt. He hurried after his companions, grabbed at the soldier's arm. 'How was it first reported?'

'I – I don't – it's everywhere! I heard – someone had come in – they'd heard—' and then an explosion and as the darkness roared they were stumbling backwards on instinct.

Silence, and then movements and shouting again, men picking themselves up from the mud, clumsy black acrobats in the torch-pricked gloom, complaints and questions. Next to the Whale was a low wooden building, a barn or a storehouse, and smoke was belching through cracks and holes in its skin, hanging and glowing fierce in the orange light.

It didn't take long to batter in the door of the little building, already damaged and now assaulted by boots and musket butts. Tarrant and Lyle were pressing in, Scot staring anxiously, Thurloe hanging back, following more slowly.

What is really happening here? What am I not seeing?

The building was empty, except for a few last strands of straw burning themselves out, and the body of a soldier, blackened in the explosion but not so ruined as to disguise the savage cut in his throat.

It silenced them, and as the news spread the men outside quietened too. Lyle stomped out, and began barking orders: a perimeter, a search. Then a shot from nearer the sea. An incoherent shout. Another shot.

An urgent voice from someone: 'The jetty!' And Lyle and Tarrant were hurrying after the man.

Thurloe followed, felt his heart kicking, and then caught himself again. *What is really happening here? What am I not seeing?*

The jetty was a long spindly finger, sloping up out of the shingle and stretching out into the darkness, on ramshackle wooden legs. At the end of it, just beyond the end of it, the sail of a ship gradually filled with wind, ghostly in the night and edging away from them. 'Stop them! Hold that ship!' Tarrant and Lyle thundering up onto the jetty, Thurloe following with long grim strides; hesitation from the two men on the jetty, standing over another body, then they were racing along the jetty again with shouts and drawn pistols as the last rope dropped from the boat.

Thurloe stumbled, an unexpected drop in the shingle, down on one knee and pushing himself up, but now there was a figure near him, a dark shape low on the beach, but not low because it was up and driving towards him. He recoiled, stumbled again and it saved his life. As he fell the outstretched blade stabbed through the last flutter of his coat and he was sprawled backwards on the stones. He gaped up, a large figure standing over him, a dextrous flick and the man had altered his grip on the knife and Thurloe waited for the plunge and knew he was dead.

More shouts, boots on the shingle, and the man hesitated, looked up and around, and Thurloe's focus shifted for an instant from the blade to the face above it.

And knew it. The face in the portrait at Astbury. The man on the horse at Nottingham Castle.

More men were crunching around on the shingle now, musketeers hurrying onto the jetty, a rowing boat being dragged down to the water. But the man had gone, and Thurloe lay flat on his back staring at the stars and trying to believe in the face.

Invisible in the darkness, his horse's head cradled against him to soothe it and muffle its breathing, Shay heard rather than saw a troop of horsemen clattering into the village of Shoreham, felt their dust billow around him.

He feared that he knew the direction they were going, and he was right. They would not find his contact at home, but it was clear that his contact was known.

Subtler movement near him. 'Shay, I congratulate you.' An earnest, exhausted face and a hand thrust into his. Shay felt his whole body sag and sigh. 'The grandest thing. Honestly, I had never thought we would manage it.'

Out at sea, the pale flicker of a sail showed in the dawn.

Something kicked in Shay, some stubborn relic of duty.

He would need support. But there was no one left now. *The last relic of the old world.* Except Teach – he would have to send for Miles Teach.

He shook his head. So old; so weary. *This is not done yet.*

Tarrant and Lyle had successfully stopped a French smuggler returning home with a cargo comprising a pair of runaway lovers. Before they had even started their interrogation of the Captain, Thurloe had troops of cavalry going east and west with named contacts to find and arrest. But the ship *Surprise* had already slipped out of Shoreham five miles to the west, and the completion of victory had disappeared with her.

Thomas Scot was exhausted by an unaccustomed night of action, and grieving. 'I cannot allow that a hotch-potch of peasants and rebels has defeated us.'

'We're hardly defeated, Master Scot.' Thurloe's voice was quiet, steady. He felt alive; he felt himself, despite the frustrations of the night, at last coming into a kind of synchronization with the world. 'Charles Stuart's run away, and he may be more convenient as an exile than a martyr. Your work will endure.' Scot didn't look as if he believed him. 'But this was no accidental collection of rebels. It's a network. Controlled by one man. One very extraordinary man, I think.'

Tarrant was scrabbling for a place in the conversation. 'What do—'

'His predecessor was George Astbury, who died at Preston. Perhaps you knew him, Master Scot.'

Scot was frowning. 'Astbury – of Astbury House, yes? I knew him, but only for a – a genteel busybody, on the edge of the old King's circle.'

'I suspect he was a better man than that. But he was nothing compared to the man who took on the role – the role of Royalism's chief intelligencer.'

'You have a name, Thurloe?' Tarrant, doubtful but interested.

Thurloe nodded. 'Shay. Mortimer Shay.' Scot's eyes went wide. 'Kin to Astbury, but with a history and daring that few men in England could match.'

'Shay!' Scot was feverish. 'But he's dead, surely. These many years. He was a notorious rogue in the old days; practically an outlaw. He can't be alive. He can't be in England.'

'I saw him in Nottingham in '48. I saw him here not three hours ago. And I've felt his presence many times between. I rather think I've been exchanging letters with him.'

'You've what?' Scot and Tarrant echoing.

'He had me as his dupe, right up to Dunbar.' Thurloe looked down, and the others did not see the smile. 'Since Dunbar, I fancy I've had his measure.'

Scot was watching him with a kind of awe; Tarrant was still grappling. 'But – surely that's trea—'

'Tarrant, we delivered the victory our masters wanted. But this war may not be done. Shay is still loose in England, and I doubt he's done fighting.'

'You have a way into this network, Thurloe?'

Thurloe felt the papers inside his coat. *These are mine. . .* Then there was illumination on Tarrant's face: 'Well, there's one definite link, isn't there?'

Thurloe's stomach lurched.

⁓

Shay had allowed himself three hours' sleep, when clouds over the moon had made it too dark to ride with even barest safety, and when exhaustion threatened to pull him off his horse in any case. Three unconscious hours in a ditch, and then he was up with the dawn and away northward again.

He'd got the King away; the Parliament men would be seeking vengeance. And the man Thurloe seemed to know something of the Comptrollerate-General now, seemed to know its systems.

He hurried on, by villages and muddy tracks, the old paths of England. The country was alive with Parliament's soldiers, those who'd been hunting the King and those still picking up fugitives from Worcester. Every town meant checkpoints and sentries, and after all that had happened even the slightest suspicion could kill him.

That seemed to matter again.

The network of the Comptrollerate-General was a passive thing; when not called or used, it disappeared back into the fabric of English life. Thurloe and his soldiers would have trouble finding any part of it, and could make little of it if they did.

But there was Astbury. Thurloe had been there. Something had led him to the Comptrollerate-General, and George Astbury and Astbury House were the most likely. Astbury couldn't disappear.

＊ ＊

Thurloe couldn't get rid of Lyle and Tarrant, and their shadows cantering beside him through the evening felt oppressive. He'd had one attempt at blithe dismissal of the relevance of Astbury House, a passing attempt at suggesting alternative lines of activity, but he knew that to say more would only increase their suspicion of Astbury – and of him. They knew of the house, and Lyle had pointed out how close it was to Leek, where the courier they'd tracked from Doncaster three years back had disappeared. So now they hurried north as a three, and Thurloe felt like an escorted prisoner.

And what am I?

The thought of Rachel faced with Tarrant and Lyle, the bitter and the implacable, was nauseating. But the frustration of the young King's escape still kicked at him. For all his cleverness with misleading letters and fake news-sheets, the network of the Comptrollerate-General still eluded him, hidden threads no doubt crossing his path even as he rode, watching him from behind these night hedges.

Rachel had chosen that world, and she was somehow part of it. It was a world he had to destroy.

The three shadows jogged onward under the moon.

— · —

Shay came at Astbury across country, down out of the hills. His horse he left a mile away from Astbury lands, and he went the rest of the way with the dewy grass brushing at his knees and his eyes fixed on the first buildings of the estate.

He trudged dull-headed, an instinct of mission moving him forward when consciousness could not. His thighs started to feel damp as the dew soaked through, and it wakened him a little.

He had to go careful. The direct road, the fastest ride, risked attention and capture. Whatever had happened to Rachel he could rectify. Even if his papers were discovered, something might be done. But if he was captured all was lost. As Astbury loomed nearer, the back façade high over the trees, he slowed again and began to look for cover: ditches, hedges and walls, the thick greenery of summer.

It had been a fast journey regardless. The network had served him well.

Now he was in the orchard, moving from tree to tree and ducking the lower-hanging apples. At the end of the ranks of trees there was a high brick wall, beyond it the first terrace of garden below the house. He glanced left and right for avenues of movement; for concealment; for escape.

The orchard: where a soldier had been buried three years before, another unexpected visitor. The strange crops of Astbury.

A fast journey, and it wasn't certain that the Parliament men would have fixed on Astbury or come with any speed. They were not as driven as he, nor as wise. There could still be time.

The last rank of trees, and he set himself behind a trunk and peered carefully through the blurring of apples and leaves.

A musketeer was leaning over the wall, staring out into the orchard.

Infinitely slowly, Shay pulled back through the trees.

At first it had been three men, cantering up the beech alley to the house. Rachel had seen them from an upstairs window, and known that something had changed, badly. The Army – Thurloe – had new information; there had been a defeat of some kind; Shay was prisoner; Shay was dead.

Three men. One of them, surely, was Thurloe.

Then more horsemen hurrying up the drive. She went cold. What threat could she and her distracted father represent? What threat did they now face?

Then the three men were standing in the hall. Thurloe wouldn't catch her eye. One of the others was sneering – 'suspected of complicity in treason' – 'hand over immediately all materials pertaining to Royalist conspiracy, and all money hidden to support it' – and her rheumy-eyed father was grinning foolishly and babbling and no one was listening.

Rachel looked shocked, and hurried away up the stairs. Through every window she could see soldiers.

Thurloe had watched her go. *Why did I come here? Do I want her to see me triumph? Do I want to see any of this?*

He wanted to be in the search. But he didn't want Rachel to see him at it. He turned and walked out of the house. Two platoons of soldiers had arrived: one to establish a cordon around the house; the other to search.

He began to wander around the outside of the house, enjoying the warmth and the peace and trying not to see the soldiers bustling past him to surround the building. There were little vestiges of routine standing out against the chaos he had brought: a pile of apples, the old man – Jacob – head down at his garden work trying to pretend there was no intrusion, kitchen waste flung out the back door in the last minutes of normality, the faint whinnying of horses, and insects oblivious to it all buzzing near him.

The soldiers unbuilt Astbury House.

Every layer of it above the brick was ripped away, in a beastly seething of men that tore and hacked until the old civilized thing stood naked among the trees. It was a savage destruction, a fast and implacable wrenching of wood and fabric, the smashing of crockery and glass, the unnecessary hurling of things from dented-lead cracked-glass windows, small pieces of furniture and trinkets that weren't worth the pilfering plummeting stupidly to earth to smash and thud. A dozen fragments of curtain plunged out of upstairs windows, the heavier cloth swooping down to shroud the mounting debris, the lighter materials catching the wind, and billowing over the lawn, blurring like tears over the scene until they hitched up on a branch. But the destruction had a remorseless knowledgeable sense to it as well: with craftsmen's understanding the soldiers went at panelling and joints and frames and tables, like anti-carpenters, reversing whole lifetimes of work.

Sir Anthony Astbury sat hunched on a bare chair in the hall, arms clamped around himself and shuddering, and watched as his whole existence was dismantled around him. The layers of luxury were ripped away with the curtains and tapestries, the layers of structure with the panelling and the random efforts the soldiers made with their knives and feet at the plaster and the floorboards. As the plague of soldiers swarmed over it, the house split and pustuled, debris and scars and blemishes. Astbury ceased to be the place he knew, and the layers of his identity peeled and shrivelled with it. In the end, Sir Anthony Astbury huddled on the chair and cried the mad, unknowable tears of a baby.

Rachel found Thurloe on the front lawn. He was forcing himself to watch the destruction now, explaining to himself the need to sacrifice beauty to principle, and suddenly his vision was the wild gold hair and cold face of Rachel Astbury, and something heaved in his gut.

She planted herself in front of him, two paces away, and stood there gazing silently into his face.

His eyes widened in faint apprehension, and then uncertainty.

She stood in front of him, gazing into his face. Her head was high, the eyes wide and shocked and defiant and somehow triumphant.

The ugly sounds of destructive men and splintering wood continued to squawk from the house, behind her, and she did not move. To Thurloe, the world was her vast eyes, and the blur of destruction beyond.

A soldier approached, briskness suppressing his unease at the strange scene: the Government man in black and the beautiful young woman, standing close and staring silently at each other from blank faces. The scene was wrong, anyway: he knew that somehow it needed remaking. Besides, pretty girl, might be a spy, there'd be ways of treating her. . . From the side he neared, hesitated, and then advanced and his arm swung up towards her. 'Soldier!'

It was the Government man, and a bitten ferocity in the word made the soldier stop, and his hand hung in the air near the woman's shoulder.

'If you touch her I'll see you hanged by evening.'

Such a strange and disproportionate idea and the soldier started to smile, and then he saw the Government man's face staring at him dead cold, and the hand hung in the air and then dropped, and he turned away.

'Your heroism is meaningless to me, John Thurloe.'

For a moment he relaxed at the return of conversation, something natural, but then he absorbed the tone of the words, bitter-bleak. He re-focused on the lovely face, and was confused to see that something in it seemed to have collapsed with the words.

'You and your kind are destroying my whole world. The life I know is no longer possible. You might as well give me to your soldiers.'

How could she be triumphant and yet somehow disappointed, somehow broken? Still Thurloe stared back at her, determined to suffer the accusation that she represented, but she was done now and uninterested, and turned and left him.

He was ashamed to find that part of his mind held clear.

Either she does not know of anything hidden here, it was thinking, *or she knows that we will not find it.*

~ ~

A gentle heartbeat on the edge of Shay's dreams. Out of place; from another world.

Still it came, a low rhythmic thump.

He woke quickly – a moment of staring stupidity in the night – and shook himself to full alertness.

A low rhythmic thump at the door.

Not a feeble knock, but a knock delivered with deliberate restraint.

He picked up his knife, took another moment for his eyes to adjust to the gloom, and then moved with long careful strides to the door.

He waited there. No more knocking; how long had his visitor been trying? Then a squawk of a creak.

He reached for the latch. He gripped it, lifted it delicately, and then with one smooth fast movement pulled the door open and stepped back to the side into the darkness.

A gasp and a little spasm of alarm from the figure now outlined clear in the doorway thanks to a candle somewhere behind it, and then Shay registered the slenderness, knew this for a woman, saw something familiar in the waves of hair. . .

'Rachel!' He held the surprise to a murmur, and then grabbed at her arm and pulled her inside. He checked behind her, picked up the candle from the corridor, and was swiftly into his room again and closing the door.

Another candle lit and the fire rekindled and her face glowed orange in the darkness. There was a wildness to her, an abandon to her hair and her expression.

'Great Gods, girl,' he muttered insistently, 'why are you come? How—'

'I hoped' – she spat the word, unpleased at the implication of dependence – 'you were nearby. If you were nearby, and couldn't get to the house, you'd be here.'

'What will these people think of you?'

Her head lifted a fraction. 'Exactly what I want them to think. They'll not be surprised that a lone traveller is visited by a whore, and they'll think nothing further of my identity.'

It was a woman's wisdom, delivered by a woman, and amid the warming frankness Shay felt a cold pang of something lost. 'You should be—'

'Astbury is ruined.'

'What?' The sense of loss was growing as he spoke.

'They have pulled it apart. My world is a shell of a building with an old broken man keening in the wreckage.' And immediately the control and the maturity strained and threatened to break. 'Every thing I have ever owned, every thing I have touched, has been. . . the soldiers have – they have touched it all – every thing, every place, is fouled.'

Two great hands clamped on her shoulders, and her chest and breath heaved and shuddered.

'You poor girl.' He knew the destruction, he knew what Astbury looked like now. He felt the loss in his gut, and he winced for these precious things he could not save. 'It's like a great part of our family has died. All we have fought for.'

'Why should you care?' The eyes were up, fierce and wet and shining. 'This is a chaos of your creation, and you have set us all adrift in it. You – you are chaos.'

Shay's face soured in the gloom, and then he gave a great mournful nod. 'Yes,' he said with finality. He watched her wild face in the weird glare of the flames. 'I am truly sorry, Rachel. I would have burned the world to protect your innocence.'

'By burning the world you have destroyed it.' She wriggled free of the powerful hands, and immediately missed them. She wanted a comfort, but no longer knew where to find it. And she wanted this big, knowing shadow to realize that he too could be vulnerable.

'But don't worry.' The bitterness stuck through the murmured words. 'Your papers are safe.' And she watched him.

A horse-kick of hope in his gut, and a slower surprise, and then caution. 'Papers?'

She gave a little snort, and then breathed in an air of superiority. With a jolt Shay saw his half-sister, scolding him out of the past. 'Perhaps, Mortimer Shay, you're not so much cleverer than George Astbury after all.' The head lifted higher. 'So little imagination, men. Like Uncle George, you had to use the one room that was kept for you. Uncle George was a man who craved stability, who thought instinctively of home, and his hiding place was in the fabric of the house. You're a man who must move to breathe, who could never be tied to one place, and the stool was one of the few unfixed things in the room.'

'And now?'

'I smuggled them out of the house, but they are safe on our land.'

A nod. 'Does anyone else—'

'Jacob. He has them. And the satchel with the jewels and our Bible. As you said.'

His mouth chewed uncomfortably. 'Thank you,' he said simply. 'Those papers are—'

'I didn't do it for your blasted papers, and I certainly didn't do it for you. If they'd found them they'd have killed us all for traitors, wouldn't they?'

He knew it, and it was another failing that clutched in his chest.

'His Majesty is safe out of England at last. He should be in Paris by now, with his mother.'

'Thank God.'

'Thank Shay. Fully six weeks the prey of every soldier in England, and he protected him and got him out.'

'We have lost the kingdom.'

'We have saved the King. The seasons will turn again. I'll wager Cromwell won't find government as easy as battle.'

'There was treachery, as Astbury thought?'

'That seems clear now.'

'And we know who it must be. Does Shay know?'

'He seems to find out these things.'

'And what then? You won't get His Majesty back on a boat for Edinburgh for a season or two.'

'England takes the strangest paths to peace. Stability needs the men back in the fields, and merchants back in London docks. Westminster is not without reasonable men.'

'Exactly. So what of Shay? Our duty. . . our duty is greater than any one man.'

'Indeed. Different ground; different horse. The Comptrollerate-General must hold the longer view.'

Shay was still awake ten minutes later, lying on the bed with futile thoughts squabbling in his head, when he heard two knocks on the shutter.

Rachel was a pale grey outline under the moon. She hissed up at him,

'My horse is lame.'

'Take mine.'

'It's too big, and it's a grey. The soldiers might notice the difference. And there are no others here.'

Shay's window was barely six feet off the ground, and he dropped into the yard with only a slight hiss at the effect on his knees. Within the minute they were trotting out of the yard, Rachel sitting behind and clutching at Shay's coat.

'Do you have to go back?' he murmured. 'I can help you; I can—'

'I don't want your help. Even if you could.' He felt her shifting behind him on the horse. 'I want my home back.'

The moon watched them onward.

Something was moving in Shay's brain: night journeys to Astbury; danger; the soldier from Doncaster coming to the house; news of Pontefract. What had he brought George Astbury that was so valuable? He probably hadn't known. But why had Astbury wanted it so badly? Was it only the report from Teach, and if so, what was there about the information that was worth risking a life for? Not just risking, but losing a life, for the soldier had been dead and buried at dawn, another contribution to Astbury's rich soil, another bit of history silently and imperceptibly absorbed.

Why, now, does this haunt me so? Is this now my dotage, to live in these past confusions and failures?

Another quarter-hour of riding and they reached a watermill, a black outline in the gloom. Rachel knew the place vaguely; a memory of a dour ferrety owner. What kind of reception would they— But Shay was already off the horse and knocking heavily at the door.

A minute, and he knocked again. From the horse, Rachel watched his silent outline against the blackness of the mill, and started to wonder more about the sentries at Astbury.

Another minute. The snap of a latch and the creak of the door and there was a thin figure shadowed against some glow inside; a glint of metal, and the beginning of an angry question, but Shay was already speaking. 'I'm a friend of Mandeville. I need a horse; black, preferably.'

A grunt. 'I've no black. A chestnut?'

'It'll do. Thank you.'

Within a minute Rachel was on a new horse and heading for home, planning paths and excuses that might serve in the misty dawn, and wondering again at the strange power of Mortimer Shay and his friends.

— ᔕ —

'Going somewhere?' The voice behind her in the stable, and Rachel whirled round, trying to swallow her heart. A soldier, a shadow in the doorway, the first of the light catching his musket-barrel.

'I was – I couldn't sleep. I needed to – I wanted to check my horse. Check you people hadn't done anything to her.' She turned away and stroked the nose of the mill-owner's chestnut. The bridle and saddle still hung on a beam immediately beside her; did they look out of place?

'I didn't see you come.'

Rachel's glance towards the tack had also showed that the horse was very definitely a him rather than a her.

She turned. The man's eyes looked stupid, or just sleepy. 'Good. I wouldn't want you to.' She pulled on a show of defiance and strode past the sentry. He reached indifferently for her arm as she passed, but she ignored him and hurried on into the house.

She managed four hours' sleep, on a mattress salvaged from the garden yesterday and laid in her bedroom on a patch of undamaged floorboards. Joanna woke her, and Rachel was immediately aware of the cold.

'Please, miss, but the man wants to talk to you. I've kept him waiting an hour, but I worried that—'

'Which man?' Looking around the remains of her room, she realized that Joanna must have tidied the worst of the plaster and laths and debris the previous evening.

'The Government man. The one who came before.'

Thurloe was sitting on the bench in the arbour. He looked up as she approached, held her eyes a moment, and looked down at the pile of papers perched carefully in his lap.

The shock had her gaping and confused.

Shay's papers. They had to be Shay's papers. *But how. . .?*

She brought her face under control. Thurloe finished looking at one page, and replaced it neatly on top of the others. He looked up.

He must know them for what they are. But how. . .?

Thurloe said, 'I assumed there were papers here. Then you were too sure. The only way you could have got something out was in the kitchen scraps. Your most logical collaborator after that was the old man.'

Was Jacob safe? Surely he hadn't—

'Jacob would not have betrayed. . . anything of us. I don't believe it.' *What can he really know? What can I say that does not incriminate?*

Still the same wretched neutrality in Thurloe's manner. 'Nor should you. That man would die for this land, and for you above all. So I told him that I knew all about the papers. I told him that unless he gave them to me I would make this whole estate a desert, and have Mistress Rachel in the Tower.' His voice softened somehow, and became more sincere. 'The principles of the good Jacob run deeper than these little vanities of political loyalty.'

'And would you?' She attempted scorn, to cover the insidious sense of vulnerability in her belly. 'Would you have laid waste to it all? Would you have seen me in one of your dungeons?'

He looked up slowly, and dour, and the words were leaden. 'My instincts are immaterial to you, surely.'

It was spiteful, and they both knew it, and suddenly Rachel Astbury wanted to scream madly at the childish, self-destructive lunacy of their world.

The destruction of the house yesterday had seemed to strip away the warmth of this life. Then her night ride to see Mortimer Shay had somehow rekindled a sense of possibility, of vitality. Now that had collapsed again and for ever. *The game is done.*

She moved to the end of the bench, and slowly sat down, and folded her hands in her lap. 'So what follows, then, John?'

His tensed shoulders dropped, and his face seemed sadder, and at last there was sincerity in the eyes. 'Rachel. . .' He sighed. 'The papers are mine now, and I must use them. They were not yours, and their treason is not yours. They were your uncle's, and your uncle is an enemy to this country, and I must find him and if I find him he will surely hang. You. . .'

His eyes searched her sadly. She felt the scorn starting to seethe in her again, but he saw it and spoke fast and earnest. 'You are vulnerable, Rachel, and I beg you to believe me. Scot and Tarrant know you for their only link to these late treasons, and if they have a fragment of evidence they will – they will. . . tax you to the uttermost to find out more. If they saw a single one of these papers and thought your fingers might have touched it, they would have you in. . . torments, in the Tower.'

They were both shaken, and stared at each other in silence, his great mournful eyes and hers wild and strained. 'If you fly they will find you, and they will know you guilty. Stay here. Stay silent. See no one who is not of the immediate household.' He watched her lost face, and something lurched in him. His hand seemed to flicker, as if he wanted to reach out. 'You must step back from the world, Rachel. Above all, do not – I beg you, do not – try to contact your uncle.'

The August night wound itself up into a storm, swirling and roaring and hurling rain horizontal out of the darkness, and the storm brought forth Sir Mortimer Shay.

Some ancient stubbornness made Jacob wait for one more hammer-blow on the planks before he opened his cottage door, dog straining at its collar under his hand. Shay was a midnight waterfall on the doorstep, streams rolling off every shadowed feature, and then a satanic grin. 'I'm the past, Jacob. We have a little unfinished business tonight.'

Jacob, after a moment, just nodded and stepped aside.

The spindly wheel-backed chair by the fire squawked as Shay dropped into it. He began to puddle, and steam. The dog sniffed around him dubiously.

Jacob stood nearby, the crevasses and outcrops of his face waiting for an expression, like barren ground before rain.

Shay watched him. Eventually Jacob settled himself cautiously on a stool on the other side of the fireplace. The dog settled next to him; its slack features slumped into sleep.

'Trouble for the garden, Jacob?'

Jacob lifted one shoulder, a suggestion of a shrug.

Shay waited.

Eventually Jacob shook his head. 'The earth don't mind. Mix a few things up. Wash out a bridge maybe.' Another shrug. 'Branches. Thatch.'

'Sometimes the wind blows from one flank, sometimes another. The tree bends and sways but does not break. Eh, Jacob? A man must shift as best he may.' Jacob watched him, warily. 'You and this land: you'll outlive all of it, won't you? All the Kings and Parliaments and battles and trickeries.'

Jacob said, 'I have broken no trust nor undertaking given freely to any man, sir.'

'I'm sure you have not.' Shay's voice was grave, but then lightened. 'Men come to you, with the newest idea, the newest fashion, and you absorb it. The newest secret. I was not the first, and I will not be the last man to trust to you and this good soil.'

Silence from the two old gnarled men. The snoring of the dog, a gentle rasping and hissing in the corner, the faint pulse of the world. The bluster and shout of the storm outside, testing the windows and moaning.

George Astbury would have burned the ephemeral papers before he burned the book. He did not burn the book with the papers. That night he was in the house with the family, the soldier arrived, the soldier died and was buried, and George left for Preston and death. In that time the book disappeared.

'We have to dig him up again, Jacob.'

Jacob glanced to the window, whining and bleared with rain.

A chewing, and a nod. 'Aye, sir.'

A decision. Rachel stood with her back to her battered home, staring out over the garden, bright and lush with summer. Small in the distance, keeping away from the house on some instinct of mourning or self-preservation, Jacob was bent to work among the flowers.

There were two visions in front of her; two possibilities. Mortimer Shay, as she had seen him in the night, an old man overtaken by his own stratagems, in a cause that looked backwards and had become self-defeating. And John Thurloe, as she had seen him in the day, brilliant servant of a power that had lost all restraint, a power whose self-preservation had become more important than its ideals, its ideals more important than humanity.

Bees humming near her, and the faint click of Jacob's blade breaking the earth.

She shook her head.

She would have to find one of them; for one last time she would have to depend on one of them.

Either would do.

She turned, and there was a man walking towards her. A moment's wonder at what fortune might have decided, and then the uncomfortable realization that it was neither of them. It was one of the other Parliament men; one of the other brutes from yesterday.

No doubt: he was heading for her. Rachel's heart began to hammer in her chest.

There was clear intent in his expression – and some underlying discomfort. Tarrant, was that the name? Instinctively, her hands clutched together against her bodice.

'Rachel Astbury.' The sneer made it a kind of accusation. 'You're coming with me. We've some questions for you.'

She nodded slowly. 'Far? For long?'

He shrugged, smiled. 'Could be.'

Another nod. 'I must just fetch. . . some necessities – for the journey. Will you come inside?' Heart hammering.

She saw him enjoy the sense of invitation, and she turned and started for the house. 'I thought I'd answered all you needed yesterday. With Mr Thurloe.'

'Mr Thurloe doesn't make the rules.'

'No. No, he doesn't.' Heart hammering, hammering, hammering against her clenched hands.

He followed a couple of steps behind her and to the side. 'I've always hated women like you.' Her stride altered, and she wondered what was coming. 'Women like you always thought I was dirt, didn't you?'

She hesitated, slowed, glanced over her shoulder at him. 'Aren't you afraid it's all women?' And she strode on towards the house, Tarrant coming behind with face twisting up into the scowl. In through the wrecked door by the pantry, the empty stone space a sudden cool, fighting to control her breathing, starting to turn, and as Tarrant stepped into the gloom and his eyes began to readjust, the dagger came free of her cuff and she stabbed him in the chest.

I have done it. Oh God what have I done?

It turned out that men don't always just die, if you stab them. Tarrant staggered back against the door, and it slammed shut, and then swung open again as its wrecked catch failed to engage and he rolled clumsily to the side and dropped. He slumped against the door pillar, feet scrabbling for purchase, gasping and calling as his hands flailed for the blade. 'You – bitch! You vicious. . . fucking bitch! You've—' and another agonized choke. His hands were scarlet, his white shirt front was scarlet, and he rolled and moaned and would not die.

The bright doorway darkened and filled. Pressed back against the wall, every muscle clenched and eyes wild, she pulled her gaze away from the writhing man on the floor.

'Tarrant, this— My Christ!'

It was Thurloe.

His eyes went rapidly back and forth between the wounded man and Rachel and he fought for words. 'Christ, what have you done?'

'She. . . bitch – she—' the words collapsed in choking.

Thurloe gazed at her. His scrutiny kindled a renewed defiance, and she fought her breaths under control and her chin came up.

He bent towards the body. 'You—' He grappled for control, for the rightness. *Tarrant's sneer at Pontefract: What are you fighting for, Thurloe?* The twisted coughing face beneath him, and the beautiful crazed pride above. One great breath, hissed out. 'You must get out of here. Now. Exactly now.'

'Yes,' she said, brittle calm. 'I must.'

Another shadow in the doorway, and Rachel gasped in a kind of relief and stepped past Thurloe and Tarrant towards it. 'Oh, Jacob! The satchel: I need it now.'

Thurloe hissed, 'We've no time!'

The old man grunted. 'In the dog's corner, miss, by the fire; in his blanket.' He caught her arm – 'Give him a pat as you go, eh?' – and she was away.

For an instant it distracted Thurloe from the moaning, rolling man beneath him. 'I'd guess you didn't give me everything, then?'

Jacob chewed on this. 'Guess you didn't ask, sir.'

Tarrant was white, and still coughing and swearing sporadically, but his breathing had evened. Thurloe, crouched over him, glanced from the face to the dark wound in the chest and up again. Tarrant's eyes followed. 'You. . . You. . .' Thurloe took another deep breath. Then he clamped his hand over Tarrant's mouth, wrenched the dagger from his chest, and stabbed him in the heart. He held his hand firm until the body ceased to spasm.

He looked up. Jacob considered the scene for a moment, and then shook his head slightly, faint bewilderment and then indifference.

'Oh, go and mind your garden, old man.'

Shay came at Astbury on foot and across country. It was enemy ground now, but he had to see how it lay.

The ruin of the place struck him first, as he peered through a screen of leaves: the smashed windows, the broken timbers, the sign of scorching above some of the openings, and the debris scattered across the lawn. The sight kicked him again for his complacency.

Then he saw the soldiers around what was left of the front door, and saw their excitement. Something unusual; the signs were immediate. The press of men, the circling of the horses, the shouts, the toing and froing. As he watched, three riders flung out from the group at a gallop and tore down the main drive. There was one man still giving orders, then in a single fluid movement he swung himself up onto a horse and pulled it round and set off down the drive himself, three more men following.

Shay watched for a moment longer, saw the energy dissipating, and withdrew into the trees.

Jacob was wheeling a barrow of leaves with steady momentum, when he heard his name murmured close by. He hesitated, and then continued until he reached a shed, where he emptied the barrow. Then he drifted into the shadow of the trees, and worked his way back.

'What's the fuss, Jacob?'

Jacob hesitated.

'If it doesn't concern Miss Rachel, it doesn't matter to you. If it does, she needs you to tell me everything.'

Jacob told him, to Shay's gathering alarm.

'And she's flying – but how? How can she—'

'There's a man with her. A Parliament man, sir.'

'He's – what, he's arrested her? Stolen her away?'

'I think he's helping her.'

It made no sense. 'Who?'

'The one called Thurloe.'

Thurloe?

'They're making for Lincolnshire, sir. Boston.'

'Why there?'

'Better for the Continent, he said. Maybe not what pursuers'd expect. He had some paper helped him decide.'

'Paper?'

'A bundle of papers, like a—'

'Like a list of names?' *Ye Gods. But how?*

'Could be. He had to hunt in it – seemed to be guessing at some names – then he hit on Boston.'

Worcester. The commandery at Worcester. Shay felt the world falling away from him. He gathered himself again, nodded towards the house. 'Who was in charge there?'

'Man called Lyle, sir.'

'What manner of man?'

Jacob shook his head.

'And this Thurloe?'

'A fair enough gentleman. One who'd try to find his way to right in the end.'

'And now he's trying to find his way to the coast, across a hundred miles of country, with Miss Rachel in his power.'

'You'd best be after them, then, sir.'

'Yes, I had.' He turned, and stopped. 'Had she a – a bag with her?'

'She did.'

Shay nodded. 'Jacob, if a man asks for me – a man on his own, not a

Parliament man or a soldier – tell him to find me in Boston. To ride like Satan himself. He'll know where.'

'Aye, sir.' The old man leaned forward, hand opening and closing in an attempt to find a gesture. 'Sir. . . she is all we have left, sir.'

— ~ —

The first stage of the journey felt like freedom: the horse pounding rhythmically and sure beneath her, Thurloe steady by her side, the wind pulling at her hair and bathing her face and seeming to blast into her, washing clean all past sense of confinement.

But by Derby, after three hours of hard riding, the aches had become permanent in her thighs and hunger and tiredness were starting to eat at her spirit. The mad euphoria of what had happened at Astbury had seeped away.

I am a fugitive.

I am a murderer.

I have deliberately abandoned the only place I ever knew safety.

— ~ —

'That was quick.' Lyle's blood was up: a mouthful of bread and wine snatched from a Derby sentry post, a fresh horse under him, and he was agitating to be away. 'You've asked everywhere she might have got a new horse?'

'Didn't have to.' The soldier pulled himself up into the saddle.

'What do you mean? Where in hell's Baines?' This to the other soldier with him. 'How long does he need for a piss?'

'I'll check.'

Lyle turned back to the first soldier. 'Well?'

'She got a new horse here.'

'Here? But—'

'There's someone with her. A Government man like yourself, sir. He got them both horses, no bother. An hour ago, no more.' Lyle's lively face showed its surprise. 'Who might that have been, sir?'

'I can't—' He snatched at the idea, rejected it, picked it up again. 'Surely not. Surely. . .' He stared at the soldier. 'There's one man it might be, but. . . but he'd have to be a hundred times more peculiar than I thought.' The third man stepped back into the yard. 'Where is he, then?'

Bewilderment. 'Baines is dead, sir. Stabbed in the throat outside, whiles we were talking here.'

Nottingham grew in front of them on the road, and Rachel bargained with her shoulders and legs that they would rest if they reached it. But when they reached it, Thurloe showed no sign of stopping, slowing to a fast trot and continuing through the side streets, aware of the great yellow shadow of the castle watching him.

She pulled up her horse. 'John – can't we stop?' A flash of pride. 'The horses—'

'They're good for a while yet.' He circled her, keeping moving.

'Even for a moment?'

'We must keep ahead of them. They can get more horses than we can, more quickly. By Derby they'll have known they were on our track. They'll have sent messengers on every road.'

'We could hide for a while. Let them pass us.'

'If they get past us, they block us. Every town they reach means more patrols looking for us. Now is all we have, Rachel.'

She looked at him, and then nodded. 'Well, then,' she said, and smiled, and kicked her horse into the canter again.

A mile after they crossed the Trent, Thurloe's horse lost a shoe. He swore, dropped to the ground, glancing anxiously back towards the town.

'We can't go back.'

He shook his head. 'And we can't look for a smith on the road, and have them catch us as they please.'

A track led to a village a mile off the main road, and with urgency and gold Thurloe had the smith at work in minutes. But the diversion cost them half an hour or more, and when they regained the main road his uneasy glances were ahead as well as behind.

Lyle had taken his anger out on his horse, and the three men changed their gasping rides at Nottingham. Lyle's feet hardly touched the ground between animals. Another great mouthful of wine and he was spitting out orders: patrols on the roads north and south, now looking for a man as well – a man claiming to be in Government pay. Then he was kicking the new horse into the gallop, and his two companions exchanged a weary glance and hurried after him, eastward for the sea with the sun starting to fall behind their backs.

Thurloe's jaw was clamped tight in apprehension as they approached Bingham, the next settlement on the road. Over a decade he had grown used to seeing soldiers everywhere, and for the last few years they had become regular contacts in his work. Now, in one act of bizarre heat by Rachel Astbury, and his own instinctive reaction to it, every uniform was a threat.

Could I somehow have done this differently? Explained away Tarrant's death? Isn't there some way I could be stability and legitimacy after all?

Tarrant's shocked face. Beside him, Rachel Astbury flying over the ground with hair billowing behind her. Somewhere out in the afternoon, men hunting him. *I can no longer explain things away. I can no longer hide behind words. In this mad day I am become the enemy of my own state.*

The first houses of the village were in sight. He slowed his tired horse to a trot, and felt Rachel matching him. He had to be normal, he had to be calmness.

Movement on the road ahead, coming from the village, and the sun coming low over his shoulder sparkled on metal.

'John—'

'Keep going. We have to keep going. Not every man and woman in England is hunted.'

Soldiers; dragoons. Half a dozen mounted men, trotting in a line, helmets and swords shining dark as they came. Twenty yards, and then ten. Was the leader looking at him? Now they met, and the leader and then some of the others had turned their heads and were watching as they passed. Thurloe forced himself to look straight ahead, caught himself in the unnatural pose, allowed a glance to the side, an indifferent nod to the eyes that he met.

But they weren't looking at him; it was Rachel they were watching. The news of his own flight hadn't travelled this far, and—

No. They were watching Rachel because she was a beautiful woman, murderess or not, and because underneath the madness they were only men.

There was a simple barrier of two crossed pikes in the centre of Bingham, and as they came nearer Thurloe saw the sentry beside it register the two of them, and then duck his head into an adjacent doorway.

'This way!' he hissed, and grabbed at Rachel's bridle and turned them into an alley; her horse, sluggish, pulled against him and came with bad grace. Twenty yards, a turn, and another turn, straight across a side street into another alley and he stopped them in an empty yard.

'You think they're waiting for us?'

'I can't be sure, but. . . It looked like – We must assume we could've been overtaken; when I lost the shoe; or on a faster road through Nottingham.'

'Perhaps they don't know us by sight.'

'Perhaps. Perhaps they've just sent gallopers with orders to set up checks and patrols. But if Lyle was at Astbury this morning he'll be after us like all the powers of hell, and he knows us.'

'And you can't risk bluffing your way through?'

'At Derby we had a head start, and it was a fair bet. Now it's too late.' He looked at her, at the big intent eyes, and then down at their two hang-necked horses. 'We need new mounts, and we need a safe place to think, even for a few minutes. It's not a big place, and we'll be noticed soon enough.'

'If I knew people near here. . . But it's too far from home.'

Thurloe alive; *people who know people*. 'What county is this?'

'What?'

Thurloe had the sheaf of papers out of his coat. 'Nottinghamshire, would you say? Or have we reached Lincolnshire?' He saw her bewildered face, and smiled heavily. 'Pray that your uncle once came this way.'

Lyle and his two companions rode hard into Bingham, and Lyle stopped only to interrogate the sentry at the barrier, and then his stolid Sergeant who came out to see what the fuss was. Had a man and a woman come through? Were there patrols out? Instructions and urgency, and then Lyle had kicked his horse into jumping the pikes and was away.

The afternoon light was starting to thin when two strangers walked warily into the dairy in Bingham, a sad-looking man and a beautiful woman, both somehow strained. The man asked for Hugh Miles, and the boy in the dairy hurried off into the shadows to find him.

'You think he'll just give us horses. So easy?'

'There is no easy any more. Perhaps there's a signal; a word of recognition. But since neither of us knows it, we have to bluff.'

The owner emerged through the shadows and the straw.

'Hugh Miles?'

'Me, sir.' Hugh Miles waited, watching the man and glancing at the woman.

The man looked around himself quickly. 'I understand that you. . . that you provide help sometimes, Mr Miles. To friends.'

Miles's face screwed up in a frown.

The stranger leaned forward, voice low and urgent. 'I need two horses.'

Miles shook his head slowly. 'I'm a dairy, sir. I don't—'

'Mandeville!' She blurted the word, surprising herself.

The man staring at her, and then stifling his own surprise; Miles uneasy.

The watermill at night. Shay unhesitant. 'I – I should say that. . . we're friends of Mandeville.'

Miles's eyes widened slightly, and he glanced beyond them. 'Of course, miss; sir. Take a little while – I have to get them from my brother – but you can rest up here.'

Half an hour after the two had departed on fresh horses, another man came to the dairy, with the same word and the same request. Something about Miles's response struck him odd, and Hugh Miles was pushed to observe, softly, that their friends were busy this afternoon.

Mortimer Shay was thrown for a moment, and then something twisted at his lips.

— ~ —

Lyle and the two soldiers with him: witches in the night, while the honest citizens of Grantham kept their doors locked and prayed for morning.

'They'll have been cautious at Nottingham, and they must have lost time at Bingham. They can't have come as fast as our gallopers, and they can't have changed horses as often. We must be ahead of them now.'

Lyle's nervy alertness wasn't shared by his weary companions. 'So?'

'So I think a little ambush.'

'Can't the patrol just pick them up?'

'These militia peasants? In the half-light? Thurloe'll turn tail and it's evens he'll get clear away. Have to cut them off. Surround them.'

— ~ —

Thurloe was fighting to keep himself alert as he rode into Grantham. The idea of rest was a cruel tease. The idea of a bed was an image of the divine. The evening was closing in, and the gloom was echoed in his head.

Had to assume they were ahead of him now. Had to be careful.

Ahead of them on the road: flames. How could that be? He slowed. Sentries, of course, with a fire to keep warm. Fifty yards away, and he could make out the intermittent orange-tinged outline of men moving in the firelight.

But there was a turning before then, to the right. Without breaking pace they took it. Houses to the left; hedges and gardens and occasional houses to the right. Skirting the centre of the town would be sensible, anyway.

The horses trudged on in the twilight.

A vestigial alertness, and Thurloe saw another fire ahead of them. The horses trudged closer. Voices, obscure, and again the suggestion of shapes and movement. He sucked in a breath of the evening, tried to revive his brain. He'd guessed the alarm would have overtaken them by now, and so it had. This was still possible. He knew it was possible. Two people could disappear into England. Nottingham; London fortress; Brighton: a man could slip into the cracks of night unseen.

Sentries on the main road behind them. Sentries ahead. No gaps to the right.

Another turning to the left, between two buildings, and again they took it without changing step.

The steady tramp of hooves was lulling Thurloe. The evening closing around him, the quiet dark backstreet, the even plod of the horse, it all felt so gentle, so easy.

The street ahead deserted, inviting; the occasional glow of a lantern. A street to slip through; a night to disappear in.

— —

'We're only three, Mr Lyle; shouldn't we—'

'It's a Government clerk and a woman. Lost your nerve?'

'So who did for Baines, then?'

'Do as you're damn' bid! Hutch blocks the road, we move in. How hard do you want it?'

And now the trudge of horses, somewhere in the darkening evening, and Lyle clutched the other's arm, pulling them back, eyes peering to pick up the first suggestion of movement round the corner.

'Mr Lyle, sir.' A murmur only, but Lyle had spun and grabbed the throat. The Captain of the local militia detachment, now a frozen alarm in the shadows. 'Sir, one of our pickets – patrol just found him – dead, sir – his throat cut.'

A ferocious hiss: 'Hold your positions!'

— —

The lure of the deserted street, a way ahead and freedom from all the sentries behind. Thurloe was fighting to clarify the shadows, and all the time the even thump of the hooves beneath matching his heartbeat.

An eruption in the steady line of the street in front, a distortion of the darkness, one of the shadows billowing out from the side and becoming a horse, and a man on the horse, and the first suggestion of a cart behind, and now the enticing backstreet was narrowing, being swallowed by the shadow. Instinctively Thurloe pushed the horse forwards, heard Rachel's gasp.

The shadow bloomed further across his vision and the light dwindled and the path was still wide enough for their horses, and then for one horse, and then it shrivelled and the night exploded in shouts and then a shot.

The shadows, the shouts, stopped for an instant at the shot. Then the outline of the man on top of the horse began to change, shrinking and toppling and disappearing, and the path between horse and wall opened again and Thurloe grabbed Rachel's reins and kicked his horse into life and in a second they were plunging through the gap and into space.

~ ~

'Hutch is down!'

'After them!'

More shots, from behind them, and shouts. 'He's getting away!' A chaos of boots and voices. 'There!'

'This way! He's killing our men!'

'Then it's him or the pox, and I don't care. There's a Royalist spy and a bloody traitor making for the sea, and I will stop them. Come on, damn you!'

~ ~

The ride to Boston was a weary unruly dream, a constant apprehension of shadows and shapes in the moonlight and the lurching and stumbling of the horses on the rough road. How long had she been riding now? Nine hours? Twelve? More than she'd ever ridden, more than should be possible. Her body was numb: hands locked on the reins, shoulders dead, her backside and her thighs sore for ever. And her head felt empty, adrift: a wasteland of sleeplessness that blurred unconsciousness and wakefulness, reality and her strange spectral fancies.

Thurloe was beside her, Thurloe was leading her to safety. But when he turned to check on her she saw the worry in his eyes, and the dead staring exhaustion.

A flickering, elusive parade hurtling past them: trees, bushes, isolated farmhouses glowing pale in the night, fences, glimpsed and reconstructed in the fog, and sometimes the pinpoint flashing eyes of animals.

A building to the left, close by, and one to the right. More buildings, hollow sockets of doors and windows gaping at her as she passed. They were in a settlement.

Thurloe slowed, stopped a moment, heaved himself up in the stirrups to get a better look at something, and then led the way into an alley and blackness. She heard him drop off his horse, and she did the same.

Some grain of strength: 'And now?'

'We find our boat.'

She looked at him, pulled herself up. 'You're very sure of yourself, John Thurloe.'

'I think a horizontal line is a bed. I think two vertical lines is a horse. But I know that the flat 'u' is a boat.' She stared at his outline. 'Come along. We'll leave the horses now. The soldiers could be all around us.' She saw his shoulders sag, saw him wrestle them up again.

—◆‿◆—

Shay eased his way around Boston by memories: old paths and old scents in the moonlight. The darkness was full of the rich sour smell of the marshes, edged with salt. The world of his younger misdeeds: assignations and trades; a place to find a lover, or to lose an enemy.

Unseen creatures whistled and shifted nearby.

Thurloe had the network now, and he was learning to use it. If he'd known how to get a horse in Bingham, he'd know how to get a boat in Boston.

Hesitation: the path was not as Shay remembered. There'd been efforts to drain the marshes in the thirties, and those had created new paths and new pools. Then the dykes had decayed or been destroyed in the forties, and again the land and the water had shifted against each other, an eternal skirmish, a perpetual blurring of the boundary.

Trying to bustle around the town looking for Rachel and Thurloe would be a dangerous waste of time. If they'd come safe to Boston, they'd be hiding out for the hour or two it would take to ready the boat. His last service to her could only be to track the boat down the river to the sea, and make sure she got on it. If Rachel hadn't come safe here, he couldn't help her any more.

A squat square ghost off to his left, perhaps half a mile, and the memory kicked warmly in him. A place of ancient sins, the old chapel, a place for forbidden love and forbidden trade. Teach knew it too, and if nowhere else he would go there. The chapel wouldn't have moved, and Shay knew he could navigate by it.

The larger question: what was Thurloe's game, now?

Again he stopped. A whispering in the gloom, animal movement or voices or just the wind. Shay stood still, listening to the spirits of the night, alone on the borderland of the world.

⁓ ⁓

Thurloe had tried to stay awake, but the knocking at the storeroom door roused him from a dead-brained doze. His nerves had him upright quickly enough, jogging Rachel out of sleep.

A boy, pale and young and silent. He beckoned to them. Rachel picked up the satchel, hung it close about her, and the two of them followed the boy out.

The understanding had been quickly spoken, but was clear enough. The boatmen did not take on their night cargoes at the wharves in town: Thurloe and Rachel would be led across the marshes to near where the Witham met the sea, and the boat would meet them there.

They were spectres in the fitful night of the town. They moved in its alleys and shadows. They never saw a front door or a human. Life was something indicated or overheard, light under a curtain, moans behind a door, a fresh heap of kitchen waste, a far-off song. They only knew the damp tramp of their feet through the slimy hidden pathways of the town, and the vague shape of the boy's back leading them away from life.

Beyond the last of the buildings they were in less danger of capture, but they kept the same cautious pace. The boy paused a moment, touched Thurloe's arm: he pointed to the faint view of the stone-strewn path, and nodded; he pointed to the darkness either side of it, and shook his head mournfully. In the silvered night, the great shadows of the marsh encircled them.

They walked perhaps half an hour, and Rachel realized that she'd begun to get the unfamiliar taste of salt in her nose. The breeze was fresher now, and sharper. Attuning herself, she could hear the whispering of water somewhere ahead: the German Sea, and the unknown world beyond the margin of England.

The sea opened up as a void to their left, and shortly afterwards they saw the river snaking out dark to meet it. The boy led them closer to it, and pointed to the outline of a jetty, ramshackle planks protruding from the path over the reeds to where the water flowed freely.

He stared at the two of them for a moment, and then turned and hurried away.

For the first time, Rachel noticed the cold, forgotten in the madness and fears of the last twelve hours. She'd dressed for a mild Astbury morning, and been transported to this anxious marshy night. The comparison jarred sick in her. That garden was gone for ever.

A minute later, from back along the path taken by the boy, a cry squealed into the night and was cut off.

She clutched Thurloe's arm. The silence swallowed them again. 'Bird of some kind,' he murmured, and neither of them believed it. Behind them England, a darkness of hunters and unknown pains. Ahead the sea, the edge of their existence. And all around the shifting world of the marsh.

When they moved their feet, they could feel the soft ground readjusting itself subtly under them.

＊　＊

Shay waited.

So soft, a click and a squelch, a few yards off to his right. His fingertips rubbed together slowly, feeling the night. He concentrated on his breathing, and then on his hearing. Silence.

The faint sucking of the marsh settling or absorbing.

If the spirits have come for me, I am ready to go. If there be men here, I may trust to myself.

He turned, and felt the prick of a blade at his throat. A thick-jacketed arm, a gauntlet, and a heavy cavalry blade shining out into his vision.

Shay swallowed his gasp.

A handsome man, alert. The eyes widened slightly. 'You must be the one called Shay, I think. Lucky day for me, then.'

Shay brought his breath under control again. 'Lucky?'

'Kill the greatest Royalist spy. Or torture you, perhaps. That might be fruitful. Then kill you. Settle with Thurloe. After this there'll be no doubting where the power in the land is.'

'You must be one of Thomas Scot's crew; his troop of snoops and thieves and cut-throats.'

'My name is Lyle, old man. And you're ill-placed to underestimate me.' The blade shivered, flashing as it caught the moonlight differently. 'By morning Scot and I will be the most influential men in England.'

'Could be a long night, though.' Just a second. Just a fraction of a second to get to the pistol. Shay's eyes flicked around for resources.

The blade pricked at his throat again. 'Easy, old man.'

'There's gold in my knapsack.'

The eyes narrowed. 'There's probably not. But once you're dead I'll find out, won't I?'

A hand clamped around Lyle's mouth and yanked the head back, a blade flashed and the handsome eyes went wide and the sword arm flapped futile, and then his throat gushed black. The body slumped to the ground, and Thomas Balfour stepped forward.

'Is there really gold in your knapsack?'

'No.'

'If you can't trust a Royalist spy, who can you?'

Shay grabbed at his shoulders. 'You, it seems. I feared you dead.'

'I've spent my life trying to die. I can't manage it.'

Shay absorbed it. 'I know the feeling.'

'The only place I knew to find you was Astbury. The old man there told me where you were headed.' A grunt. 'A hundred miles of chaos and angry soldiers. I recognized the signs.'

'I was expecting someone else, but you'll do well enough.' Shay stared into the watchful eyes, then blinked himself alert. 'Balfour, I've moments only. Listen fast.'

'I'll come with you.'

Shay shook his head. 'No. I thought I might need Teach's help to get this far, and I got yours. But the last yards I must do alone. And you must get away from this place.' His hands clutched harder at the shoulders. 'Balfour, the stability of this kingdom no longer depends on Royalism, not for a time at least. The cause that I've upheld must. . . it must take a different path for now. But the spirit of Royalism must still glow. The people must be reminded of it, and Cromwell and his minions must feel it at their heels. You will find a message waiting for you – I sent it before Worcester. Instructions. Certain contacts. Unknown to the Parliament men, whatever papers they have seized, and unknown even to my patrons abroad. Use them.'

'Very well. But—'

'There's – there's something else. Sometime – and it may be soon, for these many months have felt like – like twilight – I will at last. . . defeat life. There is a manor. In the north of Wales. A good land, and good people. I have arranged that it will be yours.'

Balfour swallowed, and fought to hold himself. 'I will. . . try to be—'

'Don't try to be anything. Just be.' Shay smiled, and pulled away. 'Tom: while you live, live proud and live fierce.'

Balfour nodded, but the old man was gone.

~~~

Rachel felt Thurloe's arm stiffen, and then she heard what he had: a change in the rhythms of the water, a thickening of the sound.

She peered into the gloom, and eventually saw it: a shadow moving across the marsh towards them, a pale spectral aura wafting around it. Her heart kicked on instinct while her brain realized that it was her boat.

Is it actually possible, after all? Am I really going to escape this place? The horror of the morning, the nightmare of the hours since. The satchel bit at her shoulder. Then, the lurking under-thought: *Can I leave this place?*

'You'll be too late, won't you?' The voice came out of the darkness of the marsh, and they both spun away from the river towards the sound.

The land was black, but out of it came a figure, a soldier with pistol extended towards them, moonlight touching the barrel as he moved closer.

An instinctive step backwards, two, and Thurloe stared around them. They were yards from the beginning of the jetty.

'Hell of a dance you've had, eh?' The barrel gleaming and flashing in the moonlight. 'Murdering spies! But two of us are enough for you, I reckon.' Thurloe was still glancing left and right, trying to see firm ground, wondering how quickly he could reach his own pistol, wondering about Rachel.

Another sound, from near behind them now. Thurloe and Rachel turned again, and a figure was climbing up onto the jetty from the soft ground beside it. This figure had a pistol levelled in their direction as well.

'That's right,' the first soldier said. 'All here together now.' And he kept on towards them, and Thurloe and Rachel moved instinctively away towards the beginning of the jetty, hesitated, two thumping hearts in the trap, and as their desperate eyes swung back and forth between the threats, the second figure, a rigid shadow and pistol, spoke for the first time, hard and low.

'Get – down.'

Rachel recognized the voice and gasped and Thurloe wrapped his arms around her and dropped and the night cracked in a shot. Rolling, fighting for purchase on the soft earth, he stared up. The first thing he saw was the soldier, arm still extended.

The pistol barrel fluttered, wavered, and fell, and the man toppled into the gloom.

Shay strode towards them, boots thumping on the jetty planks, and then past them to the soldier. He was back in a moment with the soldier's pistol and a lantern, which he lit. In its little glow, he saw that Thurloe had a pistol of his own out, pointing at him.

Shay stopped, looked at the pistol, then up at Thurloe.

'What do you propose to do with that?'

'I don't know. But since I don't know what you're doing, it seemed a sensible idea.'

Shay considered this, and nodded.

'What the hell's happening?' Another voice, hissed out of the darkness of the river behind them.

'All's well,' Shay called low; 'we're friends of Mandeville.'

'Well hurry along! We've a tide to make; militia'll be here any time.'

Shay stepped to Rachel. He looked at her for a long moment, at the curves of her hair and body in the moon. Then he bent and kissed her forehead. 'You're the last of my people,' he murmured. 'And there could be none finer. God speed.'

He stepped back a pace. She watched him, then stretched out her arm, and touched him on the chest. 'All future generations will be less,' she said quietly.

She took another step towards the jetty, and turned back. 'Why aren't you coming?' she asked. Shay and Thurloe looked at each other. 'I mean—'

Shay smiled. 'I'm afraid that even if either of us wanted to, the other wouldn't allow it.'

Rachel felt a flutter of loneliness. She looked to Thurloe, hesitated. 'Thank you, John. I don't know—'

'It's been my privilege. I was. . . I was glad to find an ideal worth fighting for.'

'Hurry, damn you!'

'Rachel,' Thurloe said. 'I'll take the satchel, please.' He took a step away from Shay and towards her. 'Call it a memento.'

His pistol was up, and pointing at Shay's stomach.

She was clutching the satchel to her chest. 'It's just trinkets. Family things.' She took an uncertain step towards him. 'Surely that's not what you care about, after all this.'

His eyes flicked between her and Shay. 'Show me.'

She glanced at Shay, and Shay nodded. Another step, and she held the satchel open.

In the lantern light Thurloe saw the dull gold gleams. Something else: he reached for it, a fat book.

'Our family Bible. Please, John!'

'We must leave! The tide turns soon, and we'll never get away!'

Thurloe glanced at Shay, but he hadn't moved. He pulled the book half out, opened the thick cover, saw in the sickly light the careful handwriting of successive Astburys filling the flyleaves, and then the distinctive cover page. He pushed it back into the satchel.

His fingers still rested on the gold shapes, one of them a bulbous lump. Another glance at Shay. 'Family things?'

'You'll hardly need them in a Republic, will you?'

Thurloe thought, and nodded ruefully. He closed the satchel and, hand still on it, looked up. 'Fare you well, Rachel. I hope we make an England you'll want to return to.'

She backed away from them, the satchel held against her breasts. 'Thank you,' she said. 'Both of you. You were both essential to me. But now I have to leave this place.' For a moment she stared beyond them into the darkness of England. 'Do what you must with it.'

Then she was striding over the jetty and dropping carefully into the boat, already starting for the open sea and freedom.

Shay said, 'If you're not going to shoot me, perhaps you'd help me tidy your friend here into the marsh.' Thurloe lowered the pistol. 'Then, since you've been hunting me these three years, I hope you'll afford me an hour's quiet talk.'

<hr />

The news of the chaos at Astbury House had sent Thomas Scot hurrying there, fed intermittently with uncertain and confusing reports of the chase across the middle of England.

When he arrived in the first grey hours of the morning, he found a solitary old man in the heart of the wrecked house, sitting on a chair, a large book clutched to his chest.

Scot knew the power of books, of words, and snatched it out of the feeble hands.

The cover was ancient – thick and gnarled. In one discreet corner of it there was a seal – a heraldic badge with which he was not familiar. He began to turn the pages.

The flyleaves were as old as the cover; stained and blotched. But then there was a break in the binding, and pages of a different quality, with the unmistakable form and language of God's holy book.

~ ~

Thurloe said: 'You've distracted me with baubles before. What did I really let go into that boat, aside from that molten relic of history?'

Shay looked up from the table, where he had just placed his own pistol and the dead soldier's. 'A book; the book. The secret register of the Comptrollerate-General for Scrutiny and Survey. And a lovely and remarkable young woman.'

'Crowns, and secrets, and beautiful women. Have we not had enough trouble?' Their eyes caught. 'And the other crown? The unmelted?'

'Oh, that's around somewhere. In case you, or someone, should find a crown useful again.'

Thurloe smiled cautiously. 'And you,' he said, 'are Sir Mortimer Shay.'

'And you are John Thurloe.' Shay extended his hand. Thurloe watched it, and his glance returned to Shay's face. He transferred his pistol to his left, and slowly reached out and shook hands.

The abandoned chapel closed around them, dank. It was barely twenty feet long, half as wide, but the ink-black corners and niches were too much for the single lantern. On the plain table – who had needed a table here, and why? – it huddled for security between the two men. On all sides the charcoal slabs ran with marsh water.

Shay said, 'Your wife's uncle was Overbury, I think; who died in the Tower in James's time.' Thurloe frowned, surprised; then nodded. Shay let out a long 'Mm' of thought, and seemed to consider the tangent for a moment.

Thurloe waited, but nothing came of it. 'We've been in correspondence two years now, I think,' he said.

'I had come to assume so. I. S. is too weak a cypher, by the by. George Astbury did the like.' Shay pointed a heavy finger. 'I think it's something in you learned men – you can't miss a chance to be clever, and it makes you stupid.' A great sniff. 'But you had me after Dunbar. I relaxed too much in my little game. Always a mistake, and this time it cost us our position in Scotland.'

'As you had played me before Dunbar. Was that your intent? Merely to manipulate a little?'

'Just a sortie of opportunity, at first. Throwing a line into a dark stream. Nine chances of ten, my letter would never have been read. But you got it, and replied to it, and so I took the chance to spread a bit of misinformation – and make the little graves of the Levellers throw big shadows.'

'You had us worrying and searching ourselves a year longer than we needed.' Shay nodded cheerfully. 'But there was more. You were trying to learn about Pontefract, and Doncaster, and the Levellers there – just as I was.'

'Yes. J. H., the melancholy Royalist, was a useful masquerade.'

'There was a real Royalist source, though.'

'No. Just me.' Shay smiled consolation.

Thurloe frowned stupidly. 'Scot was getting reports out of besieged Pontefract. I know it.'

'Low-level gossip, perhaps. A penny or a meal or a whore, for a hungry sentry.'

More earnest, confused. 'No. A very particular source. Recorded faithfully in Scot's private ledger.' The memory of his wild ruse, the frantic flicking through the pages. 'I've seen the summaries. And since before Dunbar, Scot has had direct reports of Royalist strategy. The decision to come south into England; the decision to march for Worcester rather than London.' Thurloe watched the old gaze lengthen, lost. 'You didn't suspect this? This wasn't what you were about?'

Shay's face was grim.

He glanced up, and away again. 'All along, I wondered what so obsessed George Astbury. Why he spent his last days looking towards Pontefract. Why he was so haunted.'

'He knew something?'

'He knew something was wrong.' Shay's eyes were hard, wary at the revelation. 'And for some reason he was focused on Pontefract and not the Scottish army coming south for the King.'

'And your masquerade – J. H. – was intended to learn more of this.'

Have I lost my way quite? 'I thought I was confusing you. I ended by confusing myself more.'

Thurloe was feeling his way. 'The idea of a Leveller agent in Doncaster, in contact with Royalists. After Dunbar I thought it merely a ruse in your letters: trying to unsettle us about the Levellers, trying to learn more of Pontefract and Doncaster.'

'It began as both of those things.' Shay shook his head. 'I came to realize that it built on truth; perhaps that was why it was powerful. One of your soldiers in Doncaster was sympathetic to us. The idea of an alliance was nonsense, but this man didn't like the direction General Cromwell was taking this country. He learned about the contact between Reverend Beaumont and Pontefract, and he used it to send messages in.'

'There was definitely a source? Your man Thomas Paulden – I thought he was bluffing me – said that the raid, when Rainsborough was killed, was an attempt to meet this man.'

'It was an attempt to rescue him.'

Thurloe's mind was screaming. *Surely this would be madness. The Leveller hero?* 'This makes no sense.'

'It must do, because it happened.'

'But what happened? You must know more!'

Shay laughed once, hollow. 'I'd hoped you did.' A smile. 'Between us, perhaps.' And Thurloe nodded, wary, faintly entertained.

'So, royal Pontefract is besieged, by your Army based in Doncaster. There is a strong Leveller strength in the regiments there, centred around the man Rainsborough.'

'A Leveller hero as well as an Army hero,' Thurloe put in, trying to reassure himself. 'The great orator for the new liberties.'

'And an inconvenience for your Generals, yes? The Generals he spoke against in the Leveller debates. And someone in Doncaster is unhappy enough with the direction of Army and Parliamentary policy that he decides to give information to the Royalists in Pontefract, trying to help them last out, perhaps, until a relieving army can reach them from Scotland and turn the tide in the north. Yes?'

'Yes. Scot had logged a report of someone in Doncaster passing information out.'

'Because there's also a spy in Pontefract communicating with Scot's people. And he learns that Pontefract is getting helpful messages from Doncaster, and he reports it.'

Thurloe remembered the Adjutant in Doncaster. 'There was an argument. One of Scot's men came up from London – Tarrant – asking questions. He had a – a confrontation with Rainsborough.'

'Wait. There's a step missing there, surely.'

Thurloe nodded, slowly. 'There's a report missing, in fact. Thomas Scot had torn a page out of his own private ledger, because for some reason he decided that one report, perhaps two, couldn't be allowed to stay in the records.'

'Scot's sympathetic to the Levellers. Most likely—'

'Most likely the report was from Parliament's spy in Pontefract confirming that the man communicating with the Royalists was a Leveller.'

Shay watching Thurloe intently: 'Then what?'

Thurloe rehearsing the faces and the habits: 'Lyle, in Doncaster, would have got the report. He'd have known its significance. No doubt he normally shared this material with Rainsborough, the local commander and a man to whom he was sympathetic. Not this; he rushed this to Scot in London, very alarmed. Scot was shocked, and eventually destroyed all reference to the report, and sent Tarrant to Doncaster to investigate.'

'And there's not much to investigate, but he says enough to Rainsborough to provoke an argument. Perhaps' – Shay looked at Thurloe's wary face – 'perhaps he suggests that there's suspicion coming close to Rainsborough himself. And the next thing—'

'Is the raid on Doncaster.' Thurloe nodding, hurrying on: 'Supposedly an attempt to kidnap Rainsborough, but actually an attempt to rescue the source.'

'Who must have got word out that he was under suspicion, in danger.'

'Which suggests he was well aware of what Tarrant was saying.'

'Wait.' One of Shay's fingers flicked up. 'We're supposing it's an attempt at kidnap, but we're only supposing it's an attempt at rescue too. Because what actually happens – stripping away all the chaos and the stories—'

'Is that Rainsborough was killed.'

Shay nodded. 'An agent is supposed to be rescued, and Rainsborough is killed. By William Paulden, or more probably by Austwick.'

'But why would one of—'

'Wait.' The whole hand held up now, Shay grasping for sense, scrabbling to remember a conversation in a lightless ditch. 'There's confusion, chaos. According to Austwick, he finished off Rainsborough, but the first wound came from Rainsborough's Lieutenant. In the chaos, he shot Rainsborough.'

'Wait – you mean it wasn't an accident? Rainsborough's own Lieutenant was trying to kill him?' Thurloe hissed his frustration: at his own confusion, at the madness of his world. 'Scot and Tarrant and Lyle learn that one of their Leveller friends is a traitor. Tarrant comes to Doncaster and threatens Rainsborough. The traitor decides he needs to get away. A Leveller Lieutenant attacks Rainsborough, and he dies.'

Shay whistled. 'Your friend Scot is more efficient than I thought. He set this Lieutenant as watchdog on Rainsborough, and assassin?'

Thurloe was staring into one darkened corner of the chapel. 'But how did the Lieutenant know? I can't believe it.' His head was shaking slowly again. 'Did Rainsborough do something – say something – suspicious?'

'Blackburn said that William Paulden had told his comrades to look for a signal.'

'A word of recognition from this agent?'

A slow nod from Shay. 'Miles Teach thought the man was supposed to contact Thomas Paulden, at the north bridge.'

'Thomas Paulden said his brother was giving the chance for the man to reveal himself anywhere.'

'Austwick described Rainsborough using elaborate words; a curse – intestines of Satan, or something.' Thurloe was trying to read it all: the faces of Scot and Tarrant and Lyle leering into his mind; an attempt to conjure up the scene outside a Doncaster inn. Shay pressed on. 'And immediately afterwards the scuffle started, and the Lieutenant fired at Rainsborough.'

'He'd been told to watch Rainsborough presumably, and then he finds himself in this mad escapade, being dragged off by Royalists, and then Rainsborough says something unlikely, and the Lieutenant understands that Rainsborough's identifying himself as the source.'

Shay's faced screwed up in discomfort. 'It seems too. . . There's someone else who would have wanted the source dead, isn't there? After all, who actually killed Rainsborough?'

'But the Lieutenant makes sense. For Scot and Tarrant, it would have been the end of their dreams if Rainsborough had been known for a traitor. The Leveller hero; their hero. Tarrant would have got the Lieutenant crazy with anticipation, waiting for Rainsborough to betray himself.' Shay was watching him, scratching his jaw discontentedly. 'He did betray himself, and the Lieutenant saw what was happening, and was so outraged and so tight wound that he reacted immediately, even though it might cost him his own life.'

'Which it did.'

Thurloe nodded. 'He was killed immediately.'

'Yes,' Shay said slowly. 'By Teach.'

'Yes,' said the echo. 'By me.'

Miles Teach stepped out of the blackness behind Thurloe.

Shay had known he was there, but it still had his heart pounding. Thurloe's heart all but exploded in his chest, spinning him round and thundering the blood through him.

Teach had his pistol out, levelled ready.

Shay said, 'My apologies, Thurloe. I assumed he was here and I didn't mention it. I'd wanted him along in case of difficulty, and I knew this was where he'd come if nowhere else.' The words were steady, neutral. 'This is Miles Teach; about the bravest fighter your General Cromwell has ever faced. Teach, this is Thurloe. About the cleverest man I've ever faced.'

Teach grunted. The pistol was firm. 'He doesn't look too clever at the moment.'

'It's been a night of surprises for him.'

Thurloe was sunk. A cold, hungry nausea swirled in his gut. For all his cleverness, he was still coming to terms with the plots and counter-plots. For all his caution, he'd been seduced by Shay's congeniality and forgotten him for an enemy and now he was trapped, alone, by two of the most dangerous men in the country. He gazed at Teach, and then back at Shay, seeing him afresh. Two dead stone faces, implacable.

Shay said, 'Thurloe has a pistol, Teach.'

'He should drop it.' Shay looked at Thurloe, almost scolding. Dumbly, slowly, Thurloe let his pistol drop to the ground.

Shay nodded, then glanced at the table where his own pistol and the dead soldier's remained. With another glance at Thurloe, he pulled them both closer to himself, an extra second's glance at them, mind galloping. 'Well,' he said. 'Now that things are a little more certain, we can finish that conversation.'

'You seemed to have it pretty tidy.'

Shay gazed at Teach. 'I'm not sure. It still feels wrong to me. Bits that don't quite fit.'

Teach, flat: 'But now you've run out of men to ask.'

Thurloe, forlorn, said dully: 'Thomas Paulden in the Netherlands said that if I met a man who talked of the history of Doncaster, I would learn the truth.' He added sourly, 'Why don't the two of you go and join him, and you can please yourselves?'

Shay had opened his mouth to speak, but all that came out was a stifled gasp, and then he was lost in a frown. 'Yes,' he said at last. 'Yes, I see.'

Thurloe: 'I'm so glad.'

'The history of Doncaster. Not Rainsborough.' Shay's eyes were moving between Thurloe and Teach beyond him. 'Rainsborough's Lieutenant. According to Austwick, just before the scuffle the Lieutenant started cursing too, by St Nicholas and St James.'

'The Lieutenant? But—'

'St Nicholas and St James are the old hospitals in Doncaster. That's what Thomas Paulden was telling you; that was the phrase of recognition, the signal his brother said to listen for.' A weary sigh. 'We thought that Rainsborough said something that caused the Lieutenant to attack him. But it was the opposite. Rainsborough couldn't believe how easily the raiders had got to him; he was suspicious as well as angry. Something in the words or the reaction made him realize that his Lieutenant was involved, and he went wild.' He nodded to himself. 'The Lieutenant was the man passing information out to Pontefract.' Thurloe was listening intently, caught up in the story again. 'That's much more likely than Rainsborough himself, isn't it?'

Thurloe nodded. 'And it was the Lieutenant who'd let the raiders in.' He glanced over his shoulder.

'Yes. And now it makes more sense that the man who was most awake put up least resistance. He'd sent to Pontefract for help, and help had been arranged. He made sure he was on duty. He made it all easy for the raiders to get him out.'

'But it still went wrong.'

'For the Lieutenant, yes. It did.' Shay wasn't looking at Thurloe any more. 'But not for the man who had planned the whole affair.'

Miles Teach: a face and a pistol of rock.

Thurloe started to speak, but no one was paying attention.

'Again, what actually happened that morning?' Shay's voice was grim. 'In Pontefract, there's a man passing information to Doncaster. In Doncaster, there's a man passing information to Pontefract: the Lieutenant who, through Rainsborough, would know about the information coming out of Pontefract. Two men: the spy in Pontefract, and the Lieutenant in Doncaster who'd be the one man likely to know of the spy's existence and be worried by it. That's it. And then, in the middle of a lot of meaningless chaos, the Lieutenant is killed by Miles Teach.'

Thurloe had the logic but was trying to grapple with the implications, eyes flicking back and forth between the two unmoving men.

Shay smiled, rueful, bleak. 'My mistake, Thurloe. The night's biggest surprise was for me. Miles Teach is your spy. Aren't you, Teach?'

Nothing. A flicker on Teach's lips.

'You've been on the edge of the Court for years, and when you weren't there you were in the front rank of battle. You've sold it all: royal secrets, campaign plans. Gods, no wonder George Astbury was so haunted. He knew something like this was happening. And it was you who put the Parliament intelligencers onto Ruce, the Scoutmaster. Astbury guessed there had to be someone like you; the link couldn't have been established without some middle-man who knew Ruce's weaknesses and knew someone who'd benefit. You gave Cromwell Naseby, and you gave him Preston.'

The flicker on Teach's lips thickened into a dead smile.

Shay shook his head. 'And Doncaster: the story has been eating at me for three years. Always a piece missing. You.' Teach's eyebrows shifted, indifferent. 'You claimed that Paulden and Austwick drove the affair; but it's clear from their characters that you're a much more likely leader. You and William Paulden managed communications out of Pontefract, but I think that you sent that final message to the agent in Doncaster. You claimed the agent was supposed to contact Thomas Paulden, at the bridge, but William Paulden didn't think it was so specific, and you sent Thomas Paulden ahead to get him out of the way of the inn. Even with the Lieutenant on your side, it was risky having so small a party; but you wanted to minimize the number of people – increase your command of the situation.' He shook his head. 'It was supposed to be a kidnap of Rainsborough, and a rescue of the Lieutenant, but you hadn't brought extra horses.'

At that, a slight nod of acknowledgement from Teach.

'When the man Tarrant came to Doncaster and confronted Rainsborough, the Lieutenant heard it and knew he was in trouble. He sent a frantic message to the Royalists in Pontefract for help, warning them that they had a spy among them. But the man who received this report was himself the spy: you.'

'Yes.'

For Thurloe it all made sense, but the single word from the silent Teach came unexpected.

'You set him for death. At any moment he might put something in a message to Pontefract, a message that you might not get to first, a message that would ruin you. You'd no idea who he was, and he was out of your reach, but you devised a way to lure him out and to get him to identify himself. You proposed a plan for his escape, and you gathered unknowing accomplices, and you rode in and he revealed himself and you cut him down in the gutter.'

Nothing from Teach. Very slowly, movements open and deliberate, Shay picked up the two pistols from the table, eyes on Teach. He gave one to Thurloe – it was the dead soldier's – and Thurloe took it and suddenly understood that the game had swung in his favour. He held the pistol more certainly, and stepped back, the barrel levelled at Shay's stomach.

Shay watched the movement, impassive, and then held out his own pistol towards Teach's gun hand, outside the arm: no threats, no mistakes. Teach said, 'Watch him, Thurloe,' and swiftly shifted his own pistol to his left hand and took Shay's in his right. Thurloe was concentrating hard. Once again he had Royalism's greatest agent in his control: no hesitation or over-cleverness now. But there was still something nagging at him, something odd in what he was seeing or hearing.

Shay took three steps back again. 'Astbury suspected you were double-dealing,' he said to Teach. 'He sent you to Pontefract as a test. He would have you watched, he would check your reports.'

'Yes. William Paulden was watching me. So much I realized. After the raid on Doncaster – the business of the messages in and out, and the word of recognition – he grew very suspicious. And so William Paulden died of a fever, quite suddenly.'

Shay grunted. 'Very tidy. And Astbury was already dead by then. In desperation, he'd sent a man to bring out one of your reports: not the summaries that Reverend Beaumont was making and sending out to him routinely, but one of the original documents.' He reached into his jacket – a smile at Teach's hiss of caution – and pulled out the worn page. 'This. Did your reports to him also have a message for Thomas Scot? Did something in this tell him that truth at last?'

Teach shrugged. Thurloe said, 'Lyle – Scot's man in Doncaster – had a kind of template: a page with small holes cut in it at odd intervals. If he held that over a page of writing, it would show particular letters.'

Teach smiled without warmth. 'That's right.' He let his own gun drop in its sling, and with his left hand he pulled a piece of paper from an inner pocket and flapped it open. Thurloe saw the pattern of holes. 'Like this? My messages to Beaumont and Astbury went via a church. Left in the porch at the start of service, collected from the porch at the end.' He pushed the paper into his jacket again. 'The Parliament men had time for a look in the middle, while the faithful were at their prayers.'

Shay was peering at Teach's report in his hand. 'Perhaps it's fancy, but the paper seems a little dirtier over some letters. Perhaps Lyle was a bit careless checking it: a greasy hand brushed over the template to hold it down.' He looked up. 'Perhaps, at the very end, George Astbury knew for certain that he was betrayed.'

Teach shrugged.

Then Shay was suddenly cold, and staring bleak. 'Vyse. Young Hal Vyse. He died of a fever, too, didn't he? At Worcester, quite suddenly.'

Teach nodded, impassive. 'He saw the cypher template.' He patted the pocket. 'I explained it away right enough, but he was suspicious. Kept asking questions. I knew he'd talk about it sooner or later.' He shrugged. 'Pity.'

He looked more closely at Shay, at the winter face. 'Lord, that's fallen harder than any of it. I was right. You're an old sentimentalist, Shay. I've been crossing the lines for years, selling you and your cause on the nail. And after it all, it's the death of that boy that gets through to you.'

Thurloe said quietly, 'Why did you do it, Mr Teach? Why work for us?'

'Why? For money. For myself.' He was clearly surprised at the question. 'I certainly wasn't working for you.'

Thurloe couldn't help himself. 'That was all?'

'Master Thurloe, I had a monarchy capable in the same breath of allying itself to the most stubborn Protestants and the most brutal Catholics. Shay here has worked hard to ensure English defeat at the hands of both Irish and Scottish armies. Parliament splits once a year, and now depends on the Army. The Army is a muddle of every kind of social and political nonsense. In the end, all I could rely on was myself, and all I could honestly fight for was myself.'

He smiled fully for the first time. 'Your friends have paid me most generously. As have Shay's people before now. Before Dunbar it looked like I'd be firmly back in royal pay. The Worcester campaign was never a strong bet, but you keep your options open. I wasn't sure which way tonight would go. A man can't be particular.'

The pistol was still firm, and the eyes followed it to Shay again. 'I'm afraid, old friend, I end the night on Parliament's side.' He smiled the dead smile again. 'Don't worry: once you and your uncomfortable truths are out of the way, I'll be sure to keep contact with our comrades in the Netherlands.' He nodded towards Thurloe. 'These Parliament men seem open-minded about these affairs. They've never known my identity, but they pay brisk enough.'

Thurloe couldn't escape the nagging in his head; declensions that did not seem to match; a sentence that made no sense. Dimly, he said to Shay,

'You'll be tried for—'

Shay cut in. 'I fear Teach has a swifter justice in mind. And with my own pistol.' He smiled heavily.

Thurloe looked at Teach, the steady pistol, the dead eyes. *These are the men of my world now.* He stepped back.

Shay said, 'It's all in your hands now, Thurloe,' and again the uneasy sense of something forgotten kicked at Thurloe.

The pistols. The pistols from the duel in the marsh. A gunshot out of the sea; a body toppling into the marsh.

Shay leaned back against the table, hands lightly on its edge, watching the two barrels pointing at him.

Teach said, 'Good night, Shay,' and the pistol clicked.

Empty.

An instant of irritation, no more than an instant from Teach the warrior, already reaching for his own pistol and his knife, and in that instant Shay launched himself forwards.

But as he pushed off against the table, surely so solid in place after all the years, it gave way behind him with an ungainly scrape and Shay stumbled with it, scrambling for balance and knowing he'd lost. A brief gasp from Teach, amused at his luck, and he'd time to switch the second pistol to his stronger hand and up it came ready, and Thurloe snatched at an action on instinct, and this time the blast cracked across the chapel.

Teach was bewildered, hurting: the shot had come but he'd not fired; he still couldn't see the pistol thrust under Thurloe's arm towards him, but he could feel the sting of its wound in his shoulder and the numbness in his gun arm and now Shay was on him. The great old body drove him back and off his feet and down into the dust and two hands clamped at his throat. Teach scrabbled and grappled with weakened fists and desperate knees but Shay's body would feel no injury and his big fingers clenched fierce and would never slacken and Teach flailed and choked and the flat eyes flared finally into terrified life, and for half a minute he was a desperate, spasming trapped animal, and his anguished throat managed one last crackle and failed him.

Shay rolled away, finished. Several deep gasps, and the trembling of old limbs, and then he scrambled round again and pulled the knife from his boot and stabbed Teach in the heart. 'Not for a King,' he said, hoarse and soft. 'Not for a country. But for all the lads who'll never know a future.'

He clambered to his feet, still breathing heavy, and went to the chair and dropped into it. He looked at Thurloe, at the pistol still smoking in his hand, and at the scorching in his armpit. 'That's a good trick,' he said.

'I saw it at Nottingham Castle. A long time ago.'

Real surprise. 'That was you?' And Shay chuckled. He glanced at Teach's body, and up again. 'Thank you,' he said. 'I didn't expect that.'

Thurloe was still looking at the corpse. 'Neither did I.' He looked round to Shay, and his voice came vehement. 'I am full sick of these games, old man.' Then, softer: 'I think – I think that I want truth; and this was a man become made wholly of lies.'

'Lad, I don't seek your motives; but I'll take the result.' Less briskly: 'He'd have killed you too. Inconvenient, especially now you knew his identity.'

'I could have killed you. You gave me the loaded pistol.' An uncomfortable grunt. 'You knew I'd be less danger with it.'

'Let's say that I would rather trust my fate – and this country's fate – to you than to Miles Teach. But. . . I no longer care either way. I am done.'

Thurloe nodded back towards the body. 'You seemed committed enough.'

'That? Revenge. Brute revenge. For a beautiful boy, and his beautiful mother, and all that they represented.' He let out a great breath, of sadness, of release. 'I've done my duty, Thurloe. I've saved what I could. The last things that I needed to protect went safely off in that boat tonight. The field is yours.'

'Mine? I'm a hunted man.'

'Who says so? It's been a confused day. Everyone who knew that you helped Rachel to escape is dead; my gift to you. A Royalist spy escaped to sea, but you chased as hard as you could. She had an accomplice, yes.' He pointed at Teach. 'Your prize.'

'Thomas Scot will suspect me – does suspect me.'

'I have made one or two preparations that are yet to come to fruition. You'll find that Master Thomas Scot has some disappointments coming to him. Some embarrassing failures.'

'You said. . . you don't care? You – the man who has single-handedly brought carnage across the country for three whole years? I don't believe it.'

'What I cared about is with God; or with the Dutch, at least, which is close enough for now. I have nothing left. No cause to hide behind, no cause to justify my passions. Teach was a rogue, but I cannot blame him. When the King of England invades England with Scottish soldiers, and invades again, and thousands die, where is England's stability? I... I clung to a fugitive idea of it – and in the end I lost my way.'

A soft laugh, hoarse and deep in Shay's throat, and somehow ominous. 'And now it's your time. With the end of the battles, the passions will ease a little, and the law-makers will become more important than the soldiers. Your time to make of this place what you can.'

The great chest heaved in a breath, and let it go. Thurloe's melancholy eyes watched him.

'I have no more duty in this life, and no more interest. But I've marked you, John Thurloe – Rachel marked you – for a man of heart as well as duty. I hope that you'll oblige me with one courtesy. For an old soldier – one who never feared to look life or death in the face, and give his full measure.'

Epilogue

The Passing

❧❧❧❧❧❧❧❧❧❧❧❧❧

The
WESTMINSTER GAZETTE

being an accurate record of all eſſential tranſactions of the State

PRINTED BY AUTHORITY

he pretender Charles *Stuart* is reported to have arrived in Paris, joining the reſidue of his family in their exile. Limerick in Ireland has ſurrendered to General *Ireton*. In the Iſle of Jerſey, Engliſh forces have ſecured a victory againſt the rebels there.

On the 28. of the month, Parliament declared the gathering of *England* and *Scotland* into one *Commonwealth*, for more dutiful government, better care of Chriſtian conſcience, and preſervation of peace, for all men in both places.

In Lincolnſhire, at an unnamed place on the ſea-coaſt, waſ executed by muſketeers the notorious rebel Sir Mortimer *Shay*. The tender mercy of his judges gave him a ſoldier's death, recollecting the many exploits of his youth, yet he had been alſo active in the late rebellions and unreſts, which have ſo threatened the good order of the Commonwealth, and was known for a man of infamous habits and unreftrained paffions, bloody, licentious, and wild. For his many difcreet and worthy fervices, Mafter John *Thurloe* is appointed to the office of Comptroller-General for Scrutiny and Survey.